THE ARMOURER'S SON;

OR,

The Mysteries of the Tower of London.

BEAUTIFULLY ILLUSTRATED.

COMPLETE.

LONDON:
"BOYS OF ENGLAND" OFFICE, 173, FLEET STREET, E.C.,
AND ALL BOOKSELLERS.

ARMOURER'S SON.

OR THE MYSTERIES OF THE TOWER OF LONDON

"LORD WYNCHERLEY BROUGHT THE PITCHER DOWN WITH ALL HIS FORCE ON THE MAN'S HEAD."

No. 1

THE PROLOGUE.

"Ye stones in which my gore will not sink, but
    Reek up to Heaven! Ye skies! which will receive it!
    Thou sun! which shinest on these things; and Thou!
    Who kindlest and quenchest suns!—Attest!"
                                              —BYRON.

OF THE HORRIBLE DEED COMMITTED IN THE WHITE TOWER—OF HOW LORD WYNCHERLEY
GIVES HIS CHILD INTO THE CUSTODY OF THE ARMOURER OF TOWER HILL—AND OF WHAT
THE WIZARD OF WHITEHALL SHOWED GREVILLE TREVANION IN ST. JOHN'S CHAPEL.

THE thirteenth of August, of the year 1553, and just ten days after Queen Mary made her first public entry into London, was for many years considered a "red letter" day, owing to the fact that it had been a day remarkable for atmospheric changes.

Up to twelve o'clock in the day an almost tropical sun had been pouring down on the city. So broiling were its rays, that it was almost unsafe to walk the streets.

At three o'clock in the afternoon the sun took its departure and a mist spread over the city—a blood-red mist.

This increased in density until at last a strange darkness had fallen, and it increased until it had spread throughout the whole of London.

People were startled, and superstition being rife in those days, they began to think that the end of the world was rapidly approaching.

Business was suspended; the streets became deserted, and at last the whole of London was as silent as a graveyard.

The day wore on, but this unaccountable blackness did not disappear.

Eventually the distant roll of thunder told the anxious watchers that a terrific storm was about to burst.

And burst it did, and with fearful violence.

Hour after hour it raged, the flashes of forked lightning being fearful in the extreme, and causing enormous damage, as indeed did the thunder, the reports being so loud that houses were shaken to their foundations.

Towards ten o'clock the storm began to clear off, and the citizens ventured to look from their windows and street doors, and a few, assuming an air they did not feel, sauntered off to their favourite hostelries, there to pass away an hour or so in the discussion of the "wonderful storm."

The Tower Arms, which tumble-down hostelry was opposite the frowning walls of the Tower of London, did a fine trade on this particular night.

As soon as the storm was over, the sentries off duty crowded its various rooms, all anxious to tell what they had seen from this or that part of the Tower roof where they had been stationed during the progress of the storm.

While the merriment was at its height, two gaudily-attired men rode up.

They dismounted, threw their bridals to an ostler, swaggered into the inn, and called for drink.

This having been served to them, they repaired to one of the spare rooms.

As they passed through the crowd of Tower sentinels and warders they were greeted with all sorts of jests, and, of a surety, their appearance called for it, for they looked like a couple of ugly bravos just recovering from a drunken carouse, and, if the truth were known, there is hardly a doubt, but that is just what they were recovering from.

However, they took no notice of all this, and as they interfered with no one, the sensation at their sudden and unexpected appearance soon subsided, and the two men were left alone to drink, which they did with extraordinary relish and marvellous rapidity.

The hands of the clock pointed to the hour of midnight, the hostelry was again nearly deserted and the landlord was about to give orders for the place to be closed when a horseman dashed up to the house, dismounted, and hastily entered the inn.

He was well muffled up in a long cloak, but as he crossed the threshold he threw this back, and there was revealed a most magnificent costume, adorned with gold and silver braiding and fastened at the front with gold clasps.

"Your pardon," said the host, respectfully, as he placed his huge body near the threshold of the door, "but I am now about to close the house."

"Indeed!" was the haughty reply, "then pray keep it open till I take my departure."

"Ho! and I should like to know who you are, that commands me?" said the host.

"Listen. Keep thy tongue within thy infamous lips, or ——"

"Infamous!" cried the host. "Body o' me!"

'Ay, infamous. I see you have been par

taking of a good deal of thy smuggled brandy to-night, Master Stephen Punchard, but," whispered the new comer "that should not prevent you from recognising the voice and the figure of him who raised you from what you were and helped to place you here."

If the host of the Tower Arms was under the influence of drink, and there was hardly a doubt of it, these words had the effect of instantly sobering him.

He started violently.

"Greville Trevanion!" he muttered hoarsely.

"Ay, it is. So now you know, see that I am quickly and properly attended to."

"Sir, anything you may require is yours," replied Stephen, humbly bowing, "you have but to command. The whole house and the contents ——"

"Ah, bah! of what use is the house or the contents to me? Had they been, would you have been here? Bring me a bottle of your best, and keep your tongue between your teeth —understand?"

"Perfectly, your worship."

"Do not utter my name."

"I am as silent as the grave," replied the host, bowing lowly.

Greville Trevanion stalked into the room in which sat the two men we have before spoken of.

No word was uttered, a simple signal being all that passed between them.

The host having placed the wine before Greville, and having replenished the glasses of the other two, withdrew.

A long conversation in whispers now ensued, what it was about our readers will ascertain in a few moments.

Soon after midnight Greville rose, and looking full at the men, whispered—

"Mark it well—strike hard!"

"Fear it not," grinned the men, as they touched their daggers."

"Draw your cloaks closely about you, and follow me. And remember—silence!"

At a rapid pace walked Trevanion, followed by his two hideous-looking companions, and no pause was made until they reached the Tower.

Greville Trevanion, who seemed to be perfectly familiar with all the surroundings of this ancient fortress, proceeded to the fortification overlooking the moat and which led to the "Iron Gate."

Here, let into the massive wall, was a small, low, arched doorway.

Trevanion placed a whistle to his lips and blew upon it a low and peculiar note.

In a few moments the door was cautiously opened, and a warder appeared.

"You are late," he said.

"Ay," replied Trevanion, "but I suppose that is of but little importance?"

"It does not signify to any great extent. Enter."

Trevanion and his two companions passed through the doorway and entered a small stone apartment, which was crowded with arms of all descriptions, as well as links, lanterns, chains,

armour, some of it bent and blood-stained, and also a great quantity of implements used in the Torture Chamber.

The three having entered, the warder carefully closed and bolted the door, and turned the heavy key in the massive lock.

Trevanion, after a brief pause, threw back his cloak, and took from a pocket in the inside of it five bags.

These he placed on the table.

"In each, how much?" asked the warder, who, strange to say, had turned ghastly pale, and trembled violently.

"One hundred. Count them if it so pleases you."

"Nay, I am content to believe you," replied the warder, opening a drawer in the table, and placing the bags in it; "and now that this part of the business is finished, let us proceed to the other. Listen. I warn you and your men——"

As he turned to the men he paused, a look of horror on his face.

"Why do you stop?" growled Trevanion.

"Almighty powers!" ejaculated the warder, "what murderers' faces."

And he fixed his eyes on the villainous-looking countenances of the two men.

"Never mind their faces," said Trevanion, "proceed, and quickly."

"Well, I warn you and your men to proceed cautiously. The least noise may attract the attention of the guard. And, oh, your worship, are you aware that a warrant is expected here to-morrow?"

"I expect a dozen warrants will be delivered here to-morrow."

"I mean a warrant relating to his lordship."

"No!" replied Trevanion, with a start.

"'Tis true, then."

"How know you this?"

"I overheard the lieutenant telling the chief warder so."

"By Heavens! I am not a moment too soon."

"Nay; you are right there, and——"

"Come, come. Let us delay no longer. What of the secret entrance to the cell that you spoke of?"

"I will lead your men there, and will explain it to them."

"Has his lordship been visited lately?"

"No, except by Oscar Raymond. You know him, my lord?"

"The Armourer? Oh, yes; but why on earth are his visits to his lordship so frequent?"

"I know not, except it is for company. The lieutenant, since the Armourer works for the State, allows Raymond to come and to go as he thinks proper. I have heard it said that his lordship was very good to the Armourer in the times gone by."

"Hem! well, to business."

The warder took a lantern, and, lighting it, said—

"Follow, and make no noise."

Trevanion and the two men followed.

In one of the strongest cells of the White Tower, during the foregoing conversation, stood two men.

One was of about forty years of age, tall, bronzed, bearded, and muscular; in fact, he was a very giant compared with the majority of men.

His dress was of a remarkably simple character. It consisted of a black and green doublet, much worn, cloth hose, and shoes fastened with steel buckles.

About his waist he wore a large leathern apron, round the band of which was stuck a number of instruments such as would be used by an armourer of the time.

This splendid specimen of the "Men of Old" was Oscar Raymond, the Armourer of Tower Hill.

Opposite him, looking sadly down at the floor of the cell, his arms folded across his chest, stood a finely-formed, remarkably handsome man, of about the same age as the Armourer, though, perhaps, he looked considerably the Armourer's senior.

The magnificent and costly dress he wore, even in this prison, proclaimed him to be a person of rank ; and such he was, for he was none other than the once celebrated soldier and statesman, Lord Eustace Wyncherley.

The cell was one of the strongest to be found in the Tower.

Its size was 10 feet by 8 feet.

The vaulted ceiling, the walls, floor, and recesses were all of stone, the walls being adorned with hundreds of names and initials, rudely carved thereon by the unfortunate prisoners who had, in the years gone by, occupied the gloomy apartment.

The furniture consisted of a Spanish bedstead, a stool, and a table, upon which lay a number of devotional works, together with a little heap of jewellery.

Near the door stood a huge stone pitcher, and a few wooden platters.

On the bed, fast asleep, lay a pretty little child—a boy—of about three years of age.

This was the only son and heir of Lord Wyncherley.

The pretty little fellow had been in this cell, with his father, for many a month ; but that his gloomy surroundings had not taken any effect upon his spirits was evidenced by the fact that, as he slept, a smile played about his lips.

"My Lord," said the Armourer, "the hour is late, so I must away."

"Good-bye, Oscar," replied Lord Wyncherley, gloomily, as he held out his hand, which was grasped in the horny palm of the Armourer. "Good-bye, and Heaven bless you !"

"And you, my lord, and your child !" said the Armourer, in tones of deep emotion. "I trust that when next I come I shall hear that your lordship has received your discharge."

Lord Wyncherley shook his head, gravely.

"It will not be so, Oscar," he said "At least, I fear it will not be so. My villainous cousin, Greville Trevanion, has some influence with Queen Mary, and unless I consent to do as he asks—that is, to sign away that which would rightly be my child's—my head will surely fall on Tower Hill, or what is more likely, I shall be secretly assassinated."

"My Lord," cried the Armourer, "I implore of you to dispel from your mind——"

"Nay, nay, good Oscar," interrupted his lordship, "I cannot dispel these fears. They are ever uppermost in my mind. In my dreams, I receive awful warnings that my end is approaching. But I would not fear that were it not for my poor child. I am ready to die !—quite ready, but——"

"Had not the Privy Council been disturbed from their duties by these grand *fetes*, which have been given in honour of Queen Mary, you would have had your trial, and the charges brought against you by your infamous cousin would have been investigated. But if ever aught should happen that your son should want a friend, be assured he will find one in Oscar Raymond."

Again Lord Wyncherley pressed the hand of the honest Armourer.

"Ay, Oscar," he said, with a great sob, "had I been surrounded by men as honest as yourself, I should have been happy indeed. Oh, Oscar, old friend, I——"

At this moment a loud rattle of keys was heard, and in another instant the heavy cell door was thrown open, and the warder we have before seen appeared on the threshold.

"The time is up, Master Armourer," he said, gruffly ; "and, besides, a visitor of more importance than you seeks an audience of his lordship."

"A visitor?" cried Wyncherley. "A visitor —and at this hour ? His name ?"

"Greville Trevanion,' was the reply.

The warder stepped back, and Trevanion, with a low bow, strode haughtily into the cell.

The warder pointed to the door.

"Pray go, Master Armourer,' he said. "You know your way as well as I do."

"Ay, better—much better," replied the Armourer, and once more shaking the hand of Lord Wyncherley, he strode slowly from the cell.

He walked along the narrow corridor, and halted near some broad slimy stone steps which led to a passage communicating with one of the outer gates.

"Almighty Providence !" he muttered, as he excitedly clasped his hands. "What is this feeling which is creeping over me ?

"A warning voice is whispering in my ears ! The cry of 'Murder' appears to be floating through the corridors ! What shall I do ? What shall I do ?

"This midnight visit of Greville Trevanion is made with some dreadful object in view. I feel sure of it. But I will wait below."

*   *   *   *   *

"Wait without, warder," said Trevanion, "our interview will be but brief."

The warder bowed, and went outside the cell.

"Your object in coming here—and at this hour ?" asked Wyncherley, drawing his fine figure erect.

"Why ask ? I come to repeat what I have said scores of times. This time I bring with me the necessary documents. Sign them, and you are a free man. Free as the birds of the air to enjoy during your life——"

"Ay, there you are right," interrupted Lord Wyncherley, hastily, " *during my life.* I know it well. Did I sign the papers you speak of I should sign my own death warrant !"

" Not so. I——"

'' I say yea ! And yea a thousand times ! Your idea is to get me to sign these papers which entitle you to take possession of the property at my death, thus taking from my beloved child all that rightfully would be his. And you try to persuade me that you would wait until I died a natural death ere you claimed what I had made over to you. No, no, Greville Trevanion ! I know you too well for that. I might be released from this accursed place—that I admit. But it would only be to meet my death elsewhere. Go— you have my answer—my *final* answer. Never dare to enter this chamber again. Go—and take with you my most bitter curse !"

Greville Trevanion had partially taken some papers from his pocket ; but he crammed them back, and knocked on the cell door.

It was instantly opened by the warder.

"Ere I go," said Greville, pausing on the threshold, " I would again offer you ——"

"Your offer is declined, villain !" was the stern reply. "Away, and leave me in peace."

In another moment the cell door was closed with a crash.

For some minutes his lordship paced the gloomy cell, which was illuminated only with a small lantern that threw a miserable and ghastly light around, muttering to himself.

At last he paused by the bedside, stooped and kissed the sleeping child, and then, kneeling, prayed long and earnestly.

He then rose, and extinguished the light.

The cell was now illumined only by the moon, which threw her rays through the one small circular aperture which did duty for a window.

His lordship was proceeding to undress himself when a noise, as of the shuffling of feet, caused him to pause.

He listened intently.

The noise was repeated, now low, as of the scratching of a pin, and now louder as of the scampering of rats.

A cold perspiration broke out all over his lordship's body.

What was the meaning of these sounds ?

During all the months he had been there he had never before heard the like.

His lordship, falling on his hands and knees, crawled to the door.

He listened—the noise was not there.

As he crept back he seized the heavy pitcher and held it firmly in his right hand.

Again he listened, and again came the sound, and this time he caught the indistinct muttering of voices.

"Oh, heaven !" moaned his lordship, " these sounds mean that I am to be assassinated ! And by order of my cousin ; probably by his hand ! I have heard of the secret passages in this fortress, and of the foul murders which have been committed by their aid. And I am quite un- armed ; no chance have I of defending myself. Hark !——"

"What is that ?"

A peculiar sound on his right caused him to pause, and gaze in wonder at the wall.

Solid stone it looked, but his lordship distinctly saw a portion of it move.

Another moment and it slowly, without the least sound, moved inward.

"He sleeps," whispered a voice, "and therefore we shall have little difficulty. So that's well. We shall earn our money quickly. Do you enter while I hold the door. Use your dagger, and, as *he* said, strike *hard.* And, mind, make sure of his heart ; for if you strike him there he will not cry out."

The speaker held up the lantern, and the light fell upon the faces of the two villainous-looking wretches our readers have seen with Greville Trevanion.

The one with the lantern held the secret door back with one hand, and raised the lantern aloft with the other.

His companion, a sword in his right hand and a long glittering dagger in his left, crept forward a pace and listened.

Lord Wyncherley had the presence of mind to breathe heavily as if asleep.

With a grin of satisfaction the wretch crept forward.

He had not taken two paces ere Wyncherley, with a bitter cry, dashed forward.

Raising the pitcher aloft with both hands, he brought it down with all his force on the man's head.

The villain, with a deep groan, staggered forward and fell.

Wyncherley, with the speed of lightning, snatched the man's sword from his grasp, and rushing to the bed, seized his child.

Pressing the poor little fellow, who now wide awake was uttering most pitiful cries, to his breast, his lordship dashed at the secret door which the other man was closing.

But not acquainted with its movements he had great difficulty in accomplishing this.

Before he could get it into position Wyncherley pressed his body against it, and exerting all his strength succeeded in pushing it back.

With a loud cry of alarm the man sprang back and ran along the dark, narrow passage, still carrying the lantern.

At the end of the passage was a flight of stone stairs leading to those the Armourer had descended.

Here, on the landing, Wyncherley caught up the watch, who now turned at bay, and drawing his sword, attempted to ward off the determined and most deadly thrusts aimed at him by the man he had been sent to assassinate, and who now had determined that if he was to die, he would at least die defending himself.

The clash of the steel was echoed with startling effect along the low, vaulted corridors, and this mingling with the curses of the assassin and the cries of the terrified child, made up a most fearful din.

At last his lordship got the man on the edge of the steps.

The villain missed his footing, but ere he could fall the sword of Lord Wyncherley had passed completely through his body.

Seizing the lantern Wyncherley ran down the stairs.

"I will to the lieutenant," he thought, "and lay before him what has transpired. Surely—surely I am entitled to some consideration—some mercy. Rest quiet, Roderick," he said, as he kissed his little boy, who clung so tightly to him, "your father has you, and he will protect you with his life—ay, with his life!"

Down the stairs ran his lordship—the blood-stained weapon still in his hand—faster! faster! and at last he reached the next landing.

On the landing a link, stuck in a bracket, was burning, and by its by no means brilliant light Wyncherley was enabled to some extent to see his way.

Rounding a corner, he had placed his foot on the first step, when a tall, dark, shadowy-looking figure darted from a recess.

With an appalling oath, the figure raised a dagger in the air, and then buried it in the back of the unfortunate nobleman.

A heartrending cry of mortal agony escaped his lips—a cry which rang throughout the White Tower.

He raised the sword as if to strike his assailant, then staggered, and fell across the steps.

As he fell, the lantern tumbled from his grasp, the sides flew open, and the light fell upon the fierce face of the cowardly assassin—the face of——

Greville Trevanion !

"Oh, Almighty Providence!" gasped Wyncherley, "my dreams have indeed been to some purpose. Murdered!—murdered! and by the hand of my own cousin!

"Coward! Assassin! My blood will cry to Heaven for vengeance! With my dying breath I curse you—I curse you! But my life—my child's life— Away, monster!—away, I say!"

Greville Trevanion had started forward to seize the child; but Lord Wyncherley, catching his son by the wrist, held him aloft with the one hand, while, with the other, he made frantic efforts to strike Trevanion with the sword.

"My boy!" gasped Wyncherley. "Oh, Heaven! have pity on my poor child! Help! Save him—save him!"

Trevanion drew his sword, and endeavoured to plunge it into his cousin's heart.

He was aware of the fact that his cries would —if not quickly silenced—attract attention.

As it was, the previous cries had not been heard, owing to the fact that the lions, then kept in the Tower, had been roaring somewhat loudly.

In the struggle for the possession of the child, Trevanion extinguished the light in the lantern, so that the place where the struggle was taking place, was almost in darkness.

Raising the child still higher, the noble Wyncherley, who was bleeding fast from the coward's dagger thrust, again shouted for help, but his cries were becoming more feeble every moment.

His life's blood was fast trickling down the slimy stairs.

"Oh!" he groaned. "Who will help me against this cowardly murderer? Who will save my child?"

"I will!—with my life!" cried a deep voice.

Ere Trevanion could strike again at Lord Wyncherley, a powerful pair of hands seized him by the neck and the waist and flung him head-first down the flight of stairs.

It was the Armourer!

Taking the child, he knelt down besides the now thoroughly exhausted nobleman, and whispered in broken tones—

"'Tis I, your lordship—Oscar—Oscar—the Armourer!"

"The child—the child?"

"I have the poor little fellow in my arms," replied the Armourer.

Then his courage gave way, and he burst into tears.

"Let me kiss him—let me bless him—quick —quick! I am dy—dying ——"

The Armourer placed the child's face to his lordship's lips.

"He will live to avenge me!" gasped his lordship. "Poor Roderick!— poor Roderick! Oscar—Oscar—bend down; place your ear to my lips."

The Armourer did so, and for some few moments his lordship, between his gasps for breath, whispered in his ear.

What he said it is not here necessary to repeat; we need only tell our readers that his words were instructions.

"All you have asked me I will do," sobbed the Armourer.

"Swear it!"

"I swear it!" said Oscar, as he raised his hand solemnly aloft. "As I shall answer for it at the Great Day, I swear it!"

"'Tis well. Can you find your way to the cell I have lately occupied?"

"I can."

"Take away all the articles you see on the table. But, alas! if you are caught with the child——"

"Fear it not. I know of a secret passage under the moat, by which I can make my way from the tower unobserved."

"What of Greville Trevanion?"

"Ha, he rouses himself," replied the Armourer, looking down the stairs.

"Away, then! I shall be dead, ere he returns to this spot. Farewell, Oscar!"

"Farewell!" sobbed the Armourer. "I go to save your boy from death!"

A brief pause—a firm clasping of hands, and the Armourer had parted from the nobleman for ever.

Pressing the child close to his broad chest, the Armourer turned, and fled back with the speed of a deer.

⁕ ⁕ ⁕ ⁕ ⁕

The force with which the Armourer had hurled Trevanion down the stairs was sufficient to cause him to become insensible, and to remain so for some considerable time.

Gradually, however, consciousness returned to him, and very slowly he raised himself.

Putting his hand to his head, he found that it was severely cut.

Presently, by the aid of the wall, he got upon his feet.

The clash of arms and the hurried tramping of many feet fell upon his ears.

"'Tis the guards searching the tower," he muttered, in great alarm. "And if I am seen I shall be captured."

Looking about him, he noticed a heavy chain dangling from above.

High over his head was a deep, dark recess, and he thought that if he could grasp the chain, he could draw himself into the recess, and thus escape observation.

Seizing the chain with both hands, and exerting all his strength, he placed his feet against the wall, and succeeded in drawing himself into the recess.

Nearer sounded the clash of arms, nearer came the footsteps.

Suddenly the glare of many links lit up the landing above, and a troop of the guard, headed by one of the captains, a drawn sword in his hand, stood at the head of the stairs.

The light from the links fell upon the ghastly object lying there.

The body of Wyncherley lying across the stairs, the dead hand still grasping the reeking blade.

"My God!" cried the captain, starting back. "A foul murder has been committed!"

"Murder!" echoed the men.

And "murder" was echoed again and again along the various corridors.

"Lower your links," said the captain, "and let us see who it is. By his dress he is one of our—ha! as I live! it is Lord Wyncherley! Run, one of you, and arouse the lieutenant. Tell him that Captain Scott implores him to hasten here, for a foul murder has been done."

The man had hardly got out of sight ere a loud shout behind was heard, and amid cries of wonder and horror, the dead body of a man was brought forth, and placed in front of the captain.

It was the man Wyncherley had run through the body.

The lieutenant soon made his appearance.

Ere he could ask a dozen questions, another loud shout was heard.

The soldiers made way, and presently another man was laid down before them.

This was the man Wyncherley had stricken down with the pitcher.

"He is not dead," said the lieutenant. "Give him brandy—quick!"

They raised the man's head, and poured brandy down his throat.

Trevanion craned his neck to listen the better.

The man partially opened his eyes, and looked helplessly around him.

"Speak, villain!" cried the lieutenant. "How came you in Lord Wyncherley's cell? How came you in the Tower?"

"We were paid to murder Lord Wyncherley!" gasped the man.

"Heavens! by whom? By whom? Speak! Hold him up! higher! higher!" cried the lieu-tenant, who, falling upon his knees, placed his ear to the man's lips.

"I charge you, as you are about to appear before your Maker," said the lieutenant, solemnly, "to tell me who lured you to do this most dastardly deed!"

Trevanion craned his neck still further forward.

A dead silence reigned.

Even the lions were now silent.

Trevanion's heart almost ceased beating.

His blood seemed frozen in his veins.

The assassin opened his eyes still wider, his hands clenched themselves until the nails were buried in the flesh.

Frantically did he struggle to speak, but the words would not leave his tongue.

Again and again he tried to utter the name of the man who had lured him to murder. Trevanion at that awful moment was gloating over his vain efforts, and hoping that death would quickly seize him.

Ay, and quickly seize him it did.

As he made another effort to speak, a volume of blood rushed from his mouth; his head fell forward; he was dead.

"Alas!" groaned the lieutenant. "Another Tower mystery which, probably, will never be fathomed!"

"Saved!" muttered Trevanion.

*   *   *   *   *

The bodies of Wyncherley and the two men were carried away, and search was then made for the child.

Of course, it was nowhere to be found.

This was, indeed, as great a mystery as the other.

The warders at the gates were questioned. They swore they knew nothing of what had transpired.

The only visitor to his lordship was the Armourer, and he, the warder, who had admitted Trevanion, said he had let out some two hours previously.

Our readers know he did nothing of the kind; but the man took it as a matter of course that when the Armourer left the cell he at once left the Tower.

"The child is in the hands of some one within this Tower," muttered Trevanion, who had not recovered at the time the Armourer had escaped with the child. "By Heavens!" he continued, 'I will find out who has it. I shall never feel safe so long as he lives. Ay, I will find him, and he shall die! And by this hand, as his father died."

As soon as all was again silent, Trevanion crept cautiously down, and proceeded to return the way he had come.

He might just as well have been in a trackless forest so far as finding his way out went.

And he knew that even if he made his way to the battlements, he stood a good chance of being shot down.

On he went, pausing and hiding himself at the slightest sound.

Down one flight of stairs, up another, through one gloomy corridor, and then another, crept

" The glittering eyes of the Spectre were fixed upon Trevanion."

the murderer until at last he became almost exhausted.

Still, onward he went, though it was at a snail's pace, and, finally, he paused on the threshold of what, to him, looked like an immense chamber.

As he looked within, the moon's rays poured through the windows, and then Trevanion saw that he was in a high vaulted apartment, the windows being of stained glass, and with many enormous columns supporting the roof.

Cautiously he advanced into the centre of the apartment, and looked about him.

Suddenly a cloud hid the moon, and the place was in total darkness.

But Trevanion had made out where he was, for he had been there once before.

He knew that he stood in St. John's Chapel. Alone in that sacred place—*he*—a murderer!—alone with the mighty dead!

Fear and trembling seized him; his legs shook as though he were afflicted with the ague.

He turned to fly.

He held out his hands to feel for the doorway.

Horror! The massive door was closed.

He drew back, cowering into a corner.

He was about to utter a groan of despair, when, at the further end of the chapel, a light appeared.

Of infinite smallness it was, and the flame was of a peculiar bluish colour.

Very steadily it advanced towards him, yet he could not make out who was carrying it.

The nearer it approached to him, the brighter became the light, and at last Trevanion made out a figure behind it.

The figure of a tall, dark man clothed from head to foot in a mantle of black.

There was no mistaking those large piercing black eyes; no mistaking the long beard of glossy blackness, all of which belonged to a much dreaded man—

Mervine, the wizard!

Pausing in the centre of the chapel, the wizard raised his lamp, and looked slowly about him.

The rays of the lamp fell upon the ghastly features of Trevanion, who cowered back fearful of being seen.

Whether the slight sound of his movement, made Mervine aware of his presence, or whether he was perfectly aware that Trevanion was there, we know not; but he said in deep tones—

"Stand forward, Greville Trevanion!"

"Ha!" cried Trevanion, starting forward a few paces. "I was on a visit to a friend within this Tower, and have accidently lost myself. I pray you, sir, conduct me—"

"I will call the guard to your assistance," interrupted Mervine, significantly.

"Nay, nay," cried Trevanion. "I would, if possible, depart secretly, for fear of bringing my friend into trouble.'

"Liar! Think you I do not know what has passed, and what is, at this moment passing through your mind? Yea! I do. Trevanion,

thou man of blood, look up, and listen to me. You have committed many crimes in your life; but this night you have committed the worst. Oh, Heaven! what a black soul have you! The man who has often befriended you, you have murdered! You will have to answer for it. The years during which you will be allowed to live will be full of misery. You will live until your cup of misery is full, and then—then you will *die*—surrounded by a gaping crowd, who will laugh at, and mock you!"

"What mean you?" gasped Trevanion.

"I will *show* you—look!"

The lamp went out with a hiss, and on the spot, where the wizard had stood, a white light appeared, and grew and grew until it was of great size and circular in shape.

"Listen!" said the wizard. "What do you hear?"

"The deep tolling of a bell," replied Trevanion, in hoarse tones.

"Ay, 'tis the bell of the Tower, in which you now stand, and it is tolling for *you*."

"Look!"

Within the white circle appeared a dark mass, and Trevanion saw that it was the Tower walls.

Before the walls, standing out plainly and distinctly, was a scaffold, with a block upon it.

Standing by its side, tall and grim, motionless as a statue, his hand resting on the handle of the glittering axe, the black mask upon his face, stood *the headsman*.

Presently a procession moved slowly and solemnly along the platform leading to the scaffold, and Trevanion saw that, as they moved aside at the scaffold steps the man to be executed *was himself!*

As he tottered on the platform the headsman moved slightly, then slowly raised his hand to his face.

Trevanion (that is to say, the vision of Trevanion) stood still, and looked at him.

The headsman snatched the mask from his face, and thus the pair confronted each other.

"Do you recognise the headsman?" asked Mervine.

"Ha!" gasped Trevanion, staggering forward. "*It is Wyncherley!*"

With this exclamation, he fell insensible at the wizard's feet.

"Nay," muttered the wizard, grimly. "'Twas not Wyncherley—alas! for the dead cannot return to life But *it was his son*, as he will be in years to come."

The wizard took up the lamp.

The door opened, and in stepped the warder who had admitted Trevannion to the Tower.

"There lies he for whom you search," said the wizard, sternly. "Remove him from the Tower if you value your own life, which, however, should be forfeited for your share in this night's work."

"Oh, sir——" commenced the warder, in whining tones.

Silence, villain!" interrupted Mervine. "Remove him from the Tower; and if, when you have done so you do not depart yourself, you shall be arrested."

"Sir," said the warder, tremblingly, "I search for Lord Wyncherley's child."

"Wretch! you search in vain!" replied Mervine, as he strode majestically away.

The next morning all London was thrown into a state of intense excitement by the news of what had happened at the Tower.

Every investigation was made; but of course, the whole affair was enveloped in a mantle of mystery, a mantle which there seemed no chance of penetrating. In vain was the child searched for, the Armourer summoned to the Tower, and interrogated.

He swore he knew nothing, and his word was not doubted in the least.

So the whole affair was put down as another Mystery of the Tower, and in the course of a few days, the excitement died out.

Thus the curtain falls on the PROLOGUE, and rises, after the lapse of seventeen years, on THE STORY.

CHAPTER I.

HOWS THE ARMOURER AND HIS SON AT THE FORGE AND INTRODUCES TWO EXTRAORDINARY INDIVIDUALS—HOW OSCAR WAS DESPATCHED ON AN ERRAND, AND OF WHAT HAPPENED AT TEMPLE BAR.

THE Armourer of Tower Hill had now been many, many years in business, and being a clever workman, and an honest one, he had become successful; and when we now re-introduce him, he is contractor for the manufacture of arms, and other articles, not only for the Court, but also for many eminent noblemen.

He and his son Oscar conducted the business, and were assisted by several men.

The premises, though of rough construction, were extensive, as also was the dwelling house behind them.

It was a most extraordinary thing—so people thought that—though the Armourer had been married for twenty-five years, he had only one child during the whole of that period.

And what was more singular, no one had ever seen this child until he was sixteen years of age.

"Delicate," was the Armourer's reply to all questions concerning the boy of whom the Armourer's wife spoke so fondly. Very delicate, and, therefore, he will remain in the country until he is strong enough to be able to work."

The son was brought to London shortly after he had turned sixteen, and immediately set to work.

Then people wondered at what the blacksmith had told them.

This son was no delicate youth.

Very far from it. He was a fine, tall, muscular youth, with a handsome face, and a finely-modelled figure.

"Ah," said the Armourer, "it is the country which has so improved him."

The Armourer's son is going on for twenty when we introduce him to the reader.

He was as tall as his father, and as strong.

One night the Armourer had extra business to transact.

It was a sudden order to manufacture a new scabbard to a sword belonging to Faverscourt.

"Oscar," said the Armourer, "the hour is late; but as this is somewhat important, I should be glad if you would lend me a hand at the forge."

"Certainly, father," replied Oscar, leading the way to the smithy. "And rather than rouse one of the apprentices, I will take the work home after it is finished."

"Do—do, 'twill save much delay. "'Tis a happy thought on your part, my son."

In a few moments the furnace, which was seldom entirely out, was formed into a brilliant glare, which illuminated the smithy, and the roadway.

The pair had not been long at work before a loud guffaw was heard without.

Then the latch of the smithy door was lifted without ceremony, and a loud, deep, but merry voice, cried out—.

"What! so late, Master Armourer? By the soul of the Virgin! if you go on like this, we shall soon lose thee and thy handsome son, and then—oh—what then, brother?"

"Then we should weep!" replied another deep voice. "And require many barrels of Hollands to get us to cease weeping."

"'Tis the giant brothers," said the Armourer, as a smile spread o'er his somewhat grave face. "Shall they come in, Oscar?"

"Oh, yes," laughed Oscar. "They will not interfere with us. Come in," he cried.

In another moment the visitors entered the smithy.

And such visitors! Each a very mountain of flesh and bone!

They were the brothers—Sampson and Goliar Silvester—blacksmiths of Eastcheap.

Each was of about eight feet in height, and as like each other as possible.

Marvellous men, indeed, were these huge brothers.

In order to get within the smith, they had to stoop considerably.

"Well, Sampson," said the Armourer, "and what brings you hither to-night?"

"Our feet and legs, Armourer," replied Sampson, as he caught hold of a huge anvil of enormous weight, and placed it in the centre of the smithy, "and we are surprised to see you at work so late—as also you, Oscar, who say you have such disdain for work of any description."

"I would not do this work if I had my own way in the matter," replied Oscar.

"Hem! And what would you do?"

"I would belong to the army."

"You could not, Oscar," replied Sampson, with a wink at his brother, "for the army already belongs to the Queen."

"I mean I would join the army."

"Ha, that would be a bad thing, Oscar. Very bad. The soldiers get little to eat I have heard say. Anyway, you would never get fat—like us."

"The Lord forbid it!" cried Oscar.

"Amen!" ejaculated Goliar, fervently, as he crossed his hands on his enormous stomach. "I quite agree with Oscar, brother. If everybody felt inclined to get fat, there would not be so much left for us, and that would be a serious thing, situated as we are."

"Are you hungry to-night, Sampson?" asked the Armourer.

"Very!" sighed Sampson, and his sigh was echoed by his brother. "We came out on purpose to see whether we could find a supper, but, alas! after one invitation people always give us the cold shoulder, though I am sure we do all we can to oblige them by eating and drinking as much as possible."

"Well, if it so pleases you," said the Armourer, "you may stay to supper. I have no doubt the good wife will manage to find sufficient to satisfy both your appetites."

The invitation was accepted with many thanks, for the brothers knew from experience that the Armourer kept a good larder.

At a hint from Oscar, Sampson very willingly took his place at the forge, while Oscar went to prepare for his journey.

He attired himself in his best, and placed a heavy shawl over his shoulders.

Then he returned to the smithy.

"My son," said the Armourer, gravely, as he surveyed him. "Why have you donned your best?"

"I shall call on Mervine since I shall be close to his residence."

The Armourer started.

"On Mervine? What, the Wizard?" cried Sampson, opening wide his eyes. "Holy Mary, defend us! I would rather visit the most horrid dungeons of the Tower than visit that man. By my father's soul, I can safely affirm that I am afraid of no man but Mervine, who practices the black arts. What say you, brother?"

"I say the same," said Goliar. Oscar smiled.

"I am not fearful of him," he said. "Are you, father?"

Again the Armourer started violently.

"I, my son?" he replied, slowly. "Nay, I fear him not. But——"

"You do not forbid my visit to him?"

"I forbid you nothing, my son. Go if you wish; but I warn you to be careful."

Aside, he muttered—

"The time has not yet come—the time has not yet come!"

"Give me the sword, father, and let me go," said Oscar.

"We will await you to supper," said Sampson.

"Ay, do. I shall not be very long."

Oscar took the sword, and with a nod at the two brothers, went out, and was soon lost to view in the darkness.

"Thy son is more fitted to a palace than a smithy, Armourer," said Sampson.

"Ay, he would please the Queen mightily," said Goliar.

"And the dress he wears to-night," continued Sampson, "though 'tis too rich for the son of an Armourer, becomes him well."

The Armourer was looking gravely into the dying embers on the furnace.

"I feel somewhat uneasy," he said, "and had I the feeling I have now but a few moments ago, Oscar should not have left my roof."

"Shall I go after him?" asked Goliar.

"Nay, nay," said Sampson; do not fetch him back, for that, of a surety, means ill-fortune. Bah! he will come to no harm. If any one attempts to molest him, he knows what to do right well. Odd's my life! I know not a youth in all London who is so well acquainted with the use of the sword."

"When did you see him wield the sword?" queried the Armourer, in some alarm. "'Tis the first I have heard of it."

"I saw him wield it to some tune in the apprentices' sports on the Hill but a little time back. 'Twas then playfully wielded; but all remarked that the arm that could thus playfully wield it, could wield it in a most deadly manner did occasion require."

"I trust there will be no such occasion," said the Armourer, uneasily.

"And I," said Sampson.

"And I," echoed Goliar.

"Come," said the Armourer, "and ere my good dame has quite prepared supper, Oscar may return."

Though it was not by any means the custom for an Armourer's son, even a wealthy one, to carry arms, Oscar seldom, if ever, went out at night without arming himself well.

On this occasion his arms consisted of a sword, dagger and pistol.

He was, of course, careful to keep them concealed under his cloak.

The night was profoundly dark, but Oscar was well acquainted with the streets he would have to traverse; on more than one occasion he had been molested; and, therefore, he took great pains in proceeding carefully.

Nothing of importance occurred until he arrived at Temple Bar.

His attention was then drawn to a great mob of people, many mounted, but the majority on foot, who were evidently engaged in some quarrel.

Oscar would have hurried on but that his attention was directed to an old man in the centre of the crowd.

It was an old man he knew well, as he frequently visited the Armourer for the purpose of collecting alms.

He was known as "Mad Revelle," and mad he undoubtedly was.

A sad history attached to him, for he had lost

the whole of his property—wife and children—by a fire which, years before our story commences, had broken out in the City.

He was, therefore, a man greatly to be pitied.

He was never known to harm a soul ; his madness took the shape of loud and frequent cries of anguish, and he was under the delusion that he was pursued by evil spirits.

His clothes were a mass of rags ; he was shoeless and hatless, his long white beard was uncombed.

It was evident that he had been attacked by a lot of drunken gallants, for Oscar saw that the mounted persons, at least, wore the dresses of such persons.

"Shame ! Shame !" cried a chorus of voices, as Oscar pressed forward, the better to see what was going on.

"Who cries shame ?" asked an elaborately attired youth, mounted on a black horse, and in whose right hand was clutched a heavy riding-whip. "Who cries shame ? Let the man, who first cried it, come forward, and I will serve him as I serve such mad worms as *this !*"

And amid a howl of horror the youth raised his whip, and brought the lash down with cruel force on the shoulders of the madman, who screamed with pain, and cowered back as if to hide himself.

This was more than Oscar could stand.

Pushing his way through the crowd, he placed himself in front of the poor old man, and said sternly to the youth—

"Whoever you are, you are a dastardly coward thus to attack an old and defenceless man ! Is it to be wondered at that the people cry shame upon you ?"

"Coward ?" gasped the youth. "*Coward ?* You call me coward ? Take that ! and that ! and that !"

And again and again, amid loud roars of laughter from his companions, he brought the whip down on Oscar's shoulders and face.

Oscar threw down the sword, and with a bound like a young panther, dashed upon the youth.

He seized him by the waist, and despite his frantic struggles to free himself pulled him off his horse to the ground.

Instantly the youth's companions surrounded them, some of them drawing their swords.

They might have used them had it not been for a number of sturdy apprentices, who, coming up at the moment, and learning what had transpired, threatened them with chastisement if they touched Oscar.

The crowd drew back as Oscar rose, and allowed the youth to do likewise.

"Coward ?" yelled the young gallant. "He called me coward."

"And I repeat the word," said Oscar, quietly, 'And had I a whip I would serve you as you served me !"

"By the Virgin !" roared the youth, as he stamped and raved, "you would ? Stand back, companions ! Let us see who is the biggest coward of the two."

And with an elaborate swagger, the youth drew his sword.

"A fight !—a fight !" was now the cry. "Stand back ! Stand back ! A fight ! Fair play all the world over !"

The spectators, the gallants on the one side, and the apprentices and the crowd in general on the other.

Poor "Mad Revelle" shrank back against the wall, terrified at the appearance of the naked sword.

One of the apprentices nearest Oscar recognised our hero, and was about to speak, when Oscar hastily whispered, "Do not mention my name."

"Nay," returned the young fellow. "I'll see that your name is not mentioned ; but do you know with whom you quarrel ?"

"Nay, nor care."

"'Tis the son of Lord Trevanion—one of the Queen's favourites. You have heard of him ?"

"Ay, but little, What is he to me ?"

"*Your mortal enemy !*" said a deep voice.

Oscar turned swiftly.

"Who spoke ?" he asked.

No one answered.

"I heard no one speak," said the apprentice, in surprise.

"But I will *swear* someone spoke. However, whoever it was has made a mistake so far as I am concerned."

"Do you withdraw your words ?" yelled the swaggering gallant, who was certainly young Trevanion ; and as such we will continue to call him.

"Withdraw my words ?" sneered Oscar. "Certainly not. I never speak hastily. What I said I meant."

"Catiff, draw !" cried young Trevanion, now white with rage, "or I will slit your tongue as you stand ! Draw ! though the son of a nobleman has no business to fight with one of the common hoarde."

"Your words are high flown, young sir," replied Oscar, as he drew his blade. "Beware ! this may be the last time you will ever fight with *any one.*"

"Way — way !" yelled a score of voices. "Give them room—room !"

Those of the apprentices, who carried clubs, swung them round and round, and room was soon made under the very centre of the bar.

It happened that, just before the fight commenced, a number of watermen, who carried flaming links, were attracted to the spot, and their torches threw a lurid glare over the scene which now looked remarkably strange, though picturesque.

Trevanion was accounted, at least, by his companions, a most excellent swordsman ; and, therefore, they took it as a matter of course that the fight would terminate in his favour.

The swords were crossed, on both sides, in a cautious, yet determined manner.

If young Trevanion thought himself skilful with the sword, he very soon found that he had to deal with as calm and as steady a hand as he had ever noticed.

Had it been at any other time, he might have admired his opponent's calmness and steadiness—now it only enraged him.

"Pretty play," cried a waterman, as he held his torch higher, the better to see. "Very pretty play, on my soul!"

"Play!" yelled Trevanion, "this is no idle play. Look you, catiff;" he said to Oscar, "in a moment you will find that I will delay no longer."

"Well, if you require to die quickly," sneered Oscar. "Of course, I have no objection to increase the speed."

And thereupon he plied his weapon with the rapidity of lightning, much to the alarm of the gallants, and the approval of the apprentices who, amid loud laughter, called upon Oscar to "Spit him like a fowl!"

The clashing of the weapons sounded somewhat startling under the gloomy, dark-cobwebed arch, and also they looked startling, reflected, as were the blades in the glare of the torches.

By-and-by the sounds of laughter ceased, and very soon not a movement was made, and not a sound was heard save the rapid clashing of the weapons, and the heavy breathing of one of the combatants—that is to say, Trevanion.

It was in vain that he jumped first to one side and then to another, and use every movement he had been taught, to get a chance of running his weapon into Oscar's body.

He could not get him to move from the position he had taken up.

If Oscar moved at all, it was as though he were moving on a pivot—mechanically.

At last, Trevanion began to get exhausted.

His thrusts and feints got slower and slower, and then it was that Oscar still further increased his speed.

"I would not kill this youth," he muttered half aloud. "I would spare him."

"Nay," said a deep voice, which appeared to be close at his elbow. "*Kill him! Kill him! He will be your bitterest enemy. Remember the name— Trevanion.*"

It was the voice which had spoken before.

Oscar slightly turned.

It was a fatal movement.

His foot slipped on the stones; he staggered and fell.

"Die!" hissed Trevanion, now breathless with excitement and rage, as he drew his arm back to give the fatal blow. "Die! accursed wretch!"

The sword was descending, when a dark form started forward.

Trevanion's blade was snatched from his grasp, and he received a blow which stretched him full length on the ground.

A furious rush was made on both sides, and amid cries of almost every kind, mingled with oaths and yells, a regular battle commenced between the gallants, the apprentices, and the watermen, the latter using their lighted torches with a will on the persons of the gallants, who, however, rapidly gained an advantage over their opponents, owing to their being well mounted and armed, and, in the end, they gained this victory.

Young Trevanion soon had another weapon in his possession.

"Now!" he shouted exultingly, as he endeavoured to arrange his muddy and blood-stained clothes. "Now, let me assume the command! Since I have gained the mastery over this wretch——"

"You have gained no mastery," said Oscar. "An accident only prevented me from inflicting upon you the chastisement you merited. I am quite prepared to renew the combat, and you will find that——"

"Seize him!" shouted Trevanion.

In an instant Oscar was seized, and a pair of leathern thongs having been procured, his arms were fastened behind his back.

To attempt resistance he knew would be of no use whatever.

"I may as well submit to it," he muttered, "or a dagger may very quickly terminate my existence."

Aloud, he said, as he eyed young Trevanion, with no gentle look—

"I know you, and let me tell you that in me you have found an——"

Oscar was not allowed to complete the sentence, for a drunken gallant, rolling up to him, dealt him a stunning blow on the cheek with the flat of his sword.

Suddenly a loud shout was raised, and Oscar, turning his head, saw that Mad Revelle had not taken flight with the others, but had stood under the bar, crouched up in a corner, having, no doubt, been too terrified to move.

With loud shouts of laughter the gallants dragged him out, kicking and cuffing the unfortunate old man unmercifully.

It was in vain he implored them to spare him.

"Let us teach him what his friends have done for him by their interference," said Trevanion, as he snatched a heavy whip from one of his companions. "Hold him tightly some of you."

The old man was firmly held, and despite his howls and heart-rending appeals for mercy, Trevanion lashed him with the whip until the perspiration poured down his face.

Directly they let go of him the old man, with a low moan, fell insensible in the roadway.

"Now," said Trevanion, "drag this l rat along, and we will administer a thrashing to him at the proper place. By all the saints! I should like to know who the person was who snatched the sword from my hand at the time I was about to plunge it into his heart! One of his friends, no doubt," he sneered; "but where we will now take him he will find that ten thousand friends could not rescue him!"

A rope was now procured and placed round Oscar's waist. Trevanion then mounted, as did his companions, and the young gallant, taking hold of one end of the rope, gave the word, and the gallants moved off.

Mad Revelle lay where he had dropped for fully an hour; but, at last, consciousness returned to him, and he attempted to rise.

Mad Revelle's attempt to get upon his feet was a fruitless one, and he sank back with a groan.

"I'm mad!" he muttered. "Mad! and that is why they ill-treat me so! Mad! Oh, Heaven! mad! mad! And the place is being burnt down, and I am powerless to reach those I love!

Wife, children! All!—all! All will be consumed by the raging flames! Yet, are these flames; Nay, nay; they are but spirit links which glow about me. They stare at me with their fiery eyes.

"Why am I here? Let me think! Let me think! Nay, I cannot think! I am mad! And he came and tore them away when they would have killed me! Where is he? Where are the——oh!" he cried, as he made another frantic, and, this time, successful effort to rise. "They are all gone! Was he killed? No! no! Ha! they took him prisoner. What was his name?——"

"We will name you if you are not quickly off, old ragged hide!" said a gruff voice, and two Temple watchmen slowly approached the old man. "Get home with you!"

"Home?" shrieked the unfortunate man—"home? Ha, ha, ha, ha! A prisoner—his name—his captor—was—was" (and here the old man violently smote his head with his clenched fists), "his name was—Trevanion. Ha, Trevanion!"

With this the madman, forgetting the injuries which had been inflicted upon him, took to his heels, and ran like the wind in the direction of Tower Hill.

CHAPTER II.

SHOWS HOW OSCAR WAS CONVEYED TO BLACKBURN HOUSE—HOW HE WAS PLACED IN THE "FRIAR'S CELL"—HOW HE WAS BRUTALLY TREATED, AND HOW STEPHEN STANMORE AND HIS SON WERE AUTHORISED TO TAKE CHARGE OF HIM.

AMID loud shouts of derision, Oscar was dragged along through the streets with his hands tied behind him, and the rope round his neck.

Every now and then young Trevanion jerked the rope, causing Oscar infinite pain, and the gallants delivered a continuous shower of blows on his body.

To all this, however, Oscar made no remark, deeming it prudent to keep a still tongue in his head.

At last a halt was made at St. Martin's Fields, and, looking up, Oscar saw that they had paused before a small lodge belonging to Blackburn House, once the property of Lord Blackburn, who was beheaded some three or four years previous to the commencement of this story.

This fine old mansion, which was built almost entirely of solid stone, had become the property of the Crown on the death of Lord Blackburn, and it had never been disposed of, though repeatedly offered for sale, owing to the fact that it was supposed to be haunted.

Lord Trevanion was entrusted with the care of it, as well as a great amount of other Crown property, but he was never known to visit it.

It was through him that Blackburn had come to the block, and, perhaps, he believed that the place was haunted.

Rumour had it that every midnight the shadow of the late owner of Blackburn House could be seen walking about the premises with his head in his hand.

Oscar had heard a great deal of talk about Blackburn House, and its many ghastly secrets as well as its numerous subterranean passages and vaults, but he had little dreamed that he would one day be placed in one of these vaults.

The lodge was in total darkness when the party arrived.

Young Trevanion tapped at the window with his riding-whip; but as there was no reply to this, he smashed the glass to atoms.

This noisy summons was at once answered.

The narrow door was pulled violently open, and a short, powerful, though remarkably ugly, middle-aged man, appeared on the threshold, a lantern in one hand, and a monstrous pistol in the other.

"What now!" he growled. "Will you disturb a man in——"

"Put your pistol by, Stanmore," said young Trevanion. "You should answer my summons in a more prompt manner. Perhaps you will do so in future, and so save me the trouble of breaking any more windows."

Stanmore, the lodge-keeper and watchman of the House itself, at once recognised the voice, and bowed himself almost to the ground.

"Your worship's most obedient servant," he said. "I did not know it was your worship, or you would not have had to break a window in order to summon me."

"All is well, Stanmore. Hold your lantern over this wretch's face."

And he pointed to Oscar.

Stanmore did so.

"Holy Mary!" he cried, as he caught sight of the rope round Oscar's neck. "What has he done, your worship?"

"He is a traitor to Queen Elizabeth."

"A traitor, eh? And so young!"

"Young traitors are ever the worst," observed one of the gallants.

"Ay, even so," replied Stanmore, "and what is your worship about to do with him?"

"I will tell you how it is, Stanmore," said Trevanion. "I have not yet informed his lordship, my father, of the existence of a plot against her Majesty, and in which this wretch is the prime mover, so I have decided to have him confined in Blackburn House until such time as I can furnish the proofs."

"Your worship decides very wisely," said Stanmore, who by the wink Trevanion directed at him, understood that Oscar was one of young

Trevanion's enemies. And if it is really your intention to confine the youth, I had better bring the keys."

"Do—and look you, Stanmore—where is your son?"

"Within, your worship."

"Let him accompany us then. Awake him at once, and let him bring his *tools*. Do you understand?"

"Perfectly. None so well understands how to deal with traitors to her most gracious Majesty as my son Caleb. Ho, ho!"

Oscar, whose blood fairly boiled with anger and indignation, could no longer stand it.

"A traitor!" he cried, "*I* a traitor?"

"Ay, a rank traitor!" replied Trevanion.

"You are an infamous liar!" cried Oscar. "And if Heaven spares me, I will thrust the lie down your accursed throat!"

"You may depend upon being *spared!*" sneered young Trevanion. "See yonder house," and with his riding-whip he pointed to the gloomy-looking mansion. "You will enter that place shortly: but you will never leave it alive or dead!"

"Heaven watches over me!" replied Oscar, solemnly.

"We shall see," replied Trevanion; "and mark you this—extra punishment for your abuse."

Oscar directed a scornful look at him, but made no further reply.

In a few seconds Stanmore once more appeared.

This time he carried in one hand a link, in the other a bunch of huge keys, many of them being of an extraordinary pattern.

Behind him walked his son Caleb.

He was of about the same age and height as Oscar, but he was a most extraordinary-looking object, being extremely thin, cross-eyed, and "lantern-jawed."

Added to this, his top and bottom front teeth projected to a great extent, and his hair, long and straight, was of that peculiar colour which some people call "carroty."

He carried a basket, slung over his shoulder, in which were a number of tools.

Walking deliberately up to Oscar, he poked his hideous face forward, so that his nose touched Oscar's cheek.

"A traitor, eh?" he said, in shrill treble tones. "In what a country do we live, dear fayther, that we have such awful beings surrounding us, eh?"

"You are right, my son," replied the lodge-keeper, with a wink at the gallants, who were surveying this curious specimen of humanity, as they might have surveyed the collection of monkeys in the Tower.

"And he has that peculiar smell about him like all traitors, eh, fayther?"

"Exactly, my son."

"And Lord Trevanion's good son has been fortunate enough in finding him out," said Caleb, shaking his head. "Oh, he is very cleever, fayther, eh? Ah, Blackburn House is a foine place to confine traitors. I wonder the Queen has not thought of that before now."

"I wonder no one has thought of confining you, you ugly brute!" hissed Oscar.

The hideous Caleb burst into a loud roar of laughter.

I am no traitor," he said.

"That may be," said Oscar, "but if you are no traitor, you are certainly one of the ugliest wretches I ever beheld."

"Come, Stanmore," cried young Trevanion, giving the rope a brutal jerk. "Hold your link up, and let us proceed."

"To what part of the mansion shall I take him?" asked Stanmore.

"Where should you think? One of the best bedrooms? Ho, ho! Why, lead the way to the 'Friar's Cell.' That is the place for such as he."

"True, true," grinned Stanmore, jingling his huge keys. "And if we place him in the Friar's Cell, there is certainly no chance of his escaping."

"You may be assured that I do no wish him to escape, Stanmore," whispered young Trevanion.

"What is your intention, your worship?"

"He is to die."

"Ha!"

"Yes, to die! He has grossly insulted me before a mass of people, including my friends here. We fought in the public street, Stanmore."

"Lord!"

"Yes. And of course, I being the most skilful swordsman, would speedily have run my sword through his carcase had not some wretch knocked the weapon from my grasp."

"What a pity!"

"Nay, 'twas all for the best. Had he been killed, I should not have had the opportunity of inflicting upon him the punishment he deserves, and will now get."

"True. Well, if you want any one to help you, don't forget Caleb. He is a master hand at inflicting torture. Ho! ho! But here we are."

By this time the party had traversed a long winding path, which, from not being used, was overgrown with weeds, and Stanmore paused before a narrow bridge of beams of wood, which were thrown across the moat, and did duty for the drawbridge which was in a shattered condition, and, therefore, useless.

Caleb, with the lantern, led the way, his father standing at the edge of the moat, and holding his link high aloft.

"Alas!" thought Oscar, "I feel that I shall never more breathe the pure air. Something tells me that, in this foul place, I shall die. Who knows he may intend to fling me into a dungeon, and there let me lie and starve. Oh, 'tis indeed awful to think of! What will my father say, and my poor mother who loves me so dearly?"

As he thought of his mother's kindly face, of her loving words, a sob escaped his lips, and tears started to his eyes.

The light from Caleb's lantern enabled young Trevanion to see this, and he chuckled with delight.

"I thought you would come to your senses

ere long," he said.   "Look at him, companions.
Observe his tearful face.   Ere long he will sue
for mercy,"

"Liar!" cried Oscar.   "I would die rather
than sue for mercy to such a coward as you!"

"Even if you did, 'twould be in vain," sneered
Trevanion.   "What ho! Stanmore!"

"Here," said Stanmore, who, now that all
had got across, proceeded to cross the bridge
himself.

"Hurry thyself!" shouted Trevanion.   "Let
us have the doors opened."

Stanmore and his son led the way into the
courtyard; then, instead of proceeding to the
huge gate, which was the principal entrance, he
turned to the right, pushed his way through a
number of bushes, and stopped before a low arch
in which was set a door fitted with ponderous
bolts and bars.

The whole party dismounted.

As Caleb threw the light of his lantern on the
gloomy doorway, a shudder ran through Oscar.

Many a time had the Armourer spoken of this
place to him.

He remembered him to have said how, many a
time, a foul murder was known to have been
here committed.

Having selected the key by which the door was
opened, Stanmore exerted all his strength, and
turned it.

Then he pressed his shoulder against the door,
which rolled slowly back.

A rush of damp air instantly extinguished the
torch.

"Curse it!" growled Stanmore, as he opened
the slide in the lantern to re-light it.   "Some
people would have said that it was Lord Blackburn's ghost which had blown out the link.
Ha! ha! they would not get *me* to believe in
such foolery.   Now then, gentlemen, let me go
first, and do not forget that you are going to
descend a number of steps which, though sound,
are slippery.   The slightest mistake, and you
may break your necks."

With this comforting assurance, Stanmore
walked cautiously forward.

Round and round the stone steps wound much
like a corkscrew, and they were, beyond question,
extremely slippery.

But the slime was not confined to the steps.
It ran down the walls in streams, and the smell
was horrible in the extreme.

This was accounted for by the fact that they
were passing under the moat.

At last Stanmore halted.

"Here we are," he said with a chuckle.   "Did
any of you gentlemen ever see a more lively
place than this?   Why, no; not even at the
Tower.   Whoever is placed in this cell" (and he
rapped on a narrow oaken door) "never lives
longer than a week without going *mad!* His
worship could tell you of many persons his
father has confined in this cell, who have gone
mad, and whose bones——"

"Silence!" growled young Trevanion.

Stanmore stopped with a grin, selected
another key, and opened the door.

In another moment, Oscar found himself
within a circular stone cell.

No furniture of any kind was to be seen.

There was a small stone table projecting from
the wall, and a block of wood chained to the
floor, which did duty for a chair.

The ceiling was remarkably lofty.

In the centre was a round hole, large enough
to admit of the passage of a man's body.

Oscar at once noticed this; but he saw that
it was utterly impossible for a prisoner to
reach it.

"This is the Friar's Cell, gentlemen," grinned
Stanmore, "so called because the once celebrated
Friar Stephane was supposed to have been mur-
dered by Lord Tre——"

"Silence!" shouted young Trevanion.

Stanmore at once ceased.

"And what is that round hole for?" asked
one of the gallants, pointing to the hole in the
centre of the roof.

"Oh, that," grinned Stanmore, "is the place
to lower the food to the prisoner, that is, if the
prisoner happens to be allowed food.   Now
then, Caleb, to work."

Caleb opened his basket, and took out several
implements.

Then, kneeling on the stone floor, he raised a
heavy ring, which was fixed in one of the slabs,
and, selecting another ring from his basket,
opened it.

Stanmore and several of the gallants now
dragged Oscar forward, and unbuckled the
straps.   The ring was placed round his ankle,
and then placed through the one in the floor.

A huge rivet was then passed through it, and
Caleb proceeded to fix both with a hammer.

Suddenly Oscar fell on the top of Caleb.

"Pull him off!" yelled the latter.   "Pull
him off—he will crush me!"

"He has fainted!" laughed Trevanion, picking up a pitcher of dirty water; "but we will
soon revive him."

And he flung the contents of the pitcher in
Oscar's face.

Oscar had not fainted, he had only pretended
to do so—with an object.

Before he fell he had caught sight of a small
file in Caleb's basket, and in an instant he had
it in his possession, entirely unnoticed by any
one.

After a short pause he pretended to come to,
and operations were resumed and completed.

Directly Caleb had given the last blow with
the hammer, he started up, snatched a whip
from the gallant nearest him, and dealt Oscar a
cruel slash on the face, almost blinding him.

"Curse you!" he yelled.   "Take that for falling on me!"

Oscar, uttering a loud cry, and forgetful of
the ring which secured him, launched out with
his clenched fist.

It caught Caleb on the mouth, cutting his lips
against his huge teeth, and sending him sprawling to the floor.

But the action caused Oscar to fall as well,
and he nearly lost his file.

"I will pay you anon!" roared Caleb.   "I
will pull your eyes out, I will, won't I pay
ther?"

"If you like, my dear son."

"CALEB WAS ABOUT TO DELIVER THE FIRST BLOW WHEN OSCAR STARTED UP."

"He struck me, fayther!" whined Caleb.

"Never mind, my son, you shall have your revenge."

"Yes, never mind," said one of the gallants, "you have a thick skull, that is one comfort."

"And he doesn't have to take his face to Court," laughed another.

Caleb made no reply to these satirical remarks.

He looked hard at Oscar, and gnashed his teeth.

"I will come here *when no one knows of it,*" he muttered. "Ha, ha! Father keeps the key of the door; *but I will get at him through the hole, ha, ha!* And I will torture him, ho, ho!"

"Now," said young Trevanion; "since he is secured, we will leave him, and let him have a taste of the Friar's Cell all to himself. Take your leave of him, companions, for no doubt 'tis the last you will ever see of him. Stanmore, I leave him till to-morrow in your charge. You and your son attend to him."

"Of course, your worship. And the food?"

"None!"

"Ah! Very good—very good. Come forth, then, gentlemen."

The whole party then left the cell.

"Look you," whispered Trevanion to Stanmore. "I shall part with my companions at the lodge, and then I have a word to say to you."

"Good."

At the lodge Trevanion bade his companions adieu until the following evening, and then accompanied Stanmore and his son inside.

At a signal from Trevanion, Stanmore bade Caleb retire to another apartment.

Caleb withdrew, but he did not go out of hearing.

He placed himself in such a position that he could overhear every word.

"My fayther will have all the money as usual," he muttered; "but I will see how much he gets."

"Listen, Stanmore," said Trevanion. "I mean to keep my word as to this cub."

"How do you mean?"

"Kill him!"

"Oh, ay, just so. Starve him! Send him mad! and then——"

"No, no. In this case that will not do."

"One of these gallants may, in a few hours, fall out with me, give information of what has been done, and, probably the wretch may be released."

"I see."

"Then if he is released, a nice story would soon be afloat. I should incur my father's displeasure, and be the laughing-stock of the whole Court."

"Of course you would."

"I intend he shall die——"

"By your hand! Just so——"

"No, by *yours.*"

"Hem: I have done a few things like it for your father, but for his son——"

"You will do what I ask you?"

"Eh? Hem! I don't know about that. You cannot compel me to commit *murder.*"

"Nay; but I can ask you to *dispose* of a certain person at a certain price."

Stanmore shook his head.

"Why not do it yourself?" he asked.

"I shun such a——"

Stanmore burst into a loud guffaw.

"Listen!" said Trevanion. "Do what I ask, and I will pay you five hundred crowns."

Stanmore started.

"'Tis a large sum," he said, slowly; "but how do you——"

"You would say how am I to get it? Let me tell you that it is already in my possession. Do the deed, and to-morrow the sum I name shall be yours. I swear it!"

"I don't doubt you; but I would rather have the money ere I did the deed."

"Well, well. You shall. In twelve hours I will be here with the amount."

"Good. And you shall see me do the deed if you will."

"Ay, I shall then know that all is well. Don't forget—in twelve hours."

"I shall be ready."

"Till then—adieu."

Another minute, and Trevanion had mounted and ridden away.

"He is going to kill him," chuckled Caleb, "but ere he does, I shall my little bit of sport, with him all to myself. Ho, ho! sport!"

o　　o　　o　　o　　o

Directly the door of his cell had closed, Oscar could not hear the faintest sound.

Though he listened intently he could not hear even the footsteps of his departing enemies.

Feeling about, he found the block which did duty for a stool.

The chain was of sufficient length to allow him to drag it close enough towards him.

Seating himself he gave way to thought.

How long he sat he knew not, but he was roused by a faint sound on the floor.

He placed his hand down, and found that the place was literally alive with black beetles.

Black beetles! It at once dawned upon him that it was these horrid insects which had driven so many who had been placed in that cell, mad.

Oscar started up.

He found that his limbs were fast becoming stiff and sore.

His brain seemed to grow dull his tongue was parched, and more than once he fancied that some awful shadow passed by him—anon it seemed as if a cold and clammy hand were laid upon his face.

"I have the file," he muttered. "But what if I succeed in disconnecting this link? Should I be free, then? Alas, no! And sleep steals on me! But could I sleep with this swarm of horrid insects about me? I fear not. But I will use the file."

Kneeling on the floor, Oscar at once commenced to work his file, and he soon had the satisfaction of feeling that he was making rapid progress.

CHAPTER III.

IS OF THE STRUGGLE FOR LIFE IN THE FRIAR'S CELL—OF HOW STANMORE GOES ABOUT EARNING HIS FIVE HUNDRED CROWNS, AND OF WHAT HORRIBLE EVENT OCCURRED.

SCRAPE! scrape! and screech! screech! went the file, and every scrape and every screech lessened the strength of the link which secured the ankle of Oscar Raymond.

At last the link was filed completely through, and it fell upon the floor with a clank.

"Free thus far," muttered Oscar—"free now to lay in what part of this horrible hole I may think fit; but that is all—that is all! Oh, Heaven! If I am here many hours longer, I am certain that I shall go mad! No sound—no sound whatever can I hear. I would rather attempt to compose myself to sleep amid the roar of ten thousand cannon than in this fearful silence. Yet even, at the risk of its being discovered that I have burst my bonds, I must sleep."

He threw himself on the floor against the wall, and, with his head upon his arm, fell into a sound sleep.

He slept on for several hours, and awoke at last with a start.

He leapt to his feet, shaking off hundreds of beetles, and listened.

Was it a sound he heard?

Ay, it was; and it was again and again repeated.

It was a sound as of some one moving heavy furniture overhead.

Oscar crept to the link, and fastened it on his ankle, so that it looked on one side as if it had not been tampered with.

Then he seated himself upon the block, and waited.

More distinct became the noise—faster beat Oscar's heart.

What could the noise mean.

Suddenly a light appeared at the hole above.

Oscar leaned his head on his hands, and breathed heavily as if asleep.

There was a rustling movement above as if some one were listening.

Then Oscar heard a quiet chuckle, and a voice muttered, "All is well."

In a few moments a lantern, tied to the end of a thick-knotted rope, was gradually lowered.

Oscar was able to see all this through his fingers.

The lantern eventually rested upon the ground.

Then there was another pause. The person above was evidently looking to see whether Oscar was awake or asleep.

Another moment—a moment which seemed an hour to Oscar, and the rope was violently agitated, and the figure of a man came cautiously down it

It was Caleb Stanmore.

In his mouth he carried a heavy whip, and from his pockets protruded many curiously-shaped instruments.

Directly his feet touched the ground, he again listened.

Oscar never stirred; his breathing was regular, just as if he were in a sound sleep.

With a hideous chuckle, Caleb untied the lantern, and then took the whip in his hand.

He was about to deliver the first blow on Oscar's head, when the youth, with the speed of lightning, started up, dashed forward, and clutched him by the throat.

Instantly the lantern dropped from Caleb's grasp, and once more the place was in total darkness.

Pressing his knuckles into his foe's throat, Oscar, whose blood was now fully roused, forced the wretch back against the wall.

"Dastard!" he hissed, "I am free!—free! to inflict upon you the punishment that you deserve."

Astonishment and terror had taken possession of the cowardly and brutal Caleb; but as he realised the position in which he stood, rage and fear of what might happen, lent strength to his arms, and with all the power of which he was able he struggled to release himself.

Vain the effort!

The sleep, which Oscar had snatched, had greatly refreshed him, and Caleb found it impossible to release himself.

Tighter—tighter did Oscar grasp the villain's throat until he must have been black in the face.

Suddenly Caleb made a movement with his right hand.

Oscar let go his throat with one hand, and was just in time to save himself, for Caleb had taken a hammer from his pocket, and raised it aloft.

Oscar wrenched the instrument from his grasp, and brought it down with a crash on his head.

Caleb fell weltering in blood.

"I have not killed him!" muttered Oscar. "No, no. I will not kill him if I can help it though he deserves death. Oh, for light—light! There might now be a chance of escape."

Kneeling down, he felt in Caleb's pockets, and, after taking out numerous instruments, he had the satisfaction and joy of finding a tinder box.

With the flint and steel he at once set to work, and soon kindled a light.

Lighting the lantern he held it over the bleeding Caleb.

"He is unconscious," muttered Oscar, "and from his appearance, he will so remain for a long while. Thank Heaven, I have not killed him! I would not have his blood upon my soul, wretch though he is, for the world. If he lives he will assuredly meet with a worse death than he could meet at my hands."

Oscar placed Caleb by the link, and leaned his head on the block of wood, so that., in the dim light, he looked very much like Oscar had looked when sitting there.

Placing Caleb's dagger at his own girdle, and throwing the whip into a corner of the cell, Oscar placed the handle of the lantern between his teeth, and clutching the rope, tugged at it as hard as he was able.

It was as firm as a rock.

Being assured that it was secure, he commenced to ascend.

The rope being knotted, he was, of course, greatly assisted.

Higher and higher he got, until at last he passed through the hole in the ceiling.

He stopped, and holding on with one hand, waved the lantern about with the other.

He found that he was in a room of some kind, and he stepped on to the floor.

Holding up the lantern he saw that the rope had been fixed in a chain which depended from the ceiling of the room in which he now stood.

To unfasten it was the work of a moment.

Making it into a coil, he placed it over his arm, and then raising the lantern aloft, he proceeded to survey the room.

o   o   o   o   o

The twelve hours had passed, and young Trevanion was at the lodge as promised.

Stanmore looked pale and excited.

"Ready?" asked young Trevanion.

"Ay, ay," replied Stanmore. "Quite ready. But will not your honour pause, and consider that if we——"

"Listen! There are your crowns. Count them."

"Oh, I can take your word that all is correct."

"Then why do you wish me to pause and consider?"

"Look you here," said Stanmore, producing a small black phial. "You see this?"

"I do."

"'Tis poison!"

"I guessed as much. What then?"

"Instead of plunging a dagger into the carcase of this youth, would it not be as well to put this in his water? The first draught would assuredly prove fatal to him."

"Nay, nay. Poison is useful in *some* cases, but not in this. I would see the business at once ended."

"Since it must be so," said Stanmore, "why it must be so."

"But since that poison may be useful to me at some future date," said young Trevanion, "why hand it to me?"

Stanmore handed the phial to him with a grin, and the remark that it was prepared by himself, and so if his lordship wanted any more at any time, he would remember where to go for it.

"Where is Caleb?" asked Trevanion.

"Asleep your worship. Shall I rouse him?

"Nay. You know his restless tongue. What you had done would not be a secret for any length of time.

"Right," said Stanmore. "Talking of what don't concern him is Caleb's principal failure. And, besides, the lad is tired. Now, your worship," said Stanmore, taking a lantern. "Let me know when you are ready."

"I am ready now."

"Follow me then; but you will assist me in disposing of the body?"

"Yes."

"Good. I am satisfied."

Stanmore led the way.

Noiselessly the pair descended the slimy stone steps.

"Let us listen," said Stanmore; "for 'tis more than likely he may be asleep."

"Your task will, in that case, be so much the more easy," replied Trevanion.

The pair listened intently.

No sound fell upon their ears.

"Do you hold the lantern while I open the door," said Stanmore.

Trevanion took the lantern, and Stanmore unlocked the door.

As he drew it back, the rays of the lantern fell upon—as it appeared to them—the sleeping figure of Oscar.

"'Tis well," whispered Stanmore, with a quiet chuckle, "he sleeps soundly. We shall have no difficulty with him."

"Delay no longer then!" whispered Trevanion. "Enter at once, and *strike hard*, do you hear?"

"Fear it not!" replied Stanmore, unsheathing a long dagger. "And do you hold the lantern just where you stand. For if you enter the cell with it, the light may awaken him."

Young Trevanion nodded.

With the murderous weapon clasped firmly in his right hand, Stanmore entered the cell.

An instant he listened; the next he raised the dagger on high, and plunged the blade in the throat of the figure before him.

Then plucking it forth, he drew back.

"'Tis done!" he cried. "Bring hither the lantern, your worship."

As he said this, he flung the body on its back,

Trevanion entered the apartments, and Stanmore, taking the lantern from him, held it up so that the rays fell upon the face of the figure before him.

And as those rays lit up the face, Stanmore, with a wild, unearthly cry, started back.

Young Trevanion startled, also drew back, ere he had looked fully upon the body.

Again and again Stanmore shrieked, and as he shrieked, he rushed round and round the cell like a madman.

"What ails thee, thou accursed loon?" cried Trevanion.

"Look!" yelled Stanmore, pointing at the ghastly corpse. "*Look! I have murdered my own son!*"

Trevanion started forward, stooped over the body, and looked into the white, distorted features.

Then he slowly drew himself erect—his face as pale as that of the corpse and stood still—rooted to the spot !

"My son ! My son !" shrieked Stanmore, flinging himself on his knees by his son's corpse. "*I* am not his murderer ! Nay, nay, not me, not me !"

"Fool !" yelled young Trevanion. "On whom then will you lay the blame ? On me ?"

"Yes, on you !" replied Stanmore. "For though you did not actually strike the blow, yet you prompted me to——"

"False loon !" cried Trevanion, plucking his blade from its scabbard, "dare to say that *I* am your son's murderer, and I will lay you dead at his side !"

"Do you threaten me ?" screamed Stanmore. "Do you threaten to kill *me?* And if you did, what then ? What have I to live for now that my son is no more ? Say, what have I to live for ? Wretch ! You led me on to kill my son !"

"How did your son get here ? That is the question ; you said he was asleep."

"So I thought," moaned Stanmore, his eyes fixed upon the stiffening body of his son.

"And where is he whom you came to kill, eh ? Why, 'tis as plain as plain can be. Your son came here to torture him ; he was overpowered, and the accursed youth has escaped. Ere to-morrow's sun sets, London will be ringing with this fine intelligence."

"Ay, ay, London *shall* ring !" cried Stanmore; "for I myself will spread the news, since, my son being dead, I have now no further desire to live."

"Then die, fool !" hissed Trevanion.

And starting forward, he attacked him with his sword.

Stanmore had no sword to defend himself; and even if he had, it is a question whether he would have drawn it.

As the coward rushed upon him, he simply drew himself erect, and in an instant Trevanion's blade had passed through his body.

Stanmore, with a gasping cry, fell forward upon the body of his son.

"My curse on you !" he cried, raising his hand aloft—"my curse on you ! You are a murderer like your infamous father !"

"And you will never live to tell the tale !" replied Trevanion, as he sheathed his blade.

Stanmore made no answer to him.

In another moment he was a dead man.

"And now what is to be done ?" muttered Trevanion, as he picked up the lantern. "I must away, or I may be discovered. Yes, I will away at once ; but anon, I will return and bury these two. Thus no traces of what has occurred will remain. I will so place it to my father that he, as others, will believe that Stanmore and his son have deserted their posts."

"But what of my foe, whose name I have discovered to be Oscar Raymond ? How did he escape ? Is he in league with that accursed wizard of Whitehall ? Bah !" he cried, in disgust, as he snatched the huge keys from the dead watchman's belt. "Assuredly he shall answer for it the very first time I come face to face

with him. But let me think. Since the father had the keys——"

Here glancing up, he caught sight of the aperture in the ceiling.

"The mystery is solved !" he cried. "Of course, Caleb came that way, and by means of the rope. Then this wretch, unless he has managed to get out of the barred windows, must be concealed somewhere in this building ! I will search !"

Hastily quitting the cell, Trevanion pulled the door to, and locked it.

He was perfectly acquainted with the keys of the mansion, and selecting one, he made his way up the stairs.

At the top he placed the lantern under his cloak, so that its light should not attract the attention of any one, and advanced to the principal entrance.

This door he quickly opened, entered the damp and musty smelling hall, and closed the door after him.

With the lantern in his left hand, and his naked sword in his right, the wretch ascended the stairs.

Every hole and corner he searched, and forced the point of his sword behind every curtain he came upon.

"If I meet him I am safe, for I am armed, and he is unarmed," muttered Trevanion ; "so I will not despair, for unless he has the power of transforming himself to a thing of infinite smallness, he could certainly never have escaped from this place."

    o   o   o   o   o

For a brief space we will return to Oscar.

From room to room he went, and tried the windows.

All were securely barred.

For a time he rested, and again he continued the search.

Suddenly he heard voices. He listened, and crept in the direction of the sound.

By another door he found himself in the room to which he had ascended from the dungeon.

Here the voices were very distinct.

Extinguishing the lantern, he laid himself on his stomach, and crawling to the aperture looked down.

He saw Stanmore and Trevanion and heard the former's bitter cry—"*I have murdered my own son !*"

Without moving, Oscar watched what followed.

Even could he have saved the wretched watchman, he would not have done so, for he felt that such a villain deserved death, no matter at whose hands.

When he saw young Trevanion go out of the cell, he resumed his search for an outlet.

He presently found what would prove a certain opportunity of escape, and that was a rotten bar, which, after a few shakes, he pulled from its position.

But though rotten at the ends, he saw that, taking it altogether, it was a good piece of iron, and could be relied upon.

He was to fix one end of his rope round the

bar, with the object of securing it to the two bars remaining in the window, when he heard the principal door bang.

"By all the saints!" he muttered, "the villain is about to search the place. No doubt he fancies that I have not yet effected my escape."

Oscar rapidly undid the rope, and, holding the iron bar firmly in his hand, stationed himself by the door.

Nearer and nearer came the sound of Trevanion's footsteps, and, at last, the young villain, white with rage and disappointment, entered.

Directly he entered, Oscar dashed forward, and, raising the iron bar, he smashed the sword Trevanion was carrying to pieces.

"Dastard!" cried Oscar, "he whom you seek is *here*!"

Trevanion, with a gasping cry, tottered back.

He recovered himself in a few seconds, however, and snatched his dagger from its sheath.

He had not the least idea that Oscar was armed with the weapon he had taken from Caleb.

"*Now* we are on equal terms," said Oscar, throwing away the iron bar. "Behold!"

And he plucked forth his dagger.

"Ha!" cried Trevanion.

"Advance!" said Oscar. "I await you."

But it was evident that terror had now taken possession of young Trevanion.

As Oscar stealthily advanced, he retreated.

At last he came to the door, and, with a bitter curse, he flung his dagger at Oscar's head.

Fortunately for Oscar, he anticipated the movement, and darted on one side.

Across the room flew the dagger, and buried itself an inch deep in the panelling of an oak cabinet.

Trevanion turned to fly; but, ere he could take two steps, Oscar had seized him.

"Come back, wretch!" he hissed. "Come back, thou coward! Come back, murderer! Do you seek your enemies only to turn and fly when you face them? Come back, I say!"

And, despite his struggles, Oscar pulled him back into the room.

By the dim light of the lantern, he saw that the wretch was as white as a sheet.

Indeed, he seemed almost paralysed with terror.

"Spare me!" he gasped.

"Spare you!" replied Oscar, contemptuously. "Ay, I will spare you, although you would not have spared me. You see I escaped from that dungeon. You shall go there, and it will remain to be seen whether you will escape. Give me those keys!"

"I—I——"

"Give me those keys, I tell you! Mind, your life is hanging on a thread. The keys!"

Young Trevanion threw them on the floor, and Oscar picked them up.

While stooping to do this, Trevanion made another frantic rush to gain the door.

But Oscar had him again, and this time he held him firmly.

"You are going into the dungeon in which you placed me!" said Oscar sternly. "Along with those you murdered. For at your door lies the guilt of their death."

"Oh, holy Virgin!" gasped Trevanion. "Do not place me there. Five hundred crowns shall be——"

"I cannot be bribed," interrupted Oscar; "especially with blood money."

Clutching young Trevanion by the collar and the waist, Oscar lifted him off his feet, and totally disregarding his cries and his struggles, bore him to the aperture we have described, and without any ceremony, hurled him into the darkness.

Crash he went upon the stones!

Oscar listened.

Trevanion uttered two or three deep groans, then all was still.

"He is not dead," muttered Oscar. "Villains are not easily killed. Now, I have got the keys, and the watchman and his son being dead, no one will go to him. He shall remain there, with the dead men's pale faces looking at him, until I release him, which will not be until he has felt what it is to be a prisoner in that accursed murderer's hole for many a long hour."

Picking up the lantern, Oscar left the room, and soon reached the great doors.

He found the right key and blowing out the light, he opened the door and left the house, taking the keys with him.

CHAPTER IV.

18 OF HOW THE ARMOURER GAINS SOME INFORMATION—HOW HE GETS THE ASSISTANCE OF THE GIANT BROTHERS, AND HOW THE GIANTS ENTER THE "FRIAR'S CELL" WITHOUT THE AID OF KEYS.

OUR readers will remember that when "Mad Revelle" regained consciousness, and recollected the name of Trevanion, he rushed off towards Tower Hill, his object being to inform the Armourer of what had happened, and that Oscar had been taken prisoner.

But the unhappy lunatic was doomed to meet with further misfortunes.

Rounding St. Paul's, at a terrific rate of speed, he came full tilt against one of the royal coaches proceeding from the Tower.

The concussion sent him bleeding and senseless to the earth.

The poor fellow was soon surrounded by a crowd, who, probably, would have done nothing but stand and look at him.

Suddenly the coach window was dropped, and a head thrust forth.

A head it was that was instantly recognised by the majority of persons present.

The occupant of the coach was the Lord High Chancellor of England.

"What has happened?" he asked.

"'Tis a man, my lord," said one of the footmen, "who, for the nonce, thought himself a bull, and the coach a fit thing to be tossed in the air."

"What mean you?"

"The man on the ground, your lordship, is a lunatic, who has run his head against the panelling of the coach, which 'twas a wonder he did not smash as well as his head."

"Lunatic or not, if he has met with any injury, he must be attended to. See, he bleeds. Are any of these people acquainted with the unfortunate man?"

"Yes, yes;" was the cry. "He is mad Revelle."

"Where is his home?"

"He has none, your lordship."

"Poor devil!" ejaculated the Chancellor, as he fumbled in his pockets. "Well, well, my friends, is there not a surgeon among ye all?"

No answer.

"There is an apothecary's yonder," said an apprentice, who was at the head of a dozen sturdy companions. "And if your lordship will have the kindness to give us a noble to pay for the treatment, we will convey him thither."

"Ay, that will I, my lads," replied the Chancellor, handing out two nobles, "and there is one for thyself to buy ribbons for thy sweetheart next fair-day. I like people with kind hearts," he muttered, sinking back in his seat. "Heaven's mercy on us! There are few with kind hearts in the world now. Alas! that we should have to say so."

The apprentices very carefully, yet quickly, picked up and carried the old man to the apothecary's, and the carriage, amid the cheers of the crowd, moved off.

"A good man!" said a scrivener, who had watched what had taken place. "A good man—very good. Too good for the Court as at present constituted. If he continues to be too good he will, alack! come to the block, and that soon!"

"Hence, thou false prophet!" cried several, as the scrivener, having said his say (and he had said what really came true), moved off. "Hence, thou render of mouldy parchment! Hence, thou vulture of the law! Shame on thee—shame!"

The unfortunate madman was found to be seriously injured, his head being badly cut.

As the apprentices entered the shop, the apothecary shook his head, as much as to say—

"Can give him no attention."

"Fear it not, thou bag of bones!" said the apprentice before spoken of, in tones of disgust, as he flung down the noble. "There is thy money to attend him. Do so at once."

"He will require much attention."

"Well," replied the apprentice, "here is another noble. Let thy vulture claws pick it up——"

"Let not thy tongue wag so fast, master apprentice," interrupted the apothecary, "for if at any time *you* want my attention, I may not be inclined to give it."

And beckoning to an attendant, as thin and as withered as himself, he proceeded to lift "Mad Revelle," and convey him to an inner apartment.

"Come companions," said the apprentice, gaily, "and leave old Rattlebones to his black draughts, blisters, and plague pills."

The case was so serious, that after some consideration, the apothecary deemed it advisable to detain "Mad Revelle" for some few hours at least.

Twenty hours passed, ere he was in a fit condition to leave the place.

And a terrible sight the unfortunate man looked as he tottered across the threshold, his head being enveloped in bandages.

He had not forgotten, however, where he had intended to go—that is to say, to the residence of the Armourer.

He reached the Armourer's house within half-an-hour after leaving the apothecary's, and lifting the latch of the smithy, entered.

There he found the Armourer and his wife surrounded by a number of armed citizens.

The pale face of the Armourer and the sobs of his wife showed that they were in great trouble.

"Come not here," said one of the citizens. "We have now other things to attend to besides giving alms."

"Nay, send him not away penniless," said the good-hearted Armourer. "In the midst of our troubles let us feel for others."

And he placed his hand in his pocket.

"Ay," said his wife, "and the poor man has been brutally ill-used, for, observe—his head is bandaged."

"Ay, ay, generous madam," said Revelle with a low bow. "I have been crully ill-used. Crully—cruelly. But heaven will punish them, honourable madam. Heaven will assuredly punish them, though I may not live to see it.

"Nay, noble sir, he said, as the Armourer offered him a crown. "Alms I need not now. I fear me I shall need them no more. My life will be but brief. Heaven will soon treat me with kindness, and will take my life from me, and I shall join those who so long ago were laid in the cold grave.

"But I am forgetting I had news for you, Master Armourer, hours ago—hours ago, though I forget how many," and here his voice became weak; "yet it must be very many hours ago, and it is——"

"Give him wine, good wife," said the Armourer, as he seated the man on a block of wood; "and let it be the best our cellar can afford. See, he is weak and faint from loss of blood. Alas! how sad it is that, as the world grows older, people seem to treat those who cannot help themselves, with greater unkindness. To ill-treat a man like this—a man whose life is but a few black pages of misfortune, and whose reason, in consequence, has been upset, is indeed most cruel. The curse of all true men be on them that would be guilty of such cruelty!"

"Amen!" was the reply.

Mistress Raymond, having given the old man a large glass of good wine, he seemed refreshed, and after a moment's pause, said—

"Misfortune! Ay, ay, misfortune! Alas! that I should be the bearer of such news to such a noble house as this. But, mayhap, you have heard all about it hours ago."

"About what my friend?" asked the Armourer.

"Of how they ill-treated your son."

"Heaven's mercy on us, husband!" shrieked the Armourer's wife. "He speaks of Oscar."

"Yes," murmured Revelle. "Of Oscar That was his name. A good youth. A well-mannered youth. I much fear me he is dead.

"In Heaven's name!" cried the Armourer, "what do you mean?"

All the citizens crowded round Revelle.

"'Twas Trevanion and his companions who set upon him," continued the old man, "and only because he interfered to save me from Trevanion's lash!"

Trevanion!

At the mention of this name, Mistress Raymond, with a low moan, sank into her husband's arms in a dead faint.

That the Armourer was terribly agitated could be seen by the violent twitching of his hands, and the mucles of his face.

"Speak," he said hoarsely. "Tell me—tell us all."

"Ay, all—all," cried the citizens.

But it was useless to hurry the old man. In their excitement they, for the moment, forgot that Revelle had to pause every now and then to collect his scattered thoughts.

He continued his story, and, with many a pause, concluded it.

It was very fairly told under all the circumstances.

It was sufficiently plain to the Armourer, who, putting together the disjoined sentences, made a whole of it, and retold it to his astonished friends.

"'Twas not Trevanion himself," he said, "but his accursed son, on whom may Heaven's vengeance descend! Ay, 'twas his son, Cunningham Trevanion, who, however, is as big a villain as his father, if all I hear about him be true. How strange," he mused, "that these two should thus come face to face, and at their first meeting be at once mortal enemies!"

"The question is," said one of the citizens, "to what place can he be taken?"

"I think I can tell," replied the Armourer, "and that is to Blackburn House. We must rescue him—he must be saved."

"Let us to Lord Trevanion," suggested one. "And since he is keeper of that estate, demand the keys."

"He would not oblige me," said the Armourer. "Trevanion and I are enemies. 'Tis many years since last we met. At present I have no desire to stand before him. Besides, did he know that my son was in peril, he would be glad of it, and would laugh in my face."

"Then," said one, who, with others, was attending to Mistress Raymond, "'twould be useless to attempt to enter Blackburn House without keys."

"Not so," replied the Armourer, grimly. "You surely have forgotten my friends of Eastcheap. I mean the giant brothers."

"Ha!" cried all present. "Truly, we had forgotten, indeed, Master Armourer."

"I will fetch them," cried one.

"Let me go, since I am so fleet of foot," cried another.

"Nay," replied the Armourer; "though my thanks are due to all of you, I will go myself. They will pay more attention to what I say than anyone else. Pray Heaven they have not been indulging, as is their wont."

Throwing his cloak about him, the Armourer strode off.

He quickly traversed the streets, and at length, reached Eastcheap.

In about the centre on the left from the bridge, was a small and narrow turning, and near the entrance stood a tall wooden building, from which a dingy sign projected.

On it, in letters painted awry, were the words —"Ye Jollie Smiths."

As the Armourer reached this dwelling, he was pleased to hear the merry rattle of hammers for by that he knew "the idle giants," as they were sometimes called, were at work.

While striking they were singing in loud bass voices, a song, the chorus of which ran as follows :—

"We are two jolly smiths, ring ! dong ! ding !
    And at work or play we sing—
With a bang and a clang, and a ring ! ding ! dong !
        So listen to our song,
        For 'twill not take you long.
With a bang ! and a clang ! and a ring ! ding ! dong !

Directly the huge brothers saw the Armourer, they flung down their hammers, and advancing, held out their horny hands.

"Welcome — welcome, Master Armourer," cried Sampson. "Thrice welcome——"

"If he carries a bottle of sack in his pocket," interrupted Goliar.

"Let us not think of sack now, brother," said Sampson. "Rather let us ask the Armourer what of his son. Hast thou heard ought?"

"Ay, sad news, Sampson," replied the Armourer.

"Eh, sad? It can't be sadder than that he has not yet been found. Is that the case, Master Armourer? Lord! and I loved the youth——"

"Like your own brother, eh, Sampson?" interrupted Goliar.

"Yea, like unto my own brother."

"I have heard of him," said the Armourer, in sad tones. Oscar had been seized upon by no less a person than Cunningham Trevanion and his companions."

"Heaven's mercy!" cried Sampson, "for what?"

"For defending poor old Mad Revelle by Temple Bar, where he was set upon by Cunningham, and a host of Court gallants. Revelle, who, by the way, has been most shockingly ill-treated, cannot tell where Oscar was taken; but I make no doubt, it was to Blackburn House, since that was the nearest place wherein they could imprison him."

Both the giant brothers uttered an exclamation of horror.

"Let us trust he has not been taken there," they said; "for of a surety he would never emerge alive from such a house. But since you have discovered his probable whereabouts, you will at once hasten to Lord Trevanion, and place the facts before him, so that he will order Oscar's release, and well punish his infamous son, eh?"

The Armourer shook his head.

"Nay," he said, "that would be of no use whatever. Indeed, were I announced to his lordship, I should not be admitted to his presence. Have I not, more than once, mentioned to you that Lord Trevanion and I are enemies?"

"Ay, true," replied Sampson. "Then how would you—ha! I have it, brother."

"Have what?" queried Goliar.

"We will open the doors of Blackburn House with our keys."

"So we will, brother. And, since that is decided on, let us go at once. 'Fore Heaven! I have on more than one occasion had very strong inclination to tap at the doors of that unholy place."

"What say ye, Master Armourer?" asked Sampson. "Shall we use our keys?"

"Ay, ay. 'Tis what I came here to ask you, my friends."

"Oh," said Goliar, "we require no asking, friend Armourer. If the youth is there, we will release him. So let us off."

Having extinguished their lanterns, the huge brothers left their smithy with the Armourer.

Over their shoulders they carried their enormous hammers, and as they went forth with bare arms and bare heads, and wore their leathern aprons about their waists, they attracted no little attention.

Reaching the Armourer's residence, they were warmly welcomed by the assembled citizens.

Mistress Raymond had recovered, but was in tears.

"Cheer up, noble madam," said Sampson, "if thy son is in Blackburn House, we will release him."

"May all the fiends seize upon us," said Goliar, "if we don't tear down every stick and stone to find him."

"Who was it ill-treated thee, my friend?" asked Sampson of Mad Revelle, who still sat rocking himself on the block of wood; "for if we discover them we will crack their skulls as we would crack filberts."

"'Tis no use of asking him anything," said one of the citizens, "Since the Armourer went to fetch you, he has not spoken ten words."

Mistress Raymond went and fetched two huge cans of ale for the refreshment of the giants, and having partaken of it they announced themselves ready to go.

The Armourer went first, the giants next, and the citizens after.

At a rapid pace they traversed the streets, and as they went numbers of persons followed them.

In Fleet-street they were joined by a few score of apprentices, among whom were several who had been present at the fight at Temple Bar, and seeing the Armourer, they at once remembered the circumstance, and the news as to where the Armourer and the smiths were bound was soon in everybody's mouth.

To the Armourer's great discomfiture, long before they reached St. Martin's Field, they were followed by what was nothing more nor less than a howling mob.

The name of Trevanion, too, was lustily shouted out, so that the Armourer became alarmed, lest should the news reach Lord Trevanion a company of soldiers would be sent to Blackburn House.

At length the lodge in front of the house was reached.

The Armourer knocked.

But no reply did he get.

Again and again he knocked; but as he received no reply, a consultation was held, with the result that Sampson placed his shoulder to the door and burst it open.

The whole place was in a state of disorder.

"Heaven's mercy on us!" cried the Armourer. "What a pigstye is this!"

"If 'tis a pigstye," said Sampson, "'tis certain that the owner can afford to pay for plenty of wash; for, observe the money on the table."

He pointed to the pile which had been brought there by young Trevanion.

"The fact of this money being here," said the Armourer, "only makes the absence of the watchman and his son the more mysterious."

"Ay," said Sampson. "Truly, does it? What ho?" he roared, in tones which shook the roof. "What ho! ye servants of Satan! What's come o' ye?"

"No one is here," said the Armourer; "but let us no longer delay. Take this lantern, Goliar."

"To what part shall we proceed?"

"To the Friar's cell. But let us proceed alone. This crowd can be of no service to us."

The Armourer's friends, after a great deal of persuasion, got the mob to remain where they were, and the Armourer, leading the two giants, went towards the door, which we have elsewhere described.

The Armourer took the lantern from Goliar, and held it aloft.

Stepping slightly back, Sampson struck the first blow upon the door.

Truly, it was like the roar of thunder?

Again and again Sampson brought down, upon the massive door, his huge hammer.

"By all the blessed saints!" cried Sampson, "one would think the door were made of solid iron instead of wood."

"'Twas made for resistance, brother," said Goliar; "but let us both work upon it."

Lord! to hear the blows! They sounded like the repeated discharge of artillery, and called forth loud yells of approval from the mob.

It was a long time ere the giants, with all their mighty strength, could get the door to yield.

But, at last, a panel gave way, and by this time the giant brothers, annoyed at the obstinacy of the door, had warmed to the work, and in a few more short moments, the iron bolts and huge splinters clattered down in showers, and the door was open.

The Armourer entered first.

"The Lord save us for such a vile den!" muttered Goliar. "Truly, I should like to undertake the instant pulling down of the place."

The hammers were now brought to bear upon the door of the Friar's cell.

The third ponderous blow had been struck, when suddenly the Armourer placed his hand on Sampson's arm.

"Hold!" he said, "for I could have sworn I heard a voice."

All listened intently.

The Armourer placed his ear to the keyhole, and motioned Sampson to knock. Sampson did so, and a faint cry was heard.

"'Tis the youth, I'll be sworn!" cried Goliar, joyfully.

Sampson shouted out as loud as he was able: "Bear up! bear up!"

Again they started upon the door, and with such a will, that the lock itself was shattered, and the door flew open.

The Armourer rushed in, and, raising the lantern aloft, cried out, in trembling tones·

"Oscar, my son—my son!"

But no response was given.

Suddenly Sampson uttered a loud cry of horror, and the cry was echoed by his brother.

"Look!" gasped Sampson. "As I live, here are three dead bodies!"

"Lord, have mercy upon us!" cried the Armourer. "Some foul murders have been committed. And, by the look of it, only lately. Heavens! this is, indeed, awful!"

Sampson pulled Stanmore off the body of his son.

The Armourer, holding the lantern over his face, examined his features.

"It is the watchman," he said, "and this is his son."

"And this one, covered in blood," said Sampson, dragging Trevanion forward, "who can he be?"

The Armourer held the lantern over him, and a wild cry left his lips, as he started back horror-stricken.

"It is Cunningham Trevanion," he said, "dead! dead!"

"There has, indeed, been some awful business in this foul den," said Sampson.

"And by the look of it," muttered Goliar, "Oscar, if he had been placed here, has escaped. Who knows, he may be——"

He stopped.

"You were about to say he may be answerable for this," said the Armourer, whose face was now ashy pale; "and you, I think, will not be far wrong. "Oh, Oscar! Oscar!" he moaned.

"Grieve not!" said Sampson. "If Oscar has done this, it was to save his own life. But you said you heard a voice."

"I must have been mistaken."

"Truly; unless that wretch Trevanion is not dead!"

"He is dead of a surety," said the Armourer; "but by the look of him he has not been dead long. Come, come, let us seek assistance, and have them removed."

"Nay, nay," replied Sampson, "rather let us search the house. Oscar may be in one of the rooms."

"Well, well, we will search; but my heart tells me that our search will be in vain."

Directly the three emerged into the open air, and were observed, the crowd, ignoring the entreaties of the Armourer's friends, made a rush forward.

Sampson, ere he could be stopped by the Armourer, told them of what they had found, at which a loud shout of approval was given, and loud cries of "Search the house! Down with Trevanion! Pull the house to pieces!" and other shouts were heard.

The great doors were set upon by Sampson and his brother, and soon battered down, and the whole mob poured in, scattering themselves in every part of the house; but, of course, nothing was found.

The consequence was that the mob became enraged, and they gave vent to their fury by destroying everything they could lay their hands upon.

Having satisfied themselves thus far, they left the house.

"I pray you," said the Armourer to Sampson, "to go into that vault, and bring forth those bodies. We will place them in the hall, and I will cause Lord Trevanion to be summoned."

Sampson threw down his hammer, and followed by his brother, returned to the cell.

Before many minutes had elapsed, they came rushing back.

"By the soul of my father!" cried Sampson, "One has gone!"

"What?" cried the Armourer.

"Cunningham Trevanion has gone!"

"Impossible!"

"'Tis true," said Goliar; "and so you will see for yourself if you go to the cell.

"Mystery upon mystery!" muttered the almost dazed Armourer.

"Nay, 'tis no mystery," replied Sampson. "This, no doubt, is how it happened. Trevanion's son, hearing us battering down the place, rightly took us for the rescuers of Oscar, and knowing that it would not be well for him to be caught, feigned death; and, when our backs were turned, he was up and off."

This was indeed, perfectly correct.

Trevanion's fall had rendered him unconscious for a time; but that was all.

When the Armourer and the giants entered the cell, he was perfectly conscious of all that was passing around him, and as soon as they went out, he was up and away.

Had the mob not entered the house, it is certain that he would have been stopped.

Directly the news was communicated to the rabble, they cowed down considerably, for all were well aware of the power which was then wielded by Lord Trevanion; and now that the son was proved to be alive, they knew that what had occurred would reach his lordship.

One by one they slunk away, until all had gone.

"Heaven only knows what has become of poor Oscar," said the Armourer, whose pent-up feelings giving way, he burst into tears.

"Cheer up, Master Armourer," said Sampson. "Cheer up; for when we return, he may be already at home."

"Let us trust so," replied the Armourer.

"We will leave the dead bodies of the watchman and his son where they are, and return at once."

∘   ∘   ∘   ∘   ∘

Imagine the great joy of the Armourer and the unbounded delight of the giants when, on their arrival at Tower Hill, they found that Oscar had returned to his home.

The Armourer, rushing into the sitting-room, found him in his mother's arms.

"My boy!" cried the Armourer; "safe! safe! Heaven be praised!"

In a moment Oscar was clasped to his breast.

"Yes: safe, father, so far," said Oscar, who, save that he was very pale, looked little the worse for his adventures; "but I have been cruelly used. I have heard that you and my friends, the giants, have been to Blackburn House. Pray tell me all. You burst into the caple."

"We did," replied the Armourer; "but first you must tell us your story. We want to know how it was you came to be placed in that house? We have heard something of it from Mad Revelle, but, of course, he could not give the exact version."

The giants being admitted, Oscar told his story, much to the wonderment, indignation, and horror of all.

"The bloodthirsty wretch shall answer for it!" cried the Armourer; "for ere to-morrow's sun sets, I will lay the facts before the Queen."

The Armourer now told Oscar of the way in which Cunningham Trevanion had contrived to escape.

"I am sorry we did not thoroughly examine him," said Sampson. "Had I found he was alive, I swear he should not have escaped us."

"Well, friends," said the Armourer, "since my son has returned, let us mark the occasion in a suitable manner. Both of you shall stop to supper, and it *shall* be a supper worth partaking of. I will also invite a number of my neighbours."

The neighbours were summoned, and good Mistress Raymond, assisted by her own servants, and a few servants belonging to the Armourer's friends, as well as a number of apprentices, who, it is needless to say, were delighted beyond measure at Oscar's return, set about preparing a feast on a large scale.

CHAPTER V.

OF WHAT CUNNINGHAM TREVANION TOLD HIS FATHER, AND HOW HIS LORDSHIP FORGED THE QUEEN'S WARRANT FOR THE ARREST OF OSCAR ON A CHARGE OF MURDER, AND OF HOW THE PLOTTERS SET OUT TO SEE THE WARRANT EXECUTED.

THE house of Lord Trevanion was situated in Piccadilly, and just by the spot where the Burlington Arcade now stands.

Piccadilly then (first years of Elizabeth's reign) was a very different thoroughfare to what it is now.

It is hardly necessary to tell our readers that it was considered a "suburban retreat."

The houses of noblemen were few and far between, as, in those days persons in good society preferred the neighbourhood of the Strand, Fleet Street, Holborn, and the streets abutting on those thoroughfares in which to erect their mansions.

Lord Trevanion had had many houses in his lifetime, but they were houses for which he never paid.

He preferred to get them by means frequently foul and disgraceful.

The house he held in Piccadilly had been the property of his cousin, "*the unfortunate Lord Eustance Wyncherley, who, many, many years ago, had been found murdered in the Tower of London*"—so the role, kept in the Record Office, said, and this house he called, "Trevanion Manor."

During the time which had elapsed since his cousin's death, his lordship had been highly successful in everything.

He was an especial favourite at Court with Queen Mary, but it was when Elizabeth ascended the Throne that his cup of success seemed likely soon to overflow.

As one of the Queen's favourites, he was feared by those who were not.

There were many men who, while they hated and despised this cringing nobleman, were yet bound to crawl to him. If they did not choose so to do, their petitions to the Queen and so on would meet with little or no success.

But, praised by the Queen as a good counsellor, surrounded by all the luxuries that wealth and power could command, was this lord happy?

No!

And why? Is it necessary to ask why? Was not his soul darkened by the recollections of the many dastardly deeds he had committed?

When Trevanion's only son—his only child in fact—Cunningham, was a lad of seven or eight, his lordship's wife had died—the doctor said of heart disease—and was buried amid general mourning.

Little did the crowd dream, as they looked at and pitied "his lordship," that it was by the hand of her husband that her ladyship had died.

But so it was.

In a fit of uncontrollable rage and jealousy, Trevanion had drawn his sword and had plunged it into the heart of the beautiful, but unfortunate lady.

The only witness of this awful deed was an old man, Trevanion's butler. This man happened to be passing the chamber door as her ladyship was falling with the weapon in her breast.

Lord Trevanion paid him ten thousand crowns, and swore him on the cross to preserve the secret.

Two days afterwards the servants in the establishment found the old man dead in bed—no doubt poisoned by Trevanion. But they found no crowns.

Nay, they were lying snugly enough in one of his lordship's cabinets, when the old man was taken away to the grave.

Many a noble lord, who had been foolish enough to merit Lord Trevanion's wrath had been brought to the block.

Neither the tears nor the entreaties of her, who would be the widow of the man he had condemned, could move this double-dyed scoundrel—this cringing plotter!

In the Court, surrounded by a vast crowd of all kinds, Lord Trevanion felt himself a person of some authority.

But alone in his house, what was he?

"Well, there he was one of the most miserable men on the face of the earth!

The shadow of the block, to which his cruel designs had sent many an innocent man, was ever before him.

In a room of impenetrable blackness, the dark figure of the headsman, with the glittering axe upon his shoulder confronted him.

His study, his bedroom, anywhere—everywhere was a place of terror to him.

The veriest sound unnerved him.

There was one being on earth to whom he clung, as a miser would cling to his gold, and that being was his son Cunningham.

Trevanion had never been at any pains to conceal from his son his monstrous villainy.

On the contrary, he openly paraded it before his admiring son, and trained him to walk in his footsteps.

Teaching, however, was unnecessary, for Cunningham, had inherited *all* his father's accursed nature, and *none* of his mother's, who, poor lady, had been a very angel, with a *devil* in human form for a husband!

Besides assisting his father in the carrying out of his various schemes, Cunningham formed many of. his own ; but he rarely informed his lordship of what he was doing.

When the struggle between Oscar and Cunningham was taking place at Blackburn House, Lord Trevanion was anxiously waiting for his son.

He was seated in his study, attentively engaged in endeavouring to decipher a huge pile of State documents.

Hour after hour passed by ; but Cunningham came not.

"I grow nervous!" muttered Lord Trevanion. "Where can he be? My heart misgives me! I fear he hath met with some misfortune. I would sleep, but I cannot do so unless I am assured that he is safe."

Touching a bell on the table, it was answered by a serving man.

"Have you seen my son?" asked Trevanion.

"I have not, your lordship," replied the man. "He left here some hours——"

"Yes, yes," interrupted his lordship, "I am well aware of when he left here. Can you form any idea as to where he has gone?"

"No idea whatever, your lordship."

"Did any of his companions call for him?"

"Nay, your lordship. He left here entirely alone."

"Hem! Directly he appears say that I am desirous of seeing him."

The servitor bowed and withdrew.

The hours passed, but no Cunningham came. Except those who always remained up for special duty, the servants retired, and soon the vast mansion was buried in silence.

His lordship, having partaken largely of strong wine, eventually began to nod over his documents, and, at last, his head fell forward upon the table, and he slept.

The lamp flickered and went out; and, save for the steady tramp—tramp of the sentinels placed in front of the house, and the occasional chirrup of a cricket on the hearth, no sound was heard.

Ere another hour had passed, Trevanion was in a deep sleep, and had any one listened to his strange mutterings, and seen the restless movement of his hands, they would have known that he was dreaming.

No strange thing with his lordship.

He was always dreaming—of murder, of the block—and of that man—that strange being whom no power of his could touch—the Wizard of Whitehall.

Suddenly he started up trembling in every limb.

Pressing his hands over his eyes, he groaned dismally.

"Where am I?" he whispered, staggering forward, and thrusting forth his hands. "These are not stone walls? Not the walls of the accursed Tower? No! I am in my own house —safe—safe! Yet what is that I see before me—yet—no, I can see nothing since the place is in darknes. Ha!" he shrieked, backing himself against the wall. "I see the shadow—*the Shadow of Death.* See he advances; he will seize him; 'tis he—he—Wyncherley—disguised —as the headsman. Ha! and the block—the block—the——"

He ceased ; great clammy beads of perspiration rolled down his face.

In the centre of the room a round, ghastly-white circle had appeared, and within that circle was the shadow of the headsman leaning on his axe near the block.

The glittering eyes of the spectre were fixed upon Trevanion as he cowed back against the wall.

Slowly the headsman stood erect, seized the axe in his hand, and raised it aloft.

Round his head it flew, and the next instant was buried, with a loud thud, in the block.

Then a low, deep voice, said—

Thus—but *not* thus—for the block waits— for thee, Trevanion—for *thee!*

Instantly the picture vanished, and with a groan of agony, Trevanion started forward.

With trembling hands he searched about for the tinder-box.

He found it, and with frantic haste, he kindled a light, and re-lit the lamp.

Raising it on high, he waved it on all sides of him.

"Avaunt!" he yelled. "Avaunt, accursed shadow! Die upon the block? Nay, nay! Am I not the the Queen's favourite? Care I for the Wizard and his devilish black arts? No, no! See," he said, plucking a dagger from his girdle, "with this weapon I could *cheat* the block! Bring your vision—bring all your vile plans to bear upon me, Mervine; but I laugh at you—I laugh at you! I snap my fingers at you!" he screamed. "I will one day repay you for your devilish insults! You are but a man; you *can* be nothing else, and by my hand or by the hands of my assassins, shall you die!"

He paused for breath.

And as he did so, a hurried tramping of footsteps was heard, and in another instant the door was pushed violently open, and Cunningham and Trevanion rushed into the room.

He stopped abruptly as he saw that, in his father's hand, was a glittering dagger.

"My son!" gasped his lordship.

"Yes, it is your son sure enough," replied Cunningham. "But what means this?"

And he pointed to the dagger, while, at the same time, he looked round the apartment as if to see whom it was his father was about to attack.

"'Tis naught, my son," replied his lordship, sheathing his weapon! "but that——"

"Visions again?" growled Cunningham— "visions which no one else but you can see?— visions conjured up by the contents of yonder wine bottles, and——"

"The Wizard, my son—the Wizard."

"*Curse* the Wizard!"

"Ay, I do—I do. With all my heart, I curse him! But, by Heaven's grace, you are covered in *blood!*"

This was, indeed, very true.

Cunningham was in a terrible plight, and 'twas not to be wondered at when we consider that the floor of the cell, in which he had been hurled by Oscar, was more like that of a slaughter-house than anything else.

"'Tis a wonder you see me alive, father!" cried Cunningham.

"What mean you?"

"I have been way-laid, robbed, and nearly murdered."

"By whom—by whom?"

"By one Oscar Raymond, a son of the Armourer, on Tower Hill."

Had a thunderbolt fallen at the feet of Lord Trevanion, he could not have started more violently, nor have uttered so sharp an exclamation.

"And that is not the worst of it," went on Cunningham; "for Stanmore and his son *have both been slain by this same youth.*"

A howl of rage and dismay left his lordship's lips.

"In the name of heaven!" he cried, "tell me all—all."

Cunningham told his story, and, as our readers may guess, a pretty parcel of lies it was.

To sum it up as briefly as possible, this is what it was—

He was on an excursion of pleasure, and, for safe custody, he took with him Stanmore and his son Caleb.

Near Temple Bar, without a moment's warning, they were set upon by Oscar Raymond and a lot of ruffians, robbed and cruelly ill-used.

Stanmore had the keys of Blackburn House hanging at his girdle; these were snatched from him, and the whole three of them were taken, and placed in the Friar's cell.

There, without giving them time to prepare for death, Oscar ran the watchman and his son through the body, and then attacked him (Cunningham), who, however, after a terrific struggle, managed to escape.

Such was Cunningham's story.

"For the deaths of Stanmore and his son, I care not!" said Trevanion; "for I am indebted to Stanmore in a small sum, and that I shall not now have to pay him. He also knew too much, so his knowledge dies with him. Nay, nay, I care not, so that you are safe. Oh, but you shall be avenged!—you shall be avenged, Cunningham! But—let me see. He attacked you? Where was your sword? Where your courage that you did not strike him dead at your feet?"

"My lord, the villain and his companions took my weapons from me."

"The cowards! But they shall answer for it, and—Cunningham."

"Yes, father?"

"You have heard me speak of the Armourer?"

As he uttered these words in a whisper, his lordship looked round the apartment as if afraid of being overheard.

"I *have* many times; but generally you speak of him in your sleep."

"Ha! likely enough, my son. My mind you see is never at rest, asleep or awake."

"State affairs——" commenced Cunningham in ironical tones.

But his lordship stopped him by a wave of his hand.

"The Armourer," he said, "is an enemy of mine—an enemy I should like to remove."

"Hire an assassin," suggested Cunningham, calmly.

"No, no. His death would affect me but very little. What I should like to see is this: He is a contractor for the court and by some means or other, the Queen likes the man. Now I should like to wrest this contract out of his hands, and——"

"Humble him?"

"Ay, to the dust—to the dust. So that, in fact, he will come like others, cringing and crawling, and begging and praying.

"From what I have heard, my lord, of the Armourer—and 'tis little enough, I'll warrant you—he is not, by any manner of means, a man likely to crawl and cringe to *anyone.*"

"We should see that, my son. My experience has taught me that if you strike a man, he will, in all probability, return the blow; but snatch away a man's living, and—for the sake of his family—he will humble himself, if he thinks there is a chance of regaining what he has lost."

"You may be right," said Cunningham; "but go on."

"Though what has occurred has been a misfortune to you, it will be a fortunate thing for me—for through the son, I can strike the father!"

"Very true."

"Oscar Raymond shall be arrested this very night. He shall be dragged from his bed, and safely lodged in the Tower until——"

"But what of the time? How is a warrant to be obtained, since it is utterly impossible to see the Queen?"

Lord Trevanion drew his son to him, and whispered—

"By forgery. Do you see this document?"

And he held up a small sheet of parchment.

It was covered with writing (mostly Latin), and carried the Great Seal, and the autograph of the Queen.

"I see it," replied Cunningham.

"This document then is an order for the delivery of certain State monies. This phial——" (and his lordship took a phial from a drawer in the table), "will take away all the writing that is now here, and enable me to place a substitute there."

"I see. A most excellent plan. Your lordship is certainly gifted to a most extraordinary degree."

"Truly—truly," chuckled his lordship, who now, sitting at the table, proceeded to obliterate what writing he wanted from the sheet.

This was quickly accomplished, and then Trevanion wrote rapidly for some few moments.

When he had finished, he handed the forged parchment to his son, who, on looking at it, laughed outright.

It had now the appearance of a warrant, and was, of course, duly signed and sealed in a proper manner; for the signature and the impress of the Great Seal Trevanion had not touched.

"The lieutenant of the Tower has never yet doubted my word, said his lordship; "and if he did on this occasion he has only to examine that. If he discover anything irregular in it, then my name is not—is not what it is. Ha, ha, Master Armourer! I have at last a hold upon you. And I will never loosen that hold! I swear it!"

"Look you, my lord! will you not tell me why you have a grudge against this Armourer?"

"Ay, I will. The Armourer was a great friend of Wyncherley's."

"Your cousin who was murdered in the Tower."

"Yes. And my impression is that he could, if he thought proper, tell me of the whereabouts of Wyncherley's child, which, on the night of the murder, was so mysteriously spirited away. Besides that, I fancy that the Armourer believes it was I who did the foul deed."

"Let him believe what he likes. And I was always under the impression that the child was dead."

"Well, I always try to *think* so."

"Dead or alive, what should we care? If alive, he could not prove his identity."

"Of course not—of course not," replied Trevannion hastily. "Well, well, my son, no more of this. Let us at once hasten to Whitehall. I will there obtain a proper escort, and we will then preceed to Tower Hill. Both of us shall be present to see that all is properly carried out. 'Tis a long time since the Armourer and I met. I wonder what he will say to me? Ha, ha! he shall be humbled. And you shall see his son hung from the scaffold!"

In ten more minutes, Cunningham had changed his dress, and father and son, fully armed and mounted, took their way in the direction of Whitehall.

CHAPTER VI.

SHOWS HOW THE FEAST AT THE ARMOURER'S HOUSE IS SUDDENLY STOPPED, AND OSCAR'S SURRENDER DEMANDED—OF HOW OSCAR ESCAPED, AND OF HOW HE WAS POISONED.

THE feast at the Armourer's, after some little difficulty, was laid upon the table in the largest room.

The table fairly groaned beneath the weight of fish, flesh, and fowl.

The feast proceeded merrily for some time, the appetite of the brothers Silvester causing roars of laughter.

Such enormous quantities of meat and other things did they consume, that they required nearly all Mistress Raymond's attention to keep them well supplied.

By the time the things were cleared from the table, the giants, as they imagined, were in a high good humour.

They keep the company in a roar.

Though they were not in possession of what, in those days, would be called musical voices, they could sing many a good song, and sing them they did.

So the hours passed on. As the wine went in, the wit came out, and many of the Armourer's grave neighbours found themselves attempting to compete with the giants in the shape of jokes and the singing of songs.

Oscar was highly amused; but, nevertheless, he was very restless.

Sampson was in the middle of a stirring battle song, when the youth, rising in his chair, whispered—

"Hist!"

The song at once ceased, and everyone looked hard at Oscar to ask why he had stopped it.

"What is it, my son?" asked the Armourer uneasily.

"Listen all of you! whispered Oscar.

All listened; the dropping of a pin might have been heard.

Suddenly the almost indistinct rattle of arms was heard.

Oscar started to his feet.

"What is it, Oscar?" cried Mistress Raymond, clasping her hands in terror.

"'Tis as I suspected," replied the youth. "The house is surrounded by armed men!"

"Oh, heaven!" shrieked Mistress Raymond, darting forward, and clasping Oscar to her bosom, "then they would tear you from me? Oh, husband—husband—save him! Sampson—Goliar—friends——" she cried, hysterically. "Save him—save my son!"

Sampson leapt to his feet, and from the wall reached down two two-handled swords, one of which he handed to his brother.

"By the gods!" hissed Sampson through his clenched teeth; "we will make food of them for all the wild fowl on the banks of the Thames!"

"Silence, I entreat!" said the Armourer, holding up his hand. "My son may be mistaken."

But even as he spoke, the rattle of arms was again heard, and it was evident that the men without were being placed round the house.

Then came a thundering rap on the door.

"What ho!" roared Sampson. "What want ye?"

"Open in the Queen's name!" was the stern reply.

"The Lord have mercy on us!" said a neighbour, white with terror. "We are surrounded by the Queen's troops."

"Wait a moment," said the Armourer. "Oscar, 'tis you whom they want."

"Alas! I know it," replied Oscar, "and I would not care were it not for the fact that

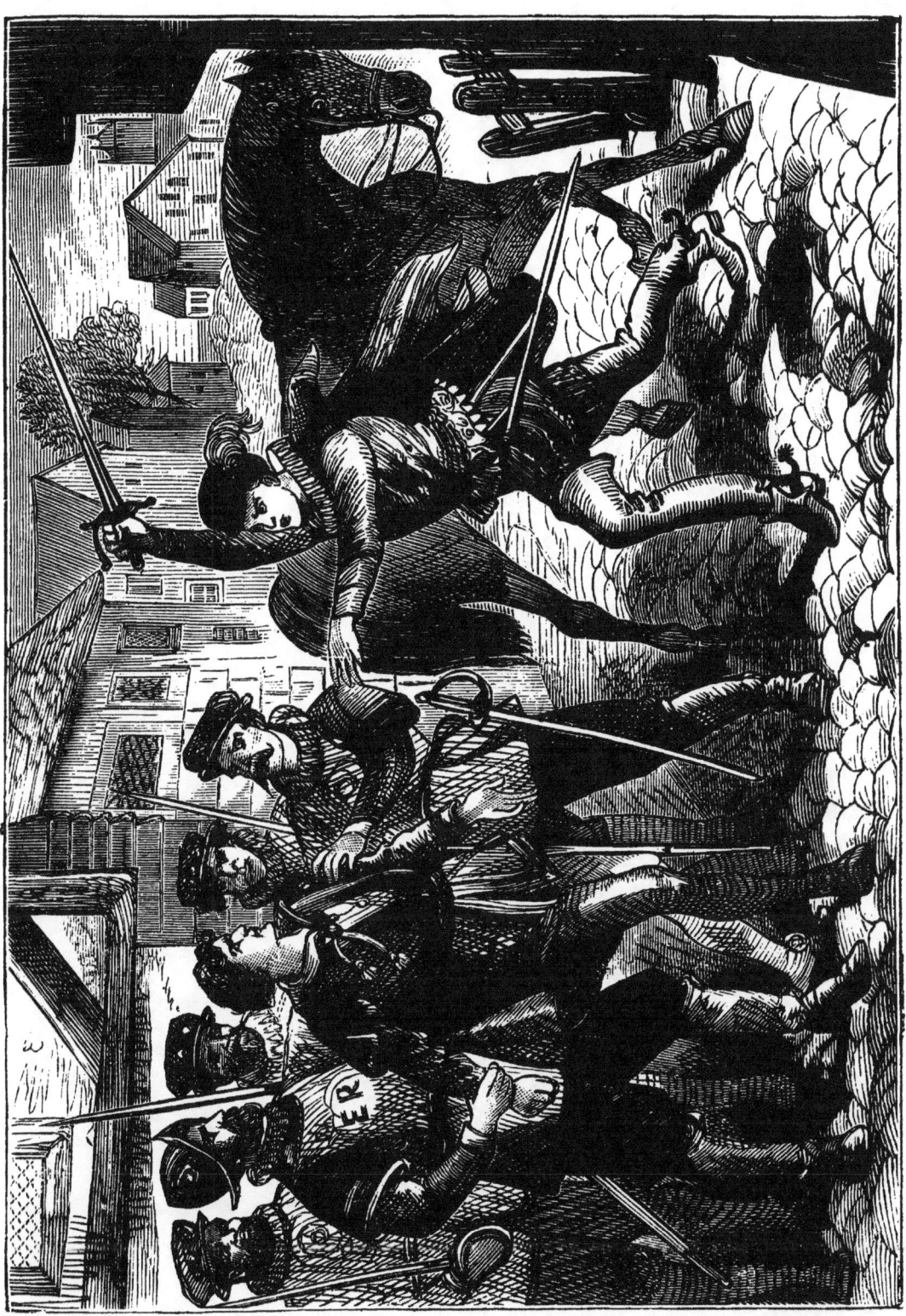

"'AGAIN I HAVE YOU AT MY MERCY,' HISSED CUNNINGHAM."

through my folly I have brought all this disgrace upon you."

"Talk not of disgrace, my son. Listen, Oscar. Until I have been able to properly lay your case before her Majesty, it would be as well that you were not taken, and for that reason——"

"Open in the Queen's name!" again cried the voice.

"Heavens!" muttered the Armourer. "I recognise that voice. 'Tis the voice of Trevanion himself."

"Oh, husband!" moaned Mistress Raymond, "if you love me, do not let them take him from me!"

But the Armourer heeded her not.

"Oscar," he said, "since you cannot pass out the back way, nor, indeed, by the front, ascend to the roof, crawl along the parapet to the roof of the smithy, and you know where to enter. Once in the smithy you can escape."

"'Tis all that can be done," said Sampson. "Fly, Oscar, and God be with you."

Oscar bestowed a hurried kiss upon his mother's lips, and darting from her, he rushed to the mantlepiece, took down a loaded pistol, placed it in his belt, and taking up a sword, buckled it on him, and saw that the blade was loose in its scabbard.

Then he ascended the stairs.

"Open in the Queen's name," cried the voice, which had first spoken, "or we will batter the door about your ears."

The Armourer opened the door, and saw that the place was alive with men of the Queen's guard, mounted, and on foot.

"What want you, my friends," asked the Armourer. "Ha, is that you, friend Malmsby?"

This was to the captain of the troop.

"It is, I am sorry to say, Master Armourer," replied Captain Malmsby.

"What is your business at this hour?"

"I have here a warrant for the arrest of a person of the name of Oscar Raymond, who, I am told, is your son."

"A warrant? A *warrant* say you?"

"Ay, here 'tis."

"By the blessed Virgin—a warrant—for what?"

"The person named in the warrant is charged with *murder*."

The Armourer was silent for a moment; then he asked—

"By whom is the information laid?"

"I will answer that," cried a voice, and Trevanion, with his son at his side, rode forward. "It was laid by me, Master Armourer, on the sworn evidence of my son, who is here with me."

"Both you and your son are infamous liars!" said the Armourer, contemptuously. "Captain Malmsby, I do assure you——"

"I am sorry, Master Armourer, that I cannot at this present moment pay heed to what you might say. You observe I have here the Queen's warrant which, if you think proper, you are quite at liberty to read."

"Nay, nay. I believe you to be an honest man enough, Malmsby."

"Sorry enough am I," said the captain. "Sorry enough am I that I should be called upon to execute a warrant at the house of so old a friend as yourself."

"I do assure you, Malmsby, that my son is not here."

These words caused a general commotion.

"Your lordship," said Malmsby, "you hear what the Armourer says?"

"Perfectly, since I am not deaf!" replied his lordship, sharply, "and my answer to that is that *he* is an infamous liar! Still what he says is of little moment. The warrant authorises you to search for, and take the person of Oscar Raymond be he alive or dead. Therefore, Captain Malmsby, do your duty."

"Why not search yourself?" growled Sampson.

"Who is that who speaks?" asked Trevanion of his son.

"'Tis one of the giants of Eastcheap," replied Cunningham.

"Ah, I have heard of them, and he who spoke had better keep his tongue silent, or perchance he may find himself within a cell which, with all his huge strength, he would fail to open."

"If your lordship would but be pleased to step within," said Sampson, "you will see what it is to be grasped by one of the Silvesters."

"If he comes within we will crack his sconce, and his son's, too, as a squirrel would crack a filbert," said Goliar.

During this conversation, the citizens, one by one, stole away; but suddenly, as one came out (he was a tailor belonging to Cheapside), Cunningham seized him by the hair of his head, and, holding a pistol to his face, said—

"Where is this Armourer's son? Speak, or I will blow thy brains out!"

Terrified beyond measure at what, had the man considered an instant, he would have known to be an idle threat, the tailor gasped—

"He went on—on—the roof to——"

He said no more.

Enraged at the man's treachery, Sampson dealt him a blow in the face with his huge fist—a blow that stretched him senseless on the ground.

This act called forth loud cries, both of horror and approval; but Trevanion allowed no time to talk of the occurrence.

"To the roof with you!" he cried.

Several men pushed forward.

"Stand by me, brother!" whispered Sampson. Aloud he said, as he swung his sword over his shoulder—

"Get back, curse you! *Back*, I say, or I will hack you to mincemeat!"

Trevanion and his son instantly backed their horses out of reach of the now furious giants.

"But one moment, friend Armourer," said Malmsby, "will you not consider whether, instead of causing blood to be shed, it would not be better to let us formally search the house?"

"*Formally!*" cried Trevanion. "Formally is not the word. It shall be done most thoroughly, or on your head be the consequences."

"The first man who crosses the threshold I will strike dead!" cried Sampson.

"Sampson, my friend," said the Armourer, "resistance would be useless. Let them search the house if they will."

In a whisper he added:

"By this time he must be safe."

Sampson and his brother stood on either side of the door.

"Pass on, my friends," said Sampson, to the soldiers. "You will find nothing in the house but some valuable property, which leave alone, or the Lord help you!"

The captain dismounted, and led his men into the house.

Up the stairs they swarmed, and searched every room.

Cunningham would have followed, but he was afraid of Sampson, who fixed his eyes upon him with no gentle look.

In ten minutes Captain Malmsby and his men returned.

"We cannot find the person we seek," said Malmsby. "Indeed, there is no such individual as in this warrant——"

"He has been concealed!" shrieked Trevanion; "but he shall not escape if——"

He was interrupted by a loud clattering as of iron falling.

Several soldiers standing near the door of the smithy had a narrow escape; for, hardly had they moved to see what had occurred, when a number of iron bars rolled off the roof of the smithy, and fell near them with a terrific clatter.

All looked up.

"Ha!" cried Trevanion, as the dim outline of a figure was seen moving slowly along the narrow parapet. "There he is—there is the person we seek, Captain Malmsby. Burst that door open—quick! A hundred crowns to the man who first seizes him!"

A hundred crowns in those days was considered to be a sum well worth having, and this promise spurred on the men.

Dashing at the door, they burst it open, and entered the smithy, which, but for a single link, would have been in darkness.

One of the soldiers snatched the link from its bracket, and, holding it aloft, saw the door, which he concluded led to the roof. So it did; but it was barred and bolted on the other side.

The chimney over the furnace, however, was wide enough to admit of the passage of a man's body, and, without hesitation, the soldier, handing the link to a companion, jumped up on the furnace, and commenced the ascent.

His boots had barely disappeared, ere Sampson, breaking through the other men, snatched hold of the handle of the bellows, and proceeded to fan the still smouldering fire into a flame.

In a few seconds the smoke came forth, and it was followed by a vast sheet of flame, which ran up the chimney.

The unfortunate soldier howled as soldier surely never howled before.

But Sampson paid no heed to him.

The more the fellow howled, with greater force did the giant blow, greatly to the diversion of Goliar, who laughed so heartily, that he was forced to sit on an anvil, and hold his sides.

The soldier's comrades felt afraid to interfere.

Presently the man came down with a rush clean on the fire.

Sampson at once caught hold of him with one hand, and hurled him to the floor.

The reason of the iron bars falling was because Oscar, not perceiving them in the dark, had touched one with his foot.

This set the others rolling with the result we have described.

Hardly had Sampson thrown the soldier (and we may remark that the man was severely scorched, as well as nearly suffocated) to the floor, ere another loud cry arose.

A great rush was made to the back of the smithy.

"He runs!—he runs!—hi escapes!" was the cry of the soldiers, as Oscar, disengaging himself from a great pile of timber, started off down Tower Hill like the wind.

Cunningham espied him, and drawing his sword, he cried—

"Follow! He who first captures him shall receive *two hundred* crowns!"

With that he plunged his spurs into his horse's flanks, and followed by Lord Trevanion and several of the mounted men, went off in pursuit.

Sampson and his brother rushed to the door, and watched them until they had disappeared.

Then Sampson said, in fervent tones—

"Pray heaven Trevanion and his son break their blessed—or, I should say—accursed—necks."

"Amen, brother!" replied Goliar.

The streets, at the time of which we are writing, being exceedingly narrow and unevenly paved, mounted men had to be very cautious how they went.

So anxious, however, was Cunningham to run Oscar down, that he forgot the precautions he should have taken, and the result was that ere he had proceeded very far, his horse stumbled, and threw him clean over his head.

He fell upon the wooden railing placed in front of a fruiterer's shop, and received an ugly gash in his face.

Lord Trevanion at once went to his assistance, and, having again mounted, the pursuit was continued.

We have no hesitation in saying that Oscar would have escaped had it not been for a hay-cart, which, suddenly appearing, stopped his further progress.

Before he could dart under the horse's head, one of the soldiers seized him.

Snatching his sword from its scabbard, Oscar proceeded to attack the man with terrific fury.

It would assuredly have been a bad night's work for the soldier had it not been for his companions, who, coming up, dismounted, and seized Oscar from behind.

Now Cunningham, his dress stained with th blood issuing from the wound in his face, thundered up, and, throwing himself from the saddle, dashed, sword in hand, up to Oscar.

"Again I have you at my mercy!" he hissed.

"Strike then!" cried Oscar; "strike coward, since you see that I am powerless to help it."

"No, no," replied Cunningham; "we will reserve you for something very different. Death by the sword of a gentleman would be too good for you. You shall die by the hand of the common hangman."

"We shall see," replied Oscar, contemptuously.

"Bind his hands behind his back," said Trevanion, who now came up, "and away with him to the Tower. But stay; Captain Malmsby and his men are coming up, Cunningham. Hand him over to his safe custody."

"Caught him?" asked Malmsby, who rode leisurely up.

"We have," replied Trevanion, "no thanks to you."

Malmsby simply bowed.

"I will be careful to report your conduct to the proper quarter," said Trevanion.

"With pleasure," replied Malmsby; "but I may as well take this opportunity of remarking that my living does not depend upon my position as an officer of Her Majesty's guard."

"I am aware of it, Captain Malmsby. You lately married Lady Stadpole, who is in possession of goodly means. I never knew Lady Stadpole to be a fool until I heard of her marriage."

"My lord," said Malmsby, calmly, "I dare you to repeat what you now have said."

"Ah, and what would you do if I did?"

"Do? I would do what any insulted man would do. I would cleave your skull in 'twain, Her Majesty's favourite though you be. Repeat what you have just said here or anywhere else, and though you be even in front of the Queen herself, I will strike you dead?"

Trevanion turned very pale.

He had no desire to make enemies of men belonging to Her Majesty's army, and he knew that he had made a mistake in saying what he had said.

He forced a laugh, as holding forth his hand, he said—

"I thought you knew me better, captain. I did but jest."

"No man should jest about such things, your lordship. 'Tis ever dangerous. Nay, I cannot shake hands with you."

"And why?"

"Because your lordship's hands are stained with innocent blood," replied Captain Malmsby.

Then, without giving Trevanion time to reply, he said to his men—

"Is the youth's arms bound?"

"Ay, ay, captain," replied the men.

"Then mount and place him between you. And look to it that you treat him well. He is Lord Trevanion's prisoner—not ours."

Trevanion and Cunningham ground their teeth, but they wisely said naught.

Before they had proceeded a dozen yards, the Armourer, the giant brothers, and others, came up.

"Cheer up, Oscar," sobbed the Armourer, "all shall be properly investigated."

"Better let me crack his lordship's skull," muttered Sampson, but in tones which he took care should reach Trevanion and Cunningham, who thereupon gave the word to move forward at a quicker pace.

The Tower was soon reached, and the party were admitted.

The lieutenant was summoned, and to him the warrant was handed.

To the lieutenant the document appeared perfectly genuine, and he said, as he placed it in his doublet:

"Unusual case, your lordship, eh?"

"It is, Master Lieutenant," replied Trevanion.

"Not State affairs?"

"At present—no. But we know not what charges may be brought against him."

"Ha—well—well. Why as I live it is THE ARMOURER'S SON!" cried the lieutenant.

"I did not know you were acquainted with him. I assure you, Master Lieutenant, he is no desirable person to know."

"Eh? Why, I know but little of him surely; but I never knew anything wrong of him. I have repeatedly remarked the youth, for to my thinking, he bears a most striking resemblance to—to—er——"

"To whom?"

"To Lord Wincherley. Your unfortunate cousin, who was so mysteriously murdered here many years ago. Does your lordship mark the resemblance?"

"I do not," replied Trevanion, sharply, and we may say uneasily, for he had marked the likeness, now that Oscar came under the glare of the lanterns.

"Well, well, my lord," said the lieutenant, "no offence is meant. But the memory of the foul murder of your——"

"If it so please you, Master Lieutenant," interrupted Trevanion, "you will say no more of the matter, but will at once order your warders to convey this youth to a place of confinement.

The lieutenant bowed.

"Wakeley," he said to one of the principal warders standing near him. "What chambers have you vacant?"

"There is the apartment in the Brick Tower——"

"That is of no use, Wakeley, as you know. It may be required for a nobleman on the morrow for aught I know."

"Well, Sir Thomas, there is a chamber in the White Tower, and there are several vacant cells below the White Tower."

"If you would please me, Sir Thomas," said Trevanion, "you will place him in one of the cells below the White Tower."

"No worse place could be found."

"That is why I select it," rejoined Trevanion, calmly.

"Monster!" ejaculated Oscar, glaring at him fiercely.

Cunningham laughed in his face.

"Well, well," said the lieutenant, somewhat

uneasily. "I have no desire to displease your lordship; but I must tell you that, as lieutenant, I am able to exercise my own judgment as to the placing of prisoners. And therefore ——"

"Therefore, you desire to displease me," interrupted Trevanion. "'Tis well, Sir Thomas."

"Nay, nay. Here, Wakeley, convey this youth to one of the cells beneath the White Tower since Lord Trevanion desires it. Yet stay—let me consider."

For some few moments Sir Thomas Davey considered.

"This youth's father," he mused, "I know well as a right worthy gentleman. A man, whom to know is to love him. And in this youth, whom I have known for some little time—though I have exchanged no words with him—I have taken a great interest. Now what care I for Trevanion? Pah! Naught!"

Turning sharply he said :

"I have changed my mind, Wakeley. Let him be conveyed to the chamber in the White Tower, and see that he is made as comfortable as possible under the circumstances."

Wakeley bowed, untied Oscar's hands, and beckoned to him to follow.

"Sir Thomas Davey," said Lord Trevanion, who could scarcely speak for rage, "you shall have reason to repent this "

"Repent *what*, your lordship? Who is lieutenant here ? Your lordship or I ?"

"At *present* you are lieutenant. If, however, you will accept my advice, you will at once make preparations for your departure."

Sir Thomas smiled contemptuously.

"Let us depart, Cunningham," said Trevanion. "Our time will come yet. Captain, lead the way. We will stay at Whitehall till morning dawns."

CHAPTER VII.

SHOWS HOW OSCAR WAS BROUGHT BEFORE QUEEN ELIZABETH IN THE COUNCIL ROOM OF THE, TOWER—OF HOW CUNNINGHAM GAVE FALSE EVIDENCE—OF HOW OSCAR STRUCK HIM DOWN IN THE QUEEN'S PRE- SENCE—HOW OSCAR WAS SENTENCED TO BE HANGED AT TEMPLE BAR—HOW SIR THOMAS DAVEY WAS DISMISSED HIS OFFICE AND OF WHAT OCCURRED AT THE FLEET PRISON.

THE chamber, to which Oscar was conducted, was, like the generality of the chambers in the Tower, but poorly furnished.

There was, however, a fairly good bed, and no sooner was Oscar alone than he threw himself upon it, and forgetting, for the time being, the dangers through which he had passed, and was likely to pass, was soon asleep.

He was awakened by a loud knocking on the door, and, jumping up, found that he must have slept many hours, for the sun was high in the heavens.

"Now then, young gentleman," said a gruff voice, and a face peered through an aperture let in the door, " come hither, and take thy breakfast. And if you will take my advice, you will be quickly with it, for I hear that you are to be taken before the Queen herself this very morning."

Oscar took the poor loaf of bread and the cup of weak wine handed to him, and said—

"I understood the Queen was at Windsor."

"She *was*—yes. But she holds a court here this very morning."

With this the man banged the shutter of the aperture to, and retired.

Oscar drank the wine, but he could not eat the bread, which certainly was almost as hard as a piece of rock.

By aid of a little water and a brush he managed to make himself presentable, and impatiently waited for the time to pass.

Before long the loud braying of trumpets, the clatter of arms, and the loud roar of cannon on the battlements announced the important fact that the royal barges had been sighted.

A third discharge of artillery showed that the Queen had reached the Tower, where she was greeted with loud cheers.

The bells commenced their clamour, and their pealing was answered by the bells in the various churches on the opposite side of the water.

Residing so long on Tower Hill, Oscar, of course, knew exactly what all these sounds meant.

He knew also that he would have to wait a very considerable time before he was conducted before the Queen, if he was to be conducted at all, which he doubted.

Two hours passed, and suddenly the clatter of arms fell upon his ears.

Nearer and nearer came the sound, and in a few moments the door of his chamber was thrown open, and a loud, harsh voice cried :

"Come forth, thou imp of Satan !"

"Whom do you call an imp of Satan ?" asked Oscar of the speaker, Brutus Gatling, the second warder of the Tower, a terrible-looking ruffian.

"Why, who else but you ?" was the reply. "Come forth !"

"Drag him out, if he will not come quietly," said another voice—a well-remembered voice—the voice of Cunningham Trevanion, who now presented himself before the door.

He was superbly attired.

In his hand he carried a jewelled rapier.

His face blazed with triumph.

Directing upon him a look of contempt, Oscar folded his arms across his chest, and left the cell.

A guard of halberdiers instantly closed round him, and led by Cunningham, the whole party moved off towards the council chamber.

Gallery after gallery they traversed, and, at length, the council chamber was reached.

A herald blew a low blast on his trumpet, the curtains which concealed the doorway were drawn aside, and the party entered.

The sight which met Oscar's gaze, was brilliant beyond description.

The room was filled with courtiers from the highest to the lowest, as well as bishops and foreign ambassadors, all attired in the richest of costumes.

All around were lines of halberdiers and Arquebusiers, each with a caliver (or musket) upon his shoulder.

At the extreme end of the chamber, beneath a golden canopy, sat the Queen, and by her side, attired in a dark velvet doublet, and covered with orders and jewels, stood Trevanion, a small roll of parchment in his hand.

As Oscar advanced, he was surveyed with considerable curiosity by all present.

From the books of the nobles and others, it was evident that the majority of them had not the slightest idea as to what was Oscar's offence; but, no doubt, they concluded it was treason, for, if not, why should he be brought before the Queen?

In a few seconds Oscar stood before her Majesty.

Cunningham Trevanion stood on his left.

Elizabeth for some few moments surveyed Oscar somewhat sternly.

Sitting erect, she said in her peculiar and somewhat harsh voice—

"My lord, this is but a very youth. Of what kind of treason is he supposed to be guilty."

"I said not treason, may it please your Majesty," replied Trevanion, bowing very low. "I——"

"Well, well," interrupted the Queen, sharply. "Perhaps we forget. What, then, is he guilty of?"

"A foul murder, your Majesty, or I should rather say murders! Your Majesty has been informed of how the watchman of Blackburn House and his son were found brutally murdered?"

"Yes; I did hear of it, truly."

"Behold the murderer, then, your Majesty!" and Trevanion, amid a loud buzz of horror, pointed his finger at Oscar, who, it need hardly be said, stood like one transformed into a marble statue.

"Odd's my life!" murmured the Queen; "we are spoken of as a reader of character, and should certainly not have guessed that this youth could be guilty of the horrible crimes you accuse him of. My lord, is it not possible you may be mistaken?"

"Nay, your Majesty," replied Trevanion, bowing very low "My son was witness of the double crime. He himself was attacked by this youth, and—but for the fact that he feigned death—he, too, would no doubt, have been murdered."

So thunderstruck was Oscar at this monstrous charge, that his tongue seemed cloven to the roof of his mouth.

The Queen turned inquiringly to Cunningham, who, receiving a signal from his father, advanced, bowed low, and said—

"I saw him drive his dagger to the haft in the bodies of the watchman and his son."

"Vile perjurer!" shouted Oscar, his face now white with passion. "Infamous liar! Though you stand in the presence of your Queen, I thus treat you."

Ere the guards could stay him, Oscar raised his clenched fist, and dealt Cunningham a crushing blow fairly between the eyes.

With a fearful shriek the lying wretch fell back into the arms of one of the courtiers.

Instantly the whole council chamber was a scene of confusion.

Swords were drawn by almost every courtier, who surrounded the Queen.

Elizabeth slowly rose.

Her face was very pale, her eyes glared fiercely, as she bit her lips in a nervous manner, which showed that she was fully roused.

Waving her hand, she said:

"Stand from before me, my lords."

The courtiers withdrew to one side.

Slowly moving her eyes round her, the Queen beckoned to a tall, grey-headed gentleman, attired in a black robe, who at once came forward.

This was Dr. Oliver Bendle, one of the Court physicians.

"Master Bendle," said the Queen, "look at this youth."

And she pointed to Oscar.

"I look at him, your Majesty," said the doctor.

"Think you he is in a sane state of mind?"

"No doubt of it, your Majesty. He is perfectly sane."

"Good. Then he is responsible for his actions. Heaven's mercy! to commit an outrage like this in our presence! By my father's soul! were this youth one of the highest nobles of the land, and did he commit such an outrage before our face, he should have his head stricken off on Tower Hill within an hour! Look you, Trevanion, let your son, as soon as he is recovered from the effects of that blow, give us a true account of all that occurred at Blackburn House. It must be quite understood, my lords, that we should not waste our time in investigating murders were it not for the fact that, in this instance, the murders have been committed in, and on property which, at present, belongs to our crown."

Cunningham, supported by a couple of courtiers, came forward, and gave the Queen the same account as our readers have heard him tell his father.

The Queen listened patiently—more patiently than was her wont, and when Cunningham had concluded, she said to Trevanion—

"And his name, my lord?"

"Oscar Raymond, your Majesty."

"What, the son of the Armourer of Tower Hill?"

"Just so, your Majesty.

"And his father such an estimable man, too? Well, Well. Listen to it. This youth is to be taken from here to Ludgate; he is to be confined within its worst dungeon for three days, and at the expiration of that time he is to be taken from there to Temple Bar. And on the very spot where your son was attacked, my lord, he is to be hung, and his body afterwards cut into four quarters, and exhibited upon the City gates. Away with him!"

Oscar was roughly seized by a host of courtiers, and a crowd of halberdiers surrounded him.

Suddenly a loud noise was heard at the entrance of the council chamber, and, in a few moments, who should appear but the Armourer and the lieutenant of the tower.

Walking rapidly up to the Throne, the Armourer prostrated himself before the Queen, and, in broken accents, craved a boon.

"It has reference to your son, Master Armourer, no doubt," said the Queen. "Well, we are sorry for you; but we cannot now listen to anything you might have to say in his behalf. He has disgraced himself. But a few minutes ago he committed an infamous outrage even before our eyes! Nay, speak not. We repeat we are sorry for you, and that is all we can say."

The lieutenant was about to speak, when Trevanion at once interrupted him.

"Your Majesty," he said, "the lieutenant, I am sorry to say, laughs at the outrage committed by such people as this. Last night he defied me."

"We will investigate the matter anon," said the Queen. "As at present the matter stands let our commands concerning that daring youth, be carried out."

Oscar was dragged from the chamber, while the Armourer, sobbing bitterly, was led forth by Lords Elkington and Stow, who sincerely sympathised with him.

Later on the Queen investigated the charge brought against Sir Thomas Davey by Lord Trevanion, and Sir Thomas, being no favourite, was ordered to be dismissed his office, and Lord Fulmore—"Brutal Fulmore, as he was afterwards called, was appointed to occupy it.

*   *   *   *

Escorted by a strong guard of halberdiers and arquebusiers, Oscar was taken bareheaded, and, with his hands securely fastened behind his back, to Ludgate, one of the old City gates, which, at the time of our story, was used as a prison.

Directly the party reached the gates, they were admitted by the turnkey.

"Who is this?" he asked, surveying Oscar

"A prisoner," replied one of the guard.

"Well, I see that!" growled the turnkey. "What is his name? and what is his offence? and what is his——?"

"Hold your cursed tongue!" thundered Cunningham. "Here, take this roll. I am the son of Lord Trevanion."

"Well," said the jailor, "I must admit him.'

Two warders, villainous-looking wretches, came forward and took charge of Oscar.

"Your services are no longer required," said Cunningham to the captain in charge of the guard, who, bowing, gave the word to his men to return to the Tower.

The two warders led Oscar along a narrow passage, and thrusting him into a small stone apartment, which was satirically called the "reception room," banged the door to.

"Ah, I see you are the men to deal with him," said Cunningham; "and let me tell you," he whispered, "you will have to be very careful of him, for he is a desperate fellow, and since he is condemned to death, would not hesitate at another murder or two."

"We will take care he does not play with us," said one.

"Take these," whispered Cunningham, as he placed a couple of crowns in the ready hands of the fellows.

The men grinned.

Having received orders from the chief of the prison, the warders opened the door of the "reception-room," brought Oscar out, unbound his hands, and one of them, taking a lantern, said—

"Follow me!"

Oscar followed without a word—to speak he knew would be useless.

The other warder walked behind the prisoner while Cunningham brought up the rear.

Down one passage, up another, and down more than one flight of stone steps, they went until a sort of crypt was reached.

On either side, at a distance of only a few feet apart, were several massive doors, each opening into a noisome cell.

"Now then," cried the first warder, as he threw one of the doors open, "in with you!"

At this instant Oscar's eyes fell upon a large piece of chain lying in a corner.

Darting forward, he picked it up, and raised it over his shoulder.

"Wretch!" he cried. "Heartless brute that you are, take that!"

Down came the chain on Cunningham's breast, and with such fearful force, that the young man fell on the floor.

Instantly the warders rushed on Oscar, who however, struggled violently with them.

One of the men proceeded to belabour him with his heavy bunch of keys, but he was soon forced to stop that, for Oscar dealt him a blow which stretched him senseless upon the ground.

The other warder, not caring to receive such a blow as his companion had, wisely let go his hold of Oscar, and drew back.

Cunningham was not severely injured.

He was soon upon his feet, and had drawn his sword.

Oscar, however, was not frightened at the sight of the naked blade.

With flashing eyes he advanced upon Cunningham.

"Springing upon Cunningham, Oscar seized him by the throat."

The rusty, but heavy chain, was slung over his shoulder again, and was grasped with both hands.

"Pause an instant!" cried Cunningham, as he placed his back firmly against a pillar. "Pause an instant. I do not want to take your life; but if you advance another step to attack me, I shall be compelled to do so."

"*You* do not want to take my life?" hissed Oscar. "You liar! But if I can, I will take *yours*, for you deserve death—a thousand deaths!"

"Go, warder," cried Cunningham, "and summon assistance."

The man placed the lantern on the ground, and rushed off like the wind.

Slowly and cautiously Oscar advanced upon Cunningham, who was compelled to keep moving round the pillar.

He would, no doubt, have rushed forward to plunge his sword in Oscar's body had he not seen that the chain was considerably longer than his weapon.

Suddenly Oscar sprang forward, and, with all his force, brought the chain down.

Cunningham raised his sword to ward off the blow, and the result was that the weapon was broken in two near the hilt.

Directly Oscar saw this, he flung down the chain, and springing upon Cunningham, seized him by the throat.

"Now!" he cried, "we are on equal terms. Dastard, you shall die."

Uttering a series of the most appalling shrieks, Cunningham frantically endeavoured to unclasp the strong fingers which grasped him.

From side to side, now against the wall, now gainst the pillars, Oscar dashed the wretch.

Suddenly Cunningham's feet touched the man whom Oscar had felled, and he stumbled over him.

Oscar, however, did not leave go his hold, but fell on top of him.

Cunningham, at this instant, snatched his dagger from its sheath; but by the dim light from the lantern, Oscar saw the movement.

Still holding him by the throat with one hand, he wrenched the dagger from him with the other, and raised it aloft to strike.

Cunningham Trevanion's career would assuredly have terminated then and there, had not the warder our hero had struck down, and who had now recovered consciousness, arrested his arm.

He seized Oscar by the wrist with his two hands, and shouted lustily for help.

He was answered.

The warder who had hurried off for assistance had obtained it.

While Oscar was struggling to release his arm from the grasp of the fel'ow who held it, loud shouts were heard, and presently a dozen or more men, some carrying lanterns, some links, and all armed with heavy bludgeons, rushed upon the scene.

Without ceremony they seized Oscar, and dragged him from off Cunningham, who instantly jumped to his feet.

And a terrible sight he looked.

His face was almost black, and his eyes seemed starting from his head.

"Hold him tight!" he gasped. "Hold him tight! Oh, he shall suffer for this! Take him to his cell instantly."

Oscar was placed in his loathsome dungeon, and Cunningham took his departure.

CHAPTER VIII.

OF THE MANNER IN WHICH THE GIANT BROTHERS VISITED THE HOUSE IN PICCADILLY— HOW THEY WERE ENTERTAINED BY THE SERVANTS, AND HOW LORD TREVANION CAME VERY NEAR BEING BOILED ALIVE.

SINCE Oscar's appearance before the Queen, the neighbours who surrounded the smithy of the giant blacksmiths had heard no merry sounds proceeding therefrom.

The joyous "Ring, ding, dong," with the everlasting accompaniment of heavy hammers on anvils, had ceased.

To sum up the matter in the proverbial "two words," the brothers were very melancholy.

Considering how kind the Armourer and his wife had been to them, this is not to be wondered at.

On the night following the day that Oscar had been committed to the prison at Ludgate, the smiths were in the smithy partaking of a small barrel of ale while thinking over what was shortly to occur at Temple Bar, when the door opened, and in walked one of the most remarkable citizens of Elizabeth's time.

This was Charles Charlesworth, an engraver on armour, who owned a little garret in Cheapside.

He was a man of about thirty years of age, about six feet in height, and thin to an extraordinary degree.

He was dressed in a doublet of red, considerably the worse for wear.

His fingers were terribly long, "made for picking and stealing," Sampson said, and his hair was fiery red.

His eyes, which Sampson said were of no colour at all, were set deeply back in his head, and were large and full of humour.

This individual was known all over the City as "Carroty Charles."

"Come in, Carroty," cried Sampson, "and take a drink of this."

"Is it good?" asked Charles, taking hold of the can offered him.

"Very good," said Goliar.

"'Tis well," grinned Charles, and placing the can to his lips, he quaffed deeply of its contents.

Setting the can down, he took a seat on a block, and said—

"Now, I've come just to ask you, Sampson, and you, Goliar, whether you have come to your senses yet?"

"Senses? What do you mean?"

"Have you got out of this melancholy fit of yours yet?"

Both the brothers shook their heads.

"It's sad business, Carroty," said Sampson, "and we have been thinking what is to be done in the matter."

"Hum! He may be reprieved."

"No fear of that," replied Sampson; "we not long ago received the news that the scaffold was being erected at Temple Bar."

"Lord save us!" ejaculated Carroty, with a look of horror. "'Tis enough to turn one's blood cold. Well, well, even now I shall hope for the best. You should really rouse yourselves, for you would be able to treat the matter better. I was about to ask you whether you would come with me to-night."

"Where to?"

"To see my beloved sweetheart."

As Carroty Charles said this, he clasped his hands, and turned up his eyes.

Sampson winked at Goliar, who said:

"You have told us about her lots of times; but you have not said where she lives, or what she is like."

"Is she fat?" asked Sampson.

"*Gloriously* fat," cried Charles, clasping his hands. "So fat she can scarcely waddle."

"She's like a duck, then, Carroty?"

"Yes, yes; she is a duck, bless her—bless her!"

"What is she?"

"Eh? She's a female, bless her— bless her!"

"What is she like, you fool?" roared Sampson. "Can't you describe her?"

"No words could describe her. She is—she is, indeed, surpassingly lovely."

"That's the reason you took to her, and she to you, eh?" said Goliar.

"It is—it is," replied Charles.

"Did she examine your hair, Carroty?" asked Sampson.

"She did—she did."

"Oh, then, it's no wonder she took to you What's her business?"

"Cook—first cook," cried Charles, clasping and unclasping his long fingers.

Sampson started, and so did Goliar.

A cook! the very thing—at least, it happened to be at the moment, for the giant brothers were somewhat hungry.

"And her residence?" asked Sampson.

"Piccadilly."

"Who is her master?"

"I am—bless her—*bless* her!"

"I mean whom is she cook to?"

"His lordship."

"What lord?"

"Lord Trevanion."

Sampson started off his seat as if he had been shot.

"Why did you not say so before," he cried.

"I wasn't aware you knew him, master giant," replied Charles.

"Why, 'twas he and his accursed son who had to do with Oscar Raymond. 'Twas his and his son's false evidence which got Oscar a sentence of death!"

"Lord, so it was!" cried Charles, uneasily, "and I had not thought of it. Well, well, it is strange of a surety. But it so happens that neither his lordship nor his son will be here to-night."

"How do you know?"

"Oh, my love told me so when I saw her this morning."

"What do you say, brother?" asked Sampson.

"As you will," replied Goliar.

"I am hungry," said Sampson.

"And I, brother," sighed Goliar.

"We had better go. The Armourer will not be here to-night. Yes, we will go, Charles, and see your beloved cook."

Charles was delighted.

"We will go at once," he said.

"But are we to walk the whole distance?" asked Goliar.

"Of a surety," replied Charles. "Where should I find horses on which you could travel?"

"Fear it not, brother," grinned Sampson. "We will not walk all the way. Let us go to old Sands and borrow his horses and his ass."

The smithy was soon closed, and the giant brothers set off with Charles.

Reaching Cheapside, they turned down Love Lane.

Here, at the sign of the "Jolly Waggoner," lived a man named Sands, an individual who spent almost all his money in drink.

Those who lived with him, including his horses, suffered in consequence.

Sampson opened the door of the stable and cautiously entered.

He came forth in a moment, a broad grin on his face.

"As I expected," he said, "old Sands is fast asleep in the manger. Keep where you are, and I will saddle the animals."

Charles did not like this business; he would a thousand times sooner have walked to Piccadilly.

But since Sampson had taken it into his head to ride, he knew very well it would be of no use saying anything against it.

Presently Sampson brought forth a sorry-looking nag, and with much laughter, told his brother to look after him, and if he attempted to run away to knock him down.

Then he brought out the other horse, a counterpart of the first.

"Observe his eyes, brother," said Sampson; "he is weeping for the sins of his drunken master!"

The ass was next brought forth, and a pretty looking animal he was, certainly.

"Observe him!" cried Sampson. "Observe

him, Carroty. He it is who steals the food belonging to these thoroughbred horses. See he turns away his face, for he knows I am speaking the truth. "Don't you?" he cried, as he delivered a spankling smack on the donkey's face, which nearly knocked him down.

"Don't ill-use the poor brute," cried Charles; "for asses are very patient."

"Come along, Carroty," cried Goliar, "and let me lift you on his back. Which way do you ride? Backwards or forwards?"

"Eh?"

"Which way do you ride? With your face to his head or his tail?"

"Oh, his head, I think."

"Good, then, on you go. Are you ready?"

"Oh, quite, thank you."

Goliar picked Carroty up like he would have picked up a child, and placed him on the saddle.

"Now, you must be very careful," said Sampson, "how you handle the reins, or he may run away with you."

Sampson and his brother now mounted their steeds.

A pretty trio they looked, as our readers may well imagine, when we tell them that had not the giant brothers lifted their feet, they would have touched the ground.

Carroty's feet, too, were only a couple of inches from the ground.

Sampson, giving the word, away they went.

The journey to Piccadilly occupied considerably longer than if the three had walked; but, although it had proved a journey of terror to Charles, it had caused the giants and some hundreds of citizens infinite amusement.

When they reached Lord Trevanion's house, they found it, as it usually was, in darkness and silence.

The only beings to be seen were two men-at-arms, who slowly paced up and down the front of the mansion.

Stern, grim-looking fellows they were; but directly the giants and Charles halted before them, they burst into a loud roar of laughter.

Sampson got off his horse, and lifted Charles off his ass.

"How do you feel now?" he asked. "I trust thy ride has not knocked all thoughts of thy cook from thy red noddle."

"Nay, nay," replied Charles. "Bless her! *Bless* her!"

"Ay, so say we," said Goliar. "Bless her, and her *joints*. I mean his lordship's joints, Carroty."

"Well, master giants," said one of the men-at-arms, as he gazed admiringly at the gigantic proportions of the brothers, "and what would you?"

"Come forward, Carroty," cried Sampson, "and describe your *duck*."

But as soon as Charles came forward he was recognised by a servant, who happened to present herself at the moment.

"'Tis our chief cook's lover," she said, 'Pray admit him."

"Well, we see no harm in a man like him," said one of the soldiers; "but we cannot admit his friends."

"Are these your friends, Charles?" cried the servant, as she eyed the huge brothers in amazement.

"Yes, I am proud to say they are my friends," replied Charles.

"Of course he is proud to own us as friends," said Sampson. "And why do you say you cannot admit us?"

"Our orders are strict," replied the soldier. "These are dangerous times, and no one is more aware of it than Lord Trevanion, to whom, as you are doubtless aware, this house belongs."

"We are, like our friend Carroty, harmless citizens," said Goliar, "as innocent as babies. We wouldn't harm the hair——"

"You have heard of us, have you not?" interrupted Sampson.

"We have, if we mistake not," replied the soldier. "You are the giant brothers of the city."

"True. Well, we are glad you know us, and in future you shall be our friends. Here, take a sip at this, 'twill put fresh life in you.'

"Well, well," said the soldier, "I see no harm in drinking with you."

"Of course not, my friends," said Sampson. "And in this bottle," handing him a wooden bottle holding about a quart, "you will assuredly find some of the finest stuff you ever tasted. Drink hearty, friends. A bottle full of good canary is a prime companion! As there is plenty more where that came from, you may keep the whole of it and welcome."

And Sampson gave his brother a sly wink.

"Thanks, friend giant," said the man-at-arms, as he handed the bottle to his comrade. "Since you are such good-natured fellows, we can have no further objection to your going in. So pray enter. But you must be ready at a moment's notice to take your departure by the back way, whither we will take your horses and the ass. Though his lordship and his son are at present absent, there is no knowing how soon they may return."

"We shall be quite ready to go," replied Sampson, "as soon as you give us notice."

Thereupon the servant, leading the way, Carroty and the giant brothers entered the mansion of the Trevanions.

Now, the liquor in the bottle was of a most powerful description; and though the giants possessed stomachs which could defy its influence, ordinary men could not.

The liquor, however, was very nice; it was a compound that the men-at-arms rarely, if ever, tasted.

They liked it much, and one took a pull, and the other took a pull, until the whole had gone.

The result was that the two men-at-arms slid helplessly to the ground, where, after vainly trying to troll a merry stave, they dropped off to sleep.

Meantime, the giants and Charles were through the courtyard, and entered the kitchen a huge vaulted apartment, in which a couple of hundred dancers could easily have been accommodated.

There were several servants present, both male and female.

Directly Charles entered he espied his sweetheart, who was busy at one end of the kitchen making "dumplings without seams."

Her bare arms were coated with soft paste, and her apron, which covered the front of her enormously stout person, was plentifully besprinkled with flour.

But as soon as Carroty entered she forgot all this, and with a wild shriek of joy opened her arms, and bounding across the kitchen, buried her face in Carroty's noble, though somewhat skinny breast.

Of course, the result of this was that Carroty got the front of his shabby doublet covered with flour.

But he did not seem to mind it.

"Bless you!" he cried "bless you!"

Suddenly the giants came through the doorway, and the whole of the servants uttered a cry of wonder.

"The Lord save us!" cried the butler, whose eyes seemed starting from his head. "Here we have a couple of statues from the abbey to keep us company."

The cook looked up.

"My friends, dearest," said Carroty; "my dear friends the——"

"Friends?" cried the cook. "Friends? Then there can be no harm in welcoming them."

And opening her arms she rushed up to Sampson, who, not relishing the idea of being smothered in flour, stepped on one side, and the cook fell into the arms of Goliar, who was not at all particular.

Placing his huge arms about her waist, he nearly squeezed the life out of her.

"Bless you!" he cried, mimicking Carroty's voice; "*bless* you. I trust your meat is as tender as yourself."

"Have you been invited to supper, my friends?" asked the butler, in surly tones.

"We *have*," replied Sampson.

"By whom?"

"By his lordship."

"Bah!"

"By Lord Trevanion I repeat."

"It is an infamous falsehood," cried the butler. "His lordship is absent, and in his absence I must see that no folly is carried on in this kitchen."

"Oh, pray let them have a little supper," said the cook, and she was supported by the other servants present.

"I say no," replied the butler, posing himself in an attitude of supreme authority. "I say no."

"You mean to say, my friend," said Sampson, "that after we have come all the way from Tower Hill to see our friend's sweetheart, we are to go away supperless?"

"Certainly."

Sampson considered for a moment.

Then he said—

"Brother, we must eat?"

"Oh, of a surety," replied Goliar.

Sampson looked round the kitchen.

Near the fireplace was a small cellar, where logs of wood were kept.

Striding up to the butler, Sampson seized him by the collar, shaking him like a dog would shake a rat.

Then he lifted him clean off his feet, and amid his loud howls for mercy, and the delighted cries of the servants, flung him, head first, into the cellar, banged the door to, and bolted it.

"Now, then," cried Sampson, "come along my pretty charmers, and get the supper on the table. I warrant you both of us are terribly hungry, as well as thirsty. I will help you. Where are the keys of the cellar—the wine cellar?"

"Try the beer first, your mountainous worship," said one of the servants.

"Well, well, replied Sampson, "beer first, brother. Where are the keys?"

"In the butler's pocket," laughed a kitchen porter.

But this did not in the least disconcert the giant.

"Which is the door, thou knave?" he asked.

The porter pointed to a low door near a copper, which was full of greasy water.

Sampson marched up to it, put his shoulder to it, and instantly burst it open, amid a loud cry of wonder at this extraordinary exhibition of strength.

Sampson now seized a lantern, and entered the cellar.

He soon reappeared with a goodly-sized barrel of ale on his shoulder.

This he placed on the table, and with his huge fist smashed the head in.

Taking down a couple of measures which hung on the nail, he filled them. One he handed to his brother, and the other he placed to his own lips, draining it at a draught.

"Truly, his lordship keeps good ale, brother," he said, smacking his lips.

"Of a truth, he does," said Goliar. "He must have thought that we should try it one of these days. And there are no better judges of good ale in all the city than you and I."

In a few moments the servants had laid the table with piles of good things.

Sampson and Goliar were delighted beyond measure.

Charles was too much taken up with his cook to pay much attention to what was before him.

And besides that he was becoming nervous at the proceedings of the giant brothers.

He knew what they were directly they had filled themselves with food and drink.

He began to wish he had not invited them.

The brothers grew playful.

They were brimful of fun, and as their fun was catching, the servants joined in with them.

The butler was dragged out of the cellar, his pockets rifled of his keys, and as he was not willing to join in with the others, he was unceremoniously thrown back again.

The wine cellar was opened, and the brothers pulled forth basket after basket and placed the whole lot upon the table until it looked like a wine merchant's counter.

Charles was no lover of beer; but he was of wine, and his sweetheart plied him with it until he was considerably more than half intoxicated.

Sampson thereupon made a space on the table between the baskets, and placed him between them, a bottle in each hand.

The laughter was now boisterous in the extreme.

The brothers were in the height of their glory.

Suddenly a loud shout was heard.

The laughter and shouting ceased as if by magic.

All turned, and beheld, in the doorway, the figures of Lord Trevanion and his son.

Lord Trevanion, as soon as he saw the condition of the place and his servants, went white with rage.

"Accursed drunken beasts!" he cried, "what is the meaning of this?"

"You have not to look far to see the meaning of it, your lordship," said Cunningham. "Look at those giants."

"Ha!" replied Trevanion. "I remember them. They are the cause of it. But they are caught—caught! By Heaven's mercy, they shall smart for this!" he shrieked, shaking his fist at the giants, who were calmly drinking his lordship's best wine.

"Ay, they would be caught if we had any one to take them," said Cunningham; "but it seems that the two men-at-arms have joined in this drunken revelry, since both are lying helplessly drunk outside the house."

"Who is this red-headed thief upon the table?" asked his lordship.

"He is my sweetheart," cried the cook.

"Then away with him!" cried Cunningham, as, advancing to the table, he seized Charles by the feet.

But Sampson, reaching forward, collared him, and dragging him to the cellar, opened the door, and flung him on the top of the butler, who fancying that it was Charles, commenced to belabour him soundly with a log.

Sampson, laughing heartily, placed his back against the door, and for some time above the cries of the servants and the shrieking of Lord Trevanion could be heard, the thuds and curses of the butler and Cunningham as they thrashed each other.

At last Trevanion, drawing his sword, ran towards Sampson, but Goliar placed his leg out, and the result was that his lordship fell on the stones.

Securing the door of the cellar, Sampson picked up his lordship, wrenched his sword from his grasp, and placed him in the copper, from which it was impossible for Trevanion to extricate himself unless assisted.

Sampson seized a light, and applied it to the shavings and wood, and in a few moments a fine fire was blazing beneath his lordship.

"There are many worse things in the world than a boiled lord," said Sampson.

"True, brother," replied Goliar, calmly, as he picked up a huge fire fork, and commenced to stir the fire." Her Majesty has been offered many a worse thing. As soon as his lordship is properly cooked, we will truss and cook his son, and both of them shall be taken to Whitehall on our ass."

His lordship's moans now gave way to fearful screams, for he felt the water becoming gradually warmer and warmer.

The servants began to get afraid that the joke, as they believed it to be, was being carried too far, and so they commenced to implore the giants to take his lordship out.

"Well, well," said Sampson, "we will at once release him if he will promise not to dismiss any of you."

"Yes, yes," cried Trevanion. "I promise! I promise!"

Thereupon Sampson drew him out of the copper, and placed him soaking wet, and more dead than alive, on the floor.

"We will now retire," said Goliar, "and will visit you again at a future time."

"Come along, Carroty," said Sampson, as he pulled Charles off the table, and tucked him under his arm. "A good night to thee all."

Laughing loudly the brothers departed, their laughter being heard long after they had got into the street.

They found the horses and the ass patiently awaiting them.

Charles, however, was so helplessly drunk that they could not get him astride the ass, so Sampson took off Carroty's doublet, tore it into strips, and his brother, assisting him, tied him upon the animal's back, his head towards the tail.

Then they managed to place their legs across their horse's backs, and, singing and laughing, they "rode" towards the city.

CHAPTER IX.

IS OF THE MANNER IN WHICH OSCAR WAS BROUGHT TO TEMPLE BAR—HOW THE GIANT BROTHERS LED THE APPRENTICES—HOW THEY BROKE THROUGH THREE LINES OF ARMED MEN, AND OF WHAT FOLLOWED.

OWING to the representations made on his behalf by the Armourer and a number of his friends, including many noblemen and gentlemen of high reputation in the City of London, the Queen granted Oscar a reprieve of one day to consider what was brought forward to prove that the statements of Lord Trevanion and his son were false.

Trevanion, as a matter of course, got to hear of this, and, urging the Queen to remember for how long he had faithfully served the State, besought he Majesty to pay no attention to those who, if they could, would ruin him and his son.

Whether it was because of Trevanion's representations, or whether the Queen had too many other matters to trouble her, that Oscar's case was almost, if not quite, unheeded by her, we cannot say.

Alarming rumours of an intended invasion by the Spaniards had reached England about this time, and so that may have been the reason that the Queen did not devote her attention to this matter.

So Trevanion and his son Cunningham had it all their own way, and everything was got ready for Oscar's execution.

In the meantime, as no chances of a pardon, conditional or otherwise, reached the ears of the giants, they resolved upon a desperate enterprise.

They swore that they would rescue Oscar.

And the giants, though rather fond of play, too much so at times, could work when they thought proper—ay, and work with a will, too, more especially if the work required to be done was in behalf of a friend.

In their schemes they were assisted by Carroty Charles.

He, of course, could be of no earthly use in an attempted rescue; but as he was a good scholar, he was of great service.

In the first place he engraved, upon a steel plate, these words—" You are invited to present yourself at the residence of the brother's Sylvester as soon as darkness sets in. This note to be destroyed as soon as read."

From this place he took fifty impressions, and with them in his pockets, made a tour of the city.

Each chief apprentice, whom he considered could be relied on, received one of these secret missives.

The result of this was that, as soon as darkness had set in, and the apprentices had seen their masters' shops closed, they set off to Eastcheap, where they found the giant brothers awaiting them.

The morning of the execution dawned at last.

Eight of the clock had scarcely struck, ere the hurried movements of many feet, loud shouts, the clatter of arms, the tramping of horses, and the well-known murmur of a vast crowd of people in the distance told Oscar only too plainly that his last hour had come !"

"At least, I will die bravely," he said. "I will not die a coward, and thus leave my dear parents open to the taunts of their enemies, few though they be."

The only thing which troubled him was whether he would be led to his doom under the eyes of the detested Cunningham.

If he thought it possible that Cunningham would not appear he was doomed to be disappointed, for presently above the clatter and the shouts in and about the prison, he heard the voice of his enemy.

Presently the door of his dungeon was thrown open, and the turnkey cried :

"Your hour has arrived, young sir. Hark to the shouts ! You have thousands to welcome you, and to cheer you on your way to execution. The whole city is in an uproar, and——"

"And on account of the execution of a paltry apprentice !" interrupted Cunningham.

"He is no apprentice !" said one of the jailers ; "but the son of the Armourer of Tower Hill, as true a man as ever breathed."

"Get about your business," cried Cunningham. He should now be on the road."

"The Lord save us !" said the turnkey. "The road to the scaffold is not very far."

"Surround him !" cried Cunningham, as Oscar, pale, but firm, stepped from his dungeon, "lest he does more mischief."

Oscar was immediately surrounded by a score of soldiers.

They were about to move on, when Cunningham cried—

"Halt !"

The men stopped.

"Take him not hence," said Cunningham, "until his arms have been securely bound behind his back."

The captain of the soldiers demurred, for he heartily sympathised with Oscar, whereupon Cunningham fiercely cried—

"Obey me, hound, if you set any value on your head !"

The captain reluctantly gave orders for a rope to be brought.

With this Oscar's hands were tied behind his back, and he was led forth.

He saw that all the passages and rooms were filled with armed men.

This, however, was not an unusual occurrence when a prisoner is about to be executed.

Outside, placed close against the door, was a cart, in which stood a clergyman, with an open book in his hand.

The cart was completely surrounded by mounted soldiers with drawn swords.

Into the vehicle Oscar was assisted, and directly he was seen a loud and prolonged cheer greeted him.

Again and again it was repeated, much to the astonishment and consternation of the soldiers who could not understand it.

Cunningham made his way to his father, who, at the back of the soldiers, was beckoning to him.

Here his horse awaited him, and he mounted.

"What is the meaning of these shouts, think you?" asked Trevanion, in uneasy tones.

"I fail to understand," replied Cunningham, "unless the majority of these present are his friends. If your lordship will look, you will see, from their flat caps and their dresses, that the majority are apprentices, and from them the shouts principally come."

"Ay, ay," replied Trevanion; "and I do not like the looks of them. And have you observed that they carry staves?"

"I have."

"My impression is, that a rescue is to be attempted. Still, if that were so, it could never be successful, for I took care to have all the available soldiers present. Come what will, I will see this execution carried out. Yet I would to Heaven the person to be executed were the Armourer himself or that accursed Ward."

"One or both may be hanged soon," replied Cunningham, significantly.

"Ay, 'twill be so, if I have *my* way in the matter, my son. But see, the cart moves."

Yes, at this moment, amid loud cries, the cart began to move.

There was a form in it for Oscar to seat himself, but that he declined to do.

Firm and erect he stood.

The sight about Ludgate and along Fleet-street, as far as the eye could reach, was extraordinary in the extreme.

Windows, balconies, housetops, everywhere, in fact, was crowded with people.

It was with the greatest difficulty that the cart could move.

It really seemed as if the people purposely obstructed its progress.

Presently the cheers gave way to groans, and there arose loud and angry cries of:

"Death to Trevanion!"

His lordship turned ashy pale, as did his dastardly son; but surrounded by soldiers, they were safe, unless anyone had the audacity to fire from the houses.

Oscar turned his eyes hither and thither, in the hopes of seeing either his father or his mother.

But they were not near the scene.

Slowly along Fleet-street the procession moved, and as St. Bride's was reached, the "death bell" commenced to toll.

It's sonorous tones were soon answered by those of St. Dunstan's bell, and the bell from the chapel in the Temple.

"It is a very singular thing," said Cunningham, uneasily, as they got halfway up Fleet street. "I called your lordship's attention to the fact, that nearly all those who shouted were evidently apprentices. But now look round, I see nothing of them."

"It is very strange," replied Trevanion; "but let us not trouble ourselves, my son. We are quite safe. Yet I would all were over."

The scaffold was reached at last, and amid terrific excitement, the cart was backed against the wooden steps which led to the platform.

Here leaning against one of the supports, stood a most brutal-looking ruffian, who was well-known by the not very enticing name of "Choking Chesham."

He was one of the public hangmen, and the most savage of the lot.

Cunningham reined up by the side of the captain in command of the troops about the scaffold.

"My father, Lord Trevanion," he said, "wishing to have this affair brought to a satisfactory and a speedy termination, desires me to say, that if you will be pleased to draw three lines of mounted men about the scaffold, he——"

"Odd's my life!" interrupted the captain. "*Three* lines? In the name of Heaven for what?"

"To guard against a surprise. His lord——"

"Tell him it cannot be done!"

"But his lordship says that if you obey him in this instance he will, as soon as the affair is over, hand you the sum of a hundred marks."

"Oh, that, of course, alters the case," grinned the captain. "Pray inform his lordship that he shall be obeyed."

In a few seconds loud words of command were given on all sides, and round the scaffold were drawn three lines of mounted men.

The movement, however, did not escape the observation of the vast crowd, who greeted it with howls of derision.

Oscar walked firmly up the steps, and reached the platform, where he was received with a grunt, and a curse by the hangman.

The clergyman followed him, and as soon as a hush fell upon the crowd, said—

"It is the wish of her most gracious Majesty that you do, before this multitude of her subjects, confess your many sins."

"Whatever sins I may have committed," replied Oscar. "I have not committed one against her Majesty, for whom I entertain the most profound respect."

"Ere you die," continued the clergyman, "you should ask pardon of your Queen and your Maker!"

"Ay," replied Oscar, raising his eyes. "I do now ask Him to pardon my sins. But I cannot ask pardon of those against whom I have not sinned."

"Confound it!" growled the hangman, displaying two rows of monstrous teeth. "Am I to remain here all day?"

"I will not detain you long," replied Oscar. "I have only to——"

He was interrupted by a tremendous shout from the centre of Fleet-street.

Again and again it was repeated, and all eyes were turned in the direction of the sound.

A rushing multitude of people could be seen, and in the centre two horsemen.

"A reprieve!—a reprieve!" was the cry.

"No!" shouted Trevanion. "No reprieve is possible. Cunningham — Cunningham — give the word to close up! A rescue is about to be attempted, captain!" he shrieked. "An extra hundred marks if you resist this attempt."

The shouts became louder and louder.

"Clear the way—stand back! stand back!" were the cries.

"By Heaven!" yelled Trevanion, raising himself in his stirrups, "a rescue *is* to be attempted! and the leaders of the howling wretches yonder are those accursed giants!"

"Lord save us, how they ride!" cried the captain. "Heaven above! what huge fellows they are!"

"Draw!" cried Cunningham, plucking forth his sword. "Draw! and resist this attempt in the Queen's name!"

A few score of swords flashed from their scabbards.

Yes, the two horsemen were certainly the giant brothers.

Each was mounted on an enormous and powerful horse,* and towering high above the crowd, they had the appearance of huge statues.

Each had fastened to his waist a large sword.

Sampson carried a tremendous hammer, while Goliar had a rusty battle axe.

Behind the brothers came an army of apprentices.

Each was armed either with a club or a heavy staff.

The crowd, with cheers of encouragement and cries of wonder, gave way before the giants.

The captains, seeing that, beyond all question, a most determined attempt at a rescue was intended, stood by the side of their men, and as the giants, followed by hundreds of apprentices, came up, the order rang out above the shouts of the multitude—

"Charge!"

The captain, to whom Cunnigham had promised the money, and who was the first to give this order, was close to Sampson, who, raising his ponderous hammer, brought it down with fearful force on the captain's head.

He smashed his helmet and battered in his head, and such was the force of the blow, that the captain's horse stumbled and fell, bringing down two or three soldier's by his side.

"Hangman! Do your duty!" yelled Trevanion.

The hangman mounted the ladder like lightning, and seized the rope, which dangled from the cross-beam.

The clergyman, who saw the deed done by Sampson, uttered a wild scream, and leapt from the scaffold among the men and horses.

---

* "Spitfire" and "Longlegs," each horse of about twice the size of an ordinary animal. They belonged to Craven, the showman, of Elizabeth's time.

He was trampled to death.

Hardly had he disappeared, ere a tall figure, clothed from head to foot in black, took his place, as if by magic.

A glittering dagger flashed for an instant, the next Oscar's bonds were cut.

"Fire!" roared Trevanion to the arquebusiers at his side. "Fire! Who is that accursed wretch? Methinks, I know that figure."

The man in black raised his hood from his face.

"Ha!" shrieked Trevanion, covering his eyes with his hands. "*The Wizard!*"

"Fire!" roared Cunningham.

The soldiers fired, the result being, however, that their balls struck down several of their comrades on the other side of the scaffold.

When the smoke had disappeared, the Wizard had vanished.

In the meantime, the soldiers, the giants, and the apprentices had become mixed up in one confused mass.

Though the apprentices laboured under a great disadvantage, they were fully roused, and did terrible execution.

The giants did wonders with their huge weapons.

They dealt death on all sides, and above the din and clash of steel, their powerful voices could be heard calling upon the apprentices to follow them.

"By Heaven's grace!" roared Sampson, as he brained one of the captains, who stood at the foot of the scaffold. "I would I were on the other side, Goliar, where I can see Lord Trevanion and his son. By the soul of my father, I would pound them into a very jelly."

"Quick, brother!" cried Goliar, as he hacked away with his battle-axe. "See, the hangman has got assistance, and the rope is already about the lad's neck. At them brother, and you love me!"

"Fear it not," replied Sampson, as he seized a halberdier's pike, which was levelled at him, and broke it in twain. "Do you see to my horse, brother Goliar."

Thereupon Sampson, who, at this moment, reached the foot of the scaffold, bounded off his horse, and knocking the howling soldiers to the right and the left of him, rushed up the stairs on to the platform.

The hangman, by Trevanion's direction, had been assisted by a number of soldiers, and had succeeded in getting the rope round Oscar's neck.

Then he had mounted the ladder, and, flinging the other end over the cross-beam, had obtained firm hold of it.

Another instant, and our hero would have been run up.

Sampson, with his heavy hammer, soon put the men round Oscar to flight.

Some of them, in their frantic haste to escape, actually flung themselves on the very points of the halberdier's weapons.

Sampson snatched the rope from the hangman's hands, and told him to descend the ladder at his peril.

Picking up a sword, he handed it to Oscar.

NOTICE.—Another Picture is Given Away with this Number.

"DESPITE HIS HOWLS FOR MERCY, THE WRETCH WAS HELD OVER."

"Defend yourself, my lad," he said ; " but remain near me."

"A thousand crowns to anyone who will capture that giant !" cried Cunningham.

"Heaven's bitter curse on you, thou hell-hound !" roared the now enraged Sampson, as, stepping back a pace, he swung his hammer round his shoulders, and let it fly at Cunningham.

It missed him, but caught Lord Trevanion's horse fairly on the forehead, killing him on the spot.

The apprentices had worked well ; but, alas ! already many of them lay weltering in their blood.

The riot had, indeed, assumed most serious proportions.

There was hardly a mounted soldier left, for the apprentices had "hamstrung" the horses, and so dismounted the men.

Directly Sampson was observed on the scaffold, the fighting appeared to cease.

So far the giants and the apprentices had won the day.

But it soon became known that reinforcements had been sent for.

Sampson paused for breath.

His naked sword was in his hand now, and he certainly looked a most formidable being.

"I have watched you ill-treat this youth !" he cried to the hangman. "I have watched you, thou ungainly lump of humanity. Come down !"

"Pah !" replied the hangman. "I am here to do my duty, and, though you were as big as a house, I would pay no attention to what you said."

Sampson was in a terrible temper.

He made no reply to the hangman, but seizing the ladder, he pulled it from its position, sending the hangman with a crash on to the platform.

Then he pounced upon him, dragged him to his feet, and despite his howls for mercy, placed the rope round his neck, and, amid wild cheers, pulled the man up until his bullet head nearly touched the cross beam.

Then he fastened the rope to one of the supports.

Wildly the hangman kicked, struggled and gasped ; but in less than a minute he hung motionless.

Follow me !" cried Sampson to Oscar, "and cut down all who attempt to oppose you."

But the fight was over.

Some few dozens of soldiers, with their horses, were lying upon the ground, some dying, but most of them dead.

"I tried to get at Trevanion and his son," said Goliar, "but no sooner did they observe me than they went off."

"They have escaped, then ? Well, well ! A time will come, I'll warrant me," said Sampson. "Oscar, mount behind me. We must hasten from London at once."

And Sampson mounting his horse, drew Oscar, who was greeted again and again with loud cheers, up behind him.

A crowd of apprentices, bloodstained and exhausted, gathered round.

"I thank you all !" cried Oscar, in a broken voice." A day may come when I will show my gratitude to you. If any of you——"

He was interrupted by a distant shout.

"Quick for our lives," cried Goliar, as he pointed in the direction of St. Clement's Church. "See, reinforcements are coming down upon us. Away !"

"Away !" echoed Sampson ; but as he saw the speed at which the soldiers were advancing, he muttered—"Too late !—too late ! Yet stay ! I will stop them. Brother, watch the lad."

Sampson again dismounted, the crowd wondering what he was about to do.

Like lightning, he rushed to the gates of Temple Bar.

With a single wrench he snapped the chain which held one half the gate, and dragged it to.

Then he did the same to the other, and dragged that to.

Only just in time, for the advancing soldiers, and a large number of them there were, fired.

The balls rattled on the massive oaken gate like a shower of hail on glass.

But Sampson left not the gate until he had drawn its huge bolts.

Vaulting into the saddle, he gave the word to press forward.

The crowd opened, and away went the brothers.

"Which way ?" asked Goliar.

"Follow me, brother," replied Sampson.

Slowly they went at first, but after they had cleared St. Paul's, they went on more swiftly, and before long they were dashing over London Bridge at a tremendous pace.

Once across the bridge, the open country was before them.

"Our horses can do ten miles without pausing," said Sampson ; "therefore, we will not stop until we have covered that distance. How dost thou feel, Oscar ?"

No answer.

"Oscar, my lad," said the giant, "dost not hear what I say to thee ?"

Still no answer.

Sampson drew in a little.

"Brother," he cried, "what ails the lad ? He clutches me tight enough, yet answers not my questions."

"Ha !" gasped Goliar. "And I had not noticed it. By my father's soul, he is covered with blood !"

Sampson uttered a cry of alarm.

He was now, of course, compelled to halt.

Dismounting, he lifted Oscar from the saddle, and placed him on the footway by the side of a ditch.

Kneeling down he examined him.

"As I live !" he said, " he has been shot !"

"Shot? By whom ?" said Goliar.

"The Lord help me, brother, how should I know ? He has been struck by a ball, which was, no doubt, intended for me. Poor lad ! Brave lad ! He has borne all this awful agony without saying a single word. I was beginning to think, brother, that he was regarding his rescue with an air of indifference !"

"Perish the thought, brother."

"Ay, ay," muttered Sampson.

"Hast found the wound, brother?"

"Ay, 'tis here in his breast. Thank Heaven, 'tis not dangerous, and if we can reach a place of safety, I can soon get some one to extract it. I will give him a draught of this.'

And Sampson pulled out his flask, and poured a portion of its contents down Oscar's parched throat.

It had the effect of rousing him to a very considerable extent.

He smiled his thanks.

"Oscar, my dear lad, said Sampson, in a broken voice, "you are sorely wounded, I am grieved to say; but if you can only manage to ride a few more miles, we shall then be in safety."

"I can do it well," murmured Oscar.

"Your will is good enough, I'll warrant," said Sampson; "but think you, your strength will allow you? Drink more of this."

"I can do it Sampson," said Oscar. "I will do it for your and your brother's sake, for you would not leave me alone."

"Heaven forbid it!" replied Sampson, "I would never leave you, while life lasted, until I saw you placed in proper hands."

Goliar raised Oscar, and placed him before Sampson, who held him firmly to his breast.

The journey was then resumed.

At New Cross a brief halt was made for refreshment, and then Sampson took the most unfrequented paths across the fields, and at last Greenwich was reached.

CHAPTER X.

HOW OSCAR WAS PLACED UNDER THE CARE OF GRIFFIN GAUNT, AND HOW THE GIANTS SET OUT FOR CANTERBURY—OF HOW QUEEN ELIZABETH FELL INTO A TRAP, AND HOW THE GIANT BROTHERS SAVED HER LIFE, AND CRAVED A BOON.

CLOSE by the side of what, at the time of our story, was considered a remarkable curiosity, the curiosity being a village church, built *entirely* of oak, and most exquisitely carved, the giants halted.

Drawing their horses into the shadow of some huge trees, the brothers threaded a very narrow lane.

Sampson went first, carrying Oscar in his powerful arms.

In about the centre of the lane stood a small, but pretty house.

On the very top of the house was perched a huge horseshoe, and by its side a hammer.

This showed that the business conducted by the proprietor of the house was that of a farrier.

At the window, very busy at a spinning-wheel sat a young girl of perhaps some sixteen years of age.

She was small and slender, but very pretty, and she boasted a most magnificent head of golden hair.

As the brothers halted before the window, at which she was seated, the girl started up, and uttered a cry of alarm.

"Grace," muttered Goliar.

"Ay, ay, brother," replied Sampson, who, walking nearer to the window, said—

"Come along, Grace, we have no time for delay. Time is now precious."

"How you frightened me!" cried Grace. "Does father expect you?"

"Why, no, my dear. You know that. If we had been expected, you would have been at the end of the lane to meet us. Would you not, Gracie?"

"'Tis more than likely. But, ha! Heavens! what are you carrying?"

"A young friend of ours, my dear, who, some little time back, met with a severe accident."

"Lord save us! He looks pale and ill. I will at once call my father."

And the girl rushed off to the back.

She speedily returned with her father, Griffin Gaunt, a tall elderly man, with a long grey beard.

"What, Sampson!" cried Griffin, holding forth his horny hand, and grasping Sampson's, "and how fares it with thee? What, Goliar! and how fares it with *thee?* Lord! I am right glad to see both o' ye. And——eh? what dost thou carry, Sampson? A youth? Odds my life! What means this?"

"And you love us, Griffin?" replied Sampson. "Delay not an instant. We will tell you and your pretty daughter all in a few moments. 'Tis sufficient for me to say that this youth is the son of a very dear friend of ours, and that he and we are in danger."

"Follow me!" cried Griffin. "Run Gracie, and prepare the first room."

In a few moments Oscar was laid upon a bed in a small, but well-kept room.

An assistant to the farrier was sent off for a surgeon.

That gentleman soon appeared, and when he had recovered from his surprise at beholding two such enormous men as the brothers, he proceeded to examine Oscar.

He produced his case of instruments, and requested to be left alone for a few moments.

When the farrier and the brothers were recalled, he said—

"I have extracted the ball. What he now requires is complete rest and quiet. Send to me in half-an-hour, and I will prepare him a strengthening and a healing cordial."

"Master Surgeon," said Sampson, as he drew a purse from his pocket, "in that you will find ten nobles. A tenth part of that sum will satisfy you?"

"It will, sir giant."

"And the rest will repay you for keeping a secret. It must not be known that this youth is here, nor that we have been seen."

"I can keep a secret without being paid for it, sir giant," replied the surgeon, proudly.

"I can see you are a worthy man," replied Sampson; "but if you will not be paid for keeping a secret, will you take the purse as a *present* from me?"

"With pleasure," replied the surgeon, as he took the purse, and placed it in his pocket, "and I will keep it in remembrance of you."

"Do, do. And now, Griffin, let us adjourn to another room. If you have no objection, Gracie might watch over him."

"I can have no objection, Sampson," replied the farrier.

"Nay, nor I," said Gracie. "I will watch over him just as though he were my brother."

"Thank you, dear Grace," said Goliar, warmly. "You will have no cause to regret your kindness."

"He is a very handsome youth," muttered the farrier, as the three left the room; "but that I——"

"Tush!" interrupted Sampson. "Do not let that trouble you. Besides, Gracie has already a sweetheart, has she not?"

"So far as I am aware, she is heart whole," replied Griffin.

"So far as you know, yes," grinned Goliar; "but maidens, as a rule, do not get very far advanced in years ere they get advanced in love."

"Ay," said Sampson, "Carroty Charles knows that. And that reminds me, brother, that we altogether missed Charles while the fight was proceeding. I much fear that the armour which he was foolish enough to put on brought him to the ground."

"If so," replied Goliar, "no harm will come to him, for he would be certain to lay on the ground until the fight was over, and some one had the kindness to help him up."

Sampson now told the farrier all that had transpired.

He listened in wonder to what he heard.

Though he was not personally acquainted with the Armourer, he knew of him as a person of high character, and was much grieved at the terrible affliction which had so suddenly and unexpectedly overtaken him.

"Your friend is my friend," said Griffin, "and I will take every care of this youth. Rely upon that."

"I do rely upon it, Griffin, and you will keep him at your house until you hear from me?"

"Ay, I will. I wish to Heaven we had accommodation here for you and your brother as well until the affair had somewhat blown over."

"Fear it not, friend Griffin, the affair is of too serious a nature ever to blow over. The country will be scoured in every direction for us. We shall go on to Canterbury to bid farewell to our parents. After that we shall take ship and sail for France."

"It is certainly the best thing that could be done," said the farrier, thoughtfully; "yet it would have been far better and safer if you could stay here, and go off to France directly the youth was well enough to travel."

"No doubt," said Sampson; "but it wou'd be wrong, indeed, to quit the country without bidding adieu to our parents."

"True, very true, indeed," replied the farrier.

Sampson and Goliar now left the house, followed by Gaunt, who bid them a hearty farewell.

*   *   *   *   *

Nothing of importance occurred until the brothers reached Wotton, some few miles the London side of Canterbury.

This was on the following night.

News travelled very slowly in those days, and not at any of the houses at which the brothers called for refreshment had the news of the riot and rescue in the city, been received.

It was near ten o'clock when the pretty village of Wotton came in sight.

"You remember the 'Bladder of Lard,' brother?" said Sampson.

"Ay," replied Goliar, "and I well remember the many casks of ale I have emptied there."

"Tony Shaw will remember us, I'll warrant," laughed Sampson.

"He will brother," grinned Goliar. "There is rather too much of us to be forgotten."

"There is one thing which is good about Tony Shaw. We can always count upon his silence. I propose we at once proceed to his place and rest for the night.

"Let us go to the 'bladder,' brother, by all means. Heaven knows we require a great deal of rest and refreshment. My throat is parched, and in good sooth, I could easily consume a few gallons of home-brewed."

"Ay, and so could I. But, Goliar——"

And Sampson drew up and looked seriously at his brother.

"Yes, Sampson?"

"This affair is beginning to weigh me down."

"So 'tis me, brother," replied Goliar, shaking his head gloomily.

"I fear me that some harm will certainly come to us. And as I came along, though I said naught, I have fancied I heard a voice in the air—a voice calling me by name. And that voice, good brother, sounded like the voice of Oscar. Something tells me that if we are not ferretted out, *he* will be."

"Let us try not to give way to these thoughts," replied Goliar. "No truer man breathes on this earth than our friend the farrier."

"He will defend the lad with his life should aught occur; but if Trevanion or his son smelt Oscar out, they would not attempt to capture him single-handed. Thinking we should be with him, they would come with a goodly number of men."

"No doubt of it. Well, well brother, let us

trust in Providence. We will return to the lad as soon as possible."

In a few more moments the giants drew up before a little hostelry, known as the "Bladder of Lard."

The brothers could see into the little parlour, beyond that reserved for the use of customers.

"By my father's soul!" ejaculated Sampson, "Tony must be doing a somewhat bad trade, brother. There is not a single customer to be seen, and Tony and his wife appear to be asleep opposite each other."

"That there should be no customers is all the better for us," replied Goliar; "but rouse them up."

Sampson gently pushed down the window, and reaching his hand over, knocked a small barrel from its shelf to the floor. It fell with a loud crash.

Instantly Tony and his wife, who had certainly dropped off to sleep, having got disgusted at the prolonged absence of customers, started to their feet, and rushed into the parlour.

"The cat, wife!" yelled Tony, seizing a stick, and darting behind his barrels. "By all the incarnate fiends, that was Master Borrell's cat. And if I *cat*-ch her, I will divide her tail from her infamous carcase! A cask of my best Rhenish destroyed! It's horrible—it's——"

"Tony—Tony Shaw—Tony the plump—Tony the fat! having a chase after a big she-cat!" cried Sampson.

Tony clutched his wife round the waist, gasping for breath.

"Spirits!" he gurgled.

"Yes, fool that you are!" replied Mistress Shaw, "and it's all running about the floor. Stand up, Tony, and be a man. Nobody shall touch you while I have a basting-spoon left in the house."

"Tony," cried Sampson, popping his head over the window.

"Here, spirit of the departed!" cried Tony, picking up a little courage, and glancing towards the window, "what would you most dread——"

He paused, and drew himself erect.

"Why, it's Sampson!" he cried. "Sampson! Wife!—wife! it's Sampson, and as I'm a living man he's grown ever so much!"

At this Sampson and his brother burst into a hearty laugh.

Of course, Tony did not see the horses.

He rushed forth, followed by his wife, and directly they saw the brothers and the enormous animals on which they were mounted, they uttered loud cries of amazement.

Sampson reached forth his huge horny hand, seized Tony's, and nearly pulled him on to the saddle.

Goliar did likewise with Mistress Shaw.

"In the name of all the saints!" cried Tony, "where did you get these horses?"

"Oh, we had them grown for us," replied Goliar. "Fine creatures, eh, Tony?"

"Verily! How much corn do they consume at a meal?"

"One load."

"Heaven's mercy! Truly they are fine animals. But come, master giants, is it your intention to stay here for the night?"

"It is, if so be you can find accommodation for ourselves and our horses."

"Well, well, no doubt we shall manage it. But your horses, Master Sampson, must remain in the open air all the night, for our stable roof is no higher than your saddle bow."

"Our horses, like ourselves, Master Tony, are ready and willing to adapt themselves to circumstances," said Goliar.

"Then they are wise animals. But I have plenty of straw for them, and if a load of corn will be of service between them, they can have it."

The giants dismounted, and led their horses to the back of the hostelry, where they assisted Tony in making them comfortable.

The brothers then entered the inn, where they sat down to a table loaded with good things provided for them by Mistress Shaw.

During the progress of the meal they related all that had happened in London.

Tony and his wife were startled beyond measure.

"The Virgin save us!" whispered Tony, in great alarm, and looking round the apartment as though he expected to find some of the Queen's Guard already there. "If you are captured you will surely be executed. Truly, truly, you never thought of a worse thing when you decided to proceed to Canterbury."

"And why so, Tony?" asked Sampson.

"You have stopped at a few hostelries?"

"Several."

"Heaven's mercy! And do you mean to say that at none of them you heard that the Queen was about to set out for Canterbury?"

"No!" cried the giant brothers.

"Such then," said Tony, "is certainly the case. By the time this must be but a few miles from here. There is one comfort, however, her Majesty rides *incognito*, and never takes with her more than a few men—noblemen, of course —who can be relied upon. I should not be at all surprised if this infamous and lying Trevanion formed one of the party."

"Do not fear, husband," said Mistress Shaw, whose nerves were considerably stronger than her husband's, "our friends will be safe enough here. None of the Queen's party ever think of stopping at our humble house. Sampson and Goliar must remain here until the Queen has established herself at Canterbury."

"For what length of time does her Majesty intend to stay?" asked Sampson.

"That," replied Tony, "is only known to herself."

"Have you any lodgers?" asked Goliar.

"None at present," replied Tony; "and even if we had, they need not see you. Come, you are both tired. I will show you to your room, a room you know of old."

"Ay, ay, Tony," replied Sampson, "we *do* know it, and we warrant you that we remember every article the room contained.

Tony led the way to the first floor, and held open the door of a very well furnished room.

It was of fair size, but the door only being

intended for ordinary men, the giants had to stoop to enter.

"Since the bedstead is of no earthly use to either of you," said Tony, "take off the clothes, and place them on the floor. There you will be able to rest. I will bring you some more bed-clothes in a moment, as well as a cask of ale."

"One moment," said Sampson. "Should any travellers come——"

"They can only be accommodated with the parlour, which is below this room," interrupted Tony; "therefore, fear nothing."

Some time after this the ale and the extra bedclothes were brought, and the giants, having consumed the former, tried to compose themselves to sleep.

•   •   •   •   •

Not a solitary customer troubled Tony to draw a cup of wine, so he determined to close his house.

Just before he could do so, however, he caught the sound of horses' hoofs.

From their rapid beating on the hard road, he knew that they were coming along at a good round pace.

"Hish, wife!" he said, as he turned very pale, "horseman are advancing, and——"

"Think you they are in pursuit of our friends?"

"I know not what to think, wife."

"Close the door!"

"Nay; let us wait."

In a few moments eleven horsemen rode up, and one of them advancing, said:

"This is the 'Bladder of Lard,' is it not?"

"It is," replied Tony; but it is too late to transact business."

"Ha, ha! list to him, companions! Too late to serve us with the wherewithal to moisten our parched throats! Look you, host, is your house full of guests?"

"Nay, we have no guests whatever. We have no sleeping accommodation at this hostelry."

"We do not require sleeping accommodation. What we want is a rest of two hours, and plenty of your best wine, for which we are well prepared to pay."

Tony consulted with his wife, and having decided that the horsemen were not after the giants, and also that they did not belong to any of the Queen's regiments, they consented to their staying a couple of hours.

The horsemen dismounted and entered the parlour.

Being served with a large quantity of wine, the leader closed the door and locked it; but before he did so, he informed Tony that another of their number was expected soon, and that directly he arrived he was to be admitted.

Now the giant brothers heard these men arrive.

Sampson at once started up, and he was followed by Goliar.

Both buckled on their weapons.

"Brother," said Sampson, "we have been tracked down it seems."

"Aye, it does."

"Well, we know what that amounts to. We will fight to the last gasp, sooner than allow ourselves to be captured. Rather let us die with sword in hand than with a rope about our necks."

"So say I. Hish! they are talking."

The brothers listened and heard what passed between the host and the travellers, and they heard them pass into the room beneath.

"Thank Heaven, brother!" said Sampson. "They are not after us, that is sure enough. Well, then, who on earth can they be?"

"Thieves!—highway robbers most likely!" replied Goliar.

"Nay, I should hardly think so. Highway robbers seldom travel in more than twos or threes, and there must be a goodly number of men below. Ha! they have locked the door! By Heaven, brother, there is some plot on foot. Ah, I have it!"

"Have what?"

Sampson pointed to the fireplace.

"You remember the pranks we have played with that, brother?"

"I should think I do," he replied; "but I had almost forgotten it. Yet I'll warrant Tony has not."

"Nay," laughed Sampson, who now cautiously crossing to the fireplace, lifting out a large piece of stone.

The voices of those below, though they were conversing almost in whispers, were now heard very distinctly.

"This," said the voice of the man, who all along had acted as spokesman, "is the greatest and boldest stroke ever made in this country."

"Ay, or in any other, I'll warrant," replied one. "Failure is impossible. Oh, by all the blessed saints, to-morrow, at this time, England will be ringing with the startling intelligence!"

Sampson turned his head, and looked in his brother's face.

"What think you?" he whispered.

Goliar shook his head.

"There's some desperate deed about to be done," he said; "but I can form no idea as to what it is."

"Well then, brother, I can."

"Eh? What is it?"

"These villains are about to stop and rob the Queen."

Goliar opened his eyes in astonishment.

"Surely not!" he said. "Whoever heard of such a thing!"

"Ha! that is where it is, brother. As you are aware, her eccentric Majesty, Queen Elizabeth, has always boasted—every one knows that —that she could travel alone, in the wildest part of the country, loaded with jewels, and no one would dare bar her way. Now, unless prevented, these men can, and will stop and rob her."

"Well, brother, I cannot say that I bear her Majesty any love, so they can e'en do as they will."

"But if we did prevent them, brother?"

"Well, what then?"

"And we saved the Queen and her escort?"

"Yes, what then?"

" We could crave a boon, and could she refuse it ? "

" They do say, brother, that there is not a spark of gratitude in the Queen."

" I'll not believe it. We could crave a boon. We could ask her for the life and the freedom of Oscar Raymond. I expect——"

" Blessed are they who expect nothing, good brother for they shall not be disappointed."

" Listen to those below, and let us see if what I think is not correct."

At this moment another horseman arrived, and entered the hostelry.

The door of the room below was instantly opened and closed again.

" Now," said the voice of the spokesman, " the news."

" She is now at Farnmere, five miles beyond the spot where we have arranged to meet her. Her intention is to stay about two hours, so that we have plenty of time."

" Good Christian watches the spot, does he not ? "

" He does. He is waiting near the ' Three Oaks.' "

" Drink up, comrades, and let us depart. Ho, ha ! to-night each of us will be enriched for life ! "

" Farnmere, brother," whispered Sampson, " Do you hear ? "

" Ay, I do."

" And the attack is to be made on the Queen. Heaven above ! they must be a bold crew. But if we stand side by side, brother, we should be a match for at least a score of such men."

" Is it then your intention to go ? "

" It is."

" Then, of course, I go with you ? We have always lived together, and will die together."

" Tush ! Talk not of dying ! If we save the Queen, depend upon it Her Majesty will grant whatever we may ask. Come, let us slip out at the back way. We will leave our horses, so that neither Tony nor his wife will know we have left our apartment."

Taking off their shoes, the brothers left the room.

They were well acquainted with the premises, and they soon reached the back of the house.

Skirting several fields, they at length reached a lane, which took them in the direction of Farnmere.

In less than an hour they arrived at the spot spoken of by the men.

It was where several roads met.

In the middle stood a rough wooden cross, and, opposite that, three huge oaks of fantastic shape.

Creeping along, the brothers caught sight of a man standing by the side of one of the trees, and intently watching the roads.

This was the individual mentioned by the spokesman of the highwaymen as " Christian."

Sampson crept up to him, and raising his open hand, brought it down on the man's face with terrific force.

He fell as if he had been shot.

" Of a truth brother," said Goliar, " you have knocked him silly. It would be better, perhaps, to put him out of his misery. A man like this is too good to live."

" Nay, nay," replied Sampson. " Let us not shed blood if it can be avoided."

With this he tore off the man's doublet, and with the strips into which he rent it, bound and gagged him, and then placed him where he could not be seen.

" Now, draw your blade, brother," said Sampson, " and let us wait."

The brothers concealed themselves behind the trunks of the enormous oaks.

Half-an-hour passed away, and then the tramping of hoofs was heard.

" They come," said Sampson. " Count them, if you can.

There was no difficulty in this, for the horsemen went right into the open.

" Twelve ! " said Goliar.

" Good ; we can manage them," replied Sampson.

The leader of the robbers called out again and again for " Christian."

" He has either become frightened," said one, " and has run away, or he has gone in a wrong direction to the ' Bladder of Lard ' "

" In either case," replied the leader " he shall suffer for leaving his post. But let us examine the spot."

The whole of the horsemen went to the middle of the road, and looked scrutinisingly upon the ground.

" All is well," chuckled the leader ; " nothing has been disturbed. Now distribute yourselves among yonder bushes. The time approaches."

In a very few moments every horseman had concealed himself.

" Brother," whispered Sampson, " what were they looking at ? "

" Odd's my life ! " replied Goliar, who was looking into the road with a puzzled expression on his face, " I cannot think."

" I see nothing."

" Nay, neither do I. But it is of little importance, no doubt."

Half-an-hour passed, and the brothers were beginning to think that, after all, the Queen would not pass that way until morning had dawned, when the distant rumble of wheels was heard.

" She comes ! " whispered Sampson. " Be ready, brother."

" Fear not ; I am quite ready."

Both brothers held in their hands their enormous swords, and they clutched them firmly, as the noise of the advancing coach grew louder and louder.

Besides the postillions only six gentlemen escorted the Queen, and they seemed to share the assurance of her Majesty ; for though all were well armed, not one held a weapon in his hand.

On they came with a rush and a roar.

Suddenly a loud crackling sound rang out, and amid shouts of terror from the postillions, and cries of affright from the escort, the six horses sank into the earth, dragging the coach on top of them.

"By heaven!" yelled Sampson, "the *Queen has fallen into a pit!*"

His cry was not heard, for, with a swift rush, the robbers dashed from their hiding places, and the leader, presenting a pistol at the nearest gentleman, cried—

"You are surrounded! Dare to draw a weapon, and all of you will be put to death."

"Treason!" cried the gentlemen, alarmed and terrified beyond description.

One of them, Sir Digby Seymour, drew his blade, but a ball, fired by one of the robbers, pierced his breast, and he fell to the ground dead.

"Come, brother," cried Sampson, dashing from behind the tree.

The two giants appeared upon the scene like magic.

Without a moment's hesitation they attacked the robbers with terrific fury.

Horses and men alike fell beneath their fearful strokes.

The gentlemen forming the escort drew their swords and pistols, and joined in the fight.

The robbers fought frantically.

The brothers gave no quarter.

Sampson at one moment came very near losing his life; for while engaged with one of the men, the leader of the robbers crept up to him, and placed a pistol to his ear.

The weapon, however, was struck up by Lord Eustance Granger, and discharged itself harmlessly in the air.

Sampson turned upon the leader, dashed his sword from his grasp, and seizing the horse by its fore legs, backed it into a ditch.

It fell, carrying the rider with it.

The leader was crushed to death.

When Sampson turned to again join in the fray, he found that the fight was over,

No less than eight of the robbers, with their horses, lay dead or dying upon the ground. The others had taken to flight.

"My lords," said a calm voice, "when you have a little leisure will it please you to assist me from this pit?"

It was the Queen.

The pit had been dug so deep, that only the upper half of the coach was above the level of the road.

The well known face of the Queen looked from the window.

She had been watching the fight without showing the slightest fear.

A wonderful woman was Queen Elizabeth.

The postillions, all three of them more or less injured, had struggled up from the pit, but they were powerless to assist the Queen.

Lord Granger and the other noblemen dismounted.

"May it please you, your Majesty," said Lord Granger, it seems almost impossible that we can assist you from——"

"Well, well," interrupted the Queen. "I pray you get assistance, for it is hardly likely I can govern a realm while imprisoned in a pit."

"The door cannot be opened, your Majesty."

"We are well aware of it, my lord. Therefore get assistance, and knock the coach to pieces. But stay—unless they are too much exhausted—those men, who came to our assistance us may be able to rescue us. Let them approach. Heaven above! What huge mountains of flesh and bone and muscle are these?"

The giants, sheathing their weapons advanced.

Sampson placed his hand upon his heart and bowed lowly.

His brother imitated him as well as he possibly could.

The Queen looked at them in wonder.

But presently this look gave place to one of anger.

In loud, stern tones she cried:

"My lords, look at these men! By the Heaven above us! do you mean to say that you have not recognised them? Do you mean to say that, in these monsters, you do not recognise the individuals who so lately threw London into a state of confusion? These men, my lords, are the men known as the giants of Eastcheap. By my father's head, we are, indeed, lucky to have met them! My lords, arrest them!"

This ridiculous order was delivered in the most impassioned tones.

Elizabeth, for the moment, quite forgot where she was, and that she was not surrounded by a large number of troops.

Lord Granger said:

"Your Majesty, we are much indebted to these giants, who have laid low those who would have robbed your Majesty, if not——"

"Say it, my lord—say it," said the Queen, as Granger abruptly paused. "You would have said that they would have slain us! Eh?" she almost screamed, as she clenched her hands. "Do you mean to tell us, my lord, that the robbers *would have slain their Queen?*"

"Your pardon, your Majesty; but such men as these own no one as queen. They are no respecters of persons; and had not these brave giants come to the rescue, it is likely that neither your Majesty nor ourselves would have reached Canterbury."

"You speak boldly, my lord."

"Your Majesty's pardon, I only speak the truth. Is it not so, my lords?" he asked, appealing to the others of the escort.

They murmured an approval.

"Sir Digby Seymour," continued Lord Granger, "was shot dead by one of the robbers."

"Say you so?" replied the Queen, in quivering tones (Sir Digby was one of her favourites), "that is sad news. 'Fore Heaven, I would Lord Trevanion had been with us instead of going, as he did, on a wild-goose chase after the youth who should, ere now, have been lying in a felon's grave."

"One day, your Majesty may have cause to repent those hard words," said Sampson.

But the Queen did not notice what he said, so advancing still closer, he added:

"Your Majesty, for what we have done, we would crave a boon."

"What!" cried the Queen.

"We would crave a boon," repeated Sampson, fearlessly.

The Queen burst into a loud laugh.

"And if your Majesty will promise that you

will grant it, we will at once release you from your unpleasant postion."

"Ho! How so? In what way do you propose to release us?"

"Your Majesty will see."

"Well, well," replied the Queen, who was very anxious to be released, "I will give you half a promise, and then if——"

"Pardon," interrupted Sampson, boldly, "we never take *half* promises."

The Queen bit her lips with vexation.

Her anxiety to be released was getting the greater, owing to the fact that the oil lamps, which hung at the sides of the coach, were rapidly burning themselves out.

"Well, I promise," she testily exclaimed.

"Help me, brother," said Sampson.

"Are the horses dead?" asked Goliar of the postillions.

"Four are dead, and the two above are nearly so, judging from their stillness," was the reply.

Sampson went upon his knees and cut the traces.

"Do you go to the opposite side, brother," he said, "and take hold of the wheels."

"Stay—stay!" interrupted the Queen. "Do you fancy that you can lift up this coach?"

"Certainly, your Majesty, easily enough."

"'Fore Heaven, we doubt it! Do you think it can be done, my lords?"

"I, for one, don't think so, your Majesty," replied Lord Granger, "for it is of enormous weight. Still these huge fellows are undoubtedly possessed of wonderful strength."

"Let them proceed."

"Are you ready, brother," asked Sampson.

"Ay, ay," was the answer.

"*Lift!*"

Slowly the coach began to rise.

In a few seconds it was standing in the road. With the exception of one or two spokes being broken, the wheels were all right.

For some few moments the Queen was speechless with astonishment; but she found her tongue directly the lords surrounded her.

"It is very wonderful," she said. "These men, my lords, should have been brought under our notice long ago. We could have found them better occupation than that of blacksmiths."

The two horses at the top were now pulled out; but they were so injured as to be quite useless.

"Which is the nearest hostelry, sir giant?" asked Lord Granger.

"The 'Bladder of Lard,' your lordship," replied Sampson, "five miles hence."

"It is a pity the 'Bladder of Lard' is not somewhat nearer," said Elizabeth.

"We will willingly act as your horses, your Majesty," said Sampson.

"Good. Let us get on then."

Sampson and his brother placed themselves where the horses should have been, and with remarkable ease, proceeded to drag the coach along.

In less than an hour they reached the hostelry, where they found Tony and his wife in a state of great alarm, for they had discovered the giants' absence.

They were almost overpowered when they found that the occupant of the coach was no less a personage than the Queen of England.

In a few minutes the whole of Mistress Shaw's cushions, rugs, and wraps were brought down and placed in the very room where a little time before the robbers had been, and thither Elizabeth was conducted.

"Why not leave what you are about to say to the Queen until a more convenient opportunity?" suggested Lord Granger.

"With all respect to your lordship," replied Sampson, "I would much rather say my say now."

"Well, then, do as you think proper. What you are about to say relates to the youth, whom you and your brother rescued from the executioner?"

"Ay, my lord."

"I am afraid that ere this he is captured."

Sampson started back.

"Captured!" he ejaculated.

"I do not say that he *is* captured," returned Lord Granger, "but I much fear me that he is. It was said that he was with you. Had he been he might, for the nonce, have been safe. Twenty hours ago Trevanion left the Tower with his son, and he took with him a very large number of men."

"I thank your lordship for the information," said Sampson.

"Follow me," said his lordship, "and you shall see the Queen."

In a few moments Sampson stood before Elizabeth, who was seated amid a pile of rugs in an arm-chair, and enjoying, or appearing to enjoy, a silver tankard of warm wine."

Sampson bent his knee before her.

But her Majesty was, so far, safe, and all her haughtiness returned.

"Rise," she said, in sharp tones, "and let us hear what you have to say."

"Your Majesty——"

"No preliminary talk," cried Elizabeth. "What is the boon you crave?"

"The life of Oscar Raymond."

Elizabeth looked at Sampson until he fairly trembled—not for himself—but for Oscar.

"So, so!" muttered the Queen, tapping her foot on the stone flooring, "this is the boon! What think you of it, my lords?"

No answer.

Their lordships shuffled their feet uneasily.

"You do not speak!" said Elizabeth; "and from that I gather that you think this man is entitled to have granted to him any boon he may ask, and for what? For saving our life, eh? Surely any man would try to save the life of his Queen? Say on, sirrah.

"That the life of this youth may be spared is all I ask," replied Sampson.

"Oh, 'tis *all*, eh? Well! And you," she said to Goliar. "Would *you* crave ought?"

"Not I, your Majesty," replied Goliar, "unless it would please your Majesty to order me a cask of home-brewed. In that I would drink to your Majesty's long life, and fight to the death to serve you."

"You shall have it, sirrah, and that at short notice," replied Elizabeth, who, instead of being offended at this, felt inclined to laugh. "Your boon is granted," she added, turning suddenly to Sampson.

Sampson threw himself upon his knees, and thanked the Queen most heartily.

Elizabeth called Lord Granger to her side, and whispered to him.

His lordship took from his doublet a piece of parchment, and Tony having procured pen and ink, Lord Granger wrote as follows :

"This is to certify that the life of one Oscar Raymond is to be spared until it is convenient for her Majesty to properly investigate all the circumstances connected with his case.
(Signed)
GRANGER."

This he handed to Sampson.

"Proceed to London with all speed." he whispered ; "for if Lord Trevanion or his son get hold of the youth before you can reach him —well, you may guess the result."

Sampson thanked him, seized his brother's arm, and hurried him out.

Directly the door had closed upon them, Elizabeth laughed heartily.

"Ere he reaches London," she said. "You may depend upon it that Trevanion, will have got hold of this youth, against whom he has such animosity."

"If that should be so, said Lord Granger, quietly, "may heaven help Trevanion."

"Oh, my lord ! heaven help Trevanion ! and why ?"

"These giants are desperate men, your Majesty."

"They may be so. But what is that to us ? Trevanion had our orders some time ago as to this youth.

"But your Majesty has now revoked those orders."

"Your lordship says wrongly ! " cried the Queen, starting up with flashing eyes. "I have only granted a boon to these men just to get rid of them. Ha, ha ! Now my lords, see about the fresh horses."

Their lordships bowed and left the Queen to her wine.

When outside, Granger said :

"After what the Queen has said, I shall feel compelled to send in my resignation. I can never faithfully serve a Queen who says one thing and means another."

In the meantime, Sampson and his brother had mounted their horses, and amid the good wishes of Tony and Mistress Shaw, had turned their heads in the direction of Greenwich.

CHAPTER XI.

SHOWS HOW LORD TREVANION AND HIS SON SUCCEED IN DISCOVERING THE WHEREABOUTS OF OSCAR—OF HOW THE FARRIER BARRICADES HIS HOUSE—OF THE ASSAULT UPON IT—HOW THE FARRIER MEETS HIS DEATH—AND HOW OSCAR AND GRACE ARE CAPTURED.

AFTER the daring rescue of Oscar Raymond, Trevanion and his son made their way to Piccadilly—utterly discomfited.

And when they reached their house, they found that their servants, male and female, had deserted them.

All had gone ; even the butler, who had for many years faithfully served his lordship, had departed.

And we may mention that this same model butler had carried off with him every article of plate he could lay his hands upon.

Trevanion and Cunningham, therefore entered a deserted house.

They first of all searched the kitchen ; they opened the cupboards, and lugged forth every article they contained in the hopes of finding food.

But they discovered not an atom.

"May all the foul fiends claim them ! " cried Trevanion. "Ere they departed, they consumed every bit of food."

"'Twas a pity it did not choke them," said Cunningham. "Well, since there is nothing to eat, we must drink. Ha ! see ! the wine cellar is open."

"So it is," said Trevanion, as he kindled a light, and entered the cellar.

There a terrific yell escaped him.

"What is it ?" asked Cunningham, hastening to his side.

"The accursed wretches have been drinking my wines, and what they could not drink they have allowed to run all over the cellar. Oh, let me get hold of them ! I will cause false charges to be preferred against them, and the noose shall be their portion."

"No doubt," sneered Cunningham, "unless the giants come to their rescue, which is not at all unlikely."

Trevanion took no notice of this.

"Follow me," he said, "though they have drank and destroyed the wine, I have plenty of brandy in my bedroom. Come, follow me. After all, brandy is more to the purpose at the present moment. It will put fire into our veins."

Cunningham followed his father to his bedroom.

There was a huge chest near the bed, and this Trevanion opened.

Taking out two bottles of brandy, and a couple of goblets, he placed them on the table, and bade his son open the bottles and drink.

"Here's to the speedy capture of this accursed

Armourer's Son!" cried Cunningham, as he raised a brimming goblet to his lips.

"And to the capture of the giants!" said Trevanion, as he raised his goblet—"to their speedy capture! And after them to the speedy capture of the Armourer, and, after him, to the capture of the Wizard, as he calls himself. For he *sha'l* be captured!

"*You lie!*"

Trevanion let his goblet fall with a crash to the floor.

Not so Cunningham.

Whether he heard the voice or not, we cannot say; but if he did, he pretended that he had not, and drank off the fiery liquid.

"What ails you, my lord?" he asked.

"Ails me?" gasped Trevanion, as he looked cautiously round the apartment. "Did you not hear a voice?"

"A voice? Pah! No sooner do you enter this house than strange fancies take possession of you. How can you hear voices when the house is deserted?"

"I *did* hear a voice, and it sounded like the voice of that fiend—the Wizard!"

"Nonsense! Drink this, my lord. It will steady your nerves."

And Cunningham refilled his goblet, and handed it to his father, who swallowed the contents at a draught.

It put a little courage into him, and, motioning Cunningham to take his seat, he said:

"Now to consider what is next to be done. Heavens! how we have been foiled! But, despite the giants, I verily believe all would have gone well, had it not been for the apprentices."

"Probably," answered Cunningham, whose hatred of apprentices was intense.

"But we have one thing to be thankful for, and that is, that a good many of them were killed."

"Ay, I am very thankful for that. Had I my way, I would slay every apprentice within the city."

"Now the question is," continued Trevanion, "To what place can these giants have taken the youth, Oscar Raymond?"

"Certainly not to the residence of his father, the Armourer," said Cunningham.

"Nay, that is not likely. They went towards London Bridge, and from there we must trace them. If it takes days to do so, we must trace them."

"I am willing, if it takes weeks or months," cried Cunningham, emphatically.

"I am glad that our repeated failures have not disheartened you," said Trevanion.

Cunningham laughed hoarsely.

"Father," he said, "you have often told me that some day I shall inherit all your riches."

"True—true, my son. And vast riches they are."

"Well, I would rather this youth died before my eyes, than that I should become the possesor of this wealth."

"Ha! Good—good! And he shall die before your eyes, my son! Ay, and before mine."

Again the mysterious voice was heard, this time louder than before.

"*You lie!*"

Trevanion turned as white as a sheet.

"Do you mean to say you did not hear that?" he cried, hoarsely.

"I certainly heard something that time," replied Cunningham who was beginning to get uneasy. "And if I hear it again, I shall begin to think that the house is haunted. But, then, by whom?"

"By the spirit of the Wizard?" replied Trevanion.

"Since he is not dead, how can his spirit walk the earth?"

"Ha! that is but one of the powers of this chief of those who practice the black arts. Mark you, my son, since Elizabeth has occupied the throne, more than one who professed to practice the black arts, has been burned alive, and for much less than what this Mervine has been guilty of. Why Queen Elizabeth tolerates him passes my comprehension."

"It *is* said by some that this Wizard has informed the Queen that she will never marry."

"So I have heard. And had it been anyone else, that alone would have been sufficient to have got them burned alive. Now to resume. My next duty would be to accompany the Queen to Canterbury. No doubt all is prepared for the journey."

"But will not the news of this terrible riot cause her to stay in London?"

"Nay, my son. Elizabeth's nerves are like iron. The news of the riot will not frighten her, and she will depart all the same. I must away to her, and excuse myself. Then we will at once commence the search. But I will take care to have with me such a number of troops that even these giants shall tremble when we encounter them."

Having drawn up their programme, father and son set out.

Obtaining an audience with her Majesty, Trevanion laid before her the particulars of all that had occurred, and begged to be allowed to organise a search after Oscar and the giants.

The Queen told him that such search would only amount to a "wild goose chase;" but as Trevanion again and again begged to be allowed to search, she told him that he might do so.

Cunningham and his father thereupon set out for the Tower.

But they took particular care that they did not go anywhere near Fleet-street, for they considered that, if recognised, they might, while the populace was so enraged against them, be torn in pieces.

Arrived at the Tower, the new lieutenant, Lord Fulmore, was taken into their confidence, and he readily offered to organise a party of troopers to accompany them.

This, however, owing to the fact that a large number of the men were off duty and enjoying themselves at the "Tower Arms," could not be done until the evening.

At length, however, and just as darkness was gathering over the city, the troopers, to the number of a hundred, were got ready to march.

All were on foot, for since they were to proceed slowly, it was considered that horses were not required.

Trevanion and Cunningham, however, retained theirs — the better to escape should danger threaten them.

Though no one had told Trevanion that the giants had really passed that way, his lordship would persist in fancying that they had crossed London Bridge.

Arrived at the bridge he inquired of several shopkeepers if they had seen the giants, but they said they did not remember having done so.

Trevanion, after a consultation with his son, entered the "Bridge Arms," a small hostelry, which stood on the bridge.

Here they found a large number of shopkeepers collected.

Trevanion offered a large bribe to the man, who could tell them which way the giants had gone.

No answer was returned for some time.

No doubt all present *had* seen the giants cross the bridge ; but then they knew who was addressing them, and none present liked Trevanion.

But money is a great tempter to some people.

As Trevanion and his son, with fierce looks, waited for a reply, a short, stumpy, greasy, and foul-smelling wretch came forward.

"Why I saw them!" he said, in harsh, cracked tones. "They were too big not to be seen, Er—er——"

"What are you ?" asked Cunningham.

"A dealer in tallow," was the reply, "and my name is Peter Paulstey."

"Go on !—go on !"

"I'm to have the money if I tell you the way they went ?"

"Yes, if you tell us correctly."

"Oh, I knows it to be quite correct. They went right over in the direction of New Cross. My son was passing on his horse as they went that way. He it was who told me, and they are the men you want, because there are no other men in London like 'em. Besides, one of them carried on his horse the youth whom they had rescued from Temple Bar."

"Good, good !" cried Cunningham. "To horse, my lord—to horse. We shall have them."

"Pardon me," cried Peter Paulstey, "you have not handed over to me the money."

"Of course not," chuckled Cunningham. "We have not yet found out whether what you have told us is correct or not."

With this Cunningham and his father made their exit.

The shopkeepers, as soon as the party had gone, greeted the discomfited tallow-merchant with a howl of derision.

"Let us seize the traitor," cried one, "and give him what he deserves !"

"Fling the wretch over the bridge !" cried the host of the "Bridge Arms." "Such a money-grubbing villain does not deserve to live ;"

In less time than it takes to write it, the wretch was collared by a dozen men.

And, despite his howls for mercy, he was carried out to the rails of the bridge, raised up, and held over.

"Let the villain live for the sake of his family," said one.

"Yes," said another ; "let the greasy varmint live, but on one condition."

"Name it—name it !" yelled the tallow-merchant. "Oh, name it !"

"That if you *do* at any time, receive any of Lord Trevanion's filthy blood-money, you hand it over to the prisoners in the Fleet."

"I agree ! I agree !"

"Swear it ! "

"I swear it ! I swear it !"

The men pulled the wretch back.

"Mark you !" said the host of the ' Bridge Arms !' " we shall know whether you do receive it, and if you do not inform us, the Lord have mercy on you."

Meantime, Trevanion, Cunningham, and the troopers proceeded at a quick pace, the two former going first and making inquiries in every direction.

But they had no longer any difficulty in finding out people who had seen the giants pass.

Almost every one had seen them.

New Cross was reached at last.

Here again no difficulty was experienced in finding out whether the giants had passed that way.

The Oak Church at Greenwich was reached, and here, at any rate, Trevanion found himself at fault.

The soldiers were brought to a standstill.

Quite a large crowd of persons quickly gathered round to see what the business of the military was.

Trevanion ordered half-a-dozen of the men who were provided with links to come forward.

The links were lighted and held aloft, and Trevanion, seated on his horse in such a manner that he could be distinctly seen, produced a small bag.

"In this," he said, holding it aloft," is the sum of twenty crowns, and that shall be the property of any man who comes forward and tells us which way two men, known as the giants of Eastcheap, went after, they reached the church some few hours ago."

A tall, ill-clad, ugly-looking fellow, pushed his way through the crowd, and said, as he stretched forth his hand—

"Give it to me. They went *that* way," pointing in the direction the brothers had taken; "but before they did so, they called and left a youth at the house of the farrier yonder. Give me the money, and I will lead the way."

Trevanion dropped the bag into the hand of the man, who, pocketing it with a chuckle, went on down the lane.

He led them to the back of Gaunt's residence, where, even at the late hour it now was, the farrier was busy at the forge.

"Yonder is Griffin Gaunt," said the man, who now withdrew.

Griffin Gaunt had not heard the party approach; his hammer, and the hammer of the man who assisted him, made too much noise for that.

Cunningham, without dismounting, went forward.

"What ho!" he shouted.

"What ho!" to you, replied Griffin.

"Hold, farrier! hold!" cried Trevanion, "put down your hammer."

Griffin paused.

Slowly he drew himself erect. He had caught sight of the glare of the torches and the glitter of arms.

A terrible fear at once took possession of him.

"The Queen's troops!" he muttered, "and they are here after Oscar Raymond. Almighty powers! what is to be done? I have not a soul who can warn him of his danger!"

"Do you hear us?" asked Cunningham.

"Ay, ay, replied the farrier, "I hear you. And have I not put down my hammer? What want you?"

"Come forth, and look at us."

"I see you plainly enough. You are some gentlemen whose horses require attention. But I have no time at——"

"Do not pretend ignorance!" shouted Trevanion. "You are well aware who we are, and for what purpose we are here. We are here to demand the person of one Oscar Raymond."

"Oscar Raymond?" answered the farrier. "In Heaven's name, what do I know of Oscar Raymond?"

"Listen, Master Farrier," said Trevannion; "let me tell you that your pretended ignorance is likely to get you into serious trouble. You had much better deliver up the person whom we are in search of, and who we know is somewhere in your house."

"I tell you," replied Griffin, stoutly, "that I know nothing of the person you are in search of."

"You are a *liar*, sirrah!" cried Cunningham.

"Pardon me," answered Gaunt, with a low bow. "I am a *farrier*."

"Ay, and a knave as well," said Trevanion. "Listen! I am one you may have heard of ere now—Lord Trevanion."

Perhaps his lordship thought that the mention of his name would strike terror into the heart of the farrier.

If he did he was wofully mistaken.

"Run, Sponsor!" whispered the farrier, pretending to stoop to pick up something. "Run and warn the youth; tell him to fly by the front—quick, for the love of Heaven—quick!"

Sponsor, the farrier's assistant, instead of trying to leave the smithy unseen, at once bounded to a small door at the side of the furnace.

Cunningham saw the movement, and, without a word of warning, the brutal ruffian drew a pistol, aimed it at the man's head, and fired.

The unfortunate man fell with a ball in his brain.

"Dastard!" yelled the horror-stricken farrier. Cowardly, bloodthirsty villain!"

"That will show you we are in earnest," said Cunningham. "And let me tell you that if you do not——"

"No more dallying!" cried Lord Trevanion, dismounting, and drawing his sword with a flourish. "Enter the house, and search it from top to bottom!"

"On, my men!" cried Cunningham, also drawing his sword, and dismounting. "On, my men, and cut down all who attempt to bar your passage!"

The farrier ran forward, took hold of his heavy folding doors, and banged them in their faces.

The huge bolts at once fell into their sockets.

"That act, my lord, said Cunningham, in exultant tones, "shows that our bird is within this cage."

"Beyond question," replied Trevanion. "And now we must to work. Do you guard this spot with half the men while I take the other half to the front."

In the meantime the farrier dashed up the stairs.

He found Oscar, who was in a fair way towards recovery (he having been wounded only in a fleshy part), seated by the window watching Grace, who was busy at her spinning-wheel.

They had heard the sound as of the firing of a shot; but as sounds of all sorts frequently came from the smithy, they thought nothing of it.

The farrier bounded into the room, crying—

"Rouse yourself, my son. Some one has betrayed you!"

With this, he went to the window, drew the shutters to, and pulled across them some heavy oak bars.

"The doors and windows below," he said, "are securely barred and bolted. They will, for a time, resist all the force that can be brought against them. But there are outside at least a hundred soldiers."

"By whom are they led?" asked Oscar, who had started to his feet in great alarm.

"By Lord Trevanion and his son—at least, I expect it *is* his son. The cowardly brute, Gracie, my dear, has shot poor Sponsor dead!"

"Holy Virgin!" cried Grace, clasping her hands; "what savagery!"

"Ay, my love. We might stand far more chance of safety were we surrounded by bloodhounds, than by those at this moment without the house. Here, Oscar," he added, as he drew from beneath the bed a large, heavy box, "here are weapons in plenty. Select what you require. Grace, my dear, many an evening I have amused myself in showing you how to load a pistol."

"Oh, father! father!" cried Grace, covering her eyes as her father placed several formidable looking weapons on the table near his daughter.

"Load them, my child!—load them!" cried Griffin frantically. "Hark at them! they are beginning upon the doors, Grace, my child, load. load as fast as you can."

Oscar took out and buckled on a sword and dagger, as also did the brawny farrier.

Grace handed a loaded pistol to Oscar, who, taking it, approached the window.

The farrier took another pistol, again urging his daughter to load quickly.

"Here," he whispered, "this is a small hole,

as also is this, and this," and he removed some small pieces of iron from the shutters. "Look through one, and fire through the other."

Oscar looked, and what he saw startled him.

Cunningham had been too impatient to wait with his men at the back, so he had joined his father.

Thus, when Oscar looked, it seemed as though the whole of the space in front, and at the sides of the house, swarmed with armed men.

Amid the clamour of arms and armour, Oscar heard Cunningham's detested voice.

"Oh, that I can but mark him!" he thought.

Aloud he cried—

"What are they doing? Ha! they have got hold of the trunk of a tree."

"Truly so," replied the farmer, who was also looking from one of the holes; "and their intention is to use it as a battering ram. It is of enormous weight, for I cut it down myself, and if I mistake not, it will eventually prove effective."

"Now then, my men!" cried Cunningham, "use all your force. Go!"

On either side the tree was clutched by a dozen men, and as Cunningham cried—"Go!" they dashed it against the door.

The force was awful.

The house trembled beneath the blow.

But the door had not moved.

Not a panel had yielded.

"Fire!" whispered the farrier as he discharged his pistol.

Oscar fired point blank at Cunningham.

Had not that young villain stooped at the moment to recover his sword, which had fallen from his hand, it is certain that his earthly career would have been terminated.

As it was, the ball struck a soldier at Cunningham's side, and he fell dead.

The bullet of the farrier had also found its billet, for one of the men having hold of the tree trunk, fell to rise no more.

"Arquebusiers advance!" roared Cunningham. "Make way there—make way. Now we shall see what our shots will do!"

At this momet one of the crowd of persons, who had accompanied the soldiers, made his way to Cunningham, and laying his hand on his arm, said—

"Your pardon, noble sir—in that house is a young girl, and——"

"Well, fool, what of her?" interrupted Cunningham.

"Why, noble sir, the balls from the soldiers may strike her."

"Let them strike her. Go from here, friend, or a ball from the girl herself may strike you."

Then turning to the arquebusiers, he said, as he pointed to the window from whence the shots had come—

"Mark well that spot. Fire!"

A score of balls rattled against the shutters.

Eagerly Cunningham looked up.

He thought, of course, to see the shutters completely riddled—perforated like the top of a pepper-box.

But he was disappointed.

It was true that the balls had, to some extent, penetrated the thick woodwork, but had not penetrated the plates of iron behind.

Hardly had the smoke from the guns of the soldiers cleared away, ere four tongues of flame darted from the shutters, four stunning reports followed, and three more soldiers bit the dust.

"By all the incarnate fiends!" cried Lord Trevanion, hastily drawing back, and pulling Cunningham with him, "this we can never stand! Try the trunk again, my men!"

"Try it yourself, your lordship!" answered one of the soldiers in angry tones. "None of us are proof against bullets so surely aimed."

"What is your number, sirrah?" cried Trevanion, who determined, at the first opportunity, to make an example of this bold soldier.

"I cannot see it in the dark!" was the reply, which called forth a chuckle from the men.

"Your duty," cried Cunningham, "is to do as you are bidden."

"No doubt of it. But none of us can move unless we have some of us to lead us."

"Cowards!" almost shrieked Trevanion. "Afraid to advance upon a barricaded house. But, Cunningham, my son, let it not be said hereafter that we had not the courage to lead the men."

Thereupon Trevanion and his son rushed to the men, and commanded them to again take hold of the trunk.

This was done, and a fresh onslaught made upon the door.

Again and again the huge trunk thundered upon the door.

Again came two shots, and another soldier fell, this time at the very feet of Trevanion.

It was evident to his lordship that whoever fired that shot intended it for him or his son.

His courageous lordship turned as pale as death.

Suddenly Cunningham uttered a loud triumphant shout.

"By Heaven!" he said, as he pointed to the lower window, almost concealed by climbing plants, "there is the place where we shall gain admittance. We had overlooked it. Come, my men, break down the fence."

The fencing was soon torn down, and, amid loud shouts, the soldiers advanced towards the window with the tree trunk.

"I thought they would miss that window," said the farrier. "Alas! they have not. Oscar, my son, you are not strong enough at present to take part in a hand to hand fight. I beg you to make your escape. 'Tis easy enough now, for I see that all the soldiers are in front. Go, and——"

"Nay, nay," replied Oscar, emphatically. "I will not leave you, and your daughter— never! I will give myself up, and so save you from further——"

"No, no!" cried the farrier, hastily. "Make good your escape, and I will then admit the men. You know as well as I do what will be your fate if arrested."

"I care not, for I am almost tired of my life. I bring misery and suffering on all who shelter me, therefore, I had better die."

"I made a solemn promise to my friends, the

giants, and that promise I will keep. Again I tell you—I beg of you—make your escape."

"And leave you to your fate! Never! Never! I swear it!"

At this instant a fearful crash was heard below; then another and another, and then followed a sound as of the fall of some weighty article.

"They have entered!" cried Grace.

"True, my child!" replied the farrier, with a groan, "and that last sound was caused by their upsetting the heavy cabinet, which I always place against the window! Follow me, Grace, keep at Oscar's side."

The farrier, drawing his sword, ran from the room, followed by Oscar and Grace.

He made for the passage on the left of the room, which led to the smithy.

But ere he reached it another deafening crash was heard, and the door at the end flew open.

Oscar clasped Grace round the waist with his left arm and clutched his sword firmly.

"They will not fire," he thought, "if they see a young girl is in danger."

Griffin ran forward.

The soldiers' links were brought to the front, and a flood of light lit up the form of the brawny farrier.

Neither Oscar nor Grace were observed by Cunningham, who, as soon as he caught sight of the farrier, cried out—

"Fire! fire!"

A deafening volley was the instant response to his cry, and the farrier, throwing up his arms, staggered back and fell, uttering the bitter cry—

"Oh, Gracie, Gracie, my child!—my child!"

Uttering a piercing scream, Grace sprang from Oscar's arms, and threw herself by her father's side.

Cunningham, thinking, perhaps, that there might be several more men in the passage, again cried out "Fire!"

"Hold!" shouted Oscar. "Hold! or you will have the blood of an innocent maiden on your souls!"

"Oh, oh!" chuckled Cunningham, "so here you are! Once more, then, we have you. Ha, ha, ha! Where is his lordship? Let him come forward and feast his eyes on this thing!"

Oscar rushed towards him.

Ignoring the halberds pointed at his breast—ignoring the levelled weapons of the arquebusiers—he would have flung himself upon the cowardly and brutal Cunningham, and so met his death at the hands of the soldiers had not Grace, starting up, thrown her arms around him.

"Don't," she sobbed, "throw not your life away thus rashly. Who knows but that, in a short time, the Queen may pardon you for whatever you may have been guilty of, and ——".

She was interrupted by a loud laugh from Cunningham and his father, who had come up at this moment.

"Pardon!" yelled Trevanion. "Pardon, say you? Ho, ho, ho, ho! the wench is mad. Cunningham, who is this hussy?"

"I am no hussy!' cried Grace, proudly. "I am the daughter of that man"—(pointing to her father)—"that honest man whom your soldiers at the bidding of this villain (pointing to Cunningham) shot dead. Poor father—dear father!"

And she burst into a flood of tears.

"It serves your father right," replied Trevanion, on whom a woman's tears had no effect whatever. "Our orders are plain and distinct enough. Whoever thinks proper to resist the Queen's troops dies—sooner or later. You have assisted your father and this young villain here in resisting us. Still we will allow you to go free. All we want is here," pointing to Oscar.

"I fear you not!" cried Oscar, hurling his sword and dagger at the feet of his lordship, "I am ready to die! I fear not death!"

"Oh," sneered Cunningham, "you fear not death, eh? So, so! Then how was it you escaped with those accursed giants?"

"Why ask so foolish a question?" replied Oscar. "Any man would escape from such a death did he see the chance. I may obtain still another chance, and then ——"

"You may obtain another chance?" screamed Trevanion. "You lie! you lie! This time you will go to the Tower, from which I swear you shall not escape. You shall be loaded with irons and flung into the most foul dungeon the Tower contains. Guards, seize and bind him!"

In a few short moments Oscar's arms were securely tied behind his back.

Turning to Grace, our hero said, in sad tones—

"Farewell, sweet girl—remember me!"

Oh, yes, yes," replied Grace, clasping her hands. "I *will* remember you!"

Cunningham gave the word, and Oscar was dragged forth like a dog.

"Your lordship," whispered Cunningham, "to this young girl I have taken a fancy."

"Eh!" cried Trevanion, sharply.

"I have taken a fancy to her," repeated Cunningham.

"Faugh!" exclaimed Trevanion, in disgust. "Pocket your fancy then! Think you that we can trouble about girls?"

"But I can, my lord."

"Not with my consent. What has caused you to take a fancy to her?"

"She is beautiful!"

"So are thousands more. What then?"

"My lord," whispered Cunningham, "you don't often have me troubling you for favours. Do you not see that this girl is certainly the lover of this youth?"

"Ha!" exclaimed his lordship, "I had not thought of that. Ha, another blow to him, and to—to——"

"To the Armourer."

"Yes! Take her—take her by all means; and do what you think proper with her. But let her whereabouts be kept secret."

"My lord, you have the keys of Blackburn House?"

"I have."

"That would be a safe place for her?"

"True—true—very true. Yes, yes, that will be safe enough; and now that her father is

"THE WRETCHES SEIZED OSCAR AND SWUNG HIM BACKWARDS AND FORWARDS."

dead, you will have no one to enquire after her if you are careful. I will proceed with the prisoner to the Tower. You take ten of the soldiers and procure a litter in which to convey the girl. As their reward to preserve silence, tell them they may return and rifle this house of whatever valuables it contains."

"Good, my lord."

"And mark, join me at Piccadilly."

"Without fail."

Trevanion gave the word, and the men, with the exception of ten, marched off.

When Cunningham had seen the march towards London commenced, he turned to Grace, who once more had thrown herself by her father's side.

"My pretty maid——" he commenced, as he touched her gently on the shoulder.

Grace started up, and fixing her flashing eyes upon him, said fiercely——

"Have you not committed sufficient outrages already?"

"Outrages, my pretty——?"

"Ay, vile wretch! Outrages! There lies *my father*."

"But I have no intention of slaying *you*, sweet mistress!"

"I care not if you do! Since my father is dead, and I have now no one left in the world to care for me, I do not wish to live."

"Talk not so. *I* will care for you if you will let me."

"*You*?" cried Grace contemptuously.

"Ay, I."

"You are the son of a nobleman!"

"Most true—most true!"

"And yet insult a girl in the presence of her father's dead body! Oh, Heaven! If this is a specimen, what hearts have England's noblemen implanted in their breast!'

"No nonsense!" cried Cunningham, impaiently. "If you will not allow me to care for you, my sweet mistress, I shall take charge of you *without* your consent."

"Monster!" cried Grace, recoiling.

"Nay, you shall find me no monster. On the contrary, you will find me as gentle and as generous and as loving as—well, as a good many would be. I pray you prepare for a journey."

"No, no! I will not leave this house!"

Cunningham advanced still closer; but Grace, with a gasping cry, sank down, and frantically clutched her father's corpse.

"Leave me alone with my dead father!" she implored. "Oh, if you have but one spark of humanity within your bosom, leave me in peace!"

"I tell you to prepare for a journey," shouted Cunningham, furiously. "If you do not at once set about it, you shall be dragged out just as you are. Mark you, I have taken a fancy to you. The daughter of a common farrier should think herself highly honoured by my attention."

"You overrate yourself, sir!" cried Grace, proudly. "I do not feel honoured in the least by your attention, and if I go hence it will be against my will. And by the Heaven above me, you will repent it! Do not imagine that I am a poor weak fool, who will put up with your insults without retaliating."

"Your spirit only causes me to admire you the more," sneered Cunningham. "But again I tell you to prepare."

"I refuse!"

Cunningham snatched off his cloak, and ere Grace could offer the least resistance, he had flung it over her head.

"One of you run and procure a litter," he cried. "Offer any sum for the use of it, but preserve silence."

"Pardon," said a soldier; "the house is still surrounded by a mob."

"No matter; keep your tongue still, and they will know nothing."

The litter was easily procured, since the soldier *did* offer a large sum for the use of it; and, somewhat under half-an-hour, the party set out, amid the jeers and the execrations of the mob, who, had they known who was within the litter, would have torn Cunningham and the soldiers to pieces.

CHAPTER XII.

IS FULL OF THE MOST EXTRAORDINARY INCIDENTS YET PRESENTED TO THE READER.

Oh, what a terrible journey was that to that "most cursed of castles," the Tower of London.

That journey Oscar never forgot during the whole of his lifetime.

Trevanion knew that he dared not ill-treat his prisoner in the public streets.

Had he dared, of course he would have done so.

But, seeing how exhausted Oscar was, the vile wretch stopped at almost every refreshment house they came to, and ordered foaming tankards of ale, or flagons of the best wine, and he made his soldiers drink in full sight of the unhappy prisoner.

It was early morning when the party, thoroughly tired out reached London Bridge.

The bridge was deserted, the whole of the tradespeople being wrapped in slumber.

At the city end of the bridge Trevanion once more gave the word to halt, and, for a brief space the soldiers allowed Oscar to rest his weary limbs against a buttress.

Poor unfortunate Oscar.

How longingly he gazed upon the dark waters of the swift running Thames.

"Were I free," he muttered, "I would mount this rail, and flinging myself in yonder water, bury all my troubles. Oh, heaven!" he moaned, "I am weary and sick unto death! Grant me a little mercy! Take my life!—take my life!"

"What is your prisoner muttering about?" asked Trevanion sternly.

Nothing my lord!" replied one of the men who, like many of his comrades, pitied, Oscar.

"Nothing, eh?" chuckled Trevanion. "By Heaven's grace he shall mutter for *something* ere long. Thank Heaven we have arrived in sight of the Tower! Look you, sirrah," he roared to Oscar. "Look your last upon earth and sky!"

Oscar made no reply; indeed, he had not the power to make a reply.

"Your lordship" said one of the soldiers, "I would suggest that we complete the journey to the Tower by water."

"Why so?"

"All of us are very tired, your lordship. Besides that, if we approach Tower Hill, we may be descried by some one who will rouse the apprentices, and then woe to us, at this present time, when we are scarce able to stand, let alone defend ourselves."

Trevanion considered a moment.

"You are right," he said; but how are we to reach the Tower by water without boats?"

"If your lordship will look over this parapet, you will see half-a-dozen barges in line."

"Yes. I see them," said Trevanion, looking over the parapet.

"Well, if your lordship will look at the arms painted on the bows, you will see that they belong to the Tower.

"You are right," replied Trevanion. "Descend with the prisoner to the water's edge."

This order was at once carried out.

Trevanion dismounted, and selecting about the most tired soldier of the whole lot, he directed him to take his horse on to the fortress, and hand him over to one of the warders.

Then he followed the party down the wooden stairs.

By Trevanion's orders, three of the barges were manned by the soldiers.

In the centre one Oscar was placed, and Trevanion seated himself in such a manner, that he could feast his eyes on the exhausted figure of the prisoner.

The soldiers on the battlements of the fortress saw the barges approaching, and they at once challenged.

They were satisfactorily answered, and preparations were made for the party's admittance.

It was perfectly wonderful how the Tower, which for hours had been buried in silence, woke up to life and activity.

Anyone would have fancied, from the terrific noise, such as the rattle of arms, the clanking of chains, the words of command, and the roll of the drum, that a political prisoner of vast importance was about to be admitted to "England's most secure of Stone Cages."

Oscar, utterly prostrated, his brain racked by many bitter thoughts, paid no attention to what was being said or done.

The soldiers drew up as well as they were able in front of the "Traitor's Gate," and presently the gate moved slowly back through the water.

A soldier in the first barge threw a rope to the warders standing on the steps, and the barges thus passed under the black and foul-smelling archway.

A dozen torches glared in the hands of as many stalwart warders, and lit up the scene with striking and terrible distinctness.

Upon the steps, in the centre of a crowd of men and officers of all grades, stood the new lieutenant, Lord Fulmore.

As the barge, containing the prisoner, touched the steps, and Trevanion stood up, Fulmore said:

"I am delighted to see that your errand has proved successful, my lord."

"Yes," chuckled Trevanion. "We had a strong fight for the possession of the wretch, however, and I grieve to say that we do not return as we left. Several soldiers were shot dead by this youth, and a man who protected him. I am happy to tell you, however, that his protector was left a corpse in his own house."

"Good, my lord," replied Fulmore ; "very good, indeed. As for several soldiers being killed, my Lord Trevanion—well—er—soldiers must *expect* to be killed, eh, eh, ha, ha! Now, Brutus Gatling, see to the safe landing o f yonder prisoner, or, perchance, to save himself from something worse, he may throw himself into the water."

The soldiers led Oscar to the bows of the boat ; but, even in that operation, the cowardly Trevanion could not let him alone.

He drew his sword, and with the point pricked Oscar in the back amid the laughter of Gatling and the lieutenant.

Perhaps Oscar's mental sufferings caused him to be indifferent to bodily pain ; anyhow, he made no cry, nor did he appear to feel the pain.

"Your lordship," said Fulmore, "is quite aware of the fact that ere a prisoner is admitted, the lieutenant must have a warrant which authorises him to receive——"

"But you, Fulmore," interrupted Trevanion, "are quite aware of the fact that in this case, no warrant is necessary, this being a recaptured prisoner, who——"

Fulmore delivered himself of one of his choice chuckles.

"I did but mention the circumstances," he said ; "and I need hardly say," he whispered, 'that any prisoner your lordship may think proper to bring here, I will accept the custody of, warrant or no warrant."

"I shall, no doubt, avail myself of your kindness," returned Trevanion, significantly.

"And, as to this youth," continued Fulmore, "you no doubt wish him to be placed in the very *best* part of the fortress."

"Say the very *worst*, my lord," replied Trevanion, "and you will not be far wrong."

"Leave him entirely to me *and my chief warder*, and we will give a good account of him."

"Into your good custody, my lord, I do leave him until to-morrow night. I shall then return with my son."

Oscar was handed over to Gatling and two of his principal assistants.

As Trevanion turned to accompany the lieutenant to his lodgings preparatory to his departure, he took a couple of nobles from his pocket, and pressing them into the ready hand of the ugly and brutal "First Warder," he whispered—

"Give me a good account of him."

"Never fear !" chuckled Gatling.

Trevanion departed with the lieutenant, followed by a scornful look from Oscar.

"Now then," cried Gatling, "away with him !"

"Whither ?" asked one of his comrades.

"Let me consider. Ha ! I have it—follow me !"

Seizing one of the links, Brutus Gatling unhooked a huge bunch of keys from his girdle, and led the way.

First they went along a low-roofed, narrow passage, then descended a flight of stone steps.

They were now in another passage similar in all respects to the first, except that it was much more damp.

Along this passage went the party, Brutus leading the way, stamping, howling, and jingling his keys to frighten away the rats, with which this part of the fortress fairly swarmed.

At last Brutus cried out—

"Halt !"

The warder stopped.

Brutus stooped, placed his hand in an iron ring set in the stone flooring, and pulled.

A large stone was lifted from its position, and the light of the torch penetrated into what to Oscar looked like a deep well.

"Look you," said Brutus, as he pointed with a chuckle at the filthy, black water. "Look at that. Do you see it ?"

"Ay," replied Oscar, "I am not blind."

"Well, then. *There*," and he pointed so a low iron door at the edge of the well—"there is your cell, and a beautiful apartment you will find it. Ho, ho ! The door is of iron ; but if, by any chance, you managed to get out, we should find you in here," pointing to the well ; "so take my advice, and do not try an escape.

"Now, you may be wondering why it is that I have taken this trouble with you. I will tell you. It is said that you are in league with the Evil One, in the shape of the Wizard of Whitehall, which most accursed of all professors of the black art is said to have the power of entering and leaving this fortress whensoever it pleases him. So, if *he* comes to rescue you, by all the incarnate fiends, we shall know where to find *him*.

"Now, you will remain in your cell until to-morrow night, when Trevanion and his son, I doubt not, will be here to make you *confess*."

"In other words," said Oscar, " to torture me !"

"Ah, if that please you better."

"My curse on him, on his son, and on *you !* for I can see that to look to you for kindness or mercy would be——"

"A piece of impertinence !" interrupted the warder, who, raising his hand, dealt Oscar a stunning blow on the face.

It sent him to the ground like a log.

The warder laughed loudly.

Brutus now replaced the stone over the well, and, opening the cell door, he stuck the link in a bracket.

"Now then," he said, " in with him !"

Thereupon the three wretches seized Oscar, swung him backwards and forwards a few times, and with another burst of fiendish laughter, *threw* him into the cell.

This was a stone apartment, in size about twelve feet by eight.

The "furniture" consisted of a small and rudely-fashioned oak table, with a stool to match.

In one corner were a number of dirty sacks, and in another a stone pitcher of water, while just above that, on a stone slab, was a loaf of bread of about the size of a brick, and almost as hard.

"Now, is not this a fine apartment ?" sneered

Brutus, "If you do not think it is, let me tell you that we have had many illustrious prisoners here, and more than *one* have had their last bath in the well, ho, ho! Now, comrades, loose his hands."

Poor Oscar!

He could only look what he would have said.

But even had he spoken, his words would have been lost on such hardened wretches as these.

But at the next order of Brutus Gatling, he was compelled to speak.

"Now, comrades," laughed Brutus, "off with his clothes!"

"Almighty Heaven!" cried Oscar, " surely you will not leave me here naked?"

"Naked? How will you be naked? Look at yonder sacks. If you feel the chill, and very likely you will, cover your carcase with them. It is quite good enough for you. And, besides, stripping you now will save us a job to-morrow; for 'tis certain that ere Trevanion applies the torture, you would have to be stripped."

The three set to work, and soon Oscar was stripped of everything he had on him.

Brutus rolled up the clothing, and handing it to one of his comrades, said—

"That will do for the old Jew anon. What we get we will equally divide. Now, come, and look you, you young villain! if any warder complains that you are making a noise, look to yourself. In a few hours I shall return, and if you are not civil, look out!"

Snatching the torch from the bracket, the three went out, their laughter ringing in the ears of our most unfortunate hero.

Having carefully locked the door, Brutus again pulled up the stone, which he now placed on one side.

"This was, indeed, a good invention," he said. "Ho, ho, ho! I wonder *who will be the next to be drowned in it?*"

In a few moments the fiendish warder and his assistants had departed.

On the bare stones, his aching back propped against the wall, Oscar sat for some time.

"I would I had died on the scaffold!" he sighed, " though it was the death of a dog, it would have been better than the death which now, I feel, awaits me. Oh, Heaven! in pity take my life—in pity take my life! Spare me not to be tortured by these vile fiends. Oh, my father! Oh, my mother! if you could but see your poor boy now! If you could see him you love so dearly—him on whom you lavished all your affection. If you could but see him now! Here in one of the foulest dungeons of the Tower!—exhausted, subjected to this gross indignity—praying for death! What would you say?"

He at last managed to crawl to the sacks.

They felt damp, and smelt most foully.

However, he managed to cover himself with them, and creeping up to the corner, leaned his head against the wall, and tried to think.

But drowsiness got the upper hand of him, and he fell into a troubled sleep.

How long he slept of course he had no means of ascertaining; but he was awakened, as it seemed to him, by being rudely shaken.

He opened his eyes—darkness everywhere.

Suddenly a peculiar sound—he could not make out what—met his ears.

This continued for some few moments, then the cell seemed to become full of vapour.

"I am dreaming," muttered Oscar. "Yet no! I am awake! ay, awake!"

The dampness made him shiver violently.

The peculiar sound he heard ceased, and a deep voice said—

"*Oscar Raymond—awake!*"

Oscar leapt to his feet, every nerve quivering with excitement.

He tried to speak, but the effort was in vain.

Again came the voice:

"*Oscar Raymond—awake, awake!*"

"I am wide awake," replied Oscar, in husky tones. "Who speaks? In the name of the blessed Virgin, who speaks?"

"Hist!" was the reply. "Let not your voice be heard."

"Ay, ay, I will not speak loud," answered Oscar, peering about on all sides—vainly endeavouring to penetrate the inky blackness.

"Do you recognise the voice of the one who is speaking?"

"My brain wanders—I cannot—yet—he! I can—I do. *The Wizard.*"

"Hush! you are right. Look up."

Oscar looked with wonder.

A small hole—it was of about twice the size of a man's fist—had appeared in the vaulted roof of the cell.

A light there appeared—vapoury, as it seemed, and Oscar tried to catch sight of the face of the Wizard—the mysterious Mervine.

In that he failed.

"Mark me," said the voice. "Are you listening?"

"Oh, yes, yes!"

"Take this."

Down the hole came a silver flask attached to a string.

"I have it," said Oscar.

"Drink—empty it."

Oscar seized the flask with both his trembling hands, and, placing it to his lips, drained it.

The contents was a liquor of a most fiery description.

It sent the blood coursing through Oscar's veins—his pulse quickened its beating.

His exhausted energy seemed to have returned to him.

He felt not the dampness now.

He seemed on fire.

"Ha!" he said, joyfully, "you have, indeed, proved my greatest friend. You have given me poison, so that I may baffle my accursed enemies!"

"Not so, my son," was the reply. "What you have drunk is no poison but a liquid prepared by myself for strengthening. Take this."

The flask was rapidly drawn up, and a parcel dropped on the floor.

Then came another and another.

"Remove those articles," said the Wizard.

Oscar at once fell upon his knees, and pulled them aside.

"Have you done that?" continued the Wizard.

"I have," replied Oscar.

"Stand aside then."

A sudden flash, and a lighted link came through the aperture.

Oscar at once picked it up.

"Place it in the bracket," said the Wizard; "but, whatever you do, hasten your movements, or all will be lost."

Oscar placed the torch in the bracket.

Then on the stone floor there fell, with a loud clank, a dagger!

To snatch it up was the work of an instant only.

"Cut the strings of the packet," said the Wizard, "you will find a complete outfit, and here are shoes" (and these also dropped through the aperture). "Don all quickly as you value your life."

The clothes, which were of a very superior description, where somewhat crumpled through being so tightly compressed; but Oscar soon smoothed them out, and then set to work to put them on.

This was quickly accomplished.

Oscar found himself attired in a costume becoming a nobleman of the first rank.

"Have you finished?" asked the Wizard

"Ay, noble sir."

"Take this."

A sword came through the aperture.

Oscar buckled it on, and also the dagger.

"Now, mark me, Oscar Raymond. Extinguish the torch, and place it in your belt. In one of the pockets of your doublet you will find a tinder-box with which to relight it when occasion shall require. Have you done that?"

"I have."

"Good. In a short time now, the warder, by name Brutus Gatling, will return, and—I am sorry to say it, for I am against the taking of life—*you must kill that man!* It is a necessary act, and in taking this man's life you will have the satisfaction of knowing that you avenge the deaths of many poor creatures—ay, many who have been murdered within the cell where now you stand. A little distance from the well without this cell, and on the right-hand side you will find an iron door. Against that you will see a large stone with a ring attached. If you use that as your brain guides you, *the warder will disappear for ever.* Do you understand me?"

"Perfectly," replied Oscar.

"Then," continued the Wizard, "with the smallest key on the warder's bunch you will open the iron door, and descend the stairs you will find on the other side. Adieu."

Ere Oscar could reply, the aperture was suddenly closed, and all was again profound darkness.

"'Tis not daylight yet," muttered Oscar. "How long can I have been here? Oh, this agony of waiting—waiting! What will follow the directions this mysterious man gave me? Oh, that I can carry them out. Alas! this man may return with several companions, and then all chances of escape would be cut off. If all ends well, I shall meet the Wizard. Yes, yes; that must be so, for, having aided me thus far, he will complete my escape. Strange, mysterious being," he mused. "What awful powers does he not possess! The draught I have swallowed seems to have put the strength of two men into my body. Oh, time! time! speed thee on!—speed thee on!"

Impatiently Oscar paced the cell, pausing every now and then at the door to listen.

Suddenly the sound, as of the distant closing of a heavy door, met his ears.

This was followed by another and another.

At last he heard a heavy tramp, and then the jingle of keys.

Nearer and nearer came the sounds, until he knew that the terrible warder must be at the cell door.

Oscar snatched the dagger from its sheath.

There was a brief pause.

Then came a clank and a thud.

It was the warder replacing the stone over the well.

Then a key was inserted in the lock of the cell door, turned, and the door thrown open.

High over his head Brutus Gatling held his torch.

He grinned maliciously.

For an instant only did the vile wretch stand on the threshold.

Oscar had shrunk into a corner, and Gatling was just about to growl out something, when our hero bounded in front of him.

High above his head did Oscar hold the glittering blade, twice it circled round his head to give greater force to the blow, and then down it came.

It was buried to the hilt in the warder's heart.

Brutus Gatling staggered back, a volume of blood rushing from his mouth.

His bloodshot eyes opened to their fullest extent.

He beat the air in a most frantic manner, gave vent to a series of horrible gurgles, and then fell with a crash to the stones—dead!

The torch, very fortunately, did not go out.

Oscar snatched it up, and placed it in a chink between the stones.

Then he plucked out the dagger, and replaced it in its sheath.

He found the stone with the ring attached in the corner as the Wizard had said.

Taking the keys from the rapidly-stiffening hand of the warder, he attached them to his own belt, and then he dragged the warder's body from off the slab which covered the well.

Stooping he placed his hand in the ring, and pulled up the stone.

"I am doing right," muttered Oscar, pausing for a moment. "Yes, yes, there can be no doubt about it. This is what the Wizard meant —'*The warder will disappear for ever.*' Those were his words."

Taking off Gatling's belt, Oscar run it through the iron ring, and then strapped it tightly round the warder's ankles.

This done he dragged the fellow to the edge of the well, and slid him into the black, stinking water.

The body of Brutus Gatling shot out of sight.

For some few seconds the bubbles danced and flashed on the top, and then the water resumed its placid appearance.

Brutus Gatling thus disappeared for ever.

Oscar replaced the stone, and now nothing was left to show what had been done, except it was a pool of blood.

The rats soon destroyed all traces of this.

Oscar selected the key mentioned by the Wizard, and inserted it in the iron door.

It opened without difficulty, and he entered the dark hole before him.

After a little consideration, he decided to extinguish the torch.

He saw the stairs before him, and noticed that they were of great length.

Closing the iron door he attached the keys to his belt, and, for a moment or two, listened.

Hearing no sound, however, he cautiously advanced, and the *greatest* caution was absolutely necessary in the place he now was, for the stairs and walls reeked with slime.

A false step, and he might break his neck down the treacherous stairs; for the Tower of London, at the period of our romance, boasted few handrails.

CHAPTER XIII.

SHOWS HOW CUNNINGHAM TREVANION SENDS HIS GUARD ON TO THE TOWER—HOW HE IS STOPPED AT SOUTHWARK FIELDS BY ROBBERS—HOW GRACE IS TAKEN FROM HIM BY CAPTAIN CARTRIDGE, AND WHAT STARTLING EVENTS FOLLOW.

NOTHING of any importance occurred for some time after the party of soldiers, with the litter containing the insensible form of Grace had left Greenwich.

Cunningham rode by the side of the litter, and every now and then he would stoop in his saddle, and take a peep inside in order to see whether the occupant was stirring.

But Grace never moved from the position in which she had been placed.

"Obstinate fool!" growled Cunningham; "but I will bring her to her senses ere long. She is a pretty wench, and now that I have her in my possession I will not part with her. Verily I believe I am right in thinking that she *is* betrothed to this Oscar Raymond. And that being so—Lord, what a stroke of luck this is! I will taunt him about her. I will tell him how loving she has been towards me. Of her kisses, her embraces, and so on!"

What were Grace's feelings during this journey?

Alas! our pen is powerless to describe them.

She did not long remain unconscious.

No; she soon recovered, and immediately all the terrible events which had occurred rushed to her memory.

"Poor father!" she sobbed, "dead! dead! dead! And left like a dog in the house! But I have one comfort in thinking that the neighbours will search the house, and they will find my poor father's body, and will decently inter it."

Several times Grace thought of thrusting her head out of the window of the litter, and shrieking for help.

But each time, as soon as thought of, the idea was dismissed.

"Who could assist me, surrounded as I am by a number of soldiers?" she thought.

Ah! who indeed!

At New Cross a halt was called.

"What house is that yonder?" asked Cunningham. "Is it not a hostelry of some kind?"

"It is," replied a soldier; "it is called the 'New Cross Arms.' The keeper of it is one Thomas Cantlebury, a surly fellow, who certainly will not condescend to serve us at this hour."

Cunningham laughed.

"Will he not?" he said. "Ha! we shall see that. I am parched with thirst, and will be served, though I pull the house down about his ears."

"We also are thirsty," grunted one of the soldiers.

"I doubt you not," replied Cunningham sharply. "And had you waited but a moment, you would have heard me say that I intended to pay for whatever you might think proper to drink. Knock at the door."

The soldiers did so.

They got no reply, however.

Again and again they thundered at the door and shutters, and at last a window above was flung up, and down came a torrent of dirty water.

Several of the men received a dose.

"Go away!" thundered a voice. "Go away, you noisy, d **unk** n brawlers—go away!"

And down went the window with a bang.

Cunningham was just about to give vent to a few of his choice curses, when he was interrupted by the soldiers, who actually burst into a roar of laughter.

Cunningham surveyed them for a few seconds in silence.

He was thinking whether they had not suddenly gone mad.

"Why do you laugh, idiots?" he asked.

"Couldn't help it, your worship," replied one of the soldiers. "That was *so* much like Cantlebury, the host."

"*Was* it?" growled Cunningham, as he

threw himself off the saddle. "We shall soon see about his impudence."

Taking a pistol from his belt, he hammered upon the door with all his might.

Up went the window again, and this time a head, surmounted with a white-frilled nightcap, was thrust forth, and a cracked female voice called out—

"Drunkards! Brawlers! Unruly imps of Satan—depart! or I will topple over the whole row of flower pots on your thick, brainless skulls!"

"Open in the Queen's name!" shouted Cunningham.

"Oh, oh!" replied the voice of the host, as he popped his head out by the side of his wife's, "that's it, is it? In the Queen's name, eh? Open? What the——what do you——Go away, and be——"

But at this instant he caught sight of the arms and the helmets of the soldiers.

"As I live, wife," he muttered, "these are, indeed the Queen's troops."

"Husband! husband!" cried the wife wringing her hands, "what have you done? Oh, of what are you guilty?"

"Nothing, fool! Hush—silence! Ho—what ho!" he roared. "What want ye?"

"Refreshments."

"Is that all?"

"Ay, that is all."

"Do you want *refreshments* in the Queen's name? Or will you *pay* for them?"

"We will *pay* for them," replied Cunningham —"that is if you are quick. If you are not, we shall batter the door down, and help ourselves."

This threat had the effect of considerably quickening the movements of the host.

In a few minutes the door was thrown open.

No sooner did Grace behold the landlord, than, thrusting her head out of the litter, she cried :

"Help! help! for the love of heaven, help an unfortunate girl. Without authority I am being forced from my home, and——"

"Silence!" hissed Cunningham, "or your life may pay the penalty of your rashness."

"My life!" replied Grace, scornfully. "What do I care for——"

"Silence, I tell you!"

"No; I will be silent no longer. Help! help! In mercy's name, help me!"

The soldiers who would, had they dared, have assisted the unfortunate girl in making her escape, looked on in silence.

The landlord, who had been joined by his wife, made an attempt to approach the litter.

But Cunningham placed one hand on his sword-hilt, and, in haughty tones, said :

"This is a prisoner of the Queen, and, at the present moment, is suffering from an attack of brain fever, and——"

"Liar!" cried Grace. "Believe him not, good people. I am nobody's prisoner but his. He would make me his mistress against my will. Oh, help me!"

Cunningham stepped up to the poor girl, and,

with the back of his hand, dealt her a stunning blow on the cheek.

Grace, with a moan of despair, fell back in the litter.

"Coward!" cried the hostess, shaking her fist in Cunningham's face.

"Hag!" retorted Cunningham. "Get hence, or your house will soon be in the possession of those who know how to keep a civil tongue in their heads!"

"Come wife," said the host, "and let us serve and get rid of this brute."

The soldiers each had a pint of wine, while Cunningham consumed at least half-a-pint of brandy."

"Your prisoner may require refreshment," suggested the host.

"Quite right," replied Cunningham. "She *may* require it, and that is all."

"May I ask your name?" said the host.

"Certainly, if it so pleases you," replied Cunningham ; but since I should not answer, it is hardly worth while to take the trouble of asking."

"Remember, sir," said the host, shaking his finger, "you called my wife a *hag*—a *hag*, sir—a *hag!*"

"I did : and you are the *husband* of a *hag!* Farewell, Mr. Host."

Cunningham left the house, followed by the soldiers.

As the last one was going down the steps, the host whispered—

"His name?"

"The son of Lord Trevanion," replied the soldier, hastily.

Immediately a confounded look rested upon the plump features of the host.

Turning to his wife, he communicated the rank of their visitor to her.

"Oh, I am not afraid!" she snapped, as she helped herself to a glass of spirits. "I daresay he thinks a great deal of himself ; but if I ever meet him without his bodkin" (the good lady meant his sword), "I will scratch his eyes out— the villain, I will!"

The party now pushed on rapidly.

Arriving within sight of London Bridge, Cunningham again called a halt.

"I shall now require the services of two of you only," he said ; "the rest can proceed at once to the Tower. I do not care which two go with me ; but whoever does will receive ten crowns."

"Which way do you intend to proceed?" asked one.

"Across Southwark Fields," replied Cunningham.

Two men readily volunteered to earn the ten crowns.

The litter was again taken in hand, and the journey resumed.

Southwark Fields was, at the time of our story, a wild waste of marshy land.

There were many spots where a horse and rider would sink and disappear, so it behoved all those who travelled that way to be very careful.

"You know your way, I suppose?" asked Cunningham of the soldiers.

"I do, your honour," replied one of the men, "and a dangerous way it is. Besides the danger of the roads, there is a chance of being pulled up by that wretch, Captain Cartridge."

"Who is he?"

"Cartridge? What, has your honour never heard of him?"

"Never that I am aware of. What is he?"

"He calls himself the tollman of Southwark Fields. He generally has a few men with him and——"

"Let us push on," interrupted Cunningham, "or we shall never reach our destination. Let Captain Cartridge be hanged! We have nothing to fear from him. If he appears he will hardly dare to stay us."

The man picked out a road across the fields, and narrow enough it was.

Cunningham rode behind the litter.

"If anything happens," he chuckled, "I can easily make my escape."

Several times poor Grace looked out of the window, but nothing met her eyes except a few miserable-looking trees, and occasionally the glimmer of a pool of water. But, after journeying about a couple of miles, they came to a clump of dwarf trees.

Here the litter was set down to allow of the soldiers resting.

Cunningham was about to address Grace, when a loud voice suddenly cried:

"Ha, ha! my merry men all—my merry men all, both great and small, look out you don't fall into these cursed bogholes! Ha, whom have we yonder?"

"The litter," cried Cunningham. "Up with it!"

The soldiers seized it.

Cunningham craned his neck, and tried to penetrate the darkness.

But he could see nothing.

He could hear the voices of several men, however, and they seemed to be getting very near.

He turned in his saddle, and looked back.

One of the soldiers noticed him do this, and he said, sneeringly—

"Don't think of turning back, your worship. If you do, you are certain to miss your way, and fall into one of these holes."

"I have no intention of turning back," replied Cunningham. "I was merely seeing whether there was room enough for the persons who are advancing towards us to pass. Can you make out how many there are?"

"No, your honour. I don't see them at all yet. Oh, ah, here they come, your worship, straight towards us."

"How many are there?" growled Cunningham.

"Nearly a dozen as far as I can make out, and all are mounted."

Again came the voice as before—

"Ha, ha, my merry men all, both great and small, look out you don't fall. May Satan and all his angels seize upon Southwark Fields, and convert them into a beautiful——ha! I told you so. We have travellers in front of us. Ho! ho! here, my jolly companions, is the wherewithal for a glorious carouse. I should not be surprised if the duchess of somewhere is before us."

Ere Cunningham could make a remark the new-comers (there were ten of them) had lit a link.

It threw a weird light on the scene.

"As I'm alive!" exclaimed one of the soldiers, "it is Captain Cartridge!"

"Ah! who calls Captain Cartridge?" said the foremost of the men, a tall, thin fellow, attired in a most fantastic garb. "For here is Captain Cartridge himself. At your service," he said, doffing his ragged hat, and placing his hand on his heart—"at your service. At the service of the occupant of the litter—if an occupant there be—at the service of the gentleman on horseback, and at his own service, which is infinitely better. Ha, hem!"

"As you are so polite," said Cunningham, sneeringly, "perhaps you will move yourselves off, and allow us to resume our journey."

"Hum!" was the reply, delivered in the most emphatic manner—"hum! We will allow you to go when you have paid the toll we demand—not before. That's the rule of the road."

"What toll do you mean?"

"Oh, we are not particular as to the amount. The larger the better. Heaven be thanked, we never travel without big pockets, and we always commence our journey with empty ones, the better to accommodate the pieces which gentlemen, like yourself, are pleased to give us."

"I know not whether you make it a rule to stop persons passing along this, the Queen's highway; but you dare not demand toll of us."

"Eh? and why not?"

"If you will use your eyes, you will see that we are of the Queen's guard."

"I am alive to that fact," answered the polite captain. "I may say that all of us are litterally alive to the fact, and——"

"And," interrupted Cunningham, "I am the son of Lord Trevanion!"

"In—deed! I am glad to hear it. All of us will feel greater pleasure in accepting toll from a lord's son than one of the common herd—you heard that companions?"

The captain's friends grunted assent.

"I refuse to pay you any toll," said Cunningham.

"I hope you don't expect us to pay you any toll," said one of the soldiers.

"Certainly not," answered the captain: "it is your duty to get as much as you can—not pay it away."

Cunningham took his pistol from his belt, and cocked it.

"But the "toll-gatherers" were too sharp for him.

Unobserved, one of them had slid off his horse, and creeping round the other side of the litter, he, just as Cunningham had prepared his pistol, snatched it out of his hand.

"Is that weapon loaded?" asked the captain.

"It is," replied the man.

"Then blow the gentleman off his horse," cried Cartridge, calmly, "that is, if he won't get off."

Cunningham was too much of a coward to risk the chance of a shot, so, with a bitter curse, he dismounted, and he was at once taken possession of.

At this moment Grace thrust her head out the window, and cried—

"Help! help!"

"All right, lady," said Cartridge, dismounting, "we will not harm you—not for worlds, your ladyship. It is one of——"

"Oh, in mercy, help me, sir," cried Grace, clasping her hands. "I am not the person you take me for. I am a poor girl who is being abducted, forced from my home by yonder wretch" (pointing to Cunningham, who was making vain efforts to escape.)

Captain Cartridge's jaw dropped in astonishment.

"Oh!" he said. Oh, oh! here's a pretty kettle of fish! Abducted, eh? and by the son of Lord Trevanion! Come out, my pretty dear, and let us look at you more closely."

He opened the door and assisted Grace to alight.

"Who is your father, my dear?" he asked.

"Griffin Gaunt, sir, who was ——"

"What?" interrupted the captain, "the farrier of Greenwich?"

"The same, sir."

"Lord! he was a friend of two worthy men I know, the giants——"

"The same, sir," cried Grace, excitedly; "the same—the very same!"

"Hum! Well, I don't know your father my dear; but I've no doubt he is a very worthy man. But the giants have been my friends. They've done me many a good turn. So I must look after their friend. But you shall tell me all anon, my dear. Jump in again. You are no longer in the clutches of yonder villain!"

"Don't search him yet," added the captain to his men. "Out with your cords; bind him hand and foot; put a gag in his mouth; fling him across his horse, and follow me. Oh, oh," he chuckled, "we'll abduct him. It's a change for him—a mighty change! ha! ha!"

With this, after bidding Gracie be of good cheer, the captain leisurely mounted his horse.

Cunningham struggled violently to release himself.

But it was all in vain.

The "toll gatherers" held him securely, and as he would not keep quiet while they were binding him, they treated him to several sound smacks on the face.

Since he found that struggling was of no earthly use, Cunningham gave vent to loud howls of—

"Robbers! thieves! murderers! help! help!"

"We are helping you," cried one of the men, as he took a gag from his pocket, and thrust it into Cunningham's mouth.

In another moment Cunningham was lying crosswise on his horse.

All being in readiness two men took the litter, another led the spare horses, and the mounted men brought up the rear.

Captain Cartridge led the way, questioning the soldiers as he went.

Without a pause they went on, and, at last, a halt was made at the entrance to a narrow lane.

Threading their way along this lane, the party stopped before a low, dingy-looking, wooden building, the steps of which commanded a view of the dark waters of the Thames, and Cartridge whistled.

A whistle answered him.

Every man dismounted, a large wooden gate at the side of the house slowly opened, and the horses trotted through it.

Cunningham was taken off his horse, which was then sent after the others, and the gate was closed.

"Now, my dear," said Cartridge, opening the door of the litter, "pray step out, and, mark it, fear nothing. Though we are rough-looking fellows, and not very graceful in our manners, nor polite in our speech, we know how to treat ladies. Go——"

"Oh, tell me—pray tell me where I am, kind kind sir," cried Grace, who, on stepping out, was somewhat alarmed at the gloomy and forbidding aspect of the house."

"Oh, I will tell you," said the captain. "I'll tell you, my dear, and welcome. "Look there," and he pointed to a signboard hanging high up on the front of the house.

"If it was daylight," he said, "you would see painted on that board a bell, and that shows, my dear, that this house is the 'Bell Tavern.' I must admit that it has not a very inviting appearance externally; but you will find the interior fairly comfortable. I will see to that," he whispered: "for the house, and the staff in it, partially belong to me. What ho! what ho! Wynn, Wynn!" he shouted.

A man hurried down the steps.

"This young lady," said the captain, "is a particular friend of my particular friends. See to it that she has the two best rooms in the house, and also she is to have Elizabeth to wait upon her, and to have whatever she wants."

"Pray follow me," said the man, making a low bow before Grace. "Elizabeth, of whom the captain has just spoken, madam, is my wife. She shall wait upon you with pleasure. Pray follow."

In a very few moments Grace found herself in very comfortable quarters with "Elizabeth" —a short, plump, fussy, good-humoured woman to attend upon her.

Directly Grace had gone, the captain turned to the two soldiers.

"To whom does this litter belong?" he asked. "The State?"

"No; to a man at Greenwich," was the reply.

"Hem! Because I was about to remark that there will not be much state about it directly

Let me see. Does my wife require such a thing? No. Thank Heaven she's got good legs and feet, and can walk wherever she wants to go, and that's never far. So, comrades, get your axes and break this lumbering thing up for firewood. But bring up the cushions, they will do for me to sit on in the parlour."

Three or four axes were brought, and the men set to work.

The litter was speedily reduced to a huge pile of firewood.

This done, the captain said—

"Now take hold of that son of a lord, and fling him, just as he is, into the little room by the wood cellar below. Lock the door after you, and come up. When we have had something to eat and drink, we will have him up and examine his pockets. I see he has a very nice lot of clothes on his back. I will exchange with him."

Cunningham was again pounced upon, bundled down the stairs, and pitched into the cellar, amid the laughter of the men.

"All right?" roared the captain down the stairs.

"Ay, ay," was the answer. "All right."

"Good—good. Come on then. Oh, we'll *lord s son* him! ho, ho!"

*   *   *   *   *

We will now return to the giant brothers.

They found the journey from Wotton a dreadful one.

For many long miles their horses went on at a good pace, but gradually their speed slackened.

Was it to be wondered at?

Think of what they had done; think of the little rest they had had.

No horse ever foaled could do such work, and not become exhausted.

The brothers arrived at Greenwich just two hours after the attack by the soldiers on the farrier's house.

As they neared the spot, they observed a large crowd of people, who hailed them with loud cries.

"Heaven's mercy!" cried Sampson. "My heart sinks within me. I fear that something terrible has happened."

"On my life, brother," replied Goliar. "I am of your opinion. Maybe the house has been burnt."

"More likely Oscar has been recaptured. You know what Lord Granger said about Trevanion and his accursed son?"

"I do. But I trust 'tis not so bad as that."

"What has happened, friends?" cried Sampson.

But for some few moments they could get no answer, for the people, forgetting for a moment what had happened, were loud in their expressions of amazement at the colossal figures of the giants and their horses.

At last a man stepped from the crowd, saying—

"My friends and I remember seeing you here before; two or three days ago."

"Quite right, friend," replied Sampson.

"You are friends of the farrier?"

"We are."

"He was a good man," said the man, sorrowfully.

"Eh?" cried Sampson. "*Was?* he *is*. But what is the meaning of all this crowd about the house?"

"The house has been besieged by a troop of the Queen's soldiers," answered the man, "From what I could gather, the farrier was hiding some one from justice. They besieged the house, I say, and the farrier, his daughter, and the person the troops were after, defended it for a long time. Many soldiers were shot dead by them. But, at last, an entrance was gained, and the person sought after taken, and——"

"Who led the soldiers, friend?" cried Sampson and Goliar in a breath.

"Lord Trevanion and his son," was the answer.

"Heaven's curse on them!" cried Sampson.

"Amen!" ejaculated Goliar.

"Go on, friend," said Sampson, excitedly.

"When all was over," continued the man. Soon after that a litter was drawn up, and a person placed within it; who it was, however, no one knows."

"But the farrier?" cried Sampson. "The farrier and his daughter where are they?"

"We think that both must be lying dead within the house!"

"Holy Virgin!" roared Sampson." "Surely such a thing must be impossible!"

"We do not think so. But we do not like at present to venture inside."

Sampson was instantly off his horse, followed by his brother.

The crowd closed round with great cries.

Every one had been afraid—actually afraid—to enter the place.

Sampson did not wait to enter by the window; seizing the trunk of the tree, the soldiers had used as a battering-ram he raised it as easily as an ordinary man would have raised a brick, and drawing back, he dashed it at the door.

The latter quivered violently.

Another thundering blow, and it flew open.

"Follow, brother!" cried Sampson.

Goliar was close at his heels, and so, indeed, was the crowd; for now they had got some one to go before them they did not mind entering the house.

Up the stairs dashed Sampson and his brother.

A small lamp still burned upon the table in the room which Oscar had occupied.

At a glance Sampson and his brother saw how the occupants had defended it.

Sampson took a torch from a bracket near the mantelpiece, lit by the lamp, and held it over his head.

"Heaven's mercy!" he groaned, "what wreck! But I see nothing either of the farrier or his daughter—poor dear little Gracie!"

He went to the other door.

The fatal door through which the farrier had rushed.

The rays of the torch fell upon the stiffened figure of the unfortunate man.

A deep, bitter groan escaped the lips of the ponderous brothers.

Throwing himself on his knees by the side of the dead man, Sampson exclaimed—

"Oh, Griffin, Griffin, it was we who brought all this upon you! Oh, Heaven!" he cried, raising aloft his clenched hand, "hear me, hear me! For this deed—for this cruel deed—*I will remember Lord Trevanion.*"

"And I, brother," added Goliar, "and I!"

The crowd had poured into the passage; but so petrified with horror were they at what they saw, so deeply impressed were they at the grief of these two enormous men—a grief which showed what tender hearts beat in their huge breasts, that they said nothing.

"There is no time for delay," said Sampson, handing the link to his brother. "The house must be searched for the daughter."

The crowd of people now moved.

"We will search," they cried.

And they scattered themselves over the house. Every nook and corner was searched, but, of course, without success.

"The person in the litter was Grace," said Sampson, emphatically. "There can be no doubt of it. What say you, brother?"

"'Tis my opinion," was Goliar's answer.

"And she is now in the clutches of that depraved, brutal beast, Cunningham Trevanion. Sooner would I see her lying dead at her father's side. But it may not be too late to save her. Let us on to London. They are not many hours in advance of us. Good friends," he added, who among you will guard this corpse and take charge of the house for awhile?"

Several at once volunteered, and from among them Sampson selected two.

He then lifted the body of the farrier, tenderly placed it on the bed, and covered it with a sheet.

Then the brothers left the house.

Mounting their horses, they set out at a good pace.

They made no halt until they reached New Cross, and it is more likely that they would not have stopped there, but that their horses sadly required water, and they themselves refreshment.

"The streets are deserted," said Sampson, "and the houses are silent. I am afraid we shall not get what we want. But wait! what is that yonder?"

"'Tis a man sitting on a doorstep," replied Goliar, "and by all the blessed saints, 'tis an hostelry, brother. Let us on!"

Goliar was right.

It *was* an hostelry, and the name of it was the "New Cross Arms" with which, and with the host and his wife, our readers have already been made acquainted.

The glass of spirits, which our readers will remember the hostess drank to relieve her overcharged feelings, had been the cause of her taking another and another.

Her husband, not wishing to see all the liquor polished off without his having at least a small share, joined his spouse, and the pair pledged each other again and again.

They drank and drank, until at last the hostess, with a deep sigh, sank in a most comfortable attitude on the floor, and the host went for fresh air to the doorstep, where, when the giants came up, he was dozing.

"Hillo, my fine fellow!" cried Sampson. "Hillo! hillo!"

The landlord looked up.

He rubbed his eyes, and fixed them upon the two enormous beings before him.

Again and again he rubbed them.

"My eyes have surely turned to magnifying-glasses," he muttered, "and yet—no—that can't be, since the house appears no larger than usual. Wake up! Wife, wife!" he cried, starting uy, "here's more *curious people*. Lord, *do* come here!"

But the hostess was fast asleep under the counter.

"What ails you, man?" asked Sampson. "Are you drunk, or what?"

"Nearly so—nearly so."

"Hem! Are you the landlord of this house?"

"I am."

"Will you be so good as to serve us with what refreshment we require?"

"I will if you pay for it. But are you sure you are real human beings?"

"No doubt as to that, my friend. Come and feel us."

"No, thank you. Rather not, I'm sure. How many barrels of ale do you require?"

"A small one between us will be sufficient for this present occasion; and, if you don't mind bringing it out to us, it will save us dismounting, and we shall be much obliged to you."

"As you are so civil," replied the host, "I will do as you require with much pleasure."

In a few moments the worthy host brought forth a goodly-sized barrel of ale, and a large can.

"Here you have it, my masters," he said, "Just hold the can, and——"

"Never mind the can, friend," interrupted Sampson, as he caught hold of the barrel, and smashed in the head. "We always drink from the wood. Now, please water our horses, and we will pay what you demand."

This being done, and the brothers having drained the barrel, the reckoning was paid.

"You haven't seen such a thing as a litter pass this way, host, have you," asked Sampson, "some two hours ago or more? It was guarded by a number of soldiers on foot, and their leader was on horseback."

To the great delight of the brothers, the host replied in the affirmative, and he did not forget to say how his wife had been called a hag.

"And she's as pretty a woman as you'd meet in a day's ramble," he said, "especially when she has her nightcap on, and is hunting for stray cats with a poker. Well, Sir Giants, if my information will prove of any service, I am glad to have given it."

Again the brothers went on.

They heard nothing further of the litter, and at last, tired and thoroughly dejected, they reached London Bridge.

"Brother," said Sampson, "though there can be no doubt that Oscar has been taken to the Tower, it would be useless for us to go there at present. We *must* take rest. If we do not, our horses and ourselves will drop from sheer exhaustion."

"Quite true, brother—quite true."

"What say you? Shall we rest?"

"I should, indeed, be thankful to do so."

"Well, though I like not all of his ways, we have found Captain Cartridge a good friend on more than one occasion ; and, since we are so close to his abode, what say ye—shall we go there?"

"Nothing better. By all means let us go."

Sampson turned, and, followed by his brother, rode across the Fields, and turned into the lane to which we have introduced the reader.

As they neared the "Bell," they heard loud sounds of revelry.

"The captain and his friends are enjoying themselves as usual," said Sampson. "Ah! what have we here?"

"A pile of firewood," replied Goliar ; "but it seems to have once been a coach or litter."

"What ho, there !" roared Sampson. "What ho !"

Instantly the window of the parlour was flung wide open, and Captain Cartridge thrust out his head.

CHAPTER XIV.

IS OF THE EXTRAORDINARY TRIAL OF CUNNINGHAM TREVANION IN THE PARLOUR OF THE "BELL TAVERN"—OF THE VERDICT AND SENTENCE PRONOUNCED BY THE GALLANT CARTRIDGE, AND OF HOW THE SENTENCE WAS CARRIED OUT TO THE SATISFACTION OF EVERYBODY EXCEPT CUNNINGHAM.

"WHO roars?" cried the captain. "Eh? who roars? Ha! as I live—here—well—by all the saints——"

"What is it?" cried the men, as they rushed to their captain's side.

A shout of recognition at once left their lips.

"The giants!" they cried.

"Ay," said the captain, "the giants! every *inch* of them! Welcome—right welcome, noble mountains!" he cried ; "but from whence did you spring? From out the earth?"

"If we did," replied Sampson, "we should certainly select better earth than is down here."

The captain rushed from the room, followed by his men, who held the stirrups while the brothers dismounted.

"Verily !" said Captain Cartridge, "this is a surprise—a *huge* surprise I may say. You are more than welcome. I was afraid that you had been captured by the Queen's troops. Know now, that we have a huge surprise for *you*."

"Ha !" exclaimed Sampson. "What is that?"

"We have a——"

At this point the captain was interrupted by the opening of the shutters above, and the appearance of Grace.

"Sampson!" she cried, joyfully. "Goliar! Oh, is it, indeed, you?"

"Gracie !" cried the brothers in a breath.

Captain Cartridge rubbed his hands, and chuckled with delight.

"I am glad to be able to do you a good turn," he said ; "but let me tell you that that is not the only surprise. We have another person in our possession—his name is Cunningham Trevanion."

"Heaven be thanked !" cried Sampson. "Still, though we are glad you have that young villain, captain, we should still be overjoyed, though you had the unfortunate girl only."

"Here, my men," cried the captain, "see that those horses—the Virgin bless us ! what monsters they are—are safely stabled—that is, if the roof is high enough, which I much doubt. And do you follow me, my big brothers, and let me set before you some refreshment."

But ere the giants would refresh themselves they had some conversation with Gracie, and from her learned all the particulars of what had transpired.

They sympathised with her in her great misfortune, and promised that they would, in future, look after her welfare.

Sweet, indeed, to Gracie was the news of what the Queen had said regarding Oscar ; but Captain Cartridge, who heard what Sampson said, shook his head.

"Trust me," he said, "the Queen does not mean it. She will easily be overruled by Trevanion.

"If she does," cried Sampson, "I will denounce her as a false-spoken Queen from one end of England to the other. But we must have patience, Gracie. All, I trust, will yet come well."

"He is safely lodged in the Tower," said the captain ; "and, no doubt, nothing more will be heard about him until the Queen returns from Canterbury."

"The paper I received from Lord Granger," said Sampson, "shall be sent on to the Tower. Neither Trevanion nor anyone else dare harm him when that paper is read."

Captain Cartridge now made the brothers acquainted with the manner in which Cunningham had been captured.

"Have you heard anything of him?" asked the captain of his men.

"No," was the reply; "he is snug enough below stairs. Is he to have aught to eat or drink?"

"Yes, he can have a drink of water if it so pleases him, but that is all. Would you like to see him, Sir Giants?"

"Nay," replied both Sampson and Goliar, "we are hungry and tired. We require a long rest, and shall be compelled to take it."

"Daylight is now dawning," said Cartridge, "so you had better set about your meal, which shall be a good one. Then a bedroom is at your disposal, and you may sleep until to-morrow evening, when the prisoner below, must, according to our rules, be brought before us. We'll *lord's son* him, comrades, won't we?"

"We will!" was the cry.

"We will do as you say," said Sampson, "and will rest in your bedroom until to-morrow night. In the meantime you will no doubt do me a favour."

"What is that, brother giant?"

"This unfortunate and cruelly ill-used girl should be returned to her home at Greenwich. She wishes to see the last of her dead father—the faithful friend who lost his life while defending a friend of ours."

"I solemnly swear to you," said the captain, "that ere you awake she shall be at her home. On one of my own horses she shall ride, and she shall be escorted by two of my most trustworthy men."

"Good—good, and you will remain at home, Gracie, until you hear from us."

"I will," replied Grace.

The giants took a most affectionate leave of her, and followed the captain into the parlour, where they were served with an excellent meal.

"There's a fine table for you!" said Captain Cartridge; "we always feed well here, though I never seem to be any the better or the stouter for it. Set to, brothers, there's a splendid chine of beef—here's half-a-dozen fat capons; here's two wild boar pies—fit for a king—here's a peacock pasty, at the other end a baron of beef, fit for Elizabeth herself, let alone Captain Cartridge, and here's a magnificent ham—I'm sorry I can't say it's a *Cunning-ham*, and other odds and ends too numerous to mention."

"As for the ale, mead, wines, or whatever you like to ask for, they shall be at once supplied, and if you are too tired to drink, my man Wynn shall stand on the table and pour the stuff into your little mouths; and yet that would hardly do since, Wynn being a good servant, I don't want to miss him, and he *may* overbalance himself, and fall down one of your throats."

While Cartridge was delivering himself of this long-winded speech, the giants had been attacking the viands before them, much to the diversion of the men, who laughed heartily at the extraordinary rapidity with which the joints and other things were disappearing.

The meal being concluded, the brothers were conducted to their bedroom; but, like the majority of beds to which they were conducted, they found those therein considerably too short

so they were compelled to adopt the system they used elsewhere—that is to say, pull off the clothes, and place them on the floor.

There they rolled themselves up, and, in a few moments, were snoring soundly.

•　　•　　•　　•　　•

When evening came round, the brothers were awakened by Captain Cartridge.

Having washed themselves, they descended to the parlour, where another savoury meal awaited them.

This was shared by Cartridge and his men and a merry and boisterous party they made.

"The young girl has been taken to her home," said Cartridge, "and money has been paid to a proper man, in order to see that the funeral arrangements are properly carried out. The men say that directly the neighbours saw Grace they flocked around her, and promised to do all in their power for her. So you may rest easy as to that. And now that we have finished our meal, let us adjourn to the court-room."

"What is that?" asked Sampson.

"It is a room next to this," replied the captain. "The men will show you into it. I will join you in a moment, and then the prisoner shall be brought before us."

Sampson and Goliar followed the men, wondering what the captain was about to do.

They concluded, from the grins on the faces of the men, that a mock trial was about to take place—a little bit of one of the captain's amusements, in fact.

In a few seconds the giants were in "the captain's court."

There were benches on both sides of the room, and at one end was a huge box, upon which was placed a desk and a chair.

At the other end, and exactly facing this, was an arrangement of thick pieces of timber.

It looked like a crate placed on end.

The giants took their seats near the box, and they were soon supplied with some good wine.

Ten men seated themselves opposite, and Wynn supplying them with ale, they commenced to enjoy themselves.

In a few more moments there stalked into the room a tall man, clothed in a long black gown, and wearing a monstrous wig, which was considerably the worse for wine stains and rough usage.

As he stalked in he bowed almost to the floor, saying—

"Greet you all, both great and small. My lords and gentlemen, you are all very welcome, including myself."

The giants started at this scare-crow for some little time; but at last they burst into such a roar of laughter, that the rafters rang again.

They recognised the captain, but it was principally by his voice; for in appearance he had altered himself wonderfully.

With a "mincing gait" he walked up the room, got on the box, and taking his seat, arranged some papers before him, and stuck a quill of extraordinary length in his wig.

Having coughed two or three times, and having swallowed a glass of brandy—"to make him more spirited in his decision," as he explained, he shouted in a loud voice—

" Bring in the prisoner ! "

Hardly had the words left his lips ere Cunningham was bundled in.

A terrible object he looked indeed.

His clothes were rumpled and dirty, his hair was disarranged, his face was black, and his eyes were wild-looking and bloodshot.

His hands were buckled behind his back so tightly that he could not move them an inch.

Being hustled into the arrangement we have called a crate, he looked round the room with a dazed stare.

Directly his eyes rested on the enormous figures of the giants, he groaned dismally.

" Prisoner at the bar ! " yelled the captain, " are you guilty or not guilty, eh ? But stay—that's wrong. Let me see what he is charged with."

And Cartridge, snatching up some papers, hastily looked at them—the wrong side up.

" Ha ! " he said, " you are charged with abducting a youthful maiden. You, a lord's son, are charged with abducting a young and innocent girl. Have you anything to say why your pockets should not be turned inside out ; No ! turn out his pockets."

Two men at once proceeded to carry out this order.

" Hold ! " screamed Cunningham. " I have something to say. Do you think that I—the son of Lord Trevanion—am to be thus grossly insulted ? I warn you that a time will soon come when you shall——"

" Turn out his pockets ! " yelled the captain, banging the papers on the desk. " Turn them out, I say."

Turn them out they did, and speedily, too.

Several articles dropped on the floor.

They were picked up and handed to the " judge."

" We have been swindled, comrades," he cried, " for there is not enough here to purchase a starved hog."

" Are there any papers of importance ? " asked Sampson—" anything to prove what a State thief he and his father is ? "

" Nay, nothing. " Ho, ho ! didst ever hear of State thieves carrying documents about—documents which would be likely to cause them to become acquainted with the inside of one of the Tower cells ? Well, comrades—I mean, my lords and gentlemen—ahem ! since he has nothing important in his pockets, we must have his attire, which we will sell for whatever it is worth. Or I may honour it by placing it on my own person—so strip him."

" Strip me ! " shrieked Cunningham. " I dare you to strip me ! Wretched mockery of a judge ! I dare you to strip me ! "

" I dare say you do," chuckled the captain, as he delivered a rapid succession of winks at the giants ; " but let me tell you that whatever I—as judge—may order to be done is done at once."

" But there is no judge who orders a prisoner to be stripped," cried Cunningham.

" Just so. And that, of course, is the very

reason I make myself an exception to the rule. My lords and gentlemen, again I say strip him."

In an almost incredibly short space of time, Cunningham was stripped from head to heel.

Upon his doublet being taken off, a great cry escaped from the lips of the men.

They surveyed what lay upon Cunningham's breast with looks of wonder.

So did the " judge " who, after a steady look of a few moments, got off his perch, and approaching the " prisoner," looked at the article.

It was a magnificent diamond and ruby head-shaped jewel.

This was suspended from his neck by a finely wrought chain.

" It is a family heirloom," groaned Cunningham. " I pray you do not take it from me."

" A family heirloom, eh ? " said Cartridge, " and a very pretty bauble, too. Detach it—companion—detach it."

Instantly it was off Cunningham's neck, and in the captain's hands.

" Yes," he said, " 'tis very pretty. I have not had so good a specimen of ' diamond paste ' in my hands for a long time. I am proud to have made its acquaintance. We will ascertain its value to-morrow, companions, dispose of it, and equally divide the result. This article may then be called the divided heirloom, ha ! ha ! "

Having pocketed this precious article (the value of it was over ten thousand crowns, and, Cunningham, to speak the candid truth, had stolen it from his father, with the idea that if he wanted money, he could easily raise it on it), the captain resumed his seat.

" Am I to remain here in this condition whined Cunningham.

" Nay, you shall be clothed directly. Listen to it. You have abducted a young and innocent girl. But before that, you gave the order to the soldiers to fire the volley which slew her father. For that you deserve death ! What say you, my lords and gentlemen ? "

" Ay," said Sampson, " he deserves the most awful death that can be thought of ! "

" We find him guilty," continued the captain, " and herewith pronounce sentence. He is to be strongly sewn up in a canvas bag, at the bottom of which two heavy stones are to be placed—taken to a boat at the end of this avenue, put in it, rowed out into the middle of the Thames, and dropped in.

A howl of terror left Cunningham's lips.

He dropped upon his knees, and with the tears streaming down his face, begged for mercy.

" Is the sentence a just one, Sir Giants ? " asked the captain.

" Very just," replied Sampson ; " but I would beg of you not to carry it out. I am not going to ask for mercy for the villain, but I would like him to be left for a future time. Let the one he has so deeply injured take his revenge."

" Well, well, Sir Giants," said the captain, " let it be as you will. But he must be punished in some way. Let us retire and consider what is best to be done."

"THE STERN, DARK FACE OF THE WIZARD APPEARED."

The giants and the captain retired to the parlour, where, over a bottle of brandy, they considered what was to be done with Cunningham.

The captain then threw off his wig and gown, and appeared in the condition we first met him.

Re-entering the "court" with the giants, he said :

"We have arrived at a most merciful decision. And let——"

"What is to be done with me ?" cried Cunningham, wildly. "Have you not sufficiently tortured me ? Have you not taken enough from me to enrich both your infamous comrades and yourself ?"

"Listen, companions !" said the captain, without taking any notice of what Cunningham said, "this lord's son is to be blacked and sent home to the Tower, where, doubtless, he is expected."

Several of the men left the room, and on returning brought with them a pail filled with a black, slimy liquid resembling pitch, and a box filled with sawdust.

It instantly dawned on Cunningham's mind what was about to be done with him.

He was about to cry aloud again for mercy, when the men seized him, and flung him on his back.

One seized a brush, and, despite the howls of the miserable wretch, he plastered him from head to heel in a thick coat of black paint.

Then they sprinkled the sawdust all over him.

Surely no one on this earth ever presented a more wretched and extraordinary appearance.

The giants were so convulsed with laughter that they rolled off their seats to the floor.

"How do you feel now, lord's son ?" asked the captain.

"Do not send me to the Tower like this," groaned Cunningham.

"Oh, no ; we will not even take you there. You would never reach there by yourself. We are about to send you elsewhere. Now, brother giants, pray get yourselves ready."

The brothers were soon ready for departure.

The two soldiers, who, during all that had occurred, had been enjoying themselves in the kitchen, were brought up to the parlour.

"The time has come for your departure," said the captain, "and I hope you have been well treated."

"We have," answered the men.

"Well, listen to me. Do not say a word where you have been. Lord Trevanion's son does not think you have been stopping here. You must say that he was captured by somebody whose name you forget. Mark it, he will be in the Tower soon ; but it will be in a very peculiar condition, and it will be by the Traitor's Gate that he enters."

"We will obey you," was the reply.

"And here," continued the captain, "are ten gowns each for you. Now depart."

The captain now informed the brothers as to how Cunningham was to be taken to the Tower, the information causing them to laugh heartily.

They then departed, thanking the captain for his kindness to Gracie, and for his princely hospitality towards themselves.

They decided to travel first to Piccadilly, and to show Lord Trevanion the paper they had in their possession.

Cunningham, crying like a child, was again bound hand and foot, then sewn up in a canvas bag, a gag being first placed in his mouth.

This bag was labelled—

"To the Lieutenant of the Tower,

"WADDING."

Wadding, for the cannon mounted on the battlements, being the only article admitted through the Traitor's Gate.

Having scribbled a few words on a huge sheet of paper, and sealed it in the shape of a letter, Captain Cartridge and two of his men attired themselves as watermen, then they took hold of the sack, and carried it to the other end of the alley, where, at the waterside, was a boat.

Into this Cunningham was placed. Cartridge and his men stepped in, and the boat was pushed off.

When within twenty yards of the Tower, the boat was shot swiftly ahead, then turned, and brought up to the gate.

Thus it would appear as if it had come from the opposite direction.

They were perceived by a sentinel, who shouted lustily to them to state the nature of their business.

"From Woolwich," roared Captain Cartridge, "with wadding."

"From the Arsenal ? '

"Yes."

"Have you any papers ?"

"Yes."

The sentinel disappeared, and soon the rattle and clanking of chains and bars was heard, and the cumbrous gate moved back, disclosing a captain of the guard, and several halberdiers on the steps.

The boat glided swiftly through the water, and as soon as it touched the steps, Cartridge rose, touching his hat.

"Well, sirrah," said the captain, sternly, "what do you call this ? What do you mean by bringing goods here at this time o' night ? Your conduct shall be reported to the lieutenant, for you have been in some tavern instead of hurrying hither."

"Your pardon, captain," said Cartridge, "we were delayed by the tide."

"Pah ! And so far as I can remember the lieutenant did not tell me that any wadding was expected. However, hand over your papers, and get you gone !"

Cartridge produced the letter, and handed it to the captain, who, without bestowing more than a glance at it, thrust it into his pocket, and waved his hand.

The "wadding," in the shape of the gagged Cunningham was bundled out on the steps.

The gate was again opened, and Cartridge and his men went off.

Silent they remained until the middle of the

river was reached, then they paused and indulged in a hearty laugh.

"Take the wadding," said the captain of the guard, "and convey it to the lieutenant's lodgings. Let it remain there until we have his orders."

Cunningham had become insensible, so that he made not the least movement; but even if he had, it is likely, considering the rough manner in which the men carried the bag away that he would have attracted no attention.

CHAPTER XV.

IS OF THE EXTRAORDINARY PROCEEDINGS IN THE HEADSMAN'S CHAMBER—OF TREVANION'S VISIT TO THE TOWER—OF WHAT MYSTERIOUS EVENTS FOLLOWED, AND OF HOW THE SACK WAS OPENED.

FOR awhile we must return to Oscar.

Down the slimy stairs he went, but at a snail's pace.

Every few minutes he paused to listen.

Sounds of all descriptions met his ears. Now it sounded like the distant banging of an iron door—now like the clatter of chains—now like the roar of a lion, then again like the sighing of the wind, now like a smothered scream, or a groan of mortal agony, then, again, like a heavy fall.

Such an effect did these sounds have upon Oscar's already terribly excited brain, that ever and anon he was compelled to hold his hands firmly over his ears.

"Oh, heaven!" he muttered at last, "deliver me from this, or mad I shall go!"

Almost immediately he heard a whisper.

It was low, but distinct—"Oscar—Oscar Raymond."

"Here," whispered Oscar in reply. "Here—here—I'm here!"

"Do not move from where you now stand," said the voice—a voice which thrilled him from head to foot— the voice of the mysterious Wizard. "Place your hand on the wall on the right."

"Yes, yes."

"What do you feel?"

"Nothing but the slimy stone which curdles my blood, and——"

"Silence!" pass your hand over the wall."

"Yes, I——"

"What do you feel?"

"My hand has touched a small knob."

"Press it."

Oscar did so, and, lo! a great piece of the solid stone wall moved quickly back.

"Enter," said the Wizard.

But Oscar had already leapt through the aperture, and the stone resumed its position.

He looked around, but could see nothing.

All was impenetrable darkness.

"Now light your link," said the Wizard.

Oscar searched for and found his tinder box, kindled a light, and set fire to the torch.

He found himself in a small stone chamber.

"Wait!" said the Wizard.

Tremblingly did he wait—appalled did he look around him.

The ARMOURER'S SON had heard much of the MYSTERIES OF THE TOWER OF LONDON; never did he dream that he was destined to become so intimately acquainted with them.

Oscar found himself in a small, square cell, the sides of which were exactly alike, and the masonry looked firm and solid.

"These cells were planned and constructed by ingenious men," thought Oscar, "and for what purpose but for the torture and destruction of their fellow men! And, alas! how many have been murdered here? Every stone, could it speak, could tell a ghastly tale! But Heaven punishes men who invent such fearful places for such terrible purposes."

Suddenly he heard a noise beneath his feet; he stepped back as a stone in the floor moved from its position, and a flood of light poured up.

The stern, dark face of the Wizard appeared.

"Give me your torch," he said, "then come down. You will feel a small iron ladder here."

Without making a reply Oscar did as he was directed, and he was soon below.

The stone was then replaced.

Oscar was about to seize the Wizard by the hand, when he suddenly caught sight of a tall, dark figure, wearing a black mask.

"Heaven!" gasped Oscar, pointing his trembling finger at this figure. "What is that —that leaning on an axe? Tell me—tell me! See! axes are on all sides of me, I——"

"Hush! Hush!" cried the Wizard, placing his hand on his mouth. "*You are in the headsman's chamber!*"

"I guessed so," replied Oscar, in horror-stricken tones. "I like not the sight of yon grim-looking man. His hands are stained with blood!"

"You are right, my son, but that they are stained with the blood of many an *innocent* man is no fault of his. You, however, have nought to fear from him. He is my friend, and, if you will let him, he will be yours. Advance, Oscar, and shake him by the hand!"

"No! no! no! I cannot! I dare not!" cried Oscar, recoiling.

"This is not like you, Oscar Raymond," said the Wizard, somewhat sternly; "but I see how it is; you are unnerved, you require rest and you shall have it directly. Advance and shake that man by the hand. You will do well to make friends with him, *for one day, you will, for a brief space, take his place.*"

"I take his place?" exclaimed Oscar. "Never! 'tis impossible."

"'Tis your destiny, Oscar Raymond."

"My destiny? Heaven grant it may not be so! No earthly power should compel me to accept the office of executioner."

"Time will show, Oscar."

Oscar hesitated no longer.

Advancing, he held out his hand, and it was at once grasped and pressed by a hand as firm and as hard as horn.

"You are my friend, Oscar Raymond," said a deep voice. "I knew your——"

"Silence!" cried the Wizard. "Silence! On your life, silence!"

The headsman placed his hand on his breast, and bowed.

The action spoke more than words.

"Oh!" groaned Oscar, placing his hand to his brow, "I am, indeed, surrounded by strange mysteries. Anon, I shall awake, and find that this is some hideous dream."

"Not so. You are wide awake, my son," said the Wizard, gravely; but now you must rest. I am compelled to leave the Tower, and were it not for the fact that you are so overcome with fatigue, you should accompany me. In this chamber you will rest until——"

"Here?" interrupted Oscar. "Rest here, with all these hideous objects surrounding me? I should never *rest*. The spirits of those whose heads have been stricken from their shoulders by these axes, would haunt me in my dreams."

"Nonsense, my son! Listen! am I not your friend? Have I not already proved myself such?"

"You have, mysterious man—you have."

"Trust to me then, and all will be well. Lord Trevanion and his son will be here to-night, and when your absence is discovered, search will be made for you, as it will for the wretch you have slain. Here no one will think of coming. Besides, the headsman goes with me, and the door will be locked until his return. Will you stay?"

"I will, I am bound to."

The Wizard motioned with his head, and the headsman placed his axe aside, and took off his mask, revealing a good-looking face.

Going to a cupboard he brought out various provisions, including a bottle of wine, placed them on a table, and told Oscar to eat and drink.

Our hero, however, could eat little; but what he had considerably refreshed him, and he was greatly cheered by the Wizard telling him that the Armourer should be made acquainted with the fact, that so far, he was safe.

The headsman now went to what looked like a small cabinet.

Catching hold of the top he pulled it forward. Two doors flew open and a small truckle bed came out.

"There is your bed," said the Wizard. "Throw yourself upon it, and rest in peace. We shall remain here for a short time."

Oscar did as desired, and he was soon asleep.

"Now let us depart," said the Wizard. "The door is fast?"

"Quite."

"Come then."

Touching a part of the wall near the fireplace a stone went back, and the Wizard and the executioner passed through.

*   *   *   *   *

At about the time that Cunningham was taken to the tower as a parcel of "wadding," Lord Trevanion was preparing to leave his silent and forlorn-looking mansion in Piccadilly.

Backwards and forwards to Blackburn House he had been the whole day.

Message after message had been despatched to the Tower.

But all with no result.

He could glean no tidings of his son.

He got frantic at last, more especially as he received information to the effect that the Queen was returning from Canterbury.

News as to what had befallen the Queen, and how she had been rescued by the giants, had reached London, and was rapidly spreading in every direction.

"Unless I take action at once!" muttered Trevanion, bitterly, "all my plans will be spoiled, for as a recompense for what these giants have done, she may pardon both them and the youth whom I have now safely in my clutches. Cursed fate! Cursed fate! Why did I not kill him then and there? But he shall die to-night! Yes, yes—soon—soon he shall die! Ha, ha! the lieutenant will aid me. It will be to his interest. We will kill him, and dispose of him in the tower, and we will give it out that he has escaped!"

"I cannot longer remain here. I must away to the Tower. Who knows I may find my son there? Oh, that it may be so. Yes, yes, I will at once away—strange sounds seem to be floatin round the rooms. I hardly dare to turn, for fear of encountering that horrible shadow. Brandy, brandy!"

With trembling hand the guilty wretch clutched a bottle of brandy, and placing it to his lips, took a deep draught.

As he replaced it he knocked the lamp over. It was instantly extinguished, and the place was in darkness.

"Ha!" he hissed, my luck is deserting me. Everything I do appears to go wrong. But I know my way—I know my way, and my horse waits. Yet I know not whom I may encounter, and I must be prepared for anything."

So saying, he drew his sword, and advancing to the window, pulled aside the heavy curtains.

He saw that the moon was well up, and the raising of the curtains caused its beams to penetrate into the room.

Thereupon he tucked up the curtains.

But as he turned, lo! a black cloud flitted across the moon, and hid it.

With a bitter oath the wretch walked towards the door.

He had not taken two paces ere he drew back.

A loud, wild cry of terror and dismay left his lips.

He tried to fly, but fear held him rooted to the spot.

The moon's rays had suddenly shot through the window again, and shone upon an object lying almost at his very feet.

That object was *a glittering axe!* And the edge of the terrible blade was turned *towards him*.

Suddenly a low, deep voice said—

"*Prepare!*"

Trevanion clasped his hand over his eyes, and groaned.

For a few moments did the guilty villain remain thus, and then he ventured to remove his hand, he found the moon's rays still in the room, but—*the axe was gone!*"

"Marvellous!" he groaned—"most marvellous! but the work of that accursed fiend in human shape, Mervino. 'Tis his conjuring—his damnable jugglery! but let him wait—let him wait!"

Placing one hand over his eyes, and holding his naked blade before him with the other, he rushed forward, scrambled pell-mell down the stairs, and entered the courtyard, where his horse awaited him.

To spring into the saddle was the work of an instant.

Forgetting, in his intense excitement, to sheath his sword, he rode forth at a terrific pace with it in his hand.

Surely the persons who beheld him must have thought him mad.

When he neared the city his attention was drawn to this by a lot of apprentices, who, as was usual with them, saw something in it to laugh at, and they bawled out to Trevanion—

"There goes the hunter of shadows—ha, ha!"

Trevanion sheathed his sword with a curse.

On he went at great speed in a circular direction, for he was still fearful of trusting himself in the neighbourhood of Fleet Street, and, at last, he reached the Tower.

He was instantly admitted, and at once conducted to the lieutenant, who was anxiously awaiting him in a large hall in the Jewel House, surrounded by a crowd of officials and soldiers, looking the picture of dismay.

"What has happened?" cried Trevanion. "Quick, keep me not in suspense."

"My lord," replied the lieutenant, "by some extraordinary means your prisoner has escaped."

"Escaped!—escaped!" yelled Trevanion. "Then to you, Lord Fulmore, I look for an explanation, and at once."

"I should be only too glad to be able to give your lordship some explanation," replied the lieutenant, who now fancied that his recently acquired position was beginning to be shaken. "He was placed in a cell from which an escape had never before been made. In that cell he was put by my most trusted man, Brutus Gatling. And what is still more extraordinary, this gaoler has *also* disappeared."

"Then you may depend upon it that they have both gone away together."

"That, my lord, is out of the question. Come forward," added the lieutenant to one of the warders who had accompanied Brutus when Oscar was placed in the cell, "and give your version of what occurred."

The man gave a version which was pretty near the truth.

"And have you not searched for the warder?" asked Trevanion.

"Every inch of this Tower has been searched," was the reply.

"You say you entered the cell where this accused youth was placed by means of duplicate keys?"

"Just so."

"Ten thousand furies! This is, indeed, a most fearful check. What is your opinion of it all?"

"My opinion is that Brutus Gatling, on going again to the cell, found that the prisoner had escaped, and knowing that he would be held responsible, he made his way out of the Tower by some secret exit."

"Did you find that the lock of the cell had been tampered with?"

"Oh, no."

"Then, by all the incarnate fiends, how do you imagine this boy could have got out?"

The lieutenant shook his head.

"Are there any secret passages in this cell?"

"Not that I am aware of. We carefully searched and sounded the walls, floor, and ceiling. No, no, my lord, there are no secret exits there."

"But then, I say!" roared Trevanion, stamping his feet violently, "how do you account for his disappearance?"

"I repeat, my lord, with all respect to your lordship, that I cannot account for it *at all.*"

"I presume you would suggest," sneered his lordship, "that the youth must be in possession of the power of getting through a keyhole?"

"Nay, I would——"

"Listen!" interrupted Trevanion. "Another search shall be made, and I will go with you. Every hole and corner above and below shall be searched. Where we cannot enter we will probe with swords and halberds. Lord! Lord!" he groaned, "to think that, after all, I am to be foiled, and made the laughing-stock of the Queen and the whole court. I would have given half my fortune had this not occurred."

"*You have rightly no fortune!*" said a low, deep voice at Trevanion's elbow.

"Liar!" shrieked Trevanion, as he dealt a soldier, at his side, such a fearful blow that the man was hurled upon the stones.

"I never spoke!" said the man, holding his hand to his forehead.

"No, that *I* can swear to," said a soldier, who had been standing at his side.

"And I, and I," was the cry. Shame! shame! to strike a man thus!"

"Well, who was it who spoke?" hissed Trevanion. "Did you not hear a voice, lieutenant?"

"I did not, your lordship."

"Nor any of you?" asked Trevanion.

"We heard someone mutter something," was

the reply of the soldiers; "but we did not understand what was said."

"It must have been the spirit of that accursed Wizard," muttered Trevanion. "And yet his spirit can hardly be in two places at the same time."

Aloud he said—

"Have any of you seen aught of Mervine, the Wizard of Whitehall lately?"

"He was seen some hours ago—at least, a soldier on the battlements, reported that he saw him in company with a strange looking man," said the lieutenant.

"Well," continued Trevanion, "has aught been heard of my son?"

"Nothing, my lord."

The reason of this was that the two soldiers whom Captain Cartridge had sent on to the Tower, had gone into one of the taverns, and there had got helplessly intoxicated.

It was consequently, most unlikely that they would return to the Tower for many hours to come.

"Truly, truly, this is most strange and unaccountable!" exclaimed Trevanion, as great beads of perspiration rolled down his face. "I should not be surprised to hear if he has been——but no, no! let me not utter the words. Fulmore, let us search the Tower."

And Trevanion, with a great flourish, drew his sword

"My lord," said the lieutenant, "with all respect to your lordship, I again say——"

"I care not what you say! I will not rest until the Tower has again been searched."

"Your lordship," said Fulmore, "is quite aware of the fact that the Tower, at this moment, is full of illustrious prisoners."

"Ay, I am perfectly aware of that important fact, since many of them are here *under my signature*," said Trevanion, in such a significant manner that there was no doubt what he meant.

"What then?"

"I was about to observe that we shall again disturb them."

Lord Trevanion laughed.

"Disturb them?" he cried. "Is that a matter which should trouble me, or you?"

"Well, since your lordship will have it so, we will search the Tower again."

In a few moments the Tower was in a state of commotion.

The whole of the soldiers, even those who were off duty, were called to arms.

The roll of many drums resounded through the long corridors, greatly to the irritation and wonderment of the "illustrious prisoners," of whom the lieutenant had spoken.

All being in readiness, a tottering old soldier, who had been in the fortress nearly all his life, and who, therefore, was credited with being acquainted with all its secrets (a great mistake, by the way), was placed at the head of the party.

Trevanion and the lieutenant followed him, and the little army of soldiers came next.

It would be a waste of our own time, and also we should weary the reader, did we attempt to give an account of the places searched by the party.

The time was, of course, lost, and Trevanion worked himself up into a violent state.

He raved, stamped, and swore like a madman.

"Is there no other place where 'tis likely the young villain may be hiding?" he asked the old soldier, who had acted as leader.

"There is not, my lord, except——"

"Ay, ay, knave—except?"

"Except the headsman's chamber; and that, my lord is always kept sacred like."

"Sacred like, eh? Sacred like! By heaven! it shall not be sacred from me!" shouted Trevanion. "Lead us to it."

The old man looked at the lieutenant, as much as to ask:

"Is this to be done?"

The lieutenant understood him.

"If it is his lordship's command," he said, "take us there."

The old man led the way through many extraordinary passages.

They went on swiftly, and Trevanion did not notice one passage more than another.

But on passing through St. John's Chapel, a deadly faintness came over him.

He gasped for breath, and had it not been for a flask of brandy, which the lieutenant offered him, it is probable he would have fallen to the floor.

How well he remembered this sacred spot.

How well he rembered the place to which he had come after the awful crime he had committed years and years ago.

Was it any wonder he should feel faint?

Was it any wonder that the villain, whose very soul was stained with blood, should tremble lest the terrible vision, which the mysterious Wizard had caused to stand before him, should again appear?

Blindly, madly, he dashed through the chapel, loudly cursing the old soldier for bringing him that way.

The lieutenant and the men followed him.

Certainly all were under the impression that he had taken leave of his senses.

Up one flight of break-neck steps and down another ran Trevanion.

Presently he stopped, and panting for breath, placed his back against the wall.

He stood now just at the top of the stairs, where years ago he had slain his cousin!

Did he recognise this spot?

Ay, only too well!

The place where the deed was committed was as firmly rooted in his memory as was the crime itself.

"My lord," said the lieutenant, on coming up with him, "I pray you calm yourself. It——"

"I hate passing through chapels!" gasped Trevanion. "I hate *all* chapels!"

"That is ever the cry of the guilty," muttered the old soldier.

Fortunately for him he was not heard.

"Lead on," said the lieutenant. "In the name of all the saints let us get this business over. Does your lordship still persist in wishing to visit the headsman's chamber ?"

"Ay, ay, I do ; I do."

The old man went on again, and at last he paused before a low archway, in which was a ponderous oak door.

"That is the chamber," he said. "When the door is open, the headsman is within ; but when it is closed, it proves that he is absent."

"You have the duplicate key ?" asked Trevanion of the lieutenant.

"There is no duplicate key of the headsman's chamber,' said several voices in chorus.

"Then,' cried Trevanion, "the door must be broken open."

"It shall be broken open," said the lieutenant, "if your lordship will only say how it is to be done."

"Fetch hammers and axes."

This order was complied with, and soon two soldiers, each provided with a heavy hammer, set to work upon the door.

The noise was fearful.

So loud was it that it reached the ears of the wild beasts in their dens, and they increased the din by loud, prolonged, and most dismal howls.

The men continued their onslaught on the door until perspiration poured in streams down their faces.

But the door yielded not.

Two other men came forward as soon as the others were tired, and urged on by Trevanion's repeated and frantic promises of a reward, they rained down the blows thick and fast.

With a sudden and most violent crash, the door suddenly flew open.

"Lights !" shrieked Trevanion—"lights !"

Ere they cou'd be brought to the door, the chamber became illuminated with a strange blue light.

So startling, so extraordinary did it appear, that an exclamation of astonishment, not unmingled with awe, escaped the lips of all who beheld it.

The soldiers would have dashed pell-mell from the spot had they not been restrained by the lieutenant, who called to them to stir at their peril.

What of Trevanion ?

He stood spell-bound—his eyes and mouth wide open—his right hand still clutched his drawn sword ; with his left he held on like grim death to the lieutenant.

The mysterious light began to fade—a rushing sound was heard—and instantly the blue light changed to a white one of startling brilliancy.

Now was heard the deep, solemn tolling of a bell.

After a few notes a black mass appeared in the centre of the headsman's chamber.

All made out the picture.

It was in the Tower walls, and before them grim and distinct was the scaffold with the hideous block, and the headsman with the glittering axe on his shoulder.

The head-man turned and fixed his flashing eyes on Trevanion ; then he snatched the mask away, and Trevanion saw the same face the

Wizard had shown him after he had murdered his cousin.

He knew what was coming, and summoning all the courage and power that remained to him, he shrieked aloud—

"The accursed Wizard ! 'tis he—'tis he——"

He started into the chamber.

The illusion vanished, and in its place stood—Oscar Raymond !"

With an appalling oath, Trevanion dashed right into the chamber.

He raised his sword ; but even as he did so a tremendous crash was heard, the chamber became filled with a bluish sulphurous smoke, and Trevanion, with a groan, staggered back and fell senseless at the feet of the lieutenant.

"The torches," cried the lieutenant, as he snatched one from the man nearest him, and, raising it aloft, entered the chamber.

But not a living soul was visible therein.

"Search this chamber," cried the lieutenant ; "search every nook and cranny. Lord ! this is, indeed, a most wonderful—a most fearful affair."

But not a single soldier could be prevailed upon to enter the place.

It was in vain the lieutenant stamped, raved, and swore.

"We have always thought the headsman was in league with the devil !" said the old man who had led the way, "and now we are sure of it."

"If it can be brought home to him," said the lieutenant, "the Lord have mercy on his soul ! The Queen will order him to be burnt at the stake ! But here, take this brandy, and pour some of it down his lordship's throat."

A large quantity of brandy having been poured down Trevanion's throat, he showed signs of returning consciousness.

His groans, when he opened his eyes, were awful.

"The Wizard ?" he asked.

"We have not seen him," replied the lieutenant. "We saw no more than you did yourself."

They assisted Trevanion to arise.

He was now deathly pale, and trembled as with the ague.

"Listen !" said Trevanion, "this headsman shall, at the earliest opportunity, be brought before the Privy Council, and made to confess what he has——"

"He has nothing to confess," said a deep voice.

All turned, and the soldiers drew back.

The tall figure of the headsman stalked through them and stood before Trevanion, who, for a few seconds, was speechless.

Over the headsman's shoulder was an axe, the edge of which, strange to say, was *towards* Trevanion.

"Where have you been ?" cried the lieutenant.

"Sharpening the axes," was the reply.

"Do you mean to say," cried Trevanion, "that you were not in that chamber but a few moments ago ?"

"Certainly not," was the reply.

"And do you also mean to say that you never heard a thundering sound as though a door was being broken open?"

"Ay, I never heard such a noise, and am astonished to see that the door of my chamber *has* been broken open. With the door of my grinding room, in the vaults, closed, and my grindstone at work, no sounds can reach my ears."

"That explanation is quite feasible, your lordship, is it not?" asked the lieutenant.

"To me it is not," replied Trevanion, emphatically. "I believe it to be an infamous lie!"

"Your lordship may believe what you think proper," said the headsman; "for whatever you do believe, or whatever you don't believe, is a matter of indifference to me."

"Do not insult me, sirrah!" cried Trevanion, "or 'twill be the worse for you!"

"I fail to see how it will be the worse for me," said the headsman. "Your threats may be feared by the many, but when you threaten *me*, your threats fall on *deaf ears*, your lordship."

With this the grim executioner stalked into his chamber.

"Your lordship, I hope, is satisfied that the youth, of whom we have been in search, is not in the Tower?" said the lieutenant.

"Nay, even now I am not satisfied of that. If he is not in the Tower, how was it he not long since appeared before all of us?"

"I am unable to say, but perhaps, all we have seen *was* the work of the Wizard. But we may get a solution of the mystery anon. You see your——"

At this moment a soldier ran up at the top of his speed, crying out—

"Your lordship, Captain Goddard requests that you will step up to your apartments at once!"

"What is the matter now, knave?"

"Oh," cried the man, his teeth chattering violently, "the Tower must be haunted, your lordship, there——"

The lieutenant interrupted the man by pushing him on one side, and with Lord Trevanion at his side, and the now thoroughly alarmed soldiers at his back, went off to his apartments.

Before the door of a small chamber, which led to the lieutenant's apartments, was a sack, and around it stood Captain Goddard (the individual who had taken the papers from Captain Cartridge), and a number of his men.

"What now, captain?" cried the lieutenant.

"Your pardon," was the reply; "but the contents of this bag, which we received as wadding from one of the Arsenal watermen, have been moving about for some little time in a most extraordinary and eccentric manner."

"Moving? *Moving*, do you say?"

"Yes, your lordship; see it—ha! it moves again!"

The lieutenant, Trevanion, and the soldiers darted back, with a cry of wonder, as the contents of the sack began to execute a series of peculiar movements.

"Wadding!" cried the lieutenant, "this is not wadding! Whoever heard of live wadding? Pah! more likely it is some beastly animal sent here by one of the merchant captains as a present to the Queen. Where are the papers? for I suppose papers were delivered at the same time as the bag?"

"Yes, your lordship," replied the captain, as he took the letter from his pocket, "and with all respect to your lordship, the sack *was* delivered here as wadding. If you will look, you will see it so labelled."

The lieutenant took the letter in his hand, and turned it over and over.

"This is no official document," he said.

"Of course it is not," said Trevanion, "the captain has be en befooled; By the Virgin! I begin to think the officials of the Tower require a hugeamount of looking after."

The lieutenant broke the seal, spread open the paper on the wall, and read—

"To the lieutenant—

"Your lordship is herewith presented with a human curiosity. It will be of great interest to Lord Trevanion should his lordship visit the Tower ere the said human curiosity ceases to exist. The writer of this would urge the lieutenant to, at once, place the present with the wild beasts. It is so curious that it would frighten even them. Adieu."

"A cursed trick has been played upon us," said the lieutenant. "Your name is mentioned, your lordship. What think you the bag can contain?"

Trevanion shook his head, but he made no reply.

"Go you, sirrah," said the lieutenant, to a soldier at his side, "and cut open the mouth of that bag."

But the man would not approach it.

The lieutenant appealed to the captain.

"I will willingly do as you ask," he said, "provided I am first allowed to discharge my pistol at it. There will then be no danger."

And he took a pistol from his belt.

The lieutenant, likely enough, would have allowed him to fire at the mysterious bag, which was all this time was moving first to one side and then the other; but Trevanion, plucking out his sword, said—

"Nay, fire not. Since my name is mentioned, let me be the one to open the bag."

He approached the sack, and taking hold of the mouth, cut the string.

Then he went to the end, and taking hold of the corners, shot out the contents.

"A man!" yelled the soldiers. "A black man—a savage negro!"

"Bring your torches here, villains!" cried the lieutenant. "Yes, 'tis a man! and bound hand and foot and gagged. The Lord save us. What hellish wretch is it who has played us this trick?"

"Suddenly, with a bitter cry, Lord Trevanion, cast himself on his knees, crying out—

"My son!—my dear son!"

"Your *son?*" said the lieutenant. "Impossible!"

There being now no further fear that the sack contained some wild beast or fiend, all crowded round, and the captain pulled the gag from Cunningham's mouth, while one of the soldiers, taking the flask of brandy from the lieutenant, poured some of the fiery liquid down his throat.

The effect was instanteous.

Cunningham opened wide his mouth, and bellowed like a bull.

Then he burst into a flood of tears, which, mingling with the black, slimy liquid and the sawdust, made him—well, our readers can form an idea as to what he must have looked like.

"Oh," cried Trevanion, raising aloft his clenched fist; "for this you shall have your full revenge, my son."

"They have robbed and nearly murdered me !" groaned Cunningham.

"Tell me—tell me—who did this fearful deed ?" his father cried.

"I will anon—I will anon. I pray you to have me at once taken to a room in the lieutenant's quarters."

A litter was procured, and Cunningham was carried to one of the lieutenant's rooms, where washing materials were placed. Two soldiers were told off to assist in cleansing him, and a tough job they found it. At the end of an hour he was led to his father, who was anxiously awaiting him for particulars.

CHAPTER XVI.

SHOWS HOW THE GIANT BROTHERS DESTROY LORD TREVANION'S HOUSE—HOW OSCAR IS ATTACKED IN THE STRAND, AND HOW THE GIANTS ARRIVE JUST IN TIME TO SAVE HIS LIFE.

WHEN the giants left Captain Cartridge, and proceeded on their journey, they had not gone far when they found that they had become famous.

Their extraordinary prowess, in connection with their rescue of the Queen from the robbers, was now all the talk of every one.

This act, coupled with their daring rescue of Oscar, had made them perfect heroes ; and as they proceeded through the streets they were hailed with loud shouts of welcome.

By the time they reached Piccadilly, quite a crowd followed them.

"If we have not risen in fortune, brother," said Sampson, "we have in the estimation of the people, and that is something. Who knows one day we may be Lord Mayors, eh, brother?"

"We should be a mighty sight too big for that, I am afraid," replied Goliar. "Still, it is something to be popular with the people, if 'tis only to turn them against this accursed Trevanion."

"Well, we have arrived at his house. How dark and silent everything looks," said Sampson, as they drew up before the mansion.

"There have been no servants in the house for a length of time," said a bystander.

"Say you so ; how is that ?"

"All have deserted. And neither Trevanion nor his son are often here now."

"What shall we do, brother ? 'Tis evident we shall not find the wretch here, so we had better get on to the tower," said Goliar.

"Nay, nay," was Sampson's reply. "Let us look about the house first. There is no telling he may be asleep in his bedroom."

"I doubt it."

"Well, there can be no harm in looking. Come brother."

"Oh, I will follow you, fear it not. There is one thing, we might find something to eat and drink within, and though 'tis not long since we regaled ourselves in a right royal manner, I nevertheless feel downright empty."

The brothers dismounted, and requested one of the bystanters to procure them torches.

This was soon done, and leaving their horses in charge of the curious onlookers, the mountains of flesh and bone stalked up the courtyard, arm in arm.

Arrived at the entrance to the kitchen, Goliar lit his torch, and held it aloft, while Sampson looked about.

There may be a servant or two left," he said, " as I see there are one or two fowls, and how thin they are ? Much too thin to live, brother, eh ?"

Sampson tried the doors ; but they were fast.

Approaching the kitchen window he rapped loudly at it.

"Hillo, my dear !" he said—"hillo ! Here's your lovers returned. Hillo, I say."

"'Tis no use, brother," said Goliar. "The place is deserted, and locked up."

"Well, we must get in by some means," replied Sampson.

Thereupon he looked round the yard, and his eyes rested upon a huge piece of marble—part of a pedestal which, probably, had once supported a statue in the hall.

Sampson took it in both his hands, raised it over his head, and sent it flying against the door, which instantly flew open.

The pair entered the kitchen, and were astonished at the air of desolation which presented itself.

"I don't wonder at it, brother," said Sampson. "No one could stop for any length of time with such a monster. But we will make the place lively enough ere we depart."

"What mean you ?"

"Why I intend to pay Trevanion part of the debt we and Oscar owe him. Ere we depart, brother, we will fire the house."

"Oh, I am quite agreeable to that," was Goliar's reply; "but first we must see what the larder contains."

"Ay, and the wine cellar."

They examined the larder first.

Nothing did they find.

Nothing whatever, except it was a few bones and several stale—frightfully stale—loaves.

Sampson groaned as he felt them.

"Truly, they are as hard as bricks," he said.

"Nothing to eat?" grunted Goliar. "This is truly dreadful!"

"I have it," cried Sampson. 'Tis a pity to leave those fowls without to starve."

"You speak truly. There are five or six of them; and though, poor things, they are somewhat attenuated, they might make us a good meal."

"They will, no doubt of it. Do you seize them, wring their necks, and pluck them, while I explore the upper part of the house."

Goliar, having lit a fire, soaked some of the loaves, and placed them in the oven to dry; then seized the fowls, killed, and prepared to cook them, while Sampson, lighting his torch, proceeded upstairs.

He entered Trevanion's bedroom, and the first thing which attracted his attention was the strong box.

The next thing was a cabinet.

Sampson, without hesitation, forced this open with his dagger.

Several bundles of papers, money, and jewels he saw; and all this he gathered up, and placed in the box, which Trevanion had neglected to lock.

After a still further examination of the place, Sampson descended the stairs with the box on his shoulder.

"Trevanion's secrets may be here, brother," he said, "and what is here may bring him to the block, eh?"

"I hope so! Perhaps Oscar may read them one of these days. Pray Heaven he is safe!"

"Amen! Well, we shall not be long before we reach the Tower. And now how are the fowls?"

"Very tender. I think, we shall find them."

In a little while the brothers had one or two of the fowls and some bread to go on with while the others were cooking.

"Very good, brother," said Sampson, stroking his immense stomach; "but the plague upon it, we never thought of the wine!"

He went to the cellar, and found it as Lord Trevanion had found it; still, there was plenty of beer, and of that the brothers partook heartily.

Having quite finished, Sampson brought out all the wood the cellar contained, placed it upon the floor, surrounded it with shavings, and then placed on the whole of the tables, chairs, and other furniture.

Goliar took the box and went forth with it, while Sampson flung one of the torches on the shavings, and then followed him.

By the time they reached their horses, the whole mass was well alight, much to the alarm of the bystanders.

"'Tis nothing, friends," said Sampson. "We have only set fire to a house, which is the property of a man who is a disgrace to his country. Let us hope it will be a warning to others."

With wide-open mouths the bystanders stood looking at the fire, which every moment became more fierce.

But they had no intention of attempting to check its progress, and even had they attempted it, their efforts would have been fruitless.

Though there was plenty of stone used in the construction of the house, there was also plenty of wood, and that being thoroughly dry, burnt with wonderful rapidity.

In less than five minutes the lower part of the place was thoroughly alight.

While the crowd was intently watching the progress of the fire, Sampson shouldered the box, and Goliar leading the horses, the brothers quietly departed.

When they got some distance they stopped, and looked at the reflection of the fire, which was becoming greater and greater every moment.

"Whither do we go with the box," asked Goliar; "for on my soul I am impatient to get on to the Tower."

"I was just thinking," replied Sampson. "I know a goldsmith in Cheapside who would be only too glad to take charge of the box; but since we are so near, I propose we take it to the Wizard's house."

"Mervine?" cried Goliar.

"Ay, he is a true friend of the Armourer, and a true friend of Oscar."

"Well, well, let it be as you wish, brother, though, I must confess, I like not his practices."

On again went the brothers, and they soon reached the Wizard's house, at Whitehall.

It was a most gloomy-looking building.

Sampson rang the bell at the gate, which was soon opened by an elderly, grey-haired man, as gloomy in appearance as the building he lived in.

"What want ye?" he asked.

"Master Mervine," replied Sampson.

"He is not within. And, even if he were, 'tis doubtful whether he would see you."

"When will he be within?"

"I cannot say, masters. I don't suppose he knows himself."

"Hem!" muttered Sampson, uneasily.

"You can trust him with it, no doubt, brother," said Goliar.

"You are Master Mervine's servant," said Sampson.

"I am proud to say I have that honour," replied the man; "and, if I mistake not, you are the giant brothers of Eastcheap?"

"Truly so—truly so, my good man."

"Master Mervine has always spoken well of you."

"He has?" cried Sampson, delighted. "Well, 'tis more than we expected, and we thank you much for telling us, my friend. Look you, you see this box?"

"Ay, ay."

"We wish to leave it for the present in charge of the Wizard. Its contents are, no doubt, of

the greatest importance you see—but come forth
a little—so—now look above—at the sky."

The old man looked and clasped his hands.

"Mercy on us !" he exclaimed, " a huge fire
is raging somewhere ! "

"You speak truly, old man," whispered
Sampson, "and the house that is burning is
Lord Trevanion's."

"Lord ! "

"Yes, and *we* fired it ! "

"Lord ! "

"Yes. But it is only a little of what will
happen to him."

"No doubt. no doubt. Alas ! he is a dreadful being ! When will the Queen open her eyes,
and see through him ? "

" Well, this box comes from yonder burning
house," continued Sampson ; "so you may guess
how important it is."

"More than *you* may think for," was the reply
in serious tones. "Pray lift it, good giant, for
it would require twenty men such as I to do so,
and follow me. It shall be placed in safety, and
directly I see Master Mervine I will call his attention to it."

Sampson followed the old man with the box,
and in a few moments it was safely deposited in
one of the many vaults beneath the house.

Soon the brothers were once more in the
saddle, and they now turned in the direction of
the Strand.

The fire they saw had now attained tremendous dimensions.

The sky above it was a brilliant red, and the
sparks were flying about in every direction.

The people were rushing towards the scene of
the conflagration.

"Lord, brother !" chuckled Sampson, "the
people ought to get us up a subscription for en-
tertaining them as we have of late. I wonder
where Trevanion is."

"Most likely—nay, we may consider it as a
certainty that he is at the Tower."

"Ay, and if he is, he will be somewhat startled
when we present the paper we have. But now
let us haste."

      ●   ●   ●   ●   ●

To return to Oscar.

He slept as soundly as a child.

His slumber was not disturbed by any horrid
dreams ; for, as our readers may have guessed,
the wine he had partaken of contained a powerful drug.

Of course, he had no idea how long he slept ;
but he was awakened by the first ponderous blows
struck upon the door by the soldiers.

In his confused state of mind this noise, for
some few seconds, sounded to him like the firing
of cannon.

But at last he realised the fact that some one
was battering down the door.

He darted from his bed, and endeavoured to
obtain a light.

He could not find one.

Above the din made by the hammers he heard
the well-known voice of Lord Trevanion.

"Lost !" he cried in despair. "Lost after all !
I am caught—fairly caught in a trap. But I
thank Heaven I am armed. If I get a chance, I
will put this good blade through Trevanion's
cowardly heart, and then—then I should indeed
die happy."

For a few moments Oscar waited, then it
occurred to him that there *might* be some secret
place in the chamber which had been left open
for him in case of danger.

He went round the walls, pressing his hands
everywhere.

But nothing yielded to them.

Suddenly that portion of the wall, where the
Wizard and the headsman had taken their departure, moved slowly back, and the Wizard,
carrying a lamp in one hand, and a small case in
the other came through.

Seeing how excited Oscar was, he said—

"You have nothing to fear—stand by my
side."

Oscar did so without a word, and the Wizard
proceeded to place several articles upon the
ground, after which he blew out his lamp.

By the aid of these articles it was, no doubt,
that when the door was burst open he
produced that extraordinary vision of the headsman.

But it was no vision of Oscar he produced—it
was Oscar himself.

When Trevanion rushed into the chamber, the
Wizard threw something towards the door, and
the result was the terrific explosion, the force of
which threw Trevanion to the ground.

Directly he had thrown it the Wizard caught
Oscar by the arm, and in another instant our
hero was on the other side of the wall, having
passed through the secret door.

"You have now no cause to fear, my son,"
said Mervine, "for they cannot trace you here.
Now listen ! you must follow me in silence and
in darkness, and I will place you without this
accursed Tower. Now this,"—pointing to a small
bundle on the ground—"is a cloak, a false beard,
and a slouched hat—assume the disguise at
once, and when I leave you go not to your
father's house, for danger lurks there; but go at
once to my house at Whitehall. Take this ring,
and if you show it to the man who will answer
the door to you, you will be admitted, and no
questions asked."

"I thank you—thank you from the bottom of
my heart !" replied Oscar, as he proceeded to don
the disguise.

It was a most effectual one, and no one could
possibly have recognised him.

He had now more the appearance of a Spaniard
than any one else.

"Are you ready ? " asked the Wizard.

"I am," replied Oscar.

"The take hold of my mantle, and mark it—
utter no word."

Oscar took hold of the Wizard's mantle, and
followed him.

How many strange passages they traversed ;
how many flights of steps they ascended and
descended, it is out of our power to say.

The Wizard's knowledge of the Tower must
have been something wonderful, for he traversed
every inch of ground in darkness.

At last he paused, stooped, and listened.

A sharp click was heard, a massive piece of stone rolled back, and Oscar saw that they had gained the open air.

"You are now at what is known as Abbot's Avenne," whispered the Wizard, "some distance from the moat, under which we have been walking; traverse this long passage as quietly as you can, and you will arrive at the other end of Tower Hill. Then for my house—for the present, farewell."

Oscar walked rapidly forward, and soon reached the spot he knew so well.

"Marvellous!" he ejaculated.

Straight on he walked, looking neither to the right nor the left.

A longing to rush to the Armourer's house, if only to say one word, came over him, but he stifled it.

He contented himself with pausing an instant, and looking in the direction of the residence of those he loved so well, then, with a deep sigh, he went on.

Suddenly he caught sight of the reflection in the sky.

"A great fire is raging somewhere," he thought. "I wonder where it is. I will ask."

Seeing an apprentice standing at his master's door looking at the reflection, Oscar asked him:

"My good lad, will it please you to tell me where the fire is?"

"Oh, a long way, off, sir," replied the lad, as he surveyed Oscar from head to foot. "A very long way off."

"At the house of a person of importance, I presume?"

"Pooh!" replied the lad, contemptuously. "Some people may think so, but I don't. I say I am glad of it. The fire is burning down the house of that brutal wretch, Lord Trevanion."

Oscar started violently.

Thanking the lad he walked on.

"I wonder whether this is the result of accident or design?" he thought. "I should not be at all surprised if the giants have had some hand in it. I may learn by and by."

On he walked as fast as possible, and nothing occurred to cause him to slacken his pace until near Charing Cross.

Here, outside the "Henry VIII," a very noted hostelry, were assembled a number of gallants.

All were, more or less, in a state of intoxication.

Oscar would have avoided them, but he found it was impossible.

Ere he could pass from the footway to the road, several had caught sight of him, and they greeted his appearance with broad grins.

"One of the models from which Will Shakespeare has taken his characters," laughed one.

"A true knight of the cloak," exclaimed another, as he gave Oscar's cloak a pull. "How much will buy you, Sir Spaniard—cloak and all?"

"Have a drink of pure English," cried another. "You have only to drink one goblet of this, Sir Foreigner, to enable you to speak English fluently so——"

He pushed the goblet unpleasantly near Oscar's face, and the result was that Oscar, raising his fist, dealt him such a blow between the eyes, that he went spinning over the table.

A loud roar of astonishment burst from all present.

"Holy Mary!" cried one, "if he is a Spaniard, he has learnt the way to strike a blow in English manner. Can you use your sword as well, Sir Stranger?"

Oscar, without speaking, attempted to move on again, but one of the gallants creeping behind him, emptied the whole of a quart of wine over him.

At the same moment another pulled his hat off.

The result of this was to pull the false beard from its position, and both that and the hat fell to the footpath.

And so did the fellow who pulled it off; for Oscar, turning suddenly, caught him a blow on the mouth, felling him.

"Cowards!" he cried, "you disgrace your cloth. Is a person not allowed to walk through the public streets without being insulted by such asses as you?"

"Surround him, companions!" cried a voice —"surround him! 'Tis Oscar Raymond—the gallow's bird—on whose head a price is set. Surround him!"

A score of blades flashed from their scabbards.

Oscar backed himself against the shutters of the hostelry.

In the young gallant, who had called out, he recognised the principal friend of Cunningham Trevanion.

"Oscar Raymond," cried Cunningham's friend, "'tis useless to draw your blade, seeing by what number of weapons you are confronted. We arrest you in the Queen's name."

"You are an infamous liar," cried Oscar. "You do not arrest me if I can help it. And besides, what authority have you to arrest me in the Queen's name?'

"We are the Queen's courtiers."

"Ay, such a thing might be. I will not dispute it. But you would have been the more correct had you said the Queen's drunken gallants, for such you certainly are."

This thrust, though true, had the effect of rousing the gallants to frenzy.

With a cry of rage they flung themselves upon our hero.

Oscar was ready, for the first at least, and the first was Cunningham's friend, who, ere he knew what had happened, was run through the shoulder.

With a bitter oath he dropped his sword, and drew back, crying out—

"Kill him! Kill him! Have no mercy on him!"

The gallants were upon Oscar with a rush, and the clash of steel became loud, fast, and furious.

Though Oscar defended himself as well as he was able, he felt that he would very soon be overpowered.

Crowds of people—attracted by the clash of steel—paused to look on, and loud were their cries of shame when they beheld what numbers were opposed to one.

It was at this moment that the giants rounded the corner after their visit to the Wizard's house.

They, from their position on horseback, were enabled to see all that was passing.

They noticed the numbers opposed to one ; but it is probable, considering how anxious they were to reach the Tower, that they would have passed on, had not Oscar, by slightly moving to avoid a dangerous thrust, brought his face under the glare of three or four torches held in the doorway of the tavern.

It was a most fortunate move—a move which saved his life.

The giants caught sight of his face.

"By Heaven, brother !" cried Sampson. "Look ! look ! 'tis Oscar."

"It is. By all the saints it is !" was Goliar's reply.

The brothers were out of the saddle in an instant.

Sampson did not wait to draw his sword, but he seized hold of a heavy oaken form, and swinging it round and round, brought down the gallants as the reaper brings down the corn.

As they fell, Goliar caught hold of them, and flung them away.

One on the top of the other they went, much to the amusement of the crowd.

Cunningham's friend, whose arm hung helpless at his side, had snatched a pistol from one of the gallants, and had crept up to within a few paces of Oscar.

He was just taking aim at our hero, when Sampson seized him.

He clutched him by the throat, dashed the weapon to the ground, and shook the gallant as a well-trained terrier would shake a rat.

"I should know your face, dastard !" cried Sampson. "Ay, I can recall it. Come, come, let me cool thy courage, thou imp of Satan !"

Amid the terrified cries of the gallant, and the screams of laughter of the assembled citizens, Sampson twisted Cunningham's friend high over his head, and dashed him into a huge horse-trough, which, being full of water, he was drenched from head to heel.

"Fear nothing now, Oscar," cried Sampson, seizing Oscar's hands in his own, "We are here, and we will not now lose sight of you. Goliar, see to him a moment ! Citizens ! do you know us ?" he added, turning to the crowd.

"We do ! we do !" was the reply from scores of throats. The giant brothers ! bravo ! bravo ! Well done, giants !"

"Look you !" said Samson, "this house is frequented by these gallants—nearly all of whom, I see, have hurried off—and yonder, in the doorway, stands Hugh Mascott, the host. A nice Englishman for a host !" he sneered, as you will all agree, if you will think for a moment, that while all these wretched specimens of Court Gallants were attacking this youth, he, stood in the doorway holding a link and laughing. Heaven's mercy, gentlemen, that cannot be tolerated, he must be punished !"

The full-bellied host turned as pale as death. "Seize him !" cried Sampson.

The host turned to fly to his parlour, but he was too late.

A ragged, but powerful tramp, standing at his side, caught him by the collar, and flung him backwards into the middle of the crowd, where he was securely held, despite his frantic struggles and his howls for mercy.

Sampson stalked into the house, and, having looked carefully round, selected a large cask of wine.

He carried it outside the house, and set it down in the midst of the crowd.

Then he told several of those present to fetch out all the mugs the house contained ; and, this having been done, Sampson lifted his ponderous fist, and, at a single blow, stove in the head of the cask.

"Thieves !" yelled the host. "Thieves !— thieves ! I will have satisfaction for this. I swear that I will cause a complaint to be laid before the Queen herself."

"Pah !" replied Sampson. "Don't trouble yourself with any such nonsense. Any documents sent to Her Majesty are used for Her Majesty's curl-papers. So ! here's confusion and bad trade to you ! In a few minutes you will find that I will place you where a petition, or a complaint, or whatever you like to call it, cannot be written to Her Majesty. Now, citizens, mugs forward !"

The citizens, screaming with laughter, seized upon the mugs, and thrust them towards Sampson to fill.

The host, vainly struggling to free himself, saw his hogshead of wine being rapidly emptied, and not the remotest chance of his being paid for it.

The sight was too much for him, and he burst into tears.

The hogshead was at last emptied.

And now every one wondered what the giant was about to do.

They were soon to be satisfied.

Sampson turned and seized hold of Cunningham's friend, who had scrambled out of the trough, and was sitting by the side of it looking a most miserable object, and lifting him up, placed him in the hogshead.

Then he caught hold of the host, dipped him in the trough, and then placed him by the side of the gallant.

This done, he took hold of the hogshead, carried it into the house, and placed it on the shelf from whence he had taken it.

He was followed by the whole crowd, and the laughter was now greater than ever.

The heads of the host and the gallant could be seen just a little higher than the rim of the cask.

Both of them knew well enough that if they attempted to scramble off, they and the hogshead would topple with a crash to the floor.

Going behind the counter, Sampson lifted up a trap door.

This led to the cellar.

"Now, host," cried Sampson, as he jumped up and stood on the counter, so that he could see them both, "you had better be careful, for the trap door is open, and if you get shifting about, you will fall through it. So we bid you a good-night, and all of us return you thanks for the liberal supply of wine you have been pleased to give us."

"Listen, good giant!" whined the host. "If you will let us——"

"Beware!" roared Sampson, "you are shifting the barrel. Another inch, and down you go!"

"Giant!—giant!" continued the host in pitiful tones. "I pray you take us down. I will give you a hundred crowns, and will say nothing about the matter if you will do so."

"Can't think of it!" replied Sampson; "but if you will remain there patiently, no doubt some one will rescue you soon. Fere thee well."

Sampson now put out the lamps, and pulled the door to.

The crowd commenced to disperse.

"You will, I am sure, pardon this delay, Oscar," said Sampson; "but it is absolutely necessary to teach these people a lesson sometimes. I will mount my horse, and you can sit behind me. We must not talk here."

Sampson mounted, and Goliar placed Oscar behind him.

The brothers then set out at a swift pace in the direction of St. James's Park.

At one of the shrubberies they halted, aed explanations followed on both sides.

Oscar was profuse in his thanks to the giants for all their care and all their trouble in his behalf.

"But, alas!" he said, gloomily, "the end will soon come. I feel it—here—here—on my heart! The document you have—will you give it me?"

"'Tis here," said Sampson, taking it from his breast, and handing it to Oscar. "Read it."

Oscar read the document, and then he deliberately tore it to pieces.

"Heaven!" cried Sampson, "what have you done?"

"Destroyed a useless document," was Oscar's reply; "for useless it would have been, Sampson. While Trevanion and his son are alive, I am never safe. Oh, that, instead of Captain Cartridge sending Cunningham to the Tower in the manner you have described, he had slain him! One villain, who lately has rendered my life wretched—one of those whose lies have rendered a once happy home miserable—would have been removed from my path."

"The day will soon come when both shall be removed, Oscar. Who knows what the documents, which I had removed from Trevanion's house, may prove?"

"They may prove a lot against him—on the other hand they may prove nothing. I fancy that Trevanion is too careful to leave anything which might ruin him, in a house with no one to guard it. However, time will prove. I am, as I said, about to proceed to the Wizard's house, where I shall probably remain for a time, for I am compelled, in consideration of what this wonderful man has done for me, to obey him. I have only one favour to ask you at present."

"And that?" asked Sampson, eagerly.

"To proceed——" (here Oscar's voice faltered) "to proceed to Tower Hill to my dear parents, and——"

"Say no more, Oscar," said Goliar, tenderly. "We will not fail to tell them everything. And now to the Wizard's house."

They turned and rode off to Whitehall.

Sampson, when they reached the Wizard's house, lifted Oscar to the ground, dismounted, and rang the bell.

The door was at once opened, and by the same old man as before.

He was about to ask a question, when Oscar held out his hand, on one of the fingers of which was the ring the Wizard had given him.

The old man bowed respectfully.

"Enter," he said.

"Heaven guard you, Oscar," said Sampson, in broken tones.

"And you, my best friends," was Oscar's reply.

"For your parents' sake, Oscar, I charge you do not give way. Though I like not the mysterious ways of Master Mervine, I know him to have great influence at Court. He has always taken a great interest in you and the Armourer. Trust in him, Oscar."

"I will—I do. Fare-thee-well."

"Fare-thee-well."

The door closed, and the brothers were alone.

They sat motionless on their horses for some few moments, and then rode slowly and thoughtfully away.

CHAPTER XVII.

SHOWS HOW LORD TREVANION OBTAINS MOST VALUABLE INFORMATION—HOW HE RETAILS IT
TO ELIZABETH—HOW SHE SHOWS WHAT A TERRIBLE TEMPER SHE HAS—HOW TREVANION
CLAIMS HIS REWARD, AND HOW OUR MOST IMPORTANT CHARACTERS ARE ORDERED TO BE
ARRESTED UNDER THE ROYAL WARRANT.

SIX days passed, and nothing of any great importance occurred.

During these six days our various characters were watching, as it were, each other.

By some means, information as to where Oscar was, reached the ears of Lord Trevanion, and, consequently, he soon came to the conclusion that it was the Wizard, who had assisted our hero to escape from the Tower.

He did not have to wait long before he got positive information as to who had fired and destroyed his house, and many were his vows of vengeance against the giants.

During the six days the Queen had removed from Whitehall to Windsor.

Festivities on a grand scale, it was supposed, were to be held at the Castle, and such, probably, would have been the case had it not been for the fact that disquieting news from Spain was being brought by almost every vessel which touched England's shores.

The Queen's high-tempered nerves were strained to the utmost.

Impatiently she waited for any scrap of news.

As soon as Windsor Castle was reached, the Council, with the Queen at its head, commenced its sittings, and the discussions were long and animated.

Then it was that Elizabeth showed of what she was really made—then, indeed, she, by her impassioned manner, by her splendid oratorial powers, showed that she possessed all the fiery blood of her royal sire, Henry VIII.

England, from its highest to its lowest quarter, was moved.

England trembled, not with fear, but with rage at the insults which were being flung at her from all quarters, and more especially by Spain.

Things were in this state on the evening of the sixth day after the incidents recorded in the previous chapter.

The day had been one of real splendour, and the prospects of a glorious harvest were only darkened by the grim shadow of the awful word —"WAR!" which, as it seemed, rested over England.

Notwithstanding the rumours flying about— notwithstanding the hurried tramp of troops through the streets, with drums rolling and banners flying—notwithstanding the rumble of cannon—albeit, then an almost certain sign of war, London itself was quiet.

Evening grew on apace, and darkness gradually stole over the city.

But though London, by degrees, became quite quiet, the Tower retained its busy appearance.

The interior and exterior swarmed with armed men, its courtyards resounded with the din of arms, horses neighed, officers roared out their commands, and the river swarmed with skiffs and barges which were either bringing officers or stores to the fortress.

On the battlement of the White Tower stood two persons.

Both were elaborately attired, and they were also well armed.

These two individuals were Lord Trevanion and his son.

Cunningham had never left the Tower since the night he was sent there in a sack by the humorous Captain Cartridge.

Though he longed to get a chance of revenge, he hardly dare leave the Tower for fear of something happening to him.

But during the six days father and son had been playing a deep game in the Tower.

By bribes judiciously bestowed, they had got into their power a man—a sort of attendant on the lieutenant—of the name of Campbell, a Scotsman, and a great lover of money.

Now this man was a personal friend—or, perhaps, we should say, a "drinking companion" —of Veleitch, the confidential servant and messenger of the Spanish Ambassador.

From this man Campbell, Trevanion and his son were waiting for a signal.

They paid but little attention to what was going on around them.

Their eyes were constantly strained towards the river.

"Be careful, Cunningham," said Trevanion, "or we shall not see it. By the Virgin, the noise these soldiers make is enough to drive a man mad! I am afraid we shall never hear the shot."

"Nay, nor see the flash if we are not careful; for see, the moon is now lost behind a bank of clouds."

"That is all the better to see the flash if we watch—remember, opposite Traitor's Gate."

Ten minutes passed.

Suddenly, far away in the distance, appeared a bright flash.

This was followed by a sharp crack.

A pistol had been fired in the air.

"*The signal,*" exclaimed Trevanion, joyfully. "And now for it! Art ready?"

"Quite."

"Wrap your cloak closely about you, and

"A BALL STRUCK SAMPSON ON THE CHEEK."

draw your hat well down over your brows. So now come."

They were about to pass down a flight of stairs which led to the lieutenant's apartments, when the lieutenant and a number of officers appeared before them.

"I was just about to seek you out, your lordship," said the lieutenant. Here, my lord, is a dispatch from Windsor."

And he handed Trevanion a small roll of parchment.

Trevanion, in great agitation, unfolded it, and read that his presence would be required in the Council Chamber at Windsor on the morrow "to discuss most urgent State affairs."

"The messenger waits," said the lieutenant.

"Let him convey a message to the Queen to the effect that I will not fail to obey her Majesty's gracious commands. We are about to leave the Tower, Fulmore, so we bid you adieu for the present. I need not say," he whispered, "that your assistance to me I thoroughly appreciate, and if I get the opportunity, which, no doubt, I shall, I will forward your interests with the Queen."

"Your lordship is too kind," said the lieutenant, placing his hand on his heart, and bowing. "I can hardly find words in which to express my gratitude to you. I am only too much aware how great is your lordship's influence at Court, and I need not say, that being, unfortunately, so poor as I am, the slightest favour your lordship is pleased to do me, will receive my heartfelt gratitude."

"Farewell then, Fulmore, and don't forget to send our horses to the 'Tower Arms.'"

"Farewell, my lord. Heaven keep you from all evil," said the hypocritical lieutenant.

"And the axe," said a voice.

"Who spoke?" cried Trevanion. "Who said the axe, I say?"

"Come, my lord," said Cunningham, taking his father's arms.

"'Twas nothing, my lord," said the lieutenant. "It was only the headsman telling his assistant to bring the block and the axe."

This was a lie, the headsman was not to be seen.

However it seemed to satisfy Lord Trevanion, for he allowed Cunningham to lead him away.

The lieutenant remained where he was, and when Trevanion had passed out of sight, he questioned those about him as to who had spoken.

Each man professed most emphatically that he had not opened his lips.

"By Heaven!" exclaimed the lieutenant, "'tis only too true that this tower is haunted. Even the very walls seem capable of hearing and speaking. Pray Heaven he does speak to the Queen of me, and she grants some favour. I would crave that I be sent to another post."

Leaving the Tower, Lord Trevanion and Cunningham crossed over to the "Tower Arms."

Avoiding the principal entrance, the pair walked round to the back of the house.

Trevanion produced a key and opened a door by the side of that which led to the kitchen, and he and Cunningham entered.

Having carefully closed the door, Trevanion stamped on the floor.

In a few seconds a short, red-faced female appeared carrying a lamp, which, with many a scrape and much blushing, she respectfully presented to his lordship.

"Mistress Punchard," said Trevanion, "your best room."

"Is all ready, your lordship?" replied Mistress Punchard. "Will your lordship be pleased to give me your commands?"

"Where is Stephen?"

"Busy in front, your lordship. The house is choke full of soldiers and warders, and such like."

"Hem! Well, the usual refreshments, and do not forget the brandy, And be quick. Also tell Stephen that when Campbell comes he is to be shown up to us at once."

Up the stairs went Trevanion and Cunningham, leaving Mistress Punchard bowing and scraping.

But she did neither as soon as they had turned the corner of the staircase.

On the contrary, she placed her fat fingers to her nose, and executed a kind of fantastic war-dance on the sanded floor.

"Got my husband under your thumb!" she muttered. "Yes, and more fool he! Oh, that I could tear off what little bit of hair you've got left on your wicked pate, you old villain! You wicked wretch you! May I have the satisfaction of seeing your head roll from the block, you infernal hypocrite you! If I thought you wouldn't find it out, I would put some poison in your brandy this very night, I would!"

A supper was served up to the pair as well as plenty of wine and brandy, and during their discussion of these refreshments the man Campbell ascended the stairs.

Being directed to enter, he opened the door, and stalked in.

He was a tall, red-headed, red-bearded, lantern-jawed fellow, of about fifty years of age, wearing a ragged costume, supposed to be Scotch.

He was armed with a "claymore" and a pistol.

Trevanion rose, and carefully locked the door, then he poured out some brandy, and handed it to Campbell, who drank it off at a gulp.

"Now your news," said Cunningham.

"Good, and of the utmost importance," was the reply. And there is no time to be lost, your lordship. It was only an hour ago that Veleitch disembarked at Wapping, where I accidentally met him. He told me confidentially that he had papers about him of vast importance, and which were to be conveyed to the ambassador at once. He said, my lord, 'there will be war against England before long.'"

"Go on."

"Acting on your instructions, your lordship, I persuaded him to come here, and pass an hour. After awhile he consented, so he will be here before very long."

"Good! good! Now, Campbell, here are ten crowns—take them,"

"My thanks to your lordship."

"And another hundred shall be yours if you get those papers from this man, and hand them over to me."

"I thought your lordship was to do that?"

"We will assist you so far as this. Look," and Trevanion took from his pocket a small phial, "this is a drug. Take it, and drop into a bottle of wine half of it. Go into the room opposite this, and wines and other things shall be sent into you. Reserve a bottle for Veleitch, which you must drug ready. When Veleitch comes, Stephen Punchard shall show him up.

Now, you understand?"

"Yes, I understand. Well, I will do it. I don't mind so long as there's no bloodshed."

"But if there was to be bloodshed, you would do it for a hundred crowns, eh, Campbell?" said Cunningham. "Remember, you have done it before."

"Not for you."

"No; but for others."

"Perhaps I have; but——"

"Say no more, Campbell," interrupted Trevanion. "Go and do as you are bid."

"But the hundred crowns?"

"I have them with me. As soon as the papers are in my possession, the crowns shall be in yours, and you may then go on to beggarly Scotland, and be hanged to you!"

"I thank your lordship," grinned Campbell, as he unlocked the door, and walked into the opposite room.

All necessary articles were provided by Stephen Punchard himself, for this man, like so many others, was in the power of Trevanion, and his lordship threatened him that if he did not do the work he wanted, instead of allowing his wife to do it, it would be worse for him.

About an hour passed, and then Stephen Punchard was heard saying—

"This way, sir—this way please. You have, perhaps, not been this way before. I assure you, 'tis more select than below. More suited to foreigners, like yourself."

"Thanks, thanks," responded a voice in broken English. "You are very kind. I shall remember your hospitality. Ha, Campbell! Well, you look snug enough. Ha, ha! this is quite enjoyable."

It was Veleitch, the Spanish Ambassador's servant, whose principal failing was a love of good wines.

Stephen Punchard ushered him into the room with all ceremony, and then pushing open the door of the opposite chamber, he whispered—

"He has arrived, and the horses have come over from the Tower."

Trevanion nodded, and Stephen descended the stairs.

"Sit down, Veleitch," said Campbell, placing a chair by the table, which had been liberally provided with wines, spirits, and eatables, "and enjoy yourself for the short time you are here."

"As I said, I cannot stay long," was Veleitch's reply, "for my message is important—the most important message in fact I have ever carried. I would not tell you so, only I know that you, as a Scotsman, have no love for the English."

"You are right there," said Campbell, as he poured Veleitch out a tumbler of wine from the drugged bottle. "If the Thames would rise and drown the lot, I should be glad of it."

"Providing you had a boat, Senor Campbell," laughed Veleitch, as he placed the tumbler to his lips, and took a pull, which nearly emptied it.

Campbell drank brandy; but while he talked and drank he narrowly watched Veleitch, on whom, however, the drugged wine seemed to have no effect, for he chatted away merrily at the prospects of a war between Spain and England.

But after another half-tumbler his eyes grew heavy, his talk became more and more confused, ond once or twice he actually yawned.

However, he seemed to know that he was becoming drowsy, for suddenly exerting himself, he sat upright in his chair.

"Strong wine this," he said. "I never felt so strange after drinking wine before. The Virgin protect me" he cried, starting up, and grasping the chair. "Ha! what is this—this feeling—mists around me? I go round and round. Campbell—this—is this some devil's trick of yours, or—is—it——. Heaven!" he screamed, "I see it—I see it—you Campbell! Traitor! False friend! I see the poison in your plaid!"

This was only too true.

Campbell had stuck the phial in his plaid, and the position in which he had seated himself had raised, and so exposed it.

"You are in the pay of the English government!" shrieked Veleitch, "and you have poisoned me! But my message shall never be known—never—never!"

He tore open his doublet.

Next his skin—exactly over his heart—were the papers he was bearing to his master.

He snatched them out, and was about to tear them to pieces, when Campbell plucked his claymore from its sheath, and rushed upon him.

But Veleitch started back with a wild cry, and drew his sword.

The weapons crossed.

Campbell was too impetuous.

Dashing forward, his foot caught in a stool, and he was thrown on his face to the floor.

The Spaniard took advantage of this.

His sword flashed, for an instant, in the rays of the lamp, and the next it was plunged to the half in Campbell's body.

"Saved!" gasped the Spaniard, swaying to and fro, as he waved the papers aloft. "Oh, heaven; but a moment to destroy them, but a moment——"

Nay, he was not allowed to destroy the fatal papers.

His face turned ashy pale, his eyes became glassy as they fixed themselves upon the precious documents, and then with a low, gurgling cry, he fell across the body of his false friend.

The phial had not merely contained a drug,

from the effects of which a man would in time recover.

No. It was a deadly poison the Spaniard had partaken of.

As he fell, Trevanion and Cunningham entered the room.

"Both dead!" cried Cunningham.

"Most fortunate," was Trevanion's reply. "Nothing is due to Campbell. See, my son, this Spanish dog has the papers clutched in his hand. "Wrench them out!"

Cunningham stooped and wrenched the papers from the fast stiffening hand of the murdered Spaniard.

Trevanion, his hands trembling as though he were afflicted with the palsy, took them.

To break off the seals which were attached to them, and to tear off the ribbons was the work of an instant.

"Come here, my son," he said, in hoarse tones, "and let us give a brief examination. So, now hold the lamp. Truly, truly, my son, good luck seems to be returning to us once more. If this proves to be the news I fancy, we are made—made for ever! Ha!"

"What is it, your lordship?"

"See here—see here. What says this? 'Tis written in Spanish. Observe, my son, this is the handwriting of the King of Spain himself. I know it well. What says he? 'Secretly our preparations for war against England have been going on for a long time. We have spent, and are spending, millions of pounds in organising a fleet of vessels which will sweep the seas clear —no matter if every nation under the sun combine to oppose us. This, our well-beloved Jerome, is a private and most secret piece of information from *ourself*, and as soon as you have read this paper, be very careful to *utterly destroy it*. We may add, Jerome, that nothing whatever can stay our resolve, though you will do well, if summoned to Windsor, to pretend that terms may be offered to us'."

"Lord!" exclaimed Trevanion, clutching the documents tightly. "Lord! here we have what is intended, in the King's own handwriting. This is the finest stroke of fortune I have ever had!"

"Fail not to turn it to account," said Cunningham.

"Fear it not, my son, fear it not!"

"I mean so that *both* of us will benefit. You seem to pay all the attention to yourself, my lord, and none to me."

"You accuse me wrongly, Cunningham. I am continually thinking of you, and of the best way of benefiting you."

"Hem! Well, you have said scores of times that you have repeatedly spoken of me to the Queen; however that may be, 'tis certain she takes no notice of it."

"Patience, my son—patience," replied Trevanion, hastily refastening the papers. "We have had ill-fortune lately, but this will be the turning point. By the Virgin, I am sure of it. Let us now hasten——"

"But what is to be done with these two?" asked Cunningham. "It would be dangerous to leave them here. It would, at any rate, be far better to bury this Spaniard, and——"

"Let us have both of them buried. Stephen Punchard will assist us. Let us summon him at once. But stay, I hear a footstep, perhaps——"

Ere he could say more, the door was very unceremoniously pushed open, and Mistress Punchard appeared.

Of course, the first things which met her eyes were the two corpses on the floor.

Holding up her hands she was about to scream, when Cunningham placed his hand on her mouth, and dragged her into the room.

"Silence, woman!" he said, fiercely. "What do you want?"

"Nothing, now," stammered Mistress Punchard. Nothing. Oh, dear, dear me! This awful sight will be the death of me. I thought I heard the clash of weapons. And I am right. Another murder at the 'Tower Arms!' Oh, dear! oh, dear!"

And the really frightened woman wrung her hands and moaned hysterically.

"Listen to me!" said Trevanion, who was somewhat alarmed lest the company below should get to know of what had occurred. "Listen to me! You are quite aware that if I think proper, I can sell this house over your head?"

"I am!—I am!"

"Well, I have no desire to do so; but, in order to retain possession here, you and your husband are to do as you are told. Now, my instructions to you are—keep a still tongue in your head. Speak to a living soul of what you see here, and, by Heaven, you shall suffer for it! Depart! and send your husband here."

Mistress Punchard descended the stairs, invoking anything but blessings on his lordship's head.

Stephen Punchard soon appeared.

"Stephen," said Trevanion, "you see those two men?"

"I do."

"They have been fighting, and have slain each other."

Stephen, without a word, turned them over, and examined them.

"I see that *one* has been run through,' he said; "but I see no wound on the other's body."

"Never mind about wounds," said Cunningham, impatiently; "they are dead, that is sufficient."

"One has been poisoned," said Stephen, significantly.

"We are quite aware of it," said Trevanion, "and so we do not want you to tell us. What we want of you is this—these men are to be taken to your vaults and buried."

"Very well, my lord. Your commands must, of course, be obeyed. But this Spaniard was the confidential servant and messenger of the Spanish Ambassador, and he may have—he must have—most important papers about his person. Shall I search him?"

"No!" yelled Trevanion. "I know what you mean well enough. I have the papers. No one knows who this man really is, not even your wife; therefore at your peril mention his name!"

"I am, as your lordship has always found me, the very essence of secrecy,"

"Yes; you have always done as you have been told, which is well for you. Do this job neatly, and fifty crowns shall be yours."

"I thank your lordship. Your commands shall be at once carried out. I will get my man to——"

"Idiot!"

"Well, I crave your lordship's pardon," said Stephen firmly; "but I cannot, and *will* not, bury these men unless I am assisted."

"*We* will assist you. You have spades and pickaxes?"

"Plenty in the vaults."

"That will do. For the nonce we will transform ourselves into labourers."

Assisted by Cunningham and Trevanion, Stephen got the unfortunate Spanish servant on to his back.

"Follow with the other man," he said, "and I will lead the way to the vaults by a secret staircase."

"Lead on, then," said Cunningham, "we follow."

But Cunningham did not hoist the dead Scotsman on *his* back.

He took off the man's belt, fastened it round his ankles, and *dragged* him along.

The vault, where the ale was kept, was soon reached, and Stephen, throwing down his burden, procured spades and pickaxes.

Assisted by Trevanion and his son, he rolled aside a couple of hogsheads, and then he and Cunningham set to work.

A grave was dug and the two dead men were flung in.

The earth and the hogshead were then replaced.

"So now that is concluded," said Trevanion, "let us have a bottle of your finest wine, and we will depart.

"Pray heaven you never return!" muttered Stephen, as he went off to fetch the wine.

He was gone some considerable time, much to the annoyance of Trevanion and his son, neither of whom could have got out of the vault unassisted.

On his return, Stephen said—

"Your lordship must be careful how you travel, for the streets, they say, are full of people, and if you are recognised——"

"Say no more, master host," interrupted Cunningham. "We are prepared to risk all. We *must* go through the streets."

Stephen made no reply to this.

He sullenly took the fifty crowns offered him, and as sullenly led the way above.

Trevanion and his son were soon in their saddles.

"Draw your cloak closely about you," said Trevanion, "and let your horse feel that you have spurs on your heels. Ready?"

"Ay, ay."

"Away then!"

The animals bounded forward, and, urged on by the repeated application of the spur, made their way through the city at a terrific rate.

At Westminster the pair halted, and put up at an inn for a few hours, their intention being to proceed to Windsor after a brief rest.

∘　∘　∘　∘　●

The morning broke fine and bright.

At ten o'clock the town of Windsor was in a state of intense excitement.

Tradesmen had neglected their shops to watch the arrivals at the castle.

Noblemen, with their ladies and their splendid trains, were continually pouring down the principal roads.

The scene in and about the castle was superb in the extreme.

A selection of soldiers from almost every regiment in England were present.

The courtyards, battlements, and corridors were full of armed men and officers.

Here and there were to be seen little knots of lords and knights discussing affairs while surrounding them, stood their esquires, pages, and other attendants.

Arms and armour flashed in the sun's rays, banners waved, clarions sounded, mounted messengers dashed hither and thither, while, above all, high up on the highest point of the castle, floated the proud banner of England.

Amid the excitement, consequent on the arrivals of the more showy trains, the approach of Trevanion and his son was almost unnoticed.

They came along the Slough-road quietly, yet swiftly, and they took no notice of what was passing around them.

Entering the castle, they placed their horses in the charge of an attendant, and then Trevanion led the way to the Green ante-room.

They found this apartment, which then led into the Throne-room, crammed with nobles of all degrees; and, from the looks on their faces, and the eager way in which they were talking, it was evident that they were discussing news of the gravest importance.

The Earl of Surrey was the first to recognise Trevanion.

"Your lordship is very welcome I should say," he said. "Her Majesty was speaking of you at intervals all day yesterday."

"Is her Majesty——"

"The Queen is in the Throne-room. She has just entered. Did you come down by the Slough-road, your lordship?"

"Yes."

"You did not chance to see the Spanish Ambassador?"

"Nay is he expected?" asked Trevanion, with as much apparent unconcern as he was able to assume.

"He is. He should have been here yesterday. Instead of him coming, however, a messenger arrived to say that the ambassador would wait until the morrow, as he expected news of the greatest importance to arrive from Spain."

"Oh, indeed."

An usher approaching at this moment, he was directed to announce Trevanion's arrival.

As soon as this was made known to the Queen,

Trevanion was directed to appear before her Majesty.

Cunningham, of course, followed him.

Almost at the same moment the Spanish Ambassador was announced.

As his tall and striking figure stalked into the ante-room, he was greeted with stern looks—they spoke plainer than words.

The Spanish Ambassador nearly always wore a smile on his face ; but on this occasion his look betokened anxiety, not unmixed with alarm.

His arrival being announced he, too, was ushered into the Throne-room, whither the whole of the nobles followed.

At the extreme end of the Throne-room, upon a raised dais, sat Elizabeth.

She was seated upon a magnificently carved, gilt throne, under a beautiful white and blue canopy, hung with pearls, embroidered with the royal arms, and bearing the inscription—

"𝔇𝔦𝔢𝔲 𝔢𝔱 𝔐𝔬𝔫 𝔇𝔯𝔬𝔦𝔱."

Her Majesty, who was attired in a robe of violet-coloured velvet, edged with ermine, and who wore upon her head a small crown studded with brilliants and pearls, was surrounded by her ladies-in-waiting, her chief nobles and advisers, and, at the back of them, four deep, were ranged lines of halberdiers.

As Trevanion advanced, and bent his knee, he took a rapid look at the face of the Queen. Never had he seen her with such a look.

It made him tremble.

Elizabeth motioned him to rise, and was about to speak to him, when she caught sight of the Spanish Ambassador, and, therefore, she waved him aside.

"What is your news ? " asked the Queen, almost before the ambassador could make his obeisance.

" I have little, your Majesty," said the ambassador. " I was expecting news from Spain yesterday and early this morning ; but I am sorry to say my messenger has not reached me. It is strange, too, your Majesty, for that he arrived in London last night I am certain, for I have seen the captain of the vessel in which he sailed."

Silence reigned for some few moments—a deep, painful silence—the dropping of a pin might have been heard.

The Queen looked fixedly at the Spanish Ambassador.

At last she said in harsh tones—

" And might we ask what news was expected ? "

" Of a surety your Majesty ! " replied the ambassador, bowing low. " The news I should have received would have been, no doubt, to the effect that the terms your Majesty's Government had proposed were accepted by my royal master, and——"

" 'Tis false ! " shouted Trevanion, taking two paces forward, snatching the fatal papers from his breast, and waving them aloft—" 'tis false ! Here, your Majesty, is the expected news—here——"

" Villain ! " cried the ambassador, laying his hand on his sword hilt. " Villain ! you——"

" Hold ! " exclaimed the Queen, starting up, and raising her hand to check the advance of the guard who, at the cry of " Treason ! " raised by one of the nobles had rushed forward. " Hold ! Withdraw, my lords and gentlemen ! Nothing is amiss. Keep back—there is no treason yet ! The Spanish Ambassador must have the respect generally given to all foreigners. When he laid his hand on his sword, he forgot, for a moment, we were present. My Lord Trevanion, hand us those papers."

Trevanion did so, but the ambassador looked as though he would snatch them from his hand.

With trembling hands, with teeth tightly set, Elizabeth tore them open, and deliberately read them one after the other.

All were written in French, with the exception of one, and that was the Spanish document Trevanion had read.

" There is nothing of any moment in these," said Elizabeth ; " but here we have a message written in Spanish, and by Heaven ! though I cannot read Spanish, I recognise here the Royal hand of Spain. Is this so, Trevanion ? "

" Your Majesty is quite correct," replied Trevanion.

" So, and you read Spanish, Trevanion ? "

" I do, your Majesty."

" And can translate this message to us ? "

" Easily, your Majesty."

" Take it, and do so. Read it aloud. We have no secrets. Go on."

Having read it to himself again, Trevanion was enabled to give a very free translation of the document.

He was interrupted several times by expressions of horror and surprise.

The Queen stood erect, and perfectly still.

When Trevanion had finished, and a hush had fallen upon all—when the ambassador, who was himself thunderstruck at such a message being sent to him, had slunk back as if to avoid the look Elizabeth bestowed on him—the Queen said—

" This is how we are treated, my lords. We, the daughter of Henry VIII. I can scarce believe it. So, your master is organising a fleet which will sweep the seas. By our father's soul, we shall see that. We shall see that, I say ! " she almost screamed, as she stamped her foot passionately on the dais. " Tell your master that the Queen of England has charged you to say that if your master were to build a fleet which would cover the sea from end to end, there would still be Englishmen left who would break through it ! "

" Nothing can stay this resolve, eh ? Nay ! Heaven forbid that *we* should utter a wish that he might stay such an insane resolve. Tell your royal master that we now refuse to make any terms—tell him that we hurl our defiance in his teeth ; tell him that the Queen of England has honest and brave men at her back, and that her nobles are ready and willing to shed their life's blood in behalf of their country ; tell him that if every one of these nobles fell *Elizabeth herself* would take a sword in her hand, and lead her troops on to victory !"

At these words a loud cheer burst from the throats of the assembled hundreds.

Still further back shrank the ambassador—fear had taken possession of him—he thought that his arrest was certain.

But he was mistaken.

" Do not forget to tell your royal master what we have said," cried Elizabeth. " You are quite certain you will not forget ? "

'There is no fear of that, your Majesty."

"Very well.   And now——"

" Pardon the interruption," exclaimed the Spaniard, " but your Majesty has not asked Lord Trevanion how he obtained possession of those papers."

" Ha, that we had forgotten.   But it is now a matter of but little importance.   Still it is——"

" The way in which I obtained possession of them, your Majesty," said Trevanion, " is very simple.   We found the servant to the Spanish Ambassador drunk in the streets, and waving these papers over his head.   People laughed at him for a drunken fool ; but we—that is my son and I, your Majesty—thinking thieves would get possession of the papers—took possession of them ourselves."

" Your story may sound well enough," said the ambassador," and it may here pass as fact, but I do not believe it.   Where did you leave my servant, your lordship ?"

" Near the Tower."

" If he can be found, no doubt he will put a different complexion on the matter."

" Ay, if he can be found," chuckled Trevanion.

The Queen dismissed the ambassador and retired to the Council-chamber,

" 'Tis war, my lords !" she muttered, fiercely. " War to the knife ! Let us, therefore, prepare for it."

Trevanion managed to intercept her, and craved a boon.

" What is it ? " asked the Queen, impatiently.

" The arrest of these persons, your Majesty. It is of the utmost importance."

And he placed a sheet of parchment before her.

But the Queen was too agitated to read it. She did not even take the trouble to look at the names of the persons Trevanion proposed to arrest.

" Is it important to us that these persons should be arrested ? " she asked.

" It is, your Majesty."

" Well, well.   I will not question your object since it is evident how devoted you are to your Queen and country.   We will sign it at once, and the Royal seals shall be attached.   But you do not intend personally to conduct these arrests ?"

" Nay, your Majesty.   My son will attend to this."

The Queen nodded, and amid loud blasts of the trumpets, entered the Council-room.

In less than an hour Trevanion joined his son.

His face was radiant with joy as he held the Royal warrant before Cunningham's eyes.

" Behold it !" he cried.   " All signed and sealed.   Now we have them ! "

Cunningham took the warrant, and carefully read it.

It authorised the arrest of the brothers Sylvester, the Wizard, and Oscar.

" Arrangements shall at once be made," said Trevanion, " for you to be accompanied by two hundred men.   Take first the giants, who will, no doubt, be found at Eastcheap or Tower Hill, then proceed to Whitehall, where there is not the slightest doubt you will find this accursed youth with the Wizard.   If you fail this time——"

" Do not fear it," grinned Cunningham. " Give me but two hundred men and a couple of reliable officers, and by Heaven I will not fail ! "

While the Council was holding its sitting, Cunningham and two hundred soldiers, under two captains, left the castle.

Trevanion watched their departure from one of the windows of the Council-chamber, and when the glitter of their arms disappeared in the distance, he breathed freely, for now he considered there was no chance of the Queen countermanding the warrant.

CHAPTER XVIII.

☞ OF THE SEARCH FOR THE GIANTS—HOW THEY WERE DISCOVERED—OF THEIR FLIGHT—HOW THEY TOOK REFUGE IN OLD ST. PAUL'S AND OF WHAT TERRIBLE EVENTS FOLLOWED.

At the period of this romance the roads from Windsor to London were poor ones in the extreme.

Cunningham was the only one of the party mounted, so that he did not become so distressed as the men and their officers.

Though fearfully impatient to push on at a rapid pace, Cunningham knew well enough it would be wise for him to make no complaint at the slow progress the men were making, so he said nothing.

Wishing to appear liberal, he called a halt at almost every alternate inn, and had refreshments supplied to the men, a course of proceeding which met with the hearty appreciation of the soldiers, who became more and more desirous of settling accounts with the Giant Brothers of Eastcheape.

The result of Cunningham's liberality was, as may be supposed, that the soldiers got into a high state of "jollity."

London, proper, was reached just after nightfall.

By that time Cunningham's men were in a most reckless condition, indeed.

At the "Henry VIII." tavern in the Strand, a halt was made for the last time.

The men were carefully regaled with brandy, and at last they announced themselves fit for anything.

Arms were looked to, especially the guns, the flints and locks of which were, one after the other, examined by Cunningham himself.

All being in readiness, the order was given to march to Eastcheap, whither we will precede them.

*   *   *   *   *

After leaving Oscar at Whitehall, the giants proceeded with their horses to the showman, from whom they had borrowed them, paid him the money he required, and then they repaired to the residence of the Armourer.

There they passed many hours, and they did not leave until they had made the Armourer and his wife acquainted with all that had transpired, and had left them quite easy in their minds as to their son's safety.

The Armourer had an enormous amount of work on hand, but not being in fit condition to carry it out, he asked the giants to do it, and receive the payment which would come to him, in advance.

The brothers readily agreed to perform the task, and the next day saw their forges in full swing.

They could work like horses when it pleased them, and on this occasion they worked as they had never worked before.

All day long, and far into the night, their forges glowed, and the tremendous din they made as they wielded their hammers could have been heard a long way off.

The neighbours were delighted at the resumption of work by the giants, on whom they seemed to look as their protectors.

Our old friend, "Carroty Charles," who was with the brothers every hour he could spare, was also delighted that the giants had returned to their old shop.

While Cunningham and his men were steadily advancing—creeping on them without the slightest warning—the brothers were hard at it.

But, though busy hammering the glowing metal into shape,—the brothers did not forget to speak of what was uppermost in their minds.

"It is strange, brother," said Sampson, "that we have received no word from Oscar."

"Ay, strange, indeed," was the reply. "But there—he is still at the house of that mysterious man, or we should have heard to the contrary."

"Though we have not heard from him, it is strange that he has sent no message to his father, the Armourer."

"Yes, you are right. But, brother, you may depend upon it, affairs are as we have for some time thought. There is some great secret between the Wizard and the Armourer."

"Ay I begin to think so, too. I have had strange thoughts about this youth lately. I am inclined to the belief that—hist! what is that noise?"

A sound, as of the rushing of many feet, had reached their ears.

Sampson went to the door, and swung it open.

He was startled to behold a great crowd of persons.

One of them—a near neighbour—cried out—

"Fly, Sampson, fly; the troops are coming to arrest you and your brother!"

"Arrest us?" "For what?"

"I know not; but the troops with Cunningham Trevanion at their head, are close here."

"How many of them?"

"Two hundred."

"Two hundred!" exclaimed Sampson and Goliar in a breath. "What a pity they did not make it *four* hundred while they were about it! But surely you must be mistaken, and you——"

"He was interrupted by a loud voice, crying—Halt—Ground arms."

In another instant Cunningham rode up to the door, a captain on each side of him.

"My name," said Cunningham, thinking it likely that the giants might not recognise him, "is Cunningham Trevanion."

"Ay, ay," replied Sampson. "There cannot be much doubt about that, for any fool could recognise your ugly face a mile off."

"Your insults will avail you naught," said Cunningham, "neither your statue, nor your strength, will prevent you from being taken and lodged in the Tower, where, ere long, the accursed gallow's bird, you for so long have been pleased to protect, will soon follow you, as well as the Wizard—the arch imposter."

"Your weak stomach is seemingly able to allow you to utter strong words, Master Trevanion," said Sampson, fiercely. "By whose orders are we to be arrested?"

"By orders of the Queen."

"I will not believe it. We rendered the Queen a great service."

"And the reward you will both get," said Cunningham, grinding his teeth, "will be a rope."

"The hemp to make a rope to fit our necks," grinned Sampson, "is not yet grown. But there—there—we have work to do, so be off with you, and take your soldiers, who——"

"Griffiths," cried Cunningham, "come forward and read the warrant."

"A warrant!" exclaimed Sampson, amazed.

Griffiths, one of the captains, stepped forward and read the warrant.

Griffiths having finished reading then drawing his sword, said—

"We arrest you—the brothers Sylvester, blacksmiths. Is it blacksmiths, your lordship?"

"*Yes!*" roared Sampson, "*blacksmiths and skull-crackers!*"

Griffiths stepped back quickly.

But he was too late!

The giant swung his ponderous hammer round

his head, and down it came with a loud and sickening crash on the captain's helmet.

The captain's head was crushed into a mass of pulp.

A loud cry of horror escaped the lips of all who witnessed this awful deed.

A soldier, standing near the unfortunate captain, raised his gun to fire, but Goliar, snatching a long rod of red-hot iron from the furnace, clapped it across his face.

It left a mark which he would carry to his grave.

"Back, brother!" cried Sampson. "Back!"

He pushed Goliar further into the smithy, and banged the door to just as a volley was fired by the soldiers."

"We have no chance against so many, armed as they are, brother," said Sampson, as he fastened the door. "But by all the fiends we will not be taken if we can help it! We must escape!"

"True, brother," replied Goliar. "A wise plan on my soul! But how?"

"I have it. The trap."

While the soldiers were hammering on the door—while Cunningham and Markham were offering huge bribes to any one who would bring hammers and axes to break open the door, and while the now excited soldiers were discharging their pieces at random through every crack they could find, the giants were throwing aside the piles of swords, daggers, spearheads, and so on, which lay in the centre of the smithy.

This was soon accomplished, and a large trap-door was revealed.

Catching hold of the iron ring, Sampson threw the door back, and then reaching down their swords from the wall, they leapt down the hole.

The trap-door led to another, which opened into the roadway a little way down.

Cunningham, who had dismounted, had, through one of the cracks, seen the giants jump into the aperture, and he appealed to the crowd of neighbours and others to tell him where it led.

But every one protested they did not know; yet our readers may be assured that the majority of them knew well enough.

"We must do it suddenly, brother," said Sampson; "it is our only chance. When I fling the door back, do you leap out, and I will follow."

Goliar was ready, and as Sampson reached up and flung back the door, he placed his hands on the sides, and lept out.

Sampson was instantly at his side.

But what little noise they made had attracted the attention of the soldiers, and also of Cunningham, who bawled out at the top of his voice—

"Fire!"

Those of the soldiers who happened to have their weapons loaded, raised and fired them, but too late, for the giants had rounded the corner.

"Follow!" roared Cunningham. "Follow, and spare not your powder!"

He did not wait to remount his horse, but placing himself at Markham's side, at the head of the men, he rushed off.

Away they went down Eastcheap and along Cheapside at a terrific rate.

The noise they made was fearful, for the soldiers kept on shouting and yelling, with all their might—

"Stop them! Stop them!"

It was not likely anyone would attempt to stop the giants, though.

Unfortunately, the bulkiness of the huge brothers prevented them from running so as to quickly out-distance their pursuers, still they kept some distance ahead.

Now and then one soldier or the other fired a ball after them, and, had the houses been constructed as they are at the present day, it is almost certain one of them would have been hit.

At last St. Paul's was reached.

The grand old cathedral appeared to be wrapped in silence and darkness.

It was evidently Sampson's intention to go down Ludgate Hill; but, as they passed the north corner of the cathedral, he saw that the door of the vestry was open, and that a light was burning within.

The verger and the sexton were discussing some matter on the threshold.

"Sanctuary, brother!" cried Sampson; and, before the startled verger could shut the door, the giants had bolted into the cathedral.

"He who enters here, when pursued by enemies, is safe, brother," said Sampson. "Good sir," he added to the verger, "for no crime whatever; for, if you will think you will recognise in us the giant blacksmiths of Eastcheap, for no crime, I say, sir, we are pursued by a swarm of the Queen's troops, and——"

"Then I am sorry for you," interrupted the verger; for though this sacred place is the temporary refuge of all who find themselves in danger of arrest, I am bound to admit the Queen's troops if the officer in command produces a warrant. Can he do this?"

"He can, sir. I—but here they are—away, Goliar, let us take our chance!"

While Cunningham, gasping for breath, was endeavouring to find the warrant which the verger would persist in seeing, the giants penetrated further and further into the sacred edifice.

Sampson and his brother were perfectly well acquainted with the cathedral, for, on more than one occasion, they had been employed in fixing the ironwork both in and outside.

Near the choir a huge brass lamp was dimly burning.

Sampson turned up the wick, and took hold of the lamp.

"Here, Goliar," he said, "is the flight of stairs leading to St. Faith's" (St. Paul's Crypt), "let us descend. Even if they follow this way we can ascend the stairs on the opposite side. Oh, that we had firearms and plenty of powder and shot. Lord, we would give them a warm reception indeed."

The door leading to the crypt was locked; but Sampson, by exerting all his tremendous strength, soon wrenched it open, and led the way.

St Paul's crypt, at the time of our romance, was the place where books and documents, belonging to the clergy and to the various schools and societies attached to St. Paul's, were stored.

There were some thousands of books of all sorts and sizes.

It was a precious storehouse of learning, and so it remained nntil the Great Fire of London, when almost every book and document was destroyed by, as Samuel Pepys has it, the "revengeful, remorseless, bloody, and unnatural flames, which for many days and nights, made London a very hell!"

"Mind the light, brother," said Goliar, "or perchance a stray spark may set fire to all these strange looking books."

"I have a tinder box in my pocket," said Sampson, "so I will blow out the lamp, and do you keep tight hold of it, for it may be useful."

"Do you propose to wait here?"

"Well, we shall see if they will search the place."

"There's not much doubt of *that*, brother."

"Then draw your blade," said Sampson, grimly, as he unsheathed his sword. "Both of us have been in too many dangers to fear death. But if the worst comes to the worst, and we see that we are safe to be captured, let us give London and the lying Queen, and the Court, cause to speak of the circumstance for many a day. Brother, I am roused as I have not been roused before! Fools that we were to rescue a Queen who could smile one moment and grant a favour, and then lie the next."

"We have indeed been most foully used," said Goliar. "Yet methinks it is not all the fault of the Queen. But hark! Do you hear them?"

"Ay, ay. They are making noise enough."

That was, indeed, true,

The whole of the soldiers were now in the cathedral, and the tramp of their heavy feet, the clash of their weapons, and the crash of heavy articles the soldiers pulled from their places to find the giants, were only too distinct.

Above these noises could be heard the voices of Cunningham and Captain Markham.

Suddenly a loud cry arose.

The giants heard the door, through which they had entered, pulled violently open, and Cunningham cry out:

"This way—this way—they have decended these stairs! Come forward you with the links."

Two soldiers, with a flaming link each, hurried forward, and soon the whole crowd of soldiers had collected.

"Now then!" almost screamed Cunningham, "do not hesitate—descend!"

But the men *did* hesitate.

Not more than two abreast could descend the stairs, and the soldiers considered it certain that the first two to go would never come up again alive.

"Cowards!" cried Markham, snatching a link from one of the men, "I will lead the way, and do you follow."

The brandy he had consumed had put a good deal of Dutch courage into Markham.

He descended the stairs, followed by the men.

Cunningham, the reader will be pleased to understand, thought it safer—very *much* safer—to keep in the background.

"They come, brother," whispered Samson. "Do you cross over and open the other door."

"But what do *you* intend to do?"

"Follow you, of course. Lord! that I was in possession of a couple of pistols! The men are being led by the other captain. Go, brother —go."

Sampson took in his enormous hand a huge Bible; truly, it was a monster, and must have weighed twenty pounds.

This he raised over his head.

Down the stairs came Markham; but, slowly and carefully, for he had never in his life before been here, and he knew not what was in front of him.

His foot had touched the last stair but one, when Sampson, stepping back a pace, the better to put all his force into action, flung the bible at him.

It hit Markham full in the face with a mighty "thwack," and the captain, uttering a loud scream of pain, toppled forward, and fell in a heap, a dozen or more men falling on the top of him.

Sampson afterwards said that no person on earth ever preached the Gospel with greater force than he flung it on this occasion.

Loud and bitter were the curses of the discomfited Markham, and frantic were his endeavours to throw off the soldiers on the top of him.

"What is the reason of this delay?" yelled Cunningham, for the narrow passage being blocked with the soldiers, he could see nothing of what had occurred. "Go on, idiots—go on! Have you found them, Markham?"

"No;" blubbered Markham. "But a large book has found me!"

What had occurred was soon explained to Cunningham, who ground his teeth his rage.

"But they cannot escape!" he muttered. "They cannot escape, for the verger swore that all the other doors were locked. By all the fiends, we shall have them yet!"

Several of Markham's teeth had been knocked out, his nose bled furiously, and altogether, in that brief space of time, he was transformed into a pretty looking object.

Certainly it was a wonder that the terrific blow had not killed him outright.

Cunningham, fearful that the giants would manage to secrete themselves somewhere, and thus cause a long search, pushed his way down the stairs.

He would not have done so, only he now felt convinced that the giants did not carry firearms, and that therefore, there was no chance of a ball reaching him.

"Rouse yourself, Markham!" he cried, "Which way have they gone?"

"How should I know?" replied Markham, as he vainly attempted to stop the blood flowing from his almost flattened nose. "It is all very well to say 'Rouse yourself!' Just look at the size of the book they flung at me. Why, it was enough to fell an ox. Had I seen it coming, I would have got out of the way."

Cunningham seized a torch, and, looking round the crypt, he espied the door through which the giants had gone.

"Look, Markham," he said, exultingly, "they have gone this way. Now we have them, for there is no other way to the choir."

But if Cunningham imagined that the doorway did not lead anywhere, he was very much mistaken.

True it was that it did not lead to the choir; but it led to a staircase by which the very roofs and tower of the cathedral could be reached.

Markham roused himself, and, again taking the link, and grasping his sword firmly, he went to the door, and pulled it open.

"'Fore Heaven!" he said; "this is, indeed, a terrible-looking hole. The thing is, to what part of the cathedral does it lead?"

"I know not. But I know this—that these continued delays will give those men every chance of escape. Lead the way, Markham; and, if they are captured, a large reward shall be yours. You have little to fear, for they have no firearms."

"Nay, that may be; but they have long swords, and devilish long arms to wield them. However, though, so far, I have received the worst of the encounter, it shall never be said that I drew back when I had two hundred men behind me. Now, you will be pleased to leave all arrangements in my hands?"

"I will," replied Cunningham.

"Good. Twelve of you," said Markham to his men—"twelve of you come forward!"

Twelve stepped up.

"Are your guns loaded?"

"They are, captain,' was the reply.

"That's well. Now, mark what I say. Where this staircase leads I know not. You will observe that is of the shape of a corkscrew. Good. At every turn six of you stop and fire upward, then retire and let the other six fire at the next turn, and so on. If that arrangement does not prove of some use, then my name is not Markham. Now forward!"

"I will see that the rest are immediately behind," said Cunningham.

At every turn six of the men paused, raised their pieces, and fired upward, as they had been directed; but no cry of mortal agony reached their ears.

The noise made by the simultaneous discharge of six guns in this narrow staircase was something tremendous; and to make the soldiers feel more uncomfortable than they were, the smoke seemed to cling round them, and to defy them to see their way any distance ahead.

Their progress, as may be supposed, was very slow indeed, and it seemed as though there was no end to this staircase, or series of staircases.

Before long it became evident to all that the staircase led to the roof.

Again and again the crash of musketry rang out, but no cry whatever followed the sullen echoes.

At last a large loophole was reached, and Markham directed one of the soldiers to lift him up, so that he might, if possible, see what height they had attained.

This was done, and, to his great surprise, the captain found that they were some distance over the clock tower, and, therefore, near the roof of the middle tower.

"Be careful now, my men," he said, "we have almost reached the top, and we shall have them in a few moments. There is one thing, they cannot now escape, unless they have wings. Forward!"

The men obeyed, but tremblingly.

Those in front were wondering whether the giants had any huge books in reserve for them.

In a few more minutes a small landing was reached.

On the right was a narrow door of massive oak.

It was slightly ajar, and, by Markham's orders, it was pushed wide open.

The men were just about to make a rush through it, when Sampson's sonorous voice was heard:

"Hold!" he cried; "you have ventured thus far, and now, if you will take our advice, you will return. If you do not, so sure as we stand here, upon the roof of this sacred building, so sure shall many of you meet with a violent death, and——"

"Stand forward," cried Markham, "and show yourselves!"

"Fool!" replied Sampson. Do you think our bodies were made for no better purpose than to be targets for your bullets?"

"Listen to me, master giants," said Markham, who peered about on all sides to get a glimpse of the giants. "Listen to me. If you will take my advice, you will no longer resist us. You are certain to be captured, for I have two hundred men behind me."

"We would not care if you had two thousand. We shall resist to the last."

Cunningham, hearing the talking, pushed his way forward.

"Why do you again pause?" he asked. "Why stop to parley with them? Forward! Yet, where are they? I see them not!"

"They are round the corner, on the roof," replied Markham.

"Then we will have them. What ho, my men!" he cried: "the first six men who succeed, either in taking or shooting these cursed giants, shall receive two hundred crowns between them! And if you, Markham, will lead, you— well, you know the large reward I have already promised."

"Fear it not," replied Markham, taking a huge drink from his flask. "I will lead them."

Again came Sampson's voice:

"You will lead, will you?" he said. Remember the fate of your comrade!"

But Markham, now maddened with what he had drunk, raised his sword, and cried:

"On!"

With a loud cheer, the soldiers, at his side, half a dozen in number rushed through the opening

In their excitement, they fired blindly, without looking to see whether the giants were before them.

The crash of the discharge had hardly died away ere two huge figures dashed into the sulphurous smoke.

Markham found himself seized in an iron grip.

In an instant his sword was torn from his grasp, and he was raised clean off his feet.

Terrible were his cries for help and mercy.

They were in vain.

It was Sampson who had seized him.

The giant, now in a most awful rage, raised him high over his head, and, with a bitter curse, *hurled him headlong over the Tower.*

Down he went, like a shot, through the darkness, crashing, with a sickening sound, against every projecting point, and, at last, he fell, a bleeding, mangled, and totally unrecognisable mass, at the very doors of the principal entrance to the cathedral.

Meantime, Goliar's sword had cut down soldier after soldier, and Sampson seized upon them one after the other, and sent them to follow their leader.

"Come forth, Cunningham Trevanion!" roared Sampson. "Come forth, thou imp of the devil! Come forth, I say, thou accursed coward! Thou hast not the courage of a worm!"

He made a mad dash at the soldiers in order to attempt to cut his way through them, and find Cunningham.

It was a mistake, for at the moment of the attempt, a number of soldiers fired, and a ball struck Sampson on the cheek.

He dropped his sword, and staggering back, fell at the feet of his brother.

Goliar, with a cry of horror, knelt at his side.

The soldiers again raised their pieces, and were about to fire, when Cunningham cried out—

"Hold! Take them alive if possible, for I would have the satisfaction of seeing them both hung together."

"Further resistance is useless, brother," moaned Sampson. "Would that both of us had been killed together, for I would have preferred death to being taken by that wretch! But since it cannot be helped, lay down your sword, and accompany them quietly. A time will come for us, brother. His triumph will be short lived."

"Can you walk if I raise you?"

"Ay, ay. I am only struck in the cheek. I would again fight, but see, we are surrounded by a perfect press of guns. If they fired, one, if not both of us, would be shot dead."

"Surrender yourselves!" cried Cunningham exultingly, "or we will show you no mercy, but will shoot you like dogs."

"We are aware of it," said Sampson, "and we will surrender ourselves, because there is no alternative. But wait, Cunningham Trevanion, your time will come!"

"Ay," chuckled Cunningham, "and so will yours, and that ere very long."

Ropes and straps were procured, and the arms of the giant brothers securely pinioned behind their backs. Each tug at the rope or strap was like knives passing into the bodies of the giants.

Goliar, during the process of pinioning, again and again called out to the soldiers to procure a bandage to bind up his brother's wound; but Cunningham warned them not to do so on pain of punishment.

So Sampson was led down the stairs, the blood from the wound flowing down and saturating his doublet.

When the party reached the cathedral front, they found that the verger had opened the front gates, and that some persons had assisted him in collecting and placing in the entrance the mangled remains of the men Sampson had hurled over.

A more horrible sight citizens surely never beheld than this.

Many hundreds of citizens had assembled, and loud were their cries of wonder as the giants were led forth.

"Apprentices, clubs, and staves," cried a loud voice, as the brothers came forth.

There was no mistaking that peculiar voice.

It belonged to Carroty Charles.

The giants, as our readers already know, were very popular with the apprentices, and the cry of "apprentices" was soon taken up, much to Cunningham's alarm.

"Hold, friends!" cried Sampson, "let me implore you to make no effort to release us. All of these men are provided with firearms, that being the reason we have been taken, and if you make any attack upon them, their leader, the detested son of the detested Trevanion, will give them orders to fire. Therefore, I beg of you to disperse quietly."

Cunningham left a few soldiers behind him to take charge of the dead men, then the remainder of the soldiers surrounded the giants, and the word was given to march.

Cunningham took the lead, and the whole party marched off towards the Tower, followed by the groans of the assembled citizens.

In a very short time the Tower was reached, and the giants, after some delay, were handed over to the care of Lord Fulmore, the lieutenant, who, after some consideration, and after consultation with his officers, decided that they were to be confined in an iron vault beneath the moat.

"There," he explained to Cunningham, "they will be perfectly safe, for though they were as big as mountains, and as strong as a dozen lions, it is certain that they could not get out."

Cunningham, however, was not satisfied until he saw the giants placed in their cell.

It was a large apartment, constructed almost entirely of iron, with steel bolts and locks.

There being no furniture of any kind, the giants were provided with a few sacks, and having been insulted by Cunningham, they were left alone in this dark, damp dungeon.

There they could hear no sounds save the dripping of the muddy water from the moat.

As may be supposed, the first thoughts of the giant brothers were of the chances of escape; but as they felt the walls, and flooring, and their hands came in contact with the cold massive iron, they thought that their chances of escape were remote indeed.

Cunningham and his men having refreshed themselves, the order was again given to march—this time to the Wizard's house in Whitehall.

The gate was opened by the old man, who, on being shown the warrant, admitted Cunningham and the whole of his men.

High and low they searched, but they found neither Oscar or the Wizard.

Cunningham alternately questioned and threatened the old man, but all he gained was that the Wizard and Oscar had left the house some hours previously, and he did not know when they were likely to return.

Cunningham left a dozen soldiers to guard the place, and arrest the Wizard, or Oscar, or both, if they returned, and then he, with what remained of his men, set out again, his intention being to rest his men for a couple of hours, and then take the road to Windsor.

CHAPTER XIX.

HOW THE ARMOURER WAS SUMMONED BY THE WIZARD—HOW THE GREAT SECRET WAS REVEALED TO OSCAR—HOW THE THREE PROCEEDED TO WINDSOR—HOW THE QUEEN WAS SECRETLY VISITED BY THE WIZARD—OF THE STARTLING REVELATIONS HE MADE, AND HOW LORD TREVANION WAS ARRESTED IN HIS BED.

THE Wizard of Whitehall was not to be caught dozing at any time.

He was always on the alert; indeed, this man was in the habit of saying that, when he slept it was always with one eye open and the other shut.

While Cunningham and his men were marching down the Strand, on the road to Eastcheap, the Wizard received, from a friend who had been listening to the soldier's conversation at the "Henry VIII.," information as to the wording of the warrant, and he made no more to do than summon his man, and tell him to at once provide him with a coach.

This useful vehicle was not to be procured at many places; but one was at last obtained from a gentleman residing at Charing Cross, and the Wizard prepared to set out with Oscar.

"Whither are we bound?" asked Oscar, moodily.

"You will soon see, my son," replied the Wizard; "but, if we wish to escape the clutches of this Cunningham, we must at once away from here."

"Better let him come," said Oscar, fiercely, as he laid his hand on his sword-hilt, "for Heaven knows how I long to get him at the point of my sword."

"Restrain your feelings, my son, I implore you," replied the Wizard. "Trust in me, my dear boy—trust in me."

"I *have* trusted you; but——"

He paused and paced the apartment with rapid strides.

"Say on, my son, said the Wizard, gravely. "Whatever you may say will not offend me, I warrant you."

"Pardon me!" cried Oscar, with much emotion, as he placed his hand in that of the Wizard. "You will pardon me, will you not?"

"I have nothing to pardon."

"My hastiness—my impatience."

"'Tis but natural, my son—'tis but natural. But the end is fast approaching. Your revenge is coming! I will be sure and certain! Lord!" cried the mysterious man, clasping his hands, "What a terrible revenge it will be! Trevanion's head will roll from the block at the first stroke of the axe *you will wield!*"

"I?" gasped Oscar. "Nay, nay. Heaven keep my hands from such a thing! Why will you persist in saying that I shall be Trevanion's executioner? It is impossible! I cannot—*cannot* think of such a thing."

"You *must*. But wait—wait. Trevanion has been your curse; he has been your determined enemy; but, oh, you cannot think what a monster he really is. Hark! the horn—the coach is ready. Come."

"One moment," said Oscar, laying his arm on that of the Wizard; "for the last time I ask you—what is the contents of that box which the giant brought here?"

"What is important to you, you shall know in an hour. Moreover, you shall see—your --your father and mother——"

This was, indeed, cheering to Oscar.

He made no further remark; but assisted the Wizard in carrying the box to the coach.

"Now, friend," said the Wizard to the driver, "with all speed to Tower Hill, and stop at the house of Oliver Allpeck, the goldsmith. Do you know it?"

"Right well, worthy sir," grinned the driver. "Every man should know the house of the City Prince. So! art ready, worthy sir?"

"Ay, drive on."

The horses were put in motion, and away went the coach for Tower Hill.

This was soon reached, and the driver drew

up before the residence of Oliver Allpeck, reputed to be the richest man in the city.

The Wizard placed a whistle to his lips, and blew a blast upon it. It was immediately answered by the goldsmith himself.

Oscar recognised him at once, for he had, on many occasions, been pointed out to him by the Armourer.

"*At last!*" he said, in what was intended to reach the ears of the Wizard only.

"Ay, my friend," replied Mervine. "*At last!*"

"I thank heaven for it!" said the goldsmith. "And the lad is here? Truly, a fine-looking youth, and very much like——"

"*Silence!*" commanded the Wizard, sternly.

The goldsmith bowed respectfully.

Several apprentices were summoned, and they conveyed the box to the goldsmith's private room, and thither Oscar was conducted.

Mervine then handed a letter to the goldsmith, who, in turn, handed it to his secretary, saying—

"The Armourer, with all speed."

"Am I to see my father here?" asked Oscar.

"Yes, my son," replied the Wizard.

"Strange," muttered Oscar. "Strange, indeed. Well, well, I am the victim of strange circumstances, so I will express no surprise at being conducted to the *house* of a stranger."

Mervine and the goldsmith conversed in whispers for some considerable time.

At last the door was opened, and Mistress Raymond, with extended arms, rushed into the apartments.

Her lips parted—she tried to speak; but her tongue failed her.

With a loud cry of joy she threw herself into Oscar's arms, and sobbed like a child.

The Armourer was no less affected.

Great fears were falling down his bronzed face as he took Oscar's hand within his own, and warmly pressed it.

"Heaven bless you, my boy," he muttered.

Turning suddenly to the Wizard, he said—

"Mysterious man—this time I can guess why thou hast summoned me.

"Yes," replied the Wizard, solemnly, "*the time has come.*"

'Oh," sobbed Mistress Raymond. Oscar, my boy—my boy—hear you not the words of yonder man of mystery? *The time has come.* That means that you are to leave us, my boy—to leave us for ever.

"Weep not, my mother," cried Oscar, who then, turning to Mervine, said, "I charge you to make me acquainted with the mystery. What is *the time* which has come?"

"The time has come, my son," said the Wizard, "when you must be made aware of the fact, that you are not what you seem—that your name is *not* Oscar Raymond—that the Armourer is *not* your father—that his wife is *not* your mother!"

Oscar started back as though an adder had stung him.

"Not my father and mother?" he gasped. "Who then am I? Some wretch whom they, out of sympathy, picked up in the gutter, and carried to their home? Some—oh, heaven! tell me who I am!"

"Hush, my dear boy!" groaned the Armourer. "Speak not so, or my already full heart will break!"

"Listen to me," said Mervine, "and you shall hear who and what you are. If I make any mistake, the Armourer, or his wife, or this worthy goldsmith, or perchance the person beside you, will correct me."

Oscar turned, and he saw standing beside him the dark figure of the headsman.

He was all attention—his glittering eyes being riveted upon the Wizard.

Oscar shuddered visibly as he looked upon this grim and silent figure.

"Many years ago," commenced the Wizard, "when you were but a little child, *your father* was arrested, charged with several serious offences against the State.

"He was an old and tried soldier, a brave man, and a gentleman, and for some time the Privy Council would not listen to the charges brought against him.

"These charges were brought forward by his cousin, a bloodthirsty, cunning, and wicked man.

"His name was *Greville Trevanion!*"

With a loud cry of wonder, Oscar started up, but the Wizard motioned him to be silent.

"As matters did not progress so rapidly as Greville Trevanion desired," went on Mervine, "the wretch caused documents to be forged, and procured witnesses to swear to their authenticity.

"The result was that your father, whose name was Lord Eustance Wyncherley, was arrested, and lodged in the Tower.

"His beautiful wife was dead, you were the only child, and at your father's earnest entreaties, you were allowed to keep him company.

"While your father was in the Tower, Greville Trevanion tried hard to get him to sign some papers, which would entitle him (Greville) to take Lord Wyncherley's property on his death, but as that would take it from you for ever (Trevanion having a son) your father declined to sign.

"In the meantime, the Privy Council had investigated the charges brought against your father, and their verdict was 'Not Proven,' and his release was ordered.

"But on the night before the day when your father was to be released, Greville Trevanion paid him another visit.

"Again your father refused to sign—though he did not know he was to be released—and this last refusal cost him his life.

"Greville Trevanion had hired two assassins, and they accompanied him to the Tower, where, assisted by a jailor, they obtained admission to your father's chamber by a secret door.

"But your father was not, as they thought, asleep.

"He overpowered the men, one of whom he brained with a pitcher, then snatched his sword from his grasp, and taking you in his arms, followed the other.

"He caught him up and slew him, and he was

about to fly to the Lieutenant, when a dagger was plunged into his body.

"It proved a fatal blow, and the hand that struck it *was the hand of Greville Trevanion!*"

Oscar started up again, trembling in every limb.

Again the Wizard motioned him to preserve silence.

"The Armourer," continued the Wizard, "who just before had had an interview with your father happened to be close by, but he was too late to prevent the dastardly deed.

"But he prevented Trevanion obtaining possession of *you.*

"From your father's arms he took you—from your father's lips he took his instructions.

"As a child you could not claim your estates, even if provided with a friend, for the State would have ordered Trevanion to take charge of you until such time as you were able to conduct your own affairs.

"Had that been so, your death would have been speedy and sudden.

"The Armourer and his wife adopted you, and have ever been an affectionate father and mother to you."

"They have! they have!" said Oscar, in broken tones, as he placed his arm about Mistress Raymond's waist, and drew her tear-stained face to his.

"Your right name," said the Wizard, "is Roderick, Lord Wyncherley. You are now of an age to claim your own—and *the time has come.*"

"But you have also to punish the man who murdered your father.

"He knows only too well that if you could prove your claim, the wealth he has so long enjoyed would be wrested from him.

"I have papers to place before the Queen—papers which will at once ruin Trevanion. He will be arrested, tried, and in due course executed, and you will be his executioner. Now, my son, are you still averse to the idea of being Lord Trevanion's executioner?"

"*No!*" cried Roderick (for such we will now continue to call our hero); "no! I will wield the axe, and, by heaven! no headsman has ever struck a truer blow than I will strike!"

"Good! good!" said the Wizard.

"Weep not, dear mother," said Roderick, in tones of deep emotion, "though the time has come for me to claim my rights and avenge my father's death, you shall still be my mother. Though it appears I am a person of title, neither you nor my father—for such I *must* call him—shall ever leave my side for any length of time. I love both of you with all my heart and soul; and I would not part with you, even though I were to be offered the Crown of England to do so!"

The headsman grunted an approval, and the Wizard said:

"Well said, my son—well said! Nobleness, gentleness, and affection are as truly planted in your breast as they were in your father's."

The Armourer again fervently pressed Roderick's hand.

"The box!" said the Wizard, as he flung the lid back. "Look here, Armourer—what see you?"

The Armourer looked into the box.

He was silent for several moments.

"What see you there, Armourer?" repeated the Wizard.

"Recollections of the past," replied the Armourer, sorrowfully. "Jewels which once adorned the person of the beautiful Lady Wyncherly—Roderick's mother; Lord Wyncherley's patent of nobility, the Order of the Garter, and——"

The Wizard stooped and picked out a square leathern case.

He pressed the spring, and handed the case to the Armourer, saying—

"And this?"

"Ha!" cried the Armourer, holding the case at arm's length, and loooking earnestly at it.

The case contained a portrait—a beautifully painted miniature—of Lord Eustance Wyncherley.

Roderick took it in his hand, and looked upon the features there represented.

"As I look," he said, slowly, "my memory grows clearer. It seems as though I remember my father."

"You will remember more clearly by and by, no doubt," said the Wizard. "Place the portrait in your breast. Now, Master Raymond, do you see this bundle of parchments?"

"I do," replied the Armourer.

"Well, this is evidence that Lord Trevanion, while pretending to be devoted to the Queen, has been privately treating with the King of Spain. In this is a letter from Trevanion to the Spanish King, in which he suggests that Elizabeth should be assassinated."

"Heaven preserve us!" cried the Armourer.

"Ay, such is part of the evidence against him."

"'Tis utterly impossible for him either to deny his own or the Spanish King's handwriting, and both are here. Master Goldsmith, will you be pleased to tell his lordship what you have of his in your possession."

"Property deeds which were handed to me by the Armourer the day after the murder of Lord Wyncherley."

"Yes," said the Armourer. "I took them from the cell, even while I held Roderick in my arms."

"What do you estimate their value at, Master Goldsmith?"

"One hundred thousand crowns; with interest, one hundred and thirty thousand."

Roderick started.

His wildest dreams of wealth had never come up to this figure.

The Wizard noticed his look of astonishment, and he said, with a smile—

"The sum may seem large, but, as the Armourer and the goldsmith will tell you, it does not represent one twentieth part of what rightly belongs to you."

"His lordship," said the goldsmith, "may instantly command any sum he chooses to name."

"He requires none at present," replied the

"'I AM HERE TO ARREST YOU ON CHARGES OF MURDER AND TREASON,' CRIED RODERICK."

Wizard. "And now, Master Armourer, when you are ready we will set out."

"I am quite ready," replied the Armourer.

"Whither are we bound?" asked Roderick.

"Windsor Castle," replied the Wizard; "and our business is with the Queen."

"Trevanion has no idea that the box is in your possession?" asked the Armourer.

"Nay! his idea is that it was consumed in the fire at Piccadilly."

"You will not be absent long?" asked Mistress Raymond.

"Nay," answered the Wizard.

Roderick took an affectionate leave of Mistress Raymond, and then entered the coach, the Armourer and the Wizard following him, and in a few moments the cumbersome vehicle rolled off.

* * * * *

The coach arrived at Windsor Castle just as the grey dawn was breaking.

The Wizard stepped out, and after some conversation with one of the captains on duty, the coach was admitted.

"Follow me," said the Wizard to Roderick and the Armourer.

Under Henry the Eighth's gateway went the Wizard, passed through the Cardinal's ward, traversed several corridors, and finally paused before an iron doorway, against which stood four halberdiers.

One of them at once advanced, but as soon as he recognised the Wizard he bowed respectfully, and stood aside.

Both the Armourer and Roderick were thunderstruck at the wonderful freedom the Wizard apparently enjoyed.

Mervine produced a key, opened the door, and when the three had passed through, he closed and locked it again.

They were now in a small courtyard, each corner of which was graced with pretty flower-beds.

A broad flight of marble steps led to a magnificent terrace, along which ran several windows.

To one of these went the Wizard, and with his key rapped upon one of the panes.

A tall, elderly gentleman, attired in a black velvet doublet, and wearing a long black cloak of the same material, round the neck of which was a gold chain of office, opened the door.

"I did not expect you," he said.

"Nay; I am several days earlier than I expected to be," replied Mervine. "Is her Majesty stirring?"

"Yes; she is with Lady Scott in the Blue-room. Shall I announce you, Master Mervine?"

"Nay; I will announce myself. My friends will remain with you for awhile."

The Wizard strode forward, and disappeared in a narrow recess.

Elizabeth—one of her maids of honour, the lovely Lady Scott at her side—was standing before a marble bust of her royal father, Henry VIII., in the Blue-room.

The expression of her face showed to what extent her mind was troubled.

He eyes flashed dangerously; her lips frequently parted as if to give expression to her thoughts; her white tapering fingers toyed nervously with the gold chain and ornaments which hung at her girdle.

"Dawn!" she muttered. "Another dawn. What will *this* day bring forth? I feel that something of importance will happen, something——"

"Pardon, your Majesty," interrupted Lady Scott. "I would your Majesty would scatter, for the time, your present thoughts to the four winds of Heaven. Your Majesty requires rest."

"Rest!" cried the Queen, fiercely. "Rest? Rest when I know that my people are being grossly insulted by a foreign power? Rest when all England has its eyes fixed on me? No! A thousand times *no!*"

Lady Scott was about to reply, but, suddenly turning, an exclamation of wonder escaped her lips.

"Look there, your Majesty," she gasped.

The Queen turned swiftly and her eyes rested upon the Wizard.

"Tush!" she said. "There is nothing to alarm you, my lady. This is Master Mervine, who has the power of appearing and disappearing at his own will. We certainly did not expect him at this hour, and in this room. Pray come forward, Master Mervine, and tell us the reason of this sudden arrival."

The Wizard looked anxiously at Lady Scott.

The Queen saw what he meant.

"Lady Scott has our entire confidence," she said. "Had we no one to whom we could tell our troubles, we should go mad, Master Mervine—mad!"

"Heaven guard England against such a calamity, most noble Queen!" was the Wizard's fervent reply.

"Well, well, your errand. Is it important?"

"Your Majesty may guess that it is, or I certainly should not have taken the liberty to intrude upon——"

"Say not that, Master Mervine. You have had our permission to have an audience with us at any hour. Say on, but be brief, for our brain is already overcharged."

"I doubt it not, your Majesty. But mark what I say, though the dawn finds your Majesty sorely troubled, yet sunset shall find you easy in your mind."

"Ha! say you so? Well, you are generally a true prophet; but we fancy that, in this instance, your prophecy will be wrong."

"Your Majesty shall see. Most gracious Queen, pardon the liberty I take when I tell you that you have in your court a terrible enemy—an infamous arch-imposter."

"Can you prove it?"

"I am here for that purpose."

"Go on."

"This traitor at the present moment, is sleeping in this very castle."

"Ha!" cried the Queen, "his name."

"Lord Trevanion."

The Queen did not start; not a muscle of her face moved.

But her eyes spoke volumes.

"Your proofs," she said, in cold, deliberate tones.

"Read these documents, your Majesty," replied Mervine, as he took the packet from his doublet, and placed it in the hand of the Queen.

The Queen took the documents to a side table, at which she seated herself.

Very slowly, and with extreme care, she read and re-read them.

She made no remarks, but her heavy breathing and an occasional gasp of astonishment, showed how moved she was.

Rising she, somewhat unsteadily, held out her hand to the Wizard, who, falling on one knee, reverently kissed it.

"You are, indeed, a faithful friend, Master Mervine," said the Queen, "and we shall not forget you. So! *this* is really how Spanish affairs stand. By my father's head Trevanion shall—but let us calm ourself. Now, Master Mervine, let us know how you came in possession of these."

The Wizard told all, and rapidly he sketched out Trevanion's history, as well as the murder of Lord Eustance Wyncherley, Trevanion's possession of the property and his persecution of our hero.

Not once did the Queen interrupt him; but when he had concluded, she said—

"And you say this youth, as well as the Armourer is here?"

"That is so, your Majesty."

"Summon them to our presence at once!"

The Wizard instantly withdrew.

He returned in a few seconds, leading Roderick by the hand.

The Armourer followed.

"Your Majesty," said the Wizard, "this is Roderick—Lord Wyncherley."

"He is right welcome to our Court," replied the Queen, as she surveyed him from tip to toe. "A fine, noble-looking youth," she muttered.

"And in this person your Majesty will have no difficulty in recognising the Armourer of Tower Hill, than whom no more loyal subject could be found in all your Majesty's dominions."

"Ay! we recognise him," answered the Queen; "And it was this man who took Wyncherley's child when he was so foully murdered by Trevanion?"

"It was, your majesty."

"He shall have his reward. Great heaven; to think what a viper we have been nursing in our bosom! And to think that this youth, who was to have been hung, should turn out to be the son of the unfortunate Lord Wyncherley. But we have Trevanion in our clutches. Oh, the double-dyed traitor!" cried the Queen, between her set teeth. "Do you remain here with us, my Lord Wyncherley. Master Mervine and the Armourer will retire while we consult with my lords, and repeat to them the strange story which we have just heard."

The Wizard and the Armourer withdrew, leaving our hero with the Queen.

In less than half an hour the whole castle was in an uproar.

The Queen had been in consultation with her lords, but Lord Trevanion was not summoned.

Before the nobles had been with the Queen very long, several soldiers were posted at the door of Trevanion's chamber.

Every one knew what that meant.

By directions of the Queen a warrant for Trevanion's arrest and conveyance to the Tower was made out.

"Now," said Elizabeth, "Lord Roderick Wyncherley, whom we have no hesitation in acknowledging and welcoming to our court, shall have a sort of revenge."

Their lordships looked curiously at her as she slowly folded the warrant up.

Handing it to Roderick, she said:

"My lord, here is the warrant for the arrest of Trevanion - Greville Trevanion—for since we have acknowledged you as the lawful son of Lord Wyncherley, Trevanion is a nobleman no longer. Without you will find the guard in readiness. And your Grace," she added to the Duke of Buckingham, "will you accompany his lordship?"

"With much pleasure," answered the duke, who hated Trevanion most cordially. "This way, your lordship."

Roderick followed Buckingham outside, where about fifty soldiers were awaiting them.

"Draw your sword," whispered Buckingham, "and take command."

Roderick did as desired, saying:

"Pray lead the way to Trevanion's room."

On went the whole party, and at last a halt was made.

The duke pointed to Trevanion's chamber.

"Is the door locked?" he asked the men on duty.

"Nay, your Grace," they replied.

Roderick turned the handle, and the door noiselessly opened.

Our hero entered, the warrant in one hand, his drawn sword in the other.

On a magnificent bed lay the traitor Trevanion, fast asleep.

Advancing to the bedside, Roderick shook Trevanion by the shoulder.

He instantly started up, and rubbing his eyes, said:

"What is this? What is this intrusion? Who—who—great heaven!—who are you, eh? The face of Lord Wyncherley! Ha! a dream! a dream!"

"Nay;" said Roderick, sternly, "this is no dream, Greville Trevanion! This is *reality*— stern reality. You are right, it *is* the face of Lord Wyncherley; but not the vision of the unfortunate nobleman you so foully murdered in the Tower of London. Nay, it is his *son*, who, at the bidding of his Queen, is here to arrest you on charges of murder and treason!"

"Liar! liar!" shrieked Trevanion, leaping to the floor.

"Nay; you shall find I am not. Behold the royal warrant. The papers you left in your strong box were not destroyed, as you fondly imagined. They were found, and at this moment they are in the hands of the Queen."

"Who placed them in the Queen's hands?" gasped Trevanion.

"*I did*," replied a deep voice – the voice of the Wizard, who, with the Armourer, had followed the soldiers to the apartment.

"Devil!" shrieked Trevanion. "Fiend! *You*, then, have dragged me down?"

"Ay, *I*. The end, Greville Trevanion, will be as I showed you in the Tower on the night of your infamous crime. The *end*, I say, Greville Trevanion, is the *axe* and the *block*, and a howling mob, who will curse you until your head falls beneath the *headsman's* stroke! And that headsman, Greville Trevanion! Remember the vision! Remember what I told you."

Again Trevanion groaned.

"Your Grace will take me prisoner?" he whined, appealing to the duke.

But his Grace shook his head.

"This is the first time you have ever asked me to do you a favour, Trevanion," he said, "and why? Because you and I have ever been enemies; because I always suspected you to be a snake in disguise—and an enemy I must ever remain. Even if it were not so, I am powerless to take you prisoner. You are arrested by Roderick, Lord Wyncherley."

"Quick," cried Roderick, "dress yourself, Greville Trevanion, or you will be dragged forth as you are."

"Oh, heaven!" cried Trevanion, as, trembling violently, he proceeded to attire himself, "the end has come!"

"Nay," said Roderick, "the end has *not* come. As Master Mervine has just told you, the end will be the block."

"Curse you!" roared Trevanion, "you shall see how mistaken you will be! I have a complete answer to the charge of treason."

"Indeed!" sneered Roderick, "and what of the charge of *murder?*"

"That I never committed."

"Well—but I will not waste words with you. Only let me say this, Greville Trevanion, I wish to heaven the Queen would let me have my revenge in my own way. Then I would place a sword in your hand, and you should have a chance of defending yourself. But that is not to be. I shall, however, have that chance with your infamous son. I shall render England a service by slaying the one who, from all appearances, is likely to follow in the footsteps of his father, if permitted to live!"

"My son!" cried Trevanion. "*You* will slay my son?"

"I shall try to. I do not mean that I will steal *behind* him, and plunge a dagger into his *back*. I mean that I will kill him in fair fight. But I now refuse to speak further to you."

One of the men was directed to assist Trevanion in donning his clothes, and this being done, he was placed in the centre of the men, and marched forth.

His appearance as a prisoner was hailed by many with shouts of joy.

The soldiers scowled at him, and cursed him in undertones.

Trevanion was conducted to the courtyard, of which we have spoken, and remained there until the duke brought Roderick further instructions from the Queen.

While he waited he implored and entreated to be allowed to go and throw himself at the feet of her Majesty and beg for mercy.

He was simply laughed at.

The duke, having given Roderick some general directions a pair of manacles were produced, and despite Trevanion's cries they were placed upon his wrists.

"I shall remain here, Roderick," said the Wizard, "for I intend, if possible, to have another interview with the Queen on your behalf. The Armourer will stay with me. I intended that we should return to London together, but since it cannot be, do you, as soon as Trevanion is safely lodged within the Tower, proceed to the Armourer's house, and there remain until we arrive."

"I will do as you wish, unless I am prevented."

"Do not get into any danger, I implore you!" cried the Armourer.

"I will not if I can help it. Farewell, then, for the present."

Turning to the captain, he gave him orders to march, and in a few moments the soldiers, with Trevanion in the centre, issued from the castle and proceeded to the river, where three State barges were in readiness to convey them to the Tower.

By the time these were reached an enormous concourse of people had assembled.

Now that Trevanion had been "hoisted off his perch," and they had no cause to fear him, the crowd greeted him with hisses, howls, and curses; indeed, but for the soldiers it is certain that they would have torn the villain to pieces.

With all speed the troops embarked, and the barges were set in motion.

Nothing of importance occurred on the river to impede the progress of the royal barges, and in due time the frowning and gloomy archway of Traitor's Gate was reached.

The huge gates were soon thrown back, and the barges shot under.

The lieutenant was absent, and was likely to be absent for some days, and, therefore Trevanion was received by the deputy-lieutenant.

"Lord Trevanion," he said, as he proceeded to open the warrant.

"Nay," said Roderick, "*once* Lord Trevanion, but *now* Greville Trevanion, simply."

"Hum! Well, we have had enough of the Trevanions at the Tower, I should say. At every turn 'tis nought but 'Trevanion this,' 'Trevanion that,' 'Trevanion's son this and that,' and so on."

"What of my son?" cried Trevanion. Have you heard of him?"

"He was here not so many hours ago," was the reply, "with a swarm of soldiers and two prisoners, the Giants of Eastcheap."

"They must be released!" cried Roderick, "and at once."

"I have no objection to release them," replied

the deputy, " and will do so if you produce the warrant authorising their release."

Cannot you release them without a warrant ?" Roderick asked. " On me shall rest the responsibility."

The deputy shook his head.

" It is impossible ! " he said.

Trevanion was handed over to the warders, who were directed to take him to the Brick Tower.

" Oh, that I could see my son ! " he groaned.

" You will never see him again," said a voice close by him.

Turning he saw, standing in a recess, the grim figure of the headsman.

Trevanion would have replied to him, but the warders, in no gentle manner, dragged him on to the chamber which was to be allotted him.

Roderick, after a few moment's consideration, was about to re-embark, and return to Windsor to get the order for the release of the giants, when he felt a hand touch his.

Turning, he beheld the headsman.

" Leave it to me," whispered the dreaded man. " A warrant will not be necessary—*files* will do quite as well."

" You will assist them in escaping ? "

" That I cannot do. But I will convey them files and other things. Fear it not ; with those the giants will require no assistance from any man."

" Well, do as you say. It will save me a journey to Windsor."

Roderick, feeling satisfied that the giants would contrive to escape, gave orders to the captain to return to Windsor with his men, while he himself went on to the residence of the Armourer.

CHAPTER XX.

SHOWS HOW CUNNINGHAM GOES OFF TO GREENWICH IN SEARCH OF GRACE--WHAT OCCURS BETWEEN HER AND CUNNINGHAM—AND HOW GRACE WAS OVERPOWERED AND CONVEYED TO VAUXHALL.

CUNNINGHAM TREVANION did not leave his couch until the sun was high in the heavens.

Hastily attiring himself, he rang the bell, and directed the landlord to bring him a tumbler of brandy-and-water.

Having consumed the brandy, he washed himself and made himself otherwise presentable, and then ordered all the soldiers to be assembled.

To the oldest among them he gave the command, telling the man that, having some business of great importance to transact, he should not then return to Windsor.

Then he called out, from among the soldiers, a man of the name of Faddle.

" I shall require you to accompany me," he said.

Thus, without further ceremony, Cunningham left them to return to Windsor.

With the man Faddle—a short, dissipated-looking soldier—at his heels, Cunningham went off.

He walked rapidly until he got to the Strand.

Diving down a narrow turning near the Savoy, Cunningham halted at the house of the —at that ti. -celebrated costumier, Hans Leitch.

To this individual Cunningham was well known.

" I require a disguise," said Cunningham, " for myself and my man. Mine must be a courtier's dress of the richest description, while the one for this man must be that of a higher servant."

" And the monish ? " chuckled the Jew.

" I have it," replied Cunningham ; " and will place it in your hands if you are quick in providing me with what I require—not without."

The costumier bustled about and placed before before Cunningham several costumes.

Cunningham selected a black velvet one slashed with red.

The one for the man having been selected, both donned their disguises.

" Whither now, honourable master ? " inquired Faddle.

" You will see if you wait," replied Cunningham. " Come—follow quickly."

He led the way to the " Savoy Arms."

Having obtained a private room, he ordered refreshments.

" Now, said Cunningham, " you should know what I am about to do, for no doubt you are somewhat curious."

" 'Tis a matter of indifference to me what you are about to do," grinned Faddle. " I am ready to accompany you wherever you may wish, providing you will excuse my absence to my chief officer when we return to Windsor."

" Oh, of course I shall do that. There is the brandy—help yourself to it ; but remember, keep yourself steady, or return to Windsor you never will."

" Eh ? " queried Faddle, pausing in the act of pouring out the brandy.

" I say, you will never return to Windsor, unless you keep steady, which means that, if you make yourself drunk, I shall simply run my blade through your carcase, and have you thrown into the Thames."

" Hum ! I thank you. 'Tis not often I meet gentlemen half so considerate."

"Listen to me," said Cunningham. "I am about to proceed to Greenwich. There resides in that neighbourhood a young lady whom I have a strong fancy for——"

"Indeed?"

"She is a very beautiful girl, though she is only a farrier's daughter. I love this girl, and I have a desire to take her to a place I have already selected, and——"

"Make her your wife?"

"That's as I may hereafter decide. Not only do I love this girl, but I would obtain her so that a rival—an accursed apprentice—should not have her."

As Cunningham uttered these words, a face appeared at the partly-open window at the other end of the room.

That face belonged to one of the goldsmith's apprentices, who had been on business to the keeper of the hostelry.

Probably he would not have listened to what was being said, had not the words "accursed apprentice" caught his ears.

"I should have thought," said Faddle, "that a gentleman like you would have had such a paltry rival removed. There are plenty of men willing to make away with a man for a few crowns."

"I am aware of it; but since the State will strangle him very soon, I shall not have the trouble of hiring anybody."

"Have you seen the er—rival—the apprentice lately?"

"No."

"May I ask his name?"

"His name is now a well-known one—Oscar Raymond, the Armourer's son."

Faddle stared.

The face at the window pressed closer to the sill.

"Why," said Faddle, "that is one of the names mentioned in the warrant."

"Just so."

"Well, it was a pity we did not capture him."

"A thousand pities; but his capture will soon be effected, fear it not."

A smile of derision lit up the face at the window.

"My intention is to remain here until night-fall," continued Cunningham; "for it would never do to attempt to capture the girl by daylight; then take a boat at the Savoy steps for Greenwich."

"A wise plan," observed Faddle. "And what does your worship intend to do in the meantime?"

"Go into the card-room and play. During the interval fortune may smile on me, and I may rise a winner of a thousand or two. You can join the watermen below, and try your luck. Here are twenty crowns. Play, but don't drink, and above all things, preserve strict silence as to who you are, what you are, and what is your business."

"Don't mention it, your worship. I am as silent as the grave. I say nothing."

"But I do," muttered the apprentice, as he turned from the window. "I fancy I can understand a little of what was said. Oscar Raymond—now Lord Wyncherley—then the person, so richly dressed, must be Trevanion's son Cunningham. I see. I will at once inform my master."

He hastened back to his master's shop, and informed the goldsmith of what had occurred, and that worthy gentleman went off to the residence of the Armourer, thinking it likely that Roderick had returned.

He had returned, but had gone off on business of importance, so Mistress Raymond said, and he was not likely to return for some hours.

Now our hero had informed Mistress Raymond all about Grace; indeed, he had declared to her that he loved the girl, and Mistress Raymond had been thinking of having her brought to her house.

Her alarm for the girl's safety was great. She, however, had no alternative but to wait and to hope that Roderick would return before her intended.

Cunningham Trevanion played on longer than he had intended.

Fortune had not smiled upon him.

On the contrary, he eventually lost, and when he rose at eleven of the clock he had lost all but a few crowns with which to pay the watermen.

On calling his man he found that he, too, had been unlucky and had lost all.

Added to this, he was considerably the worse for what he had imbibed.

Having hired a wherry the two entered, and the tide being favourable, they were soon going down to Greenwich at a good rate.

Poor Gracie Gaunt!

Sad and lonely indeed was now the home of her childhood.

How often she thought of our hero!

How often she wondered how he fared.

Many were the bitter tears she shed as she thought of the dreadful fate which she felt sure would overtake him.

She would have visited the Armourer and his wife—for our hero had told her all about them—only, as she did not know them, she thought that such a visit might be looked upon in the light of intrusion.

She grew pale and nervous—shuddered at every sound.

Though Grace made no demonstration of her grief, her sad face constantly attracted the attention of the neighbours, and, at last, an elderly lady, called the Widow Wallace, who had known Gracie when she was an infant, called upon her, and offered to stay with her.

The kind offer was willingly, thankfully accepted: and the Widow Wallace, closing her own house, took up her quarters with Grace.

Almost at the same moment that Cunningham Trevanion and his man set out from the Savoy steps, Grace and the Widow were preparing to retire for the night.

"Let us trust, my dear child," said the Widow, "that you will hear from your friends, the giants, to-morrow."

"Oh, that I may!" replied Grace. "Last night I scarcely slept for thinking of them. I pray every hour that nothing may have befallen them."

"You look weary enough to-night, my dear; no doubt you will sleep."

"I shall if the wind is not high. Its sighing and moaning round the house disturbs my slumbers. It puts me in mind of someone groaning in agony."

"Ay, ay, my dear. It is because you are so continually thinking of the fine youth who has stolen your heart. Is it not so?"

Gracie blushed, but made no reply.

"Well, well," continued the widow, cheerily, "all of us girls, or grown-up women, have, or have had, hearts to lose. Come, my dear," she added, as she opened a shutter, "see what a lovely moonlight night it is; and there is not sufficient wind to move a bough: so you will sleep well. Now, come."

The pair went into Gracie's bedroom.

Grace had soon disrobed, and, falling on her knees, she offered up a fervent prayer for the safety of the giant brothers, and prayed that Heaven would guard him she had learned to love so earnestly—our hero.

In a few more moments Grace and the widow were in bed, and a few minutes later both were asleep.

*   *   *   *   *

Just after midnight the wherry, containing Cunningham and Faddle grated on the sand by the side of the landing-stage at Greenwich.

"You will await us here," said Cunningham to the waterman. "I have paid you your fare."

"True, your worship," answered the waterman; "but only for *one* way."

"Ah, I had forgotten. Cursed luck! I was thinking that the crowns I saved were sufficient for both ways. Faddle, have you no money at all?"

"Not a single piece. I lost all."

"Ay, and what you did not lose at the tables you lost in drink, you drunken hound! Well, waterman, at present I have no more money, but I can faithfully promise——"

"With all respect to your worship," interrupted the waterman, "I never take promises, for I find they are always broken."

"But I am the son of Lord Trevanion," replied Cunningham, proudly.

"Well, that's likely enough, and I always find that courtiers are always the worst for keeping promises."

"What do you require as your return fare?"

"Ten crowns, that is the proper night fare. Day fare would be but half the money. Then there is the time I shall be waiting. That would be five crowns an hour at night, by daylight——"

"Here," interrupted Cunningham, haughtily, as he snatched a diamond ring from his finger, "take this. To-morrow I will settle your claim and redeem it."

The waterman took the ring, critically examined it, and being satisfied that it was genuine, expressed his satisfaction.

"And now," said Cunningham, "which is the most direct way to Greenwich Church?"

"If your worship will turn and look to the right, you will see that the moon is shining on the spire of it."

"Ay, I see. Be ready to move off at a moment's notice, and reserve the stern of your boat for the female of whom I spoke."

So saying, Cunningham turned abruptly on his heel and strode away, followed by Faddle.

Arrived at the old wooden church, Cunningham paused and looked about him.

"If you have lost your way——" began Faddle.

"Silence!" thundered Cunningham. "I have *not* lost my way. Why, you chicken-hearted poltroon! if you stare at me in that frightened manner, I will ring your cursed neck!"

"Frightened!" replied Faddle, looking cautiously around him. "Why, I am as brave as a lion."

"Follow me then," said Cunningham, who by this time had found out the turning.

He soon reached the farrier's house, and standing under a tree opposite, he carefully surveyed it.

"Securely locked and bolted," he said.

"It is," replied Faddle, "and you may depend upon it that there's no one within."

"I am of opinion that there is."

"How are we to gain an entrance?"

"Let me think. Ah, I have it—the smithy."

Off went Cunningham to the smithy.

The doors were held together only by a broken piece of iron which Cunningham very soon detached.

He motioned to Faddle to follow.

The man did so, casting nervous glances on all sides of him.

Cunningham noiselessly closed the doors, then took a tinder-box from his pocket, and kindled a light.

Looking round the smithy, he found the best half a link.

This he lit, and handing it to Faddle, said—

"Now follow me carefully and noiselessly, you white-faced loon. By the Virgin! never did I deal with a more cowardly villain in my life."

Cunningham was cowardly enough, but this soldier was infinitely worse.

His knees knocked together as he followed Cunningham through the door in the smithy which led to the house.

Very cautiously Cunningham led the way.

On the first landing Faddle knocked against two or three long iron rods.

They fell with a crash to the floor, and Faddle falling with them, the torch was extinguished.

"Clumsy wretch!" hissed Cunningham. "If I fail it will be through you, and you shall suffer for it, by heaven you shall!"

"I could not help it your worship," whispered Faddle.

"Silence!" replied Cunningham, laying one hand on the man's arm and drawing his sword with the other. "I heard a voice."

"Nay," gasped Faddle.

Cunningham shook him, whispering—

"Draw your blade. No doubt she has friends with her. Spare them not ; but harm not a hair of the girl's head."

○ ○ ○ ○ ○

Grace and the Widow Wallace slept soundly, and, likely enough, soundly they would have slept till morning dawned had nothing occurred to arouse them,

The crash of the falling iron awoke them both.

Grace started up with a low cry of alarm.

"Hark !" she said.

"Hush, my dear," said the Widow, as she raised herself. "Probably it was the cat who has——"

"The cat would never knock down those heavy bars on the landing," replied Grace, struggling hard to keep herself calm.

"I will see," said the Widow, as she slid out of bed. "Do not be frightened, my dear. The house was too securely fastened for any one to enter without us hearing them."

The Widow was not a nervous woman, but yet her hands trembled as she lit the little brass lamp on the table.

"Do not leave your bed, my dear," she said.

"I cannot stay in it," replied Grace, as she leapt from it, and threw a long dressing-gown around her.

The Widow unlocked and opened the door, and, raising her lamp over her head, boldly stepped on to the landing.

The rays of the lamp fell upon two dark forms and two glittering blades.

A piercing shriek instantly escaped the Widow's lips.

"Merciful Father !" she cried. "Who and what are you, villains ?"

"Silence, my good woman," replied Cunningham, and no harm shall happen to you. We——"

"Harm !" cried the Widow, as she suddenly stooped and snatched up one of the bars of iron. "Harm shall come to you if you do not tell me your business. Midnight ruffians—murderous wretches, who are you ?"

At this moment Grace, who had advanced to the landing, uttered a despairing cry.

"'Tis the wretch who slew my father !" she said. "The villain of whom you have heard—Cunningham Trevanion."

The Widow placed the lamp upon a sideboard.

"Let me deal with them," she said.

"I will to the window," cried Grace, "and cry for help.

The Widow, holding the bar of iron in both her hands, and raising it high above her head, dashed it upon Cunningham.

But, as the bar descended, Cunningham darted to one side, and the iron fell upon the shoulders of Faddle, but it did him no harm.

Ere the Widow could recover herself, Cunningham raised his sword, and, with a bitter curse, drove it clean through the heart of the unfortunate woman.

"Oh, Gracie," she moaned. "Heaven help you. Oh, God, receive my soul."

"Go !" cried Cunningham to Faddle. "The girl !"

Grace had opened the shutters, but ere she could cry out, she heard the death shriek of her kind friend.

Rushing to the mantelpiece, she reached down a pistol and cocked it.

It was loaded, and the flint was perfect

Grace hurried towards the door, but ere she reached it, Faddle rushed in.

He had not taken two paces into the room ere Grace raised the weapon and fired.

The startling crack of the pistol was echoed by an unearthly shriek from Faddle, who had received the bullet in his throat.

Staggering forward, he fell dead at the feet of the heroic girl.

Grace stooped, and snatched the sword from his grasp.

At that moment Cunningham hastily entered—the lamp in his hand.

An exclamation of rage escaped his lips as he beheld his man lying dead on the floor and the girl he had come to abduct standing erect and firm—like an avenging angel before him – the glittering blade of the dead man firmly clutched in her white hand.

"Vile wretch !" cried Grace, " thrice accused ruffian ! Where is my friend ?"

"Dead. And you have killed my man, I see. Well, if you don't feel the loss of your friend more than I do that of mine, there will be no harm."

"Dead !" gasped Grace. " Dead ! Oh, unhappy wretch that I am. Oh, that the balls of your accursed followers had pierced my breast instead of my father's."

"Cease this nonsense," said Cunningham, advancing " I have a few very impor——"

"Advance another step at your peril !" cried Grace, "for though I am a woman, you shall find that I know well how to wield a sword."

"Very pretty, I must admit," sneered Cunningham. "And it is most amusing to me I do assure you. Will you listen to me while I—"

"Listen ! I listen to you ? No ! a thousand times no ! Infamous ruffian that you are, I would not listen to one word you said."

"I have come here at great risk," said Cunningham, fiercely ; "and do you imagine that, now that I have you within my grasp, I will quit this house unless you accompany me ? No ! Put down that sword."

"I will not," said Grace : "and, if you advance to touch me, I will drive this weapon through your heart !"

"I like your courage."

"Tempt me not to prove it. Back ! Back ! I say !" cried Grace, as Cunningham again moved towards her.

Placing the lamp on the table, and summoning up all his courage, Cunningham, who now knew well enough that he had a desperate girl to deal with, commenced to approach Grace.

Ere he had advanced many paces, Grace, with a bitter cry, raised her pistol, and flung it with all her force at the dastardly ruffian.

The aim was true.

The butt of the pistol struck Cunningham on the mouth.

Two of his front teeth were knocked down his throat.

He staggered back with a gasp, and, his feet coming in contact with the body of his man, he fell to the floor.

Gracie raised her sword.

"Heaven has placed you at my mercy," she said, "and now I— But, no—I cannot strike. Rise and begone."

She lowered her sword, and pointed to the door.

Cunningham rose and turned, as if about to quit the chamber.

But suddenly he turned again, rushed upon Grace, and seizing her by the throat, hurled her against the wall.

Nevertheless, brave Grace tried to use her blade.

But she was now powerless, for Cunningham seized her wrist, and wrenched it in such a way, that she was compelled to drop the sword.

Then, with a brutal oath, he hurled her to the floor.

By this time he was completely exhausted, and for some seconds, leaned his back against the wall, and panted violently.

Grace never moved.

Her head had come in contact with the floor, which rendered her unconscious.

"If she had not shot Faddle," he muttered, "I might have got her to the boat very quickly. But as I shall have to carry her myself, it will take much longer. She may come to, and scream for assistance.

"I don't know what to do, unless I gag her, and— But, no. By Satan, I remember! I have with me a drug I bought from old Porter, that cunning old rogue who charged me its weight in gold.

"A nice sight I must look with my teeth knocked out. The pain is fearful. But no matter. I am the victor, and can bear it."

As he spoke, he took from his pocket a small packet, and opened it.

It contained a white powder.

He looked at it for some moments, as if trying to think what he was told to use of it.

Then he searched for, and found, a glass and water.

Placing a little water in the glass, he poured into it about a tenth part of the powder.

Then kneeling, he raised Gracie's head, and, after some difficulty, forced her to swallow it.

"Now, my beauty," he chuckled, "we shall see soon who is master—you or I."

Having wrapped her in a counterpane, he went upon the landing, light in hand.

Its rays fell upon the body of the poor old woman.

Immediately a fiendish idea occurred to him.

"No doubt," he muttered, "Oscar will soon come here—and he shall see something. If I fire the house, the bones of the old woman here will be found, and no doubt mistaken for the bones of Grace.

"But then there is the body of Faddle. No matter. His bones will be taken to be those of a friend. Ho, ho! this is a glorious idea."

He easily raised Grace in his arms, and carried her to the smithy.

Returning, he piled up all the articles he knew would burn well on the landing, and set fire to them.

He then descended, once more took Grace in his arms, and left the smithy.

As he passed through, he could hear the crackling of the wood, and knew from that that the flames were getting a strong hold.

The streets were apparently quite deserted, but, in case anyone should be about, he pretended to be speaking to Grace as he went on, and intended—if, by any chance, he *should* be questioned—to say that he was carrying his sister to a doctor's.

But, though before he reached the river, one or two persons passed him, no one attempted to question, and he reached the river in safety, and with Grace still unconscious.

The waterman was still there, standing up in his wherry, and eagerly watching.

In a second or two, Cunningham was in the wherry, and laid Grace in the stern.

"Where is your friend?" asked the waterman.

"What friend?"

"The man you had with you."

"I know not. I have missed him, and cannot wait to look for him."

"To what part am I now to take you, your honour?"

"By Satan," thought Cunningham, "that is exactly what I have not thought about."

After a little consideration, he said—

"Do you know Vauxhall?"

"Ay, your honour, I should think so, since I was born there. But it is a fearful distance from here. It is impossible I could row all the way there without stopping."

"We will take it in turns to row."

"Very well. Then I will do the journey. The ring you handed me will, no doubt, pay—"

"It is worth more than two hundred crowns, so you will see that you are on the safe side. You will give me your address, and to-morrow I will call upon you and redeem the ring."

It was a long and weary journey to Vauxhall, and the greatest care had to be used the whole way, for the river was exceedingly dark, and in consequence dangerous in many parts.

Little did the young ruffian dream, as he passed the gloomy Tower, that his father was a prisoner within it.

Reaching the steps at Vauxhall, he told the waterman to remain there for a short time.

Then, having ascertained that Grace still remained totally unconscious, he ascended the steps, and walked rapidly through the narrow turnings.

"It is lucky I thought of Master Porter," he muttered, "or I should scarcely have known where to take her. No doubt he will give me the accommodation I require—if I pay for it."

Meanwhile, the waterman, after a few minutes had elapsed, struck a light, and looked into Grace's face.

"A beautiful creature," he thought—"a lovelier face I never beheld; and yet I row a goodly number of Court dames. And, as I live, she is in her nightdress! There's some rascality about this, I'll be sworn."

"This is an abduction, and a cruel one, too, for the girl is drugged—yes, and her head has been bleeding. I am certain that this young man is a villain. Well, if any inquiries are made, and I hear of it, I will give what information I can."

Whipping out his knife, he cut off a small portion of her hair.

Then he looked at her fingers.

Upon one of them was a ring of peculiar workmanship.

This he took off, and placed hair and ring in his pocket.

* * * * *

The house of Master Porter was distant not many hundred yards from the river, and Cunningham was glad to see a light shining through the chinks of the shutters.

Master Porter himself answered his knock.

He was a tall, thin, sharp-featured old man, with a pair of deep-set eyes, which seemed to be darting in all directions at the same time.

He carried in his left hand a small piece of taper, and in his right, a short, heavy iron bludgeon.

He thrust the taper before Cunningham's face, and scanned it.

"Oh," he said, "it's you, is it? Well, who the deuce would have thought of seeing *you*, eh? You surely don't want any more yet?"

"What?"

"Powder."

"Not I. I want accommodation this time."

"Accommodation! Well, that is a thing I don't deal in. What do you expect me to do—turn my house into a hostelry?"

"No doubt you wish you had the *chance* to do so, for you could use a few of the barrels of spirits you have below."

"Hish! hish! You may be overheard."

"It is not so risky to talk of spirits as powder."

"Anyone hearing me talk of powder, would think I meant gunpowder."

"Anyone knowing you as well as I do, would be perfectly certain that *you* are not a man who deals much in that article. But the accommodation I want is for a young girl."

"Oh, oh! For a— But you don't mean to tell me it is for the young girl of whom you have so often spoken?"

"No other."

"Eh? Upon my soul, you astonish me."

"I've no doubt of it. But it *is* the same girl. At this moment, she is lying unconscious in a boat at the steps."

"I know not what to do. I am—and you know I always *have* been—willing to oblige you, but my wife is in bed, and she is a demon if aroused from her sleep. It is impossible that I can take charge of a young girl."

"Rouse her, explain what is wanted, and tell her that I will pay her well."

Old Porter, after some consideration, did as desired, and went to his wife.

He soon returned, and said that she consented to take charge of the girl, on the understanding that she was to be thoroughly well paid.

Thereupon Cunningham, delighted with the result of his visit, returned to the boat, and the waterman placed Grace in his arms.

But Cunningham did not ask him for his address.

In his excitement, he forgot all about it, and the waterman did not remind him.

Cunningham strode on rapidly through the streets, and congratulated himself again and again on the fact that no one was about.

He had not the faintest idea that he was followed. But he was.

The waterman shadowed him every inch of the way, and noted the house at which he called.

He then returned to the wherry, and pulled away to his own home for a well-earned rest.

CHAPTER XXI.

SHOWS HOW THE GIANTS GET OUT OF THE TOWER—OF HOW THEY PARTOOK OF A MAGNIFICENT REPAST AT ALDGATE, AND OF THE WONDERFUL STORY TOLD BY SAMPSON.

WE must now return to the giant brothers.

Two hours after they had been placed in their cell, they got thoroughly tired of it, and seating themselves on the cold iron flooring, they gave themselves up to bitter thoughts.

"Caged at last!" muttered Sampson.

"Ay, and securely, brother," replied Goliar; "for, from what I can make out of it, it is utterly impossible we can get out of here. The lions in their doubly barred cages may just as well try to escape. May Satan claim that son of Trevanion's ere long, say I."

"So say I, brother, with all my heart. And the foul fiend claim Trevanion also. I say, brother!"

"Ay, ay."

"I would rather die than remain a prisoner here for any length of time."

"Ah, so would I."

"Though you cannot see the roof any more than I can, you can hear the dripping of water, eh?"

"Yes; and as I stretch forth my hand, I can feel the wet on the floor."

"Just so. We are immediately beneath the moat. Now, do you think our united strength would force away that solitary bar at the grating which communicates with the next cell?"

"No. For the reason that we could not get hold of it."

"Ah, I had forgotten."

"What were you thinking of doing?"

"I was thinking that, if we forced the bar out, we might use it as a pick, and having picked a hole in the roof, the water would, of course, rush in—"

"And drown us like rats! Heaven save us from such a fate. Or, if we are to die by water, at least, let it be *clean*, and not the muddy, foul-smelling stuff in the moat."

"The water would rush in, brother, and force away sufficient of the roof for us to try and escape."

"I don't think so. We have not got much thinner yet. And that reminds me that I am fearfully hungry."

"Let us try— Hush!"

"Eh?"

"A footstep. A warder, perhaps, with some food."

Both listened, but no key was placed in the lock.

But a deep voice said—

"Sampson!"

"Here," replied Sampson, in a whisper, as he got upon his knees and crawled to the door. "Here—speak—who are you?"

"Is your brother asleep?"

"Nay, by all the saints he is not," whispered Goliar, as he crawled to his brother's side.

"Sampson, if you had the tools, you could pick a lock?"

"By heaven, friend, try me!" replied Sampson, with difficulty restraining his excitement.

"Place your hand at the bottom of the door."

"I have done so. Ha, I have it."

"What?" asked Goliar.

"A file, brother."

"Praise be to heaven!" ejaculated Goliar. "It is at the present time of more importance than food."

"Feel again," whispered the voice.

Sampson did so, and his hands rested upon several files of all sizes, as well as several other instruments used for picking locks.

Again he felt and found several small pieces of torches—*very* small they were, certainly, for the door was too near the ground to allow of large pieces being placed under, and there was a flint and steel, and a piece of rag.

"Thanks—thanks, friend," said Sampson; "you have indeed done us a great favour. With these we can pick the lock, and— Ha!"

"What?"

"The bars *without*."

"I have unfastened them."

"My blessing on you. And now, friend, your name?"

"The headsman."

"What name, brother?" whispered Goliar.

"The headsman."

"Lor'! Well, he must be a good-natured fellow, though, for my part, I always took him to be the devil in disguise. We thank you, Master Headsman," he said aloud.

"When you get out," said the headsman, "turn to the *right*, go straight on, ascend a flight of stone steps *silently*, overpower the men on duty at the *Water Gate*, and—you know the rest.

"One word more. Trevanion is arrested, and is now lodged in the Tower. By the Queen's orders, he was conducted here by Oscar, now Lord Wyncherley, his proper—"

"*Who?*" cried Sampson. "His name— Oscar's name is—eh? *Hi!* HERE! What did you say his—"

"He has gone, brother," interrupted Goliar; "but no matter, we shall learn all soon if we are lucky enough to get out. Quick! let us light this link, and set to work."

"Trevanion arrested—here in this Tower at this moment?" cried Sampson. "Oh, that I could have the satisfaction of just placing this right hand round his infamous throat."

"Oscar a lord! Did he not say a *lord?*"

"Yes; but I always thought there was some mystery about him."

"Ay, ay; but hasten, good brother."

The brothers, having kindled a light, set to work upon the massive lock.

To most men, the attempt to pick such an enormous lock would have seemed ridiculous; but though the brothers looked at it seriously, they did not despair, for many hundreds of locks they had picked in their time.

We will not weary our readers with an account of how they progressed.

After working at it some four hours, they heard footsteps.

The brothers extinguished their link, and in a few moments, the heavy iron slab in the door was flung back, two black loaves of bread were thrown in, and a gruff voice said—

"More to-morrow at this time. Pitcher of water in the corner."

"We *know* it, ruffian," answered Sampson; "and if you don't quickly close that mouse-hole, I will fling the pitcher in thy ugly face."

The warder and his assistants laughed as they banged the little door to; and, strange to say, they departed without noticing that the bars had been unfastened.

"Big as you are," yelled the warder, "you can't get out of this."

"All the better for your bones," roared Sampson.

After a little rest, the giants again set to work.

For a long time they continued; but, as the time went on, their spirits rose, for they were succeeding in picking one of the best locks ever made.

At last the door moved slowly back.

Just as the brothers crossed the threshold, the great bell of the Tower struck the hour of one.

"An hour past midnight," whispered Sampson. "Let us hasten."

They traversed the passage silently, and on reaching the steps, stopped.

"Two halberdiers are at the Water Gate," said Sampson.

"Two? Well, that is of no importance," replied Goliar.

"Nay—our safety is everything. We will not strike them. Let us throw them into the moat. If they can swim, they will be all right."

The two halberdiers were deep in conversation, and they did not hear the brothers approach them.

Suddenly Sampson sprang upon one, while Goliar threw himself upon the other.

"Utter a cry," said Sampson, as he clutched his man firmly by the throat with one hand, and snatched the fellow's dagger from its sheath with the other—"utter one cry, and you are a dead man. The keys of the gate!"

"The gate is open," gasped the man, who had turned deathly pale.

"Good. Then you must swim for your life."

And raising the man over his head, he hurled him into the moat.

Goliar did the same with his man, and ere the two had risen to the surface, the brothers had pulled open the gate, and were rushing over the little wooden bridge.

With almost incredible speed, they bounded away across Tower Hill.

On the opposite side they were seen by four warders, who were just about to enter the Tower.

Without thinking of the great strength possessed by the enormous brothers, they pounced upon them.

But they went down like ninepins before a well-placed ball; and, for many a day afterwards, had every reason to regret attempting to stop Sampson and Goliar.

The giants continued to run until they had put about a mile between themselves and the Tower, and then they paused, and leaned against a wall to gain breath.

Neither spoke for a few seconds.

They only looked at each other.

At last, Sampson said—

"Brother Goliar, I feel faint—not from the exertion, mark you, but from want of food."

"Ay, ay, and a cask of ale, or a dozen bottles of wine— But here we are, brother Sampson, without money to get anything. But how is your wound now?"

"Oh, I think nothing of that. But my stomach is grumbling. It reminds me that it requires attention."

"Ah, if Oscar would pass this way."

"Lord—er—something now, brother. He would take compassion on us, I am sure. A title will not cause him to forget old friends."

"Not it—never! Ah, he has a true heart. But now, what shall we do? That is the question."

"You are correct, it is. Now, if we could— But let me wait. We are close to Aldgate?"

"Yonder stands Aldgate Pump."

At this, both simultaneously burst into a loud laugh.

"Ah, that pump!" said Sampson. "Many is the drink we have had there, when we could get no ale. I propose that we drink now."

"Impossible! It may be as vile as what we have had in the Tower. And besides, our stomachs are too cold to contain water; but, as we are at Aldgate, what say you if we go on as far as Dick Horsley's?"

"Ho, ho!" laughed Sampson; "I was about to propose it myself. Come along, brother. No doubt old Dick will be *pleased* to see us."

On they went about half-a-mile past Aldgate, and they then dived down a narrow, dark turning, at the end of which was a large hostelry, picturesquely constructed of oak.

This house, it was said, contained some of the largest beams ever used in the construction of a house.

The owner was Dick Horsley, a man who had dabbled in many things during his life, but who certainly never prospered until he came into possession of the "Green Dragon"; but as to *how* he came into the possession of it, was a mystery to all his acquaintances.

The brothers were perfectly familiar with the place, and, in the first instance, they went round to the back.

They passed into the stables, and here there was a little window, which looked into the large public room.

The moment they entered the stable, they were convinced that, in defiance of the hour, there were many men present.

They were overjoyed at this, because they considered it more than likely that they should see one or two whom they knew.

The window was partly open, and they not only saw into the chamber, but heard what was said.

They were not at all surprised to hear that the conversation was upon the throwing into the Tower of "Lord Trevanion."

"I am right glad," said one, "to know that the old rogue has been seized. It is certain that he will go to the block."

"And his son will be hanged," said another.

Said a third—

"This Trevanion has plenty of friends, and it may be that some attempt will be made to rescue him."

At this moment the host entered.

A repulsive-looking fellow was Horsley, and as much unlike a host as it is possible to imagine.

"For my part," he said, "I care not whether he escapes or not. But there are two in the Tower who, I happen to know, will *not* get out, big as they are."

"You mean the giant brothers?" said one of the men.

"I do."

"Well, I hope they *will* get out, for they are jolly good fellows—rather rough sometimes, it is true, but good-hearted for all that. They've got out of many a scrape, and they may get out of the Tower."

"Never. It is but a few hours ago that one of the warders called here on his way to Epping, whither he has gone to carry a message. He told me that the giants had been placed in a cell, from which it is utterly impossible that they can get out.

"They will swing, my friends, you can depend on that. And if I have to close my house, I will go and *see* them hanged."

"What have they done to you?"

"No matter what—they are my enemies. I tell you I would not give them a sup, nor a crust, if they were starving."

"A good-hearted man is Dick Horsley, brother Goliar," whispered Sampson.

"Truly he has the heart of an angel, brother Sampson. But he is only a little man, and, as we are so hungry, I propose that we eat him," replied Goliar.

"No, no—the morsel would not be delicate enough. But he said he would not give us bite or sup if we were starving. Well, as we are so hungry, we will *take* what he has. Come, let us to the front."

Sampson picked up a halter as he left the stable, and put it in his pocket.

Round to the front they went and looked in.

No one was about, and so they entered.

The moment they pushed open the door of the chamber in which the men were, there was a great shout of astonishment.

As for the host, he dropped a tray, filled with tankards, and started back.

He came in contact with a stool, and over he went with a crash to the ground.

Sampson picked him up for all the world as he would have picked up a rabbit, and placed him on the table.

"Why, my friend," he said, "whatever made you fall so heavily? Are you drunk, my dear friend, Dick Horsley?"

Horsley replied not.

He could only stare with all his might.

Goliar turned to the astonished men.

"My friends," he said—"and I see there are among you more than one who know us—we are glad to see you. I am sure you will be glad to know that we easily got out of the cage on Tower Hill."

At this, the whole of the men, without exception, burst into a cheer.

"And my friend Dick, here," said Sampson, "is, I am perfectly certain, delighted. What say you, Dick, eh?"

No reply came from Horsley.

"My friend Horsley has lost his tongue," continued Sampson, "or it wants loosening; so I will loosen it for him."

Thereupon he dealt him such a smack on the face, that Horsley went sprawling across the table, amid the loud laughter of the men.

"The fact of it is," said Goliar, "we were hungry, and we went in the stables in search of some oats with which to quench our thirst—"

"Hunger, brother, hunger," said Sampson.

"Ay, to be sure, hunger; and we chanced to overhear Dick Horsley say that he would like to see us hanged. What an uncharitable expression, my friends, eh? Fancy anyone desiring to see two innocent little children like us strung up at the end of a rope! But our time has not come for that."

"No," said Sampson, as he took the halter from his pocket, "but Horsley's has."

Horsley uttered a loud yell of terror.

"Mercy," he said—"have mercy on me. What I said was only in fun."

"It will not do," continued Sampson; "we know the difference between fun and earnestness. You expressed a wish to see us hung. Moreover, you said that if we were starving, you would not offer us a bite or sup; and for what

you said, you shall suffer. I think we shall hang you to your sign-post without."

Again Horsley yelled for mercy, and appealed to the men to rescue him.

But they only laughed the more.

"But first," continued Sampson, "we must eat and drink, for I assure you that we have had little enough at the Tower. Do you hold the rope, brother Goliar, the while I speak to the cook."

The woman chanced to be up, and when she was called, she came into the chamber.

She was a middle-aged woman, short, and fearfully fat, with a wonderful double chin.

The moment she saw Horsley with the halter round his neck, and noted the expression upon his face, she burst into a fit of laughter, which seemed nearly to double her up.

Then she looked at the giants.

"Saints!" she ejaculated, "what monsters of men! Good sirs, may it please you to tell me how much you can eat at a sitting?"

"Oh," replied Sampson, "we can eat sitting or standing. It is a matter of no importance to us."

"You must be the giant brothers—Sampson and Goliar?"

"True, my pretty maid," said Goliar. "And you have never seen us before?"

"Never, but I have heard of you."

"Never seen us before!" said Sampson. "Then your education has not been complete until to-night—or, rather, this morning. We have been here many times to see our friend Horsley. We like him so much, that we can't bear him to go out of our presence; and so, as you see, we detain him with a rope.

"And now, Mistress Cook, will it please you to tell us what you have in your larder? Master Horsley, with his usual kindness to us, has given us full permission to have whatever we desire. Is that not so, Dick Horsley?"

Horsley made no reply, until Goliar pinched his leg.

Then he said—

"Ye-yes."

"Of course," continued Sampson. "A kinder-hearted man than Dick Horsley never breathed the breath of life. Well, Mistress Cook, do you bring here the whole of the contents of your larder. We will then make a selection."

The cook made no inquiry of Horsley whether she should do as requested.

Off she went, and the while she was gone, Sampson went in search of something to drink.

He soon returned with a small barrel of ale.

This he placed upon the table, and with a tankard, burst in the head, which he threw away.

Then he offered the barrel to Goliar, who took a big drink, and rubbed his stomach with satisfaction.

Sampson, to the astonishment and great amazement of all present, then finished the remainder.

"Ah, yes," he said, "that ale must have been specially reserved for us. On my soul, I never tasted better."

At this moment, the fat, shiny-cheeked cook

made her appearance, carrying a tray of eatables

Truly there was a goodly collection, and the eyes of the brothers sparkled as they beheld them.

They were spread upon the table, and the brothers, after warning Horsley not to move, sat down.

Never, since the house was built, had the place rung with such hearty peals of laughter as on this occasion.

And no one could have helped laughing at the giants as they ate.

Huge pieces of meat and bread, as well as daintily-made pies, disappeared with marvellous speed.

The cook could scarce believe her eyes.

She stood rooted to the spot, and every now and then she burst into a loud laugh.

Her outbursts, of course, called forth a scowl from Horsley, but she took not the faintest notice.

Sampson rose, after a few minutes, entered the serving-room, and brought out half-a-dozen bottles of wine.

"Here is a good brand, brother Goliar," he said. "I know the marks well."

Yes, and so did Horsley.

It was the finest brand he had got.

He groaned as he recognised them, and then burst out—

"It's a robbery—a vile robbery."

"Ah, wait—wait, my friend, Dick Horsley," said Sampson; "you will not miss them long."

"I will give information about you."

"To be sure. We are prisoners escaped from the Tower."

"*You* are?" cried the cook.

"We are, fair cook—we are. And our friends round about would, I am sure, like to know how we got out."

"We should," was the cry.

"Well, I will tell you. But first, brother, what say you to this tasty-looking fowl?—as fat as yonder buxom beauty, the cook."

"Well, truly," replied Goliar, "it is a fine bird, and it would be a pity to waste it; so, while you tell how we got out of the Tower, I will cause it to disappear."

Sampson, having poured down his capacious throat nearly a whole bottle of wine, gave the following parcel of elaborate lies, with the gravity of an old judge.

"Well, you see," he said, "it was just past the hour of twelve—at least, so I judged, for, of course, we could not hear the clock—and my brother had dropped off to sleep on the steel floor—when a strange sound fell upon my ears.

"It seemed like the rattling of bones."

"Truly," assented Goliar, "just like the rattling of bones."

"How did you hear it, when you were asleep?" asked the cook.

"Oh, I only *dreamt* that it was so."

Sampson continued—

"Then the iron walls, and the steel bolts, and the *tons upon tons* of heavy chains which fettered us, shook violently, and Goliar awoke."

Goliar nodded.

"True—very true," he said. "It was a wonderful experience. Go on, brother."

Sampson went on—

"Then there was a noise in the roof of the cell, and in a few moments, a light appeared, and we could see a hole.

"We were wondering what on earth could be the matter, when the figure of a woman appeared.

"Oh, she was clad all in white, and looked the very incarnation of loveliness. When I think of her I feel thirsty."

So saying, he picked up another bottle of wine, and half of it went the way of the other.

"Don't drink otherwise than hearty, brother," said Goliar. "Be assured there is plenty more in the house."

Sampson resumed—

"This most exquisite dream of loveliness said that she had come to rescue us. We fell upon our knees, raised our hands, and blessed her."

"Did you see the *whole* of her figure?" asked the cook.

"To be sure we did."

"Through that hole?"

"No, bless you, she floated in the air."

"Ha, ha!"

"Eh?"

"Ho, ho! Ha, ha, ha!"

"Upon my word, it is too bad. Brother Goliar, I appeal to you whether I am telling the truth or not."

"Gospel truth—nothing else. I never knew you to tell a lie yet, brother Sampson; and I have known you longer than your father."

Sampson was persuaded to go on again, and he did so as follows—

"Her voice was like the tinkling of a silver bell. She promised to rescue us on condition that, in less than a week, we should place upon her father's grave in Bishopsgate churchyard an iron cross, which we were to construct ourselves.

"We agreed, you may be sure, and at once our fetters dropped off us."

At this the fat cook was so convulsed with laughter, that she dropped to the floor.

But she was not the only one who laughed.

Every man present was highly diverted by this marvellous extempore story.

But Horsley laughed not at all.

A fierce scowl rested upon his sharp, repulsive features.

He was, of course, thinking of the vast quantity of his choicest provisions and wine which had been swallowed by the giants, and he was also wondering what next they would choose to devour.

"Ah," said Sampson, "it is a pity that a man like me should be doubted. But I will continue, for I would have you know the end of the story.

"As I have said, the fetters fell off us. Then this angelic lady dropped into the cell.

"Oh, what a sight! She seemed surrounded by a halo of light."

"What is that?" asked the cook.

"Don't you know what a halo of light is?"

"I don't."

"A beautiful light like the moon. Well, she said, 'Follow me.'

"Then she touched the ponderous iron door, and it flew open. At once two warders on duty darted forward.

"The lady raised her hands, and moved them backward and forward, and what was the result? The two men became immovable. Was it not so, brother Goliar?"

"It was. They stood like statues."

"Ay, like statues. The lady went on opening every door without keys, and causing every warder to become petrified. And so we went on to the great gate at Tower Hill.

"We passed through, and then turned to thank the lady; but, lo! she had vanished.

"That is the true story, my friends, and if I have entertained you, I am pleased."

"Oh, we have been *mightily* entertained," said the cook; "and here I dub you King of *Liars*."

"Thank you. Such a title, coming from such ruby lips, and—"

"Hold—hold, Master Giant. "I am not accustomed to such compliments."

"Then you *ought* to be. But tell me this—have you a husband?"

"No."

"Then, by St. Mary, you *ought* to have. But fear it not. I am unmarried, and want a sweetheart. What better could I find than the one who has placed before us this morning such exquisite viands?"

"But you would make *six* of me."

"Ay, ay, but the more the merrier. But now, brother Goliar, we must be moving. Dick Horsley, are you ready to be hung?"

Horsley gave a great gasp, but made no reply.

"What!" cried the cook, "do you mean to say that you intend to hang him?"

"Ay, ay. And I will marry you, and together, we will keep Dick Horsley's hostelry. One advantage in my being a host is that, if no customers come, I can drink their share."

"But what has he done?"

"He said that he hoped to see *us* hung. Moreover, he said that, if he saw us starving, he would not give us bite or sup."

"*Did* you say so?" the cook asked Horsley.

Horsley shook his head.

"Take back the title you have bestowed on me—that of King of Liars," said Sampson—"and bestow it upon *him*."

Two or three of the men nodded to the cook, signifying that he *had* said so.

But the cook was serious now.

"Good giants," she said, "in consideration of the excellent fare I have placed before you, I pray you release him. If you will do so, I am sure that Master Horsley will agree to let me supply you with a good meal whenever you chance to pass this way."

"Brother Goliar," said Sampson, "can we refuse to listen to the supplications of so charming a woman?"

"I think we cannot, brother Sampson. But I think that Dick Horsley should pay a ransom for his release."

"Ah, a good idea! Dick Horsley, do you agree to pay—no, we will not say pay—agree to *advance* us the sum of twenty crowns?"

"I have no such sum," growled Horsley.

"Eh? No such sum! You who can buy your spirits and your wines at one-third the price that most can?"

"It is false!"

"Not so, Dick Horsley; it is the truth. But no matter. As soon as we have leisure, we will lay certain information before the proper authorities."

"Listen," said the cook: "I have twenty crowns in my box, and I will advance them to you."

"My pretty cook," said Sampson, with a low bow, "it is impossible that we can take money from a lady."

"Twenty crowns is but a small amount," said one of the men. "I will advance it."

"We have no security," said Sampson.

"No matter. I can trust you."

"Thanks, friend. We accept your offer."

"Well, then," said the cook, "since you will not let me advance the money to you, let me make you a present of it."

"Truly," said Sampson, "you are a good-hearted woman. But all we will accept of you is six kisses each. What say you, brother Goliar?"

"With all my heart," replied Goliar.

The fat cook made no objection, and, amid loud laughter, and hideous scowls from Horsley, the giants solemnly gave her the kisses. Truly they sounded like the loud smacking of a whip.

Sampson then took the halter off Horsley's neck.

"My friend Dick," he said, "you have been saved by a miracle."

"No, no," said Goliar, "by a woman."

"Ah, true, by a woman. But it was not my intention to hang you. No, we do not commit murder, but we should have placed you in one of your own barrels, taken you to Aldgate Pump, and there pumped upon you as long as a drop ran from the nozzle."

"Yes, yes," said Goliar, "he has escaped being pickled in cold water."

The twenty crowns were then handed over, together with the address of the lender; and the brothers, after consuming two more bottles of wine, took their departure.

"He brought down his dagger, and buried it deep in Sweetman's heart."

CHAPTER XXII.

IS OF WHAT HAPPENED AT THE HOUSE OF MASTER PORTER AT VAUXHALL.

As may be imagined, before many hours had passed, London was ringing with the extraordinary escape of the giant brothers, and several of the warders were placed under arrest, on suspicion of having assisted them.

Several persons came forward to say that they had seen the brothers in the streets, and at last they were traced to the "Green Dragon," the host of which gave a full, and highly-coloured and elaborate account of them.

But at the "Green Dragon," all trace of them was lost.

Search was made in every direction, but without result; and the most singular thing was, that no one in the neighbourhood remembered them having passed.

Oscar, with the armourer and others, searched for two days, but they failed to trace them, and they came to the conclusion that they had gone into the country.

But the while search was being made by both friends and warders, a special messenger was on the road to Windsor; and, at the expiration of the second day, he returned with a warrant, which made the giants free men, and a copy of it was posted up in scores of hostelries; also criers were hired in various towns to proclaim the fact of the warrant having been obtained, as well as a proclamation to the effect that the giants' friends were most anxious to welcome them.

On the evening of the third day, Oscar hurriedly departed to Greenwich.

His despair can be far better imagined than described when, instead of the house where poor Grace had lived, he saw a mass of ashes.

Several persons were round the spot, and to one of them Oscar addressed himself.

"Ah, sir," said the man, "it *was* a fire, I can tell you. In half-an-hour after the flames were first seen, the place was burned to the ground."

"By heaven, it is fearful!"

"Did you know the young girl, sir?"

"She was to have been my wife." said Oscar, with difficulty uttering the sentence, for the tears were fast falling down his face; "but it cannot be that she lost her life?"

The man gravely shook his head.

"Young sir," he said, "I am exceedingly sorry for you, but I fear that Mistress Grace *did* lose her life. Many bones were found yesterday among the ruins, and they were conveyed to Doctor Wood, whose house is yonder—there with the tall spire.

"It is well known that he has been making an examination of them, but what the result is I know not, nor do I think anyone else knows at present."

Bowed down with grief, and feeling certain that Cunningham was the author of the mischief, Oscar made his way to the doctor's.

It was not long before he was admitted to the doctor's presence, and unreservedly he told him all.

"My young friend," said the doctor, who had listened, with rapt attention, to him, "my investigations have been concluded, and I am enabled to ease your mind.

"The remains found were in excellent preservation, and not one of the bones are those of a young girl. Anatomy has been the study of my life, and I cannot make a mistake.

"The bones that were brought here were those of a man and a woman."

"A man!"

"Yes, a middle-aged man. The other was that of an elderly woman. Who the man was is a mystery, but there was staying with Mistress Grace an elderly lady—whose house was close here—called the Widow Wallace. Did you know this lady?"

"I did not."

"She was a most estimable person. Just about four hours before this disastrous fire broke out, she called upon me—for she suffered from a weakness of the heart—and informed me that she had taken up her quarters with Mistress Grace, as she knew she was so lonely.

"The girl's father was well known to me, and I was so interested in the fire and her disappearance, that, at my own expense, and in my presence, I had the ruins thoroughly searched.

"The result is as I have said. No bones of a young girl have been found.

"If you, sir, had been a student of the human frame, I would show you the bones, and explain how I arrive at this conclusion. It is simple enough to a lifelong student of anatomy, as I have been.

"No, sir, Grace was most decidedly not in the house at the time it was burned down. What can have become of her, heaven only knows.

"You say that your opinion is that this atrocious young rogue, Cunningham Trevanion, is at the bottom of it, and I should say that you are correct.

"Now that I know all, I don't think there is any doubt but that this youth—probably with some associates—abducted the unfortunate girl, and then fired the house.

"It is also probable that the man whose bones are in my possession, lost his life at the hands of the widow, or Mistress Grace.

"If I were a young man, I would most willingly assist you in trying to discover what had become of the poor girl, but I am old and feeble."

"I thank you sincerely," replied Oscar, in tremulous tones; "but you see there is absolutely no clue to work upon."

"I entirely agree with you. There is certainly no clue. I know not what advice to offer, but I should say that you must trace this young ruffian, Oscar Trevanion. I suppose you have no idea where he is to be found?"

"I have not, at this present moment. But you may depend that I shall leave no stone unturned to find him out, and when I do—"

"Hand him over to the proper authorities," interrupted the doctor.

Oscar shook his head, saying—

"No, I shall not trouble the authorities. Whenever and wherever I meet him, he fights for his life. Sir, I am extremely obliged to you for your kindness.

"I leave here fully convinced that, at any rate, Grace never perished in the fire. But for the information with which you have supplied me, I verily believe I should have gone mad."

The doctor, uttering words of encouragement, accompanied Oscar to the door.

After a short conversation there, Oscar departed, promising to let the doctor know if he were successful in his search for Grace.

Days flew by, and inquiries were made on all sides—no expense being spared.

But it was without result.

Nothing whatever was heard of Grace, and nothing was seen of Cunningham.

To the latter we return.

Knowing now that his father was a prisoner in the Tower, he, of course, considered it certain that a warrant was out for himself; and for some few days he kept himself in hiding in one of the very lowest dens in Vauxhall.

Here, with another, and the last ring he had, he borrowed some money, played, and won a considerable amount.

He was thus enabled to disguise himself, and he did so in a most complete manner.

He then, one night, ventured forth, and took his way to Master Porter's.

He was met by that person himself and his wife.

The latter was a short, wiry old woman, older than her husband by some few years.

Her appearance was most extraordinary, for she was nearly bald.

Porter was about to speak, but the old woman waved her bony hand as a warning to him to preserve silence.

"Listen to it," she said to Cunningham, when the door was closed: "This is not the proper way to treat us, is it?"

"To treat you!"

"How is it you have not been with any money?"

"Do you mean to say that your husband has not told you?"

"How should *he* know?"

"Yes, yes," said Porter; "I told you that his father was a prisoner in the Tower, and that, no doubt, he was afraid to come out, lest he, too, might be taken."

"That is just it," said Cunningham.

"*Is* it?" croaked the old woman. "Well, if you didn't come yourself, how is it you did not send?"

"Would it be advisable to trust money with a stranger? Besides, I have not yet been able to go to my goldsmiths?"

"When *will* you bring money here?"

"To-morrow night, without fail."

"How much?"

"Well, let us say one hundred crowns. That will, no doubt, suit you for the present."

"It will. But you understand that this girl requires close attention, and she requires also good food?"

"No doubt. As to the latter, let her do without it."

"*What?*"

"I say, let her do without it."

"But you don't want to marry a bag of bones, do you?"

"*Marry* her!" said Cunningham, with a coarse laugh. "What do you take me for—a fool?"

The old woman grinned, showing her toothless gums.

"I was given to understand that it was your intention to marry her."

"So it was—at one time. But it is not now."

"She is very beautiful."

"I am aware of it. *She* is also well aware of it, and so is the one she chooses to call her lover. Ho, ho! I'll lover her."

"What do you propose to do?"

"Tame her, and make her my slave."

"And suppose you fail?"

"I will cage her, and treat her like a wild beast. I will lash her with the heaviest thong I can get."

The old woman chuckled hugely at this.

"Well, well," she said, "if you do that, you are bound to make her—"

"As ugly as *you* are," said old Porter.

But he wished, the next instant, that he had *not* said it, for the old woman dealt him such a terrific slap across the face, that he went staggering.

"I'll wager *you* will be ugly enough before long," she said. "I have had *too* much of your impudence lately, Jack Porter, and your money won't save you if you are not careful.

"Now," she added to Cunningham, "if you want to see her, follow me. I daresay, in defiance of your disguise, she will know you."

"No doubt of it. She will *feel* that it is me."

"I don't think so."

"Eh?"

"She told me she would not touch you with a fireiron. So it's not likely she will *feel* that it is you."

"Bah! But go on, I follow you."

Gracie had been placed in a small, poorly-furnished chamber at the very top of the house, the only ventilation to which was admitted through one small circular window.

The old woman never failed to lock the door upon her, and escape was, therefore, utterly impossible.

But, even if there had been several chances, it is doubtful if Grace could have availed herself of them, for she was so weak.

One glance into her pale face would have convinced anyone of the anguish she had endured since she had been in that house.

Cunningham at once noted the great change.

"Ah," he thought, "she is in such a condition now, that I can twist her round my little finger."

Aloud he said—

"Do you know who I am?"

"If I could not have penetrated your disguise, I should have recognised your voice. Ah, cowardly villain! Abandoned, brutal ruffian!"

"And what have you brought me here for? Do you fancy you can terrify me into submission to your wishes?"

"You will be compelled to do exactly as I say."

"Never."

"Ah, we shall see. It will be either submission or death."

"The latter is ten thousand times more preferable."

"The idle words of a foolish girl."

"You will find that they are not idle. But remain where you are," she added, as she seized a large jug, "or, as true as there is a heaven above, I will hurl this at your head!"

Cunningham turned to the old woman.

"Did you ever see such a vixen in all your life?"

"Patience, patience!" grunted the old woman; "she will turn directly. She is of an age when girls give off fine speeches. They like to hear themselves talk. But what she has said to you is nothing. You should have heard what she has said to me! Ho, ho! if I could only remember it all."

"She has called me everything."

"It is false!" said Grace. "I have said but little, for the simple reason that I decline to have anything to say to you."

"Ay, ay," hissed the old woman, "so you have said before. But be careful, lest I may be tempted to slit your tongue. Understand that I have had to do with persons of far better position than you.

"Anyone, to watch you with your airs and graces, would fancy that you came of a Royal family."

Cunningham laughed aloud at the old woman's rage.

Then he turned to Grace.

"No doubt," he said, "you would much like to know where you are?"

No reply.

Cunningham continued—

"But you will not know. And let me tell you this: You are now in my possession, and in my possession you remain."

"For a time."

"For ever. If you act properly, you shall be treated as a lady; if you do not, you will be treated as a dog."

"Yes, yes," said the old woman, "as a dog; and there is a nice vault below this house where you can be placed. And a sound thrashing will do you good."

"Do with me as you will," said Grace— "torture me, but I will never yield to a brutal ruffian."

"No doubt," sneered Cunningham, "you fancy that you will be rescued by Oscar; but dispel such an idea from your mind. You are where no human soul can rescue you. You are in a spot where no one would think of looking for you."

"I am willing to believe," said Grace, with great calmness, "that your devilish plans have been well laid. Ah, but even now I do not despair."

"Pah! you are a fool. But I will talk to you again to-morrow."

"It will be a pity to waste your valuable breath, since whatever you may say will not have the faintest effect upon me."

To this Cunningham made no reply.

To the old woman he said—

"Come, let us leave the fool. What we shall do directly will have some effect upon her, I'll warrant."

They rejoined old Porter, who was soothing the pain caused by the smack on the face with a bottle of wine.

But he was not allowed to consume the whole of it, for his wife, without the slightest ceremony, took up the bottle, and drank off what remained in it.

"Good!" said old Porter; "there is none left for Cunningham."

"No matter," said Cunningham, as he threw down four crowns, "go into the cellar and get some more. Here is the money to pay for it."

The throwing down of the money made a great impression upon old Porter and his wife.

"To be sure," said the latter, as she darted upon the money. "Seat yourself, Master Cunningham, and I will soon place good wine before you."

"Put down that money!" thundered old Porter.

"Not I," replied the old woman. "You have enough, you miserly old rat. And you take care to keep it to yourself, don't you, eh?"

"And what will be the good of it, eh? You will die, and—"

"Not before you," interrupted Porter, savagely. "I will see to that."

"Don't be too sure."

"Eh?"

"Too sure."

"What do you mean by that?"

"I mean what I say."

"Ah, marvellously clever woman! Mind you don't overreach yourself."

"Be careful how you talk to me, or I will give you another such a slap across the face that will send you silly. But you can go for the wine yourself now."

"Ay, so I will. But hand over the money."

"Not I."

Old Porter lit a lantern, and left the chamber, muttering what he would do before long.

"Husbands and wives always quarrel when they get to a certain age," grinned Cunningham.

"Well, it so happens that I am not his wife."

"Not?"

"No."

"I always understood you were."

"No doubt. So has most people. But I am not. I hate the old rogue."

"Well, then, why don't you leave him?"

"I have often made up my mind to do so, but I don't see why I should go without some of the money I have helped to put in his pocket."

"Is he worth much?"

"Thousands. Look here," hurriedly whispered the old woman as she rose, "let us share it between us."

There was a pause of a second or two, and Cunningham said—

"Agreed! agreed! Is the money in the house?"

"Ay, the whole of it, in a cabinet in the bedchamber. Quick!—seat yourself. I hear his footsteps. Mind, what you do, *you must do at once.*"

"I understand you. And we share equally?"

"Yes, equally."

Old Porter came in, carrying a couple of bottles of wine.

"Here you have it," he said; "and I will guarantee that it is worth drinking."

The old woman opened one, and filled two or three goblets.

Cunningham emptied one of them at a draught.

"Ah, by all the saints," he said, as he took up the other bottle, "this is a splendid wine."

Porter held up the lantern close to the bottle.

"Yes," he said, "it has been in this house more than ten years."

Cunningham pretended to admire its colour for a few seconds.

Then he replaced it on the table.

But, as the old man turned to place the lantern beside the wall, he seized it by the neck, and raising it high over his shoulder, brought it down with all his force on Porter's head.

The blow was a fearful one, and the old man, with but one gasping cry, staggered back, bathed in blood, and fell with a crash to the floor.

Neither Cunningham nor the old woman moved for some few minutes. They stood looking down upon old Porter.

His limbs moved convulsively, but before long he lay perfectly still.

Then Cunningham looked at the old woman.

"What say you?" he whispered.

"You have done well. I had no idea that a bottle would kill a man so soon. Is he dead?"

"Not yet; but he will be in a very short time. There is no head that can stand a blow like that. Leave him where he is, and let us overhaul the cabinet you spoke of. Of course you know it will never do to remain here."

"Why not? we can put his body beneath the ground in one of the cellars. Oh, yes, I shall remain here. Then, you must remember the girl."

"It would be madness to take her from one place to another."

"Well, well, we will place him below."

The old woman took up the lantern and led the way upstairs.

The house was of remarkable construction, and contained, on each floor, peculiar recesses, most of which were filled with all sorts of articles.

Indeed, not only the recesses but every room was more or less filled with a miscellaneous collection of articles.

There was, however, one exception, and that was a room—a very small one—which led into the bedchamber.

The floor sounded so hollow as Cunningham crossed it that he paused in astonishment.

The old woman laughed.

"Ah," she said, "I will wager that you do not guess what is beneath this floor."

"I shall not try to guess; but what is it?"

"Water."

"Water? That sounds curious."

"No doubt. But look here," she added, as she led the way into the bedchamber, "you see that rope with the ring?"

"I do."

"Well, if that is pulled, the floor in the next chamber parts in the centre, and whoever is on it is precipitated into a deep tank of water."

"How deep?"

"Oh, quite twenty feet. You see, some five or six years ago this house was broken into by several masked men. They entered this bedchamber and took away a lot of money, but not one thousandth part of what belonged to old Porter.

"But after that the old man consulted a carpenter, with the result that several small chambers were utilised, a deep tank placed at the bottom one, and this flooring was made.

"It is worked by springs, which are acted upon by this rope.

"If the old man heard the slightest movement he would pull it—so."

As she spoke she pulled the rope, and placed the ring on a hook below it.

Then she held aloft the lantern and told Cunningham to look.

"Don't you think it ingenious?" she chuckled.

"Very ingenious indeed," replied Cunningham, who, however, took precious good care that he did not get too close.

The old woman returned to the bedchamber, and let go the ring.

The flaps were heard to close with a bang.

The old woman then went across the room to a tall, quaintly-carved cabinet.

"Have you the keys?" asked Cunningham.

"I will show them you in a moment."

She stooped, placed her hand at the bottom of the cabinet, and a long, exceedingly narrow drawer slid noiselessly out from the side.

It contained a bunch of keys only.

Cunningham took them out, and, after a few seconds, opened one of the drawers.

The contents consisted of a number of papers, but, at the bottom, was a small case, and this was found to contain a very valuable diamond brooch.

As Cunningham looked at it, he thought—

"There is not the faintest doubt but that, besides a pile of money, there are a number of valuable articles of jewellery here. Am I to have half? No, I will have the lot."

He told the unsuspecting old woman to hold up the lantern. Suddenly he started.

"Hark!" he said.

"What is it?"

"I could have sworn I heard a footstep. Surely the old man has not recovered?"

"Not he. A footstep? I never heard it. But we will go and see."

Downstairs they went.

The old man was dead.

They searched all the place below, but of course nothing was seen.

As the reader has guessed, Cunningham had heard no noise at all.

"Are you satisfied?" asked the old woman.

"Aye, aye, all is right. Lead the way back and let us set to work."

The old woman, raising the lantern, hastened back, Cunningham being close at her heels.

As they entered the bedchamber Cunningham, by a rapid movement, pulled down the cord and placed the ring on the hook.

Thus, once more, the flaps in the adjoining chamber were open.

The old woman now placed down the lantern and took the keys.

"Now for the money," she said, "and we will count it and divide it—"

"*Never!*" roared Cunningham, as he seized the old woman by the throat. "Never, I tell you—the money is mine!"

The old woman uttered no cry for mercy.

Her rage was fearful.

Her eyes seemed to flash fire, as she in turn seized Cunningham with her long, bony hands.

"Curse you!" she gasped; "I will strangle you!"

She tried hard to get her hands about Cunningham's throat, but failed.

But she caught hold of him in other places, and, in but a few seconds, Cunningham's clothing was torn almost to shreds.

Backwards and forwards they struggled, hurling to the ground first one article and then another, until the bedchamber presented the appearance of having been in a state of siege.

The old woman cursed in an appalling manner.

But Cunningham said nothing.

He had but one object in view, and that was to force the old woman to the door.

She of course did not know this, nor did she see that the ring of the rope was upon the hook.

The struggle continued for fully a quarter of an hour, and then the old woman—strong though she was—began to get exhausted.

Here was Cunningham's chance, and he forced her to the door.

For the first time the old woman dropped one of her hands, and that was to clutch the woodwork for support.

"Release me," she gasped, "and the whole of the money shall be yours."

Cunningham released her.

"You swear it?" he said.

"Yes, yes, I am too—too much exhausted to continue to—"

"I *know* it," interrupted Cunningham, "but your exhaustion is *over!*"

As he spoke he made a sudden rush, and pushed the old woman backwards.

Down through the open flooring she went, her cry ringing through the house

The next instant there was a loud splash, and that was followed by other piercing screams.

But Cunningham speedily silenced them by releasing the rope.

The flaps, as before, closed with a bang—a singular thing when it is considered that they opened without the slightest noise.

Cunningham went upon his knees and placed his ear to the woodwork.

He heard a faint moaning and what sounded like the splashing of water.

But it lasted only for a few moments, and there was then perfect silence.

"Good!" muttered Cunningham, as he rose, "and so the money is mine. But, by all the fiends, I have had to work for it.

"Never, in all my life, did I come across a woman with such strength. I thought, more than once, that she was getting the best of it. Ah! but the old fool never thought of the flaps."

He went into the bedchamber and picked up the lantern, and held it up before the mirror.

"I look a sight, sure enough," he muttered— "a perfect scarecrow. I must not present myself to lovely, charming Grace again to-night.

"Ah, if I could get someone to persuade her to drink some wine! I have in my pocket the remains of the drug. But that, of course, is impossible."

He went to the cabinet, and opened drawer after drawer.

But he found in them nothing which would prove of any value to him.

There were all sorts of papers, and mysterious-looking black M.S. books in foreign languages.

These he flung in every direction over the floor.

The principal thing to open now was the large doors in the centre of the cabinet.

But he found no key that would fit the lock.

So he took the heavy fireirons, and literally smashed the doors to pieces.

Inside was a large sheet of parchment, and upon it was written these words—

"To CATHERINE STONE, otherwise 'Mother Porter.'

"You are foiled! I well knew that one day you would make an attempt to get possession of my money, but I have long been prepared for you, and my money has been placed where neither you nor anyone else can get possession of it.

"And mark it: if any harm comes to me, you will be suspected, and your arrest will follow.

"So what do you think of this, Catherine Stone?"

This was all.

Cunningham, after reading this over two or three times, hurled it, with a bitter curse, to the ground.

"No," he cried, "it is not the old woman who has been foiled, it is *me*. What have I done for nothing? Well, next to it.

"The brooch will fetch, perhaps, three or four hundred crowns. But there is not another article of jewellery here. By Satan, I am unlucky. But no matter. There are plenty of things in the house which I can turn into money.

"But I shall retain possession of the house for the present. It will, no doubt, be of service to me. At any rate, it will always be a safe refuge."

Downstairs he went, lantern in hand, and made his way to the cellars.

Here he quickly found the place where the wines and spirits were kept.

Taking a bottle of the latter, he went to the chamber where lay the body of the old man.

"What am I to do with this?" he thought, as he looked at it. "Had I better dig a grave below and—but no: I will drop it into the cistern.

"Oh, oh! It would, after all, be a pity to separate such a *loving* old couple!"

In the first place, he knelt down and searched the body.

His search was a successful one, for he found several other articles of jewellery, including a massive gold chain with a large locket attached, and a number of letters and other papers, the whole of which he pocketed.

He then dragged the body to the bedchamber.

This was a work of great difficulty, but it was accomplished at last, and once more he caused the flaps to open.

Another moment and he had hurled the body below.

The wretch chuckled loudly as the body struck the water.

"It was a mighty fine invention," he muttered, "and no doubt the old man little dreamt that it was where he would find a resting-place.

"And this reminds me. It is more than likely that I will serve charming Grace in the same way. Oh, what a splendid revenge, to hurl her down this trap, and then let Oscar know where she is to be found!

"This I will consider. But it is more than likely that I shall do it. And now for the spirits. While I am enjoying them, I will look at the papers, for they may give me some clue as to the name of the goldsmith in whose care the old man placed his money.

"After that, I must look about for some clothes."

CHAPTER XXIII.

OF HOW CUNNINGHAM MEETS WITH AN OLD "FRIEND"—AND OF HOW HE AND CHARLES PORTER LOST THEIR LIVES.

THE papers contained no reference whatever to a goldsmith.

The letters caused Cunningham some astonishment, for they were headed, "My dear father."

There were four of them, and each thanked "my dear father" for sums of money received.

Each was signed, "Your affectionate son, Charles."

"Now," thought Cunningham, as he read the letters for the sixth time, "who can this person be who signs himself 'Charles'?

"Surely it cannot be that old Porter had a son? No, I don't think that can be possible. I have known him for a long time, and he never mentioned such a thing to me.

"I suppose that some person to whom he advanced money—and I know that he *did* advance money—placed them in his hands for some purpose."

Having finished the spirits, Cunningham reascended to the bedchamber, calmly laid down, and went to sleep.

When daylight came, he awoke, and searched the house for some clothes.

He found a quantity in a large box in one of the chambers, and what he selected fitted him fairly well.

In this box, too, were several well-mounted pistols.

He took two of them, and was about to place them in his belt, when he noticed a name upon them.

That name was—

"CHARLES PORTER."

"Ho, ho!" chuckled Cunningham; "then it seems that he *had* a son. It occurs to me that this son is bound to keep out of the way for some reason. Well, it is of no importance to me."

The next thing he did was to make a good meal of the provisions he found.

What he left he took to Grace, and, after torturing her by his presence for nearly an hour, he hurled the broken food at her feet.

"As a dog you shall be treated," he said; "and I will break that proud spirit of yours, or break your neck. I can see, from the expression upon your face, that you are in hopes of being released.

"I have told you before that it is impossible. You are in my house—"

"It is false!"

"Eh?"

"False. This is *not* your house."

"Oh, oh! You know better than I do?"

"I know it is not your house. The wicked old woman you thought proper to place over me told me it was *her* house."

"Ah, ah! What a lie! But we will not argue that point now. There, on the floor, is your food. Eat it."

"I will neither eat nor drink anything that has been in *your* hands."

"Then *leave* it, and be cursed to you!" yelled Cunningham, as he banged the door to, and bolted it.

He did not go out until night, and he then made his way to "The Three Goats," the hostelry to which he went after he had placed

Grace in the care of old Porter, and the house at which he had played and won.

It was a fearfully low place, in one of the worst quarters of Vauxhall, but it was very handy to the house, the distance not being great.

He played again and won, and won again on the following night.

For four nights in succession he played, and with success.

It was wonderful where the dissipated, hulking scoundrels who frequented the house got the money from.

The total amount Cunningham won was not great, of course, but he knew that it would last him some considerable time.

He took plenty of refreshments from the hostelry to the house, and regularly supplied Grace with what he did not want.

And he never failed to heap upon her all the vile abuse he could think of.

Secretly rejoiced was he to see that she was getting thinner, and that she had evidently abandoned all hope of being rescued.

Now, on the night of the sixth day, about an hour after Cunningham had taken his departure, a young man wearing a slouched hat and a heavy cloak approached the house.

To watch his movements one would have thought that he had some idea of being followed.

After some hesitation he knocked upon the door.

Getting no answer, he knocked a second and a third time, and then went to the back.

This young man, we may at once inform the reader, was none other than Charles Porter, the only child of the old man.

It was the first time he had been near the house for twelve months, and he would not have been there then only that a letter he had been expecting had not arrived.

Charles Porter had not been a saint by any means.

He had been connected with a gang of ruffians, who had committed many a crime for which the penalty was death.

Twelve months before we introduce him to the reader's notice, he, with others, had been engaged in a gigantic series of barefaced frauds.

They were caught absolutely "red handed," and lodged in prison.

But old Porter's money proved the proper key for the release of his son.

In other words, one of the jailers was heavily bribed, and he was the means of the escape of Charles.

But the money proved useless to the jailer, for he was suspected, arrested, tried, convicted, and hanged.

Search was everywhere made for Charles Porter, but without result—thanks again to old Porter's money.

Charles remained in hiding for months, and the authorities got tired of the search after him.

He went from place to place, and at last reached Birmingham; and it was to that place that his father sent the letters containing money.

The old man's affection for his son was very strong.

He sent him money with pleasure, and was quite happy and content to receive in return a letter of acknowledgment and thanks.

Charles was, of course, familiar with every part of the premises.

He went to a small shed and took from it a ladder.

This he placed against one of the windows.

Ascending, he easily opened it and shouted out—

"What ho! what ho!"

This he repeated half-a-dozen times.

Getting no answer, he muttered—

"This seems strange to me. My father was never a heavy sleeper. Has anything happened? Well, I shall soon see."

Getting through the window, he took out flint and steel, struck a light, and made his way to the bedchamber.

He uttered a loud cry of astonishment when he saw the state it was in, and that it was unoccupied.

He searched for, found a taper, and, lighting it, went over the house.

He started from the chamber in which his father had lost his life.

Ashy pale went his face as he saw the pool of blood, and noted the fragments of the bottle, for Cunningham had not attempted to remove anything.

He traced the blood up the stairs, and into the chamber containing the flaps.

There he stood for some few moments, lost in thought.

Next he ascended to the top, and he at once noticed that one of the attic doors was bolted.

In an instant, he shot the bolts, and opened the door.

But Grace did not come forward.

The reason was simple enough.

She thought it was Cunningham.

Charles raised the taper aloft.

"Is anyone here?" he asked.

Grace came forward, and as the rays of the taper fell upon her, Charles started back.

No word left his lips for a few seconds.

He stood as if rooted to the spot.

But at last he said—

"Who, mistress, are you?"

"A prisoner."

"A what?"

"A prisoner."

"You astound me, mistress. Do you mean to tell me that my father has confined—"

"I don't know your father."

"Master Porter."

"I have had no dealings with him."

"Who then?"

"His wife."

"Wife! No, the old woman."

"Ay, she is an old woman."

"She is not my mother. But do you tell me that it was she who caused you to be confined here?"

"No, she is my keeper."

"Keeper! This is astonishing indeed. By whom was she bribed to keep you here?"

"By a wretch called Cunningham Trevanion."

"I have heard the name many a time. When did you last see him?"

"But a few hours ago."

"When did you last see the old woman?"

"Some *days* ago."

"Ah! and you have not seen the old man?"

"Not at all."

"By heaven! Some terrible crime has been committed, I feel sure; and the one who has done it is this Cunningham Trevanion."

"He is capable of committing *any* crime."

"But you, lady, are no longer a prisoner. You are free to go where you will."

"Free?" cried Grace.

"Free as the air, mistress."

"Oh, sir, how can I thank you?"

"Thank me? I want no thanks, mistress. I say that you are free—go. I will deal with this Cunningham Trevanion, if I can find him. Come, let me show you from the house."

"In what part is this house situated?"

"What! you do not know that?"

"I do not."

"Vauxhall."

"I thank you."

"Come, mistress. But first — and you will pardon me I am sure—have you money?"

"None whatever; but I care not for money so that I am out of the clutches of Cunningham Trevanion."

"I am worth but a small sum, but here are ten crowns. Accept it, mistress, as a small loan."

"No, no—"

"I insist. It is impossible that you can pass through the streets without money."

"Well then, I accept. But tell me to what part I shall return the money."

"Return it when you will, to—but no. I shall probably meet you again some day. Go, mistress, at once. But wait—I will escort you a few hundred yards from the house."

He conducted her below, and before they left the house he procured for her a thick, heavy mantle, which almost concealed her figure and face.

Having seen her some five hundred yards from the house, he returned, closed the door, and again went over the house.

"Cunningham Trevanion, eh?" he muttered, as he drew a long dagger and felt the point. "Aye, I shall have something to say to him. Murder has been done, and that I can swear to."

In the bedroom he found the paper written by Master Porter, and read it a dozen times.

"I can't understand it in the least," he muttered. "From this it would seem as if the old man was suspicious of being murdered by the old woman. Can it be— But I will wait. Cunningham Trevanion can't be far off."

In darkness he remained, dagger in hand, waiting.

*   *   *   *   *

In the meanwhile, Cunningham ordered wine, and took possession of the most comfortable seat in a small "private" room at the hostelry.

But he was to be disturbed.

He had not been seated more than half-an-hour, when the door was unceremoniously opened, and a tall, thin, peculiar-looking man of about six-and-twenty entered.

His costume was decent, but showed signs of hard wear, and he wore a long slender rapier.

He was about to quit the chamber again, when Cunningham chanced to turn. At once he uttered an exclamation of astonishment.

"*What!*" he cried, "is it possible? Do I really, once more, behold the redoubtable Cunningham Trevanion?"

Cunningham scowled as he replied—

"What the fiend do you mean, eh?"

"Come, come," said the man, with a grin, "you don't intend to deny that you are Cunningham Trevanion, do you?"

"To be sure I do."

"Well, then, I must be mistaken, of course. So I will wish you a good-night. I am sorry that you are *not* Cunningham Trevanion, because I have an important letter for him."

"Who from?" asked Cunningham, eagerly.

The man grinned from ear to ear.

"You betray yourself," he said. "I am now convinced that you *are* Cunningham Trevanion."

"I'll not deny it. Hand over the letter."

"I'm sorry that I can't."

"Why not?" scowled Cunningham.

"Because I have not got one."

"You infernal fool!"

"Not at all. What I said was a catch. But let us continue to be friends, Master Cunningham. I may be of service to you in the future, just as I have been in the past."

"Well, well, that is true. But your sudden appearance here startled me. I was under the impression that what I heard was true."

"What was that?"

"That you had been hanged."

The man laughed aloud.

"Ah," he said, "so many have been under that impression."

"Then it must have been that precious cousin of yours?"

"It was Robert Sweetman—the same name as myself. You see, he took a fancy to four horses belonging to Lord Harvey—"

"Where were they?"

"In his lordship's stables. He was leading them away when two ostlers espied him. He was arrested, tried, and hanged. Poor Robert! and for four miserable horses. But you don't offer me a drink."

"Call for what you like."

Robert Sweetmen did not fail to do so, and he ordered the very best.

"I would rather have seen the devil himself than this man," thought Cunningham. "A more dangerous man does not live. That I have proved—that my father has proved. It is true that I shall want assistance, but I would not employ *him*—not I.

"He would sell me for a paltry sum, I'll swear. There is only one thing to do with a man like this, and that is to *remove* him. And the finest way of removing him is to poison him.

"No doubt I shall be able to get what I want somewhere in the neighbourhood. I will pay *any* price for it.

"But I must pretend to be extremely condescending."

The wine was brought, and Sweetman started on it, quickly consumed it, and asked if he should order another.

"Oh, yes," replied Cunningham; "I don't mind paying for more, for I fancy you will be useful to me. The fact of it is, I have a little *business* on hand."

"Near here?"

"Not far off."

"Don't you want some assistance?"

"I do; and you, I know, I can trust."

"That you can."

"It is of a delicate nature, and requires careful handling. If you assist me I will pay you handsomely."

"Here's my hand on it. I am hard up, and shall be glad to do anything."

"Listen: Do you remain here a short time. I shall return within an hour, and then I will tell you exactly how you can assist me."

"Good," said Sweetman.

Cunningham quitted the hostelry and returned to the house.

Producing flint and steel, he kindled a light, searched for and found a lantern, and with that proceeded upstairs.

He had scarcely reached the first landing before there was a sudden rush, as if a bundle of canvas had been hurled across the floor, and Cunningham found himself seized by the throat.

"Hound!" hissed Porter, "I have you. I have you, Cunningham Trevanion."

Cunningham wildly shook his head.

"What!" thundered Porter, as releasing one hand, he raised aloft the dagger, "do you mean that you are *not* Cunningham Trevanion?"

Cunningham again shook his head.

"Can this be so?" Porter asked himself. "Is this only one of the bloodthirsty, villainous dogs?"

Releasing Cunningham, he said—

"Mind, beware how you reply. You mean to say that you are not Cunningham Trevanion?"

"Oh, no, no, I am not. No, sir—I am not," gasped Cunningham.

"Who, then, are you?"

"I—I—was here—"

"You are one of his men?"

"Yes, yes, I will not deny it, your honour, if you will not hurt me. I have been running messages for him. I had no hand in the crimes committed by him. Oh, no, sir; I am not so bad as that."

"Where is my father?"

"Your father?"

"My name is Porter."

"Ah, sir, alas! your poor father was murdered—yes, murdered by Cunningham Trevanion. And so was his wife. I was not here when it was done, but Trevanion told me about it, only a little while back, at 'The Three Goats,' and when I told him that I would have nothing further to do with him, he dealt me a terrific blow in the face, and kicked me out of the hostelry.

"I only came back here to get a few things."

"Tell me this: what was done with the bodies?"

"He said that he had buried them through the flooring somewhere. Ah, he is a terrible man, your honour."

"Describe him—describe the hound."

Cunningham instantly gave the description of *Sweetman!*

He added—

"He will return soon, your honour, for he has a girl somewhere here in the house, and he said he was going to search for the old man's money."

"Ay, ay, I will search him! He said he hurled the bodies through the flooring, did he? I know what he means. But I will attend to that anon.

"Listen: You have done with him for good?"

"Done with him, your honour? I would not have anything further to do with him for any amount. If I did, I am certain to get into gaol—or perhaps I might fare worse."

"Take this. Five crowns are here. For this amount, you will go to the hostelry and watch him. If, when he leaves the hostelry, he goes in a direction opposite to this house, come here at once and let me know."

"Yes, yes, I understand. I will go at once, your honour."

Accordingly, Cunningham left the house, and returned to the hostelry.

"A narrow squeak, by Satan!" he muttered. "Ho, ho! but I have a very excellent plan."

There was actually a smile on the villain's face as he entered the chamber in which Sweetman awaited him.

He whispered in his ear—

"All is well, and if you act entirely as I tell you, we are likely to benefit to the tune of several thousand crowns.

"You see, a short distance from here, is the house of a miser—I will show you the place; and I have succeeded in entering by the window, and opening the door.

"Now what we shall do is to make a sudden rush into the place—you by the door, and I by the window. The moment we are heard, the old man will rush from his bedroom.

"You will throw yourself upon him, and I will finish him."

"Good. When do we start?"

"At once. Do you follow me. But wait, and I will borrow a taper from the host."

This having been done, they went on to the house, and Cunningham pointed out the door.

Then he crept round to the back.

Sweetman, suspecting no danger, pushed the door open, entered, and lit the taper.

He waited a few moments, and hearing no noise, crept up the stairs.

Porter, from the stairs above, saw him, and immediately recognised the description given him by Cunningham.

He waited for him to ascend still farther, and then, with one spring, he was upon the landing.

Not one word did he utter.

He brought down his dagger, and buried it deep in Sweetman's heart.

Cunningham saw what took place, for he had ascended the ladder placed against the window by Porter, though that young man did not see him.

When Sweetman fell, he descended, and after waiting a few moments, entered the house by the door.

He called out—
"What ho!"
Porter answered—
"Come up."
Cunningham ascended.
"Look," said Porter, "there lies the wretch. He is dead, and I have avenged my father's death."
"Ay, ay, that you have. It serves him right."
"I will now examine the place where my father was hurled. Follow me."
Cunningham did so, and he expressed the greatest surprise at the secret flaps.
When Porter had them safely open, he said—
"Do you remain here the while I get a rope."
He quickly found one, and tying a lantern to one end, lowered it.
Presently its rays glittered upon the surface of the water.
The next moment, the face of old Porter was seen, and then that of the old woman.
"I will fetch up my father's body," said Porter, "and in its place, put the body of Cunningham Trevanion. As to the body of the old woman, it can remain there."
As he said this, he was lying upon his stomach, the better to see the bodies below.
"Yes," said Cunningham, "and I will help you. You are sure it is the body of your father?"
As he said this, he, unseen by Porter, rose.
"I am *certain* of it," answered Porter, looking eagerly down. "He was evidently hurled, all of a sudden, down into the water. And there is no chance of escape—none."
"You are *right!*" cried Cunningham.
Like a flash he seized Porter by the legs, and hurled him below.
There was nothing to clutch at. Porter like, his father, was doomed.

Cunningham, with a fiendish howl, threw himself upon his stomach.
"*I* am Cunningham Trevanion," he cried. "Do you hear it, eh?"
There was no reply.
All that could be heard was a low gurgling sound, and the splashing of water.
But this speedily ceased, and perfect silence reigned.
Cunningham rose, entered the bedchamber, found a taper and lit it; and he at once caused the flaps to resume their proper position.
"Triumphant again!" he chuckled; "but I don't remember ever having such a narrow escape before. And now for darling Gracie. Ho, ho! I will have my way this time and no mistake. And then I—yes, by all that is good, I will serve her in the same way.
"Then it would not be a bad idea to take away as much of value as I can carry, and fire the house."
He ascended to the chamber in which Grace had been placed, and kicked the door open.
"What, ho! Lady Pride!" he cried; "here I am once more, and—"
He paused suddenly, as he saw that the chamber was tenantless.
Rooted to the spot, he stood for some considerable time. Then he muttered—
"Ah! yes, I see it all. She has gone. Old Porter's son released her—of that I feel sure. Well, no matter—I shall have her again. Yes, I shall have her again. And the next time there will be but little ceremony.
"But, confound it! I wish she were here now. I am in the right humour. But it will be dangerous to stop here longer. I will be off."
Collecting as many articles as he thought were of value, he placed them in a bag, slung it over his shoulder, and left the house.

CHAPTER XXIV.

IN WHICH IT IS SEEN THAT GRACE FALLS INTO ANOTHER DANGER, AND OF HOW SAMPSON AND GOLIAR GET HER OUT OF IT.

MEANTIME Gracie went on, but it was slowly, so weak was she.
Occasionally she paused to lean against some doorway.
"I have heard," she thought, "that when a person is suffering from extreme exhaustion, a small quantity of spirits sometimes acts like magic. But how can I obtain such a thing? I cannot—dare not enter a hostelry. Alas! I feel so ill."
"What ails you, mistress?" asked a voice.
Gracie turned, to find a tall, elderly man beside her.
From the tone of his voice, and the splendid cloak he wore, he appeared to be a gentleman.
"I feel ill," replied Grace, raising her face.

As she did so her mantle fell from it, and her face was fully revealed.
"On my soul!" muttered the gentleman, "she is exceedingly pretty. It is not often that one sees such a pretty girl as this alone in the streets."
Aloud he said—
"I am sorry for you. If I can be of any service, command me. Have you far to go?"
"Not very far. I think, if I had a little spirits, I could manage to proceed."
"Yonder is a hostelry. Let me take you there, and—"
"No, no; I must not enter a hostelry."
"Well, then, I will go and procure you some. I shall not be more than a few minutes."

"Oh, thank you, kindly."

The gentleman went off, but it was not long before he returned with a tiny vessel containing spirits.

This he handed to Grace, who drank it, feeling assured that it would so act upon her that she could continue her journey.

She again thanked the gentleman for his trouble, and bade him good-night.

Then once more she tottered on.

But she did not get far.

A strange, choking sensation came upon her, with a feeling of terrible sickness.

Hard she tried to throw it off, continuing to walk as she did so, and totally unconscious of the fact that the man who had brought her the spirits was following her like a shadow.

She stopped at last, and staggered to a doorway, the post of which she tried to clutch.

It was a failure.

She fell like a log to the ground.

The reader is able to guess what had been done.

The spirits had been drugged.

From one terrible danger poor Gracie had fallen into another.

The man approached her, stooped, looked into her face, and then, raising her in his arms, walked rapidly away.

He did not go far.

Stopping at a house not more than a hundred yards from the Abbey, he rang the bell, and the door was answered by a short, singularly grave elderly man, who started back in great surprise.

"Your lordship—returned?" he said.

"Yes," was the reply; "I changed my mind. Instead of proceeding to the Tower, I went elsewhere, and—"

"But, in heaven's name!" interrupted the butler—for such was the man's vocation—"what has your lordship got?"

"If you will have the kindness to speak when I have spoken," was the reply, "it is possible that you may hear. Returning, I found this young lady—"

"Lady?"

"I presume she is, though, to be sure, her attire is not very elaborate. I found her in the street. As you see, I have taken compassion upon her."

As this conversation was proceeding Lord Gordon Herries, for that was the gentleman's name, entered the fine hall and the butler closed the door.

Lord Herries continued—

"Tell your wife what I have told you, and add that she is to place this lady, at once, in the Crimson Room."

"That bedchamber, your lordship, is in a state of disorder because of the repairs, and the—"

"Do as I tell you."

The butler bowed and went below.

The very first words he said to his wife were—

"More villainy—at least, so I suspect."

"What now?" asked his wife.

"His lordship has returned, and has brought with him—actually in his arms—a young girl."

"What! a girl?"

"Yes, a girl."

"But, where, in heaven's name, did he bring her from?"

"He said he found her in the streets, took compassion upon her, and brought her here."

"Compassion? Lord Herries took compassion? No, no; the world is not coming to an end yet! As you say, it is more villainy. The sooner we are away from here the better."

"True. But I will not go until I have seen this girl away from the house."

"Right, John, right."

"You had better go up and obey his orders, or he may dismiss us at once; and that would be all the worse for the girl, perhaps."

Within half-an-hour Gracie, totally unconscious, was lying upon the bed in a magnificently furnished apartment designated the Crimson Room.

Consciousness returned to her before very many hours had passed.

But she lay on the bed like a poor, worn-out child, scarcely able to say anything.

Lord Herries continually visited her, and Gracie, weak and worn out though she was, was easily able to understand that she was in the clutches of a villain—a titled vagabond, who was simply awaiting her recovery to pester her with his "attentions."

John Kennard, the butler, and his wife saw this as plainly as possible, and the latter watched Gracie as keenly as a hawk watches a sparrow.

For two days Gracie said very little indeed.

She was not certain about the people who came in and out of the chamber, but, satisfied at last that Mistress Kennard and her husband were to be trusted, she told them of how she had been the prisoner of Cunningham Trevanion; how she had escaped, with assistance, from the house; and of how Lord Herries had procured her some spirits, which she had no doubt had been drugged.

That same night John Kennard left the house to procure her—unknown to Lord Herries—some medicine.

On the way he called at the "Shield," the very hostelry at which Lord Herries had procured the spirits for Grace.

While drinking a small goblet of wine, Kennard heard sounds of uproarious merriment in an adjoining chamber.

He enquired of the host the cause of it.

The host grinned.

"Do you look in," he said.

Kennard did so, and started back.

"Great heaven!" he said; "what enormous men!"

"Aye," whispered the host, who stood beside him, "there are only two men so big in the world. One is called Sampson, and the other Goliar."

Again Kennard started, and an exclamation of joy almost left his lips as he thought—

"The giants that poor girl spoke of!"

Aloud he said—

"But the two men with them, and the men at the tables?"

"Oh, yon two men with them," replied the host, with a laugh, "are a couple of lawyers. The rogues, for a long time past, have been defrauding a number of poor people. The giants got hold of them, and they are playing a game with them."

Kennard entered.

The sight presented was decidedly very peculiar and highly laughable.

The two lawyers were elderly men, clothed in black—a very shabby black indeed—and as thin as laths.

Both of them were vultures, who preyed upon the poor, and for years they had haunted Westminster.

The brothers heard all about them at the hostelry, and, strange to say, while the host was telling them about the lawyers, they came in—not for wine, but for shelter from a number of people who were following them, yelling and shaking their fists at them.

At once the giants pounced upon them, much to the delight of the crowd, and took them into the room.

Just as Kennard entered, the brothers had the lawyers upon their knees.

"Why, you see," said Sampson, "these are the devil's imps. Presently we will see how they can stand fire."

At this the two lawyers yelled with terror.

"Injure us at your peril," said one, "and we will set the law in motion against you."

"Oh," said Goliar, "we don't intend to injure you."

As he spoke, he took the lawyer from his knees, and pitched him over to Sampson.

"Certainly not," said the latter, as he banged the lawyers' heads together, "we would not hurt them for any sum. My friends, what shall we do with them? You see there is a fine fire on the hearth, and it is big enough to roast one at the time."

Again the lawyers uttered loud cries of terror, and the cries were echoed by loud shouts of laughter from the onlookers.

"Well," said Goliar, "as they object to be roasted, what say you to boiling them? I have never yet seen how a boiled lawyer looks, but I daresay very nice."

Sampson shook his head.

"These two would look very bad," he said, "for they have very little meat on their bones."

"If they haven't much meat on their bones, they have plenty of money in their pockets."

"It is false!" said one of the lawyers. "There are no poorer men in London."

"Out with what you have."

"Eh?"

"Out with it."

"What?"

"The money—quick! Look around. There are fifteen people here, and— Host! What ho, host!"

"Here, your honour."

"How much is fifteen bottles of good wine?"

"No," said Goliar, "five for us—that will be twenty."

"Twenty crowns," said the host.

"A very reasonable amount. Now, you devil's imps, out with it."

Both the discomfited lawyers protested that they had no such sum about them.

"Well, then," said Sampson, as he started up, "on the fire you go."

He was about to seize one, when he took a purse from his pocket and threw it upon the floor.

Sampson picked it up, opened it, and counted the contents.

"Twenty-one crowns, exactly, Master Host," he said; "so that is one for yourself."

Turning to the lawyer, he pulled him round.

"Now," he said, "say after me. Do you hear it?"

"Ye—yes—yes."

"Say, 'Master Host, do you get these poor people twenty bottles of good wine. I give it them freely, and with all my heart.'"

The lawyer groaned, but did not reply.

"Speak out!" thundered Sampson.

No reply.

Thereupon Sampson seized the lawyer and hung him up in the air by his feet.

Upside down the lawyer said what he was told to, and he was lowered to the floor.

"Both of you can go now," said Goliar, "and mark it, if you are seen in Westminster again, you will be brought here and roasted. Be off with you."

The lawyers waited not to be told a second time.

They darted to the door and were on the other side of it in an instant.

"Well, said Sampson, "they have had a lesson. I don't fancy they will trouble the poor of Westminster much more. And now, my friends, drink. See, here is the host."

Kennard gradually made his way to Sampson.

He got close to him at last and touched him.

"Well?" said Sampson; "who are you?"

"A few words with you, Master Giant."

"Ay, ay, say on."

Kennard whispered a few words in his ear, and Sampson started up.

"By the thunder of heaven!" he cried, "is this possible? Brother Goliar, we must away. Quick—drink!"

A bottle being disposed of by each they bade the people at the hostelry good-night and quitted it in company with Kennard.

"What is it, brother Sampson?" asked Goliar.

"Poor Gracie!" replied Sampson, in tremulous tones; "she is not far from here—a prisoner, or little better. You have heard of that scoundrel, Lord Herries, who is said to be the only person who knows what became of a certain three girls who lived near the Tower?"

"Ay, ay; who has not?"

"She is in his clutches. But this man, who is the butler, will tell us all."

Kennard hastily did so.

"Oh, yes," said Sampson, "it is our poor Gracie, sure enough. Great powers! what would Oscar say?"

"We must have her away from that house, brother Sampson," said Goliar, "even if we pull the house down."

"Oh, we shall not have to do that. How many are in the house?"

"My wife only."

"Good. Not that we should care if there were a dozen. But come on, my friend, and as we go, we will form a plan how to act. You and your wife are an honest, kind-hearted couple, and you may rest assured that you will be well rewarded."

In the meanwhile, something had been taking place at the house.

About a quarter of an hour after Kennard had departed, his lordship rang for the wife.

Slowly she ascended to the chamber in which he sat.

"Well," he said, "and how is our patient now?"

"About the same."

"The same! Nonsense. But where is John?"

"Out."

"Where has he gone?"

"I have no idea, but I do not think he will be long."

"He had better *not* be long. He had no orders to leave the house. But now see that the girl is properly attired, and bring her here."

"When, your lordship?"

"As quickly as possible."

"She is not in a fit condition to—"

"Depart, and at once carry out my orders. That is what you are here for."

It was not long before Mistress Kennard returned, escorting Grace.

His lordship rose as she entered, and eagerly scanned her features.

"Well," he said, "and how do you feel now?"

"I feel well enough to quit the house, and I will now say adieu."

Lord Herries smiled.

"Is it thus you repay a kindness?" he asked.

"A kindness! Is it a kindness to drug a girl?"

"Drug! Do you insinuate that I drugged you?"

"I am certain of it."

"Who put such a thing into your head?"

As he asked this, he looked at Mistress Kennard.

"It was not necessary for anyone to put it into my head," she said; "my feelings tell me that."

"Listen to me: I am a gentleman who—"

"If you are a gentleman," interrupted Grace, "allow me to depart."

"Not by any means. Here you remain so long as it pleases me. The fact of it is, I have taken a fancy to you. And when I take a fancy to anyone, I am in no hurry for their departure. You may go, Mistress Kennard. I have a great deal to say to this young lady—alone."

"I have no desire to be alone with you," said Grace.

"And why?"

"Because I am sure that you are not a man to be trusted."

"I warn you to be careful what you say to me. It is in my power to make you a lady to be envied, or destroy you."

"You are a coward to say such a thing. I demand—"

She paused, as a knock came upon the door.

The next moment John entered.

He paused in astonishment as he saw Grace, and Lord Herries noticed it.

"John Kennard," he said, "it is my opinion

that you and your wife have been trying your very hardest to set this girl against me."

"What makes your lordship—you who are almost old enough to be the girl's grandfather, say so?"

"I have every reason to say so. Tell me—or on your head rest the consequences—what you have been saying to her."

"Your lordship would not care to know."

His lordship's face became distorted with rage.

"Dog!" he roared; "what have you been saying?"

"I warned her to be careful of you, for you were a dangerous man."

Lord Herries darted across the room towards Kennard, and as he did so drew his sword.

But John was out of the chamber first.

Lord Herries was about to cross the threshold when he found it barred by an enormous form—a form which towered head, shoulders, and chest higher than himself, and completely filled the doorway.

It was Sampson.

Behind him was Goliar.

Lord Herries knew them at once, for he had often seen them.

Sampson seized him by the collar, wrenched his sword out of his hand, and passed it over his shoulder to Goliar, who broke it as he would have broken a toothpick.

The blade he threw away, but observing that the hilt was jewelled he put that in his pocket, with the remark that it might be of use.

Grace, the instant she saw who had arrived, uttered a loud cry of joy.

"Thank heaven!" she said, as the tears fell down her cheeks. "Thank heaven!"

"Ay, you are quite safe now, Gracie," said Sampson; "and you shall go with us. But I beg of you not to be in a hurry."

As he spoke, he lifted his lordship clean off his feet, and carried him farther into the chamber.

Then he gave him such a stunning clout on the ear, that his lordship was sent flying several yards away, and fell to the ground.

"You are a pretty lord," said Goliar. "You are after the style of another one we know—one who will have his wicked, ugly head struck off anon."

"It seems to me, brother Goliar," said Sampson, "that we have arrived just in time."

"Ay, ay—thanks to this good man."

Lord Herries staggered to his feet.

In hoarse tones, he said—

"Do you wait! My time will come. I have but to go to the Court—"

"They can do without the likes of you at Court, I'll warrant it. What do think the Queen would say if she knew what you had done? But I will take care that you don't go to the Court for the present. A wretch like you deserves to be punished, and punished you *will* be."

"You dare not lay a hand on me."

"But I have *already* laid a hand on you."

Lord Herries was trembling in every limb with terror.

"Leave my house!" he gasped.

"Oh, you can be assured that we will not take it with us."

Sampson and Goliar conversed in whispers for a few seconds.

Then Sampson said to Kennard—

"Fetch a razor, my friend."

A wild cry left his lordship's lips, and he cried—

"Murder!"

Sampson smiled.

"Oh, no," he said, "we are not going to murder you, though a man like you don't deserve to live. Go on," he added to Kennard, "bring a razor, a long piece of rope, and a cloth."

Kennard was not long in procuring these articles.

Lord Herries then altered his tones, and appealed for mercy.

"I will give you a thousand crowns to leave me alone," he said.

"Keep your money," said Goliar; "we would not take ten thousand."

Sampson once more seized Lord Herries.

Resistance was absolutely useless.

He was like a mere infant in Sampson's hands.

He was forced into a chair, and in a few moments, Goliar had pinioned him with the rope in such a way, that it was impossible for him to free himself.

Then Sampson took the razor, and with the rapidity and dexterity of an experienced barber, shaved off the hair from his face and head.

He then looked a perfect scarecrow.

Sampson next tore one of the mirrors from the wall, and held it towards him.

"What!" he said, "would you have me believe that you would go to Court like this? No, no—not for one moment would I believe it."

Lord Herries groaned as he saw his reflection in the mirror.

"He ought to thank his lucky stars that he has not had his head cut off, instead of his hair," said Goliar.

"There's time enough for that," said Sampson.

Goliar next took the cloth, and gagged his lordship.

"There," he said, "I think we have now made you fairly comfortable. In that position you will remain until someone enters the house and releases you. If no one comes you will die."

"Now, my friend," said Sampson to Kennard, "do you bring up three or four bottles of his lordship's best wine. This young lady will partake of a small quantity the better to enable her to keep up."

Grace was indeed very thankful for a small portion of the wine.

Sampson insisted on Kennard partaking of some, and he and Goliar finished the remainder.

Goliar then told Kennard to assist his wife in packing what few articles they required.

When this was done Sampson picked up one of the costly rugs from the floor, completely wrapped Grace in it, and took her in his arms.

"Come along, my child," he said; "you look tired and worn. We will go to the Armourer's house, and I will carry you every step of the way."

Goliar extinguished the lights, and the whole party departed.

CHAPTER XXV.

OF HOW OSCAR IS ACCOSTED BY A WATERMAN—OF WHAT TRANSPIRED BETWEEN THEM—AND OF HOW THEY WENT TO THE HOUSE AT VAUXHALL.

WE must retrace our steps somewhat.

Our hero, as may be supposed, was nearly distracted.

Though inquiries had been pursued in every direction, and most unceasingly, no tidings were heard of Grace.

About the hour of eight on the same evening that the giant brothers rescued Grace from the clutches of Lord Herries, Oscar strolled to the river.

By its banks he remained some time, lost in thought.

Bitter thoughts were his—very bitter indeed.

Gracie was alive—that he fully believed, and that she was in the clutches of Cunningham Trevanion he had no doubt at all.

But to what part had she been taken?

"Ah!" he considered, "I might search night and day and never find her. I do not fancy—"

"A boat, your honour?" said a voice.

Oscar turned, to see a waterman beside him.

"No, my friend," he said, "I don't want a boat. I was thinking of having one as far as Greenwich, but I have altered my mind."

"I am glad of it."

"Glad?"

"Why, yes; for I have no desire to go so far. And another thing, I don't like Greenwich. Only yesterday I rowed there. I took two gentlemen, or at least so they appeared to be. But they were quarrelling nearly all the way, and just as we arrived off Greenwich, one drew a pistol and shot the other dead."

"A more extraordinary thing I have never heard of. Well, who did they turn out to be?"

"Ah, that is not known at present, your honour. Perhaps it never will be. I handed the body over to the authorities, and shall have to go to Greenwich again. The journey took me a long time, and I got nothing for it.

"Greenwich is an unlucky journey—at least it has proved so to me. It was not so long ago that I took two men to the steps and had to await their return.

"'NOW,' HE SAID, AS HE DREW A PISTOL, "WHERE IS YOUR MONEY'"

"One only came back, and he had a girl in his arms. Ah, that was a mysterious affair, and I have never been able to make it out."

At this Oscar started.

Of course Grace was continually uppermost in his mind.

The waterman continued—

"I rowed the pair back to Vauxhall, and there the man landed, saying he would return in a few minutes. The girl he left in the wherry.

"Thinking that something was wrong, and that it might, hereafter, be to my advantage, I cut a lock of hair from the girl's head and took a ring from her finger, and so—"

Oscar seized him by the wrist.

"My friend," he said, "your story has the greatest interest for me. I am now looking for a young girl who was taken away from Greenwich by a consummate villain. I will give you five crowns to show me the hair and ring."

The waterman at once pulled the articles from his pocket.

"Five crowns," he said, "is, of course, a considerable amount to me, but I would show you or anyone else the articles, because I am anxious to find out who she was."

It was with a very trembling hand that Oscar took the articles.

The waterman produced flint and steel, and kindled a light, so that Oscar could see them distinctly.

"Gracie's hair!" he cried. "Gracie's ring! These articles belonged to the lady I seek."

"Then, by heaven, sir, your words could not fall on more welcome ears."

"Alas, alas! of what use are these to me? How can I tell—"

"One moment, your honour. The man returned to the boat in a few minutes, and took the girl—who remained quite unconscious the whole time—away with him.

"Ah, but I followed, and I could, this moment, point out the house to which the girl was taken."

Oscar took both the waterman's rough, horny hands and pressed them warmly.

"You, above all other men, are the one I require," he said—and the waterman could tell how deeply he was affected. "You will show me this house, and what you demand I will pay you."

"I will show it you, your honour, most certainly. As to payment for the time occupied—well, I will leave that to you. But, though I am a poor man, you may depend that I shall demand nothing excessive. Here is my wherry, your honour. Jump in, and I will soon land you at Vauxhall steps."

He did, too, pulling with all his might, but he left himself sufficient breath to tell Oscar all that had transpired between him and his mysterious fare, who, Oscar knew, was none other than Cunningham.

Vauxhall being reached, the waterman fastened his boat to a rope, and bade Oscar follow him, and he conducted him, almost without a pause, to the house.

At a little distance from it, they stood and watched.

Suddenly the waterman said—

"Look, your honour. I think that is a light moving about."

"It is. It is the light of a taper, unless I am very much mistaken. At any rate, it proves that someone is in the house."

Oscar tried the door.

It was fast.

Thereupon they went to the back.

Singular to say, the ladder was still there, but the window was closed.

"I will ascend," whispered Oscar, "and if I succeed in entering, do you follow me."

"Without fail, your honour. But are you armed?"

"Fairly well."

"Good."

Oscar ascended, and easily raising the window, noiselessly entered.

The waterman followed him, and soon stood beside him on the landing.

Oscar drew his sword, and both stood side by side, listening.

For some few minutes not the faintest sound was heard, nor was a light seen.

Then the sound of footsteps—heavy footsteps—was heard below.

Oscar looked over the banisters, and saw a tall, badly-clad man, of middle age, examining some articles on the wall by the light of a taper.

In this examination he took some considerable time, but at last he ascended.

When he reached the top of the stairs, Oscar sprang forward, and caught him by the throat.

As may be imagined, the man was staggered.

But at last he said—

"Oh, oh, even in a house I am not safe. People seem to spring from all sorts of unsuspected places. Of a truth, I am the most unlucky man in the world!

"But why point your sword at my heart, your honour? Surely I have not done *you* any harm? Why, I declare that this is the first time I have ever set eyes upon you."

"Who *are* you?"

"Eh?"

"I say, who *are* you?"

"Oh, as to that—"

"Be careful, or I swear that I will drive this blade through your body."

"Odds my life! this is a fine thing. Surely I am a most unlucky man."

"Whom do you serve?"

"Serve! What, do you think I have a master? Not I."

"You have."

"You are a—I mean, it's a mistake."

"Your master is Cunningham Trevanion."

"Who? Cunningham Trevanion! What a huge joke. I have heard of such a person, it is true, but I have never seen him. I can see there is a mistake here. Release your hold, master, and perhaps I can set it right."

Oscar released his hold.

Something told him that he was not associated with Cunningham Trevanion.

"It is my business to ask who the deuce *you* are," said the man; "but I will not, in case you give my throat another clutch with your iron fingers. But I will tell you who *I* am. My name is Dick Haversford. Ever heard that name before?"

"No."

"Nor did I until the other day."

"The man is evidently a fool," thought Oscar.

"Dick Haversford" continued—

"I've had *several* names, you see," he said, "but none of them have been any good to me. All I have been compelled to change, and I was at a loss for a new one, when I heard that a man named Dick Haversford had been taken from the Thames. So I took that name."

"I want to know how you got *here*."

"Oh, ay. Well, I'll soon tell you that. Last night, I came along the path at the back of this house, and I saw a ladder against one of the windows.

"I was tired out and wanted a rest, and thinking that this house was unoccupied, I watched for a time. Seeing no light, I ascended the ladder and entered, and I soon found that there was no one in the place—at least, no one alive. At the bottom of the stairs, there I found a man, dead. I looked at him, and came to the conclusion that he had been murdered. If not, then I'm a Dutchman.

"But I've seen so many dead men in my time, that I did not trouble, and I went to bed.

"In the morning, I searched the house. Well, I would not do it again in any house I found myself. Ah, this is a house with a history, if you like. I—"

"Tell me this—quick! Did you find a young girl here?"

"A young girl! No, and no signs of one. But I found an old woman, or rather, her body. Oh, what a sight—what a sight!"

"Go on—go on."

"I also found the body of an old man."

"By heaven! this is indeed a house of death."

"It is, upon my word. I never saw a thing like it in all the whole course of my life. Were you acquainted with the owner of this house?"

"Not at all. But a young girl was taken here, and it is for her I search."

"I see. Well, as I have said before, there is no young girl here—at least, not alive. There may be some place I have not explored, in which another may be found. But for your sake, I hope not. If you decide to search the place, I will help you willingly. I hope you are now convinced that I have nothing to do with this Cunningham Trevanion?"

"Yes, I am satisfied as to that. Where did you find the bodies of the old man and woman?"

"In one of the most extraordinary places I ever beheld. I will show you, and I think you, too, will be pretty well astonished."

He took them to the bedchamber, and showed them the ring.

"I thought it peculiar," he said, "and pulled it—like this—and then put it on this hook. Now do you look here."

He then, raising high a lantern, showed them the cistern.

Oscar and the waterman stood looking at it in astonishment.

"This has been a house of crime, I should say," he said. "Why should such a place have been constructed at all? Get a piece of rope, and let me lower the lantern."

The waterman produced a thin piece of cord, and at one end the lantern was fastened and lowered.

As soon as it reached the water, a great cry burst from the three.

"By all the saints!" gasped Haversford, "there are *three* bodies altogether. It is evident that one has not long risen to the surface."

"I feel perfectly certain that Cunningham Trevanion is at the bottom of all this," said Oscar. "I don't say that he has committed these murders, but he is the author of them."

"What do you advise, your honour?" asked Haversford. "Shall I give notice to the authorities?"

"No—*you* had better not do that, or you may be closely questioned as to your movements for the past few days."

"Ay, ay, that is true, your honour."

"I will myself give the necessary notice. Now to search the place."

Search was made in every hole and corner.

"I feel perfectly satisfied," said Oscar, "that she is not here, dead or alive. The wretch has taken her with him, but I will never rest, day or night, until I have found her. Come, my friend," he added to the waterman, "let us quit the place."

To Haversford he said—

"My advice to you is, to put a mile or two between yourself and this house. It might be awkward for you if you were caught here."

"I will take your advice."

Oscar and the waterman returned to the wherry.

"You can now row me to London Bridge," said the former.

When they arrived there, Oscar handed the waterman a sum of money, took his name and address, in case he should be wanted to prove anything, and made his way to the Armourer's.

A great cry of joy left his lips when the door was opened by Sampson, and he saw Goliar behind him.

But what sort of cry escaped him when Sampson, grasping him by the waist, and raising him up on high, said—

"She is safe, Oscar—we have her here. Yes, Grace is here, safe and sound."

Thank heaven!" said Oscar.

"Ah," said Sampson, sorrowfully, "but we have not come across that hound, Cunningham Trevanion. I would we had, for we would have sat on him until every bit of breath had left his carcase. But don't let us detain you—go to Gracie."

Away darted Oscar, and—but we will draw a veil over the scene that ensued.

It was a long, long time before Oscar and Grace could tear themselves away from each other.

When they did so, Sampson told how they had rescued her.

Oscar, the tears standing in his eyes, thanked them again and again.

"But what have you been doing with yourselves all this time?" he asked.

"Oh, we have been hiding most of the time," said Sampson. "We did not want to be put in the Tower again. Not likely."

"But you have been pardoned by the queen. You are free men, and notices to that effect have been posted on the Tower gates."

"So we have just heard. But pardoned! We have done nothing to be pardoned for. Ah, well, it doesn't matter. We are free to walk the City, and that is something."

"Sampson, my friend, and you, Goliar, shall have the finest meal, and the best ales and wines that can be bought for money."

Both the giants stroked their stomachs.

"Ah," said Sampson, "how welcome will a fine meal be."

"Ah, welcome indeed," said Goliar. "We have eaten nothing for a whole day, and as for wines—well, they are very scarce. We have forgotten the taste of them."

"We hope," said Sampson, "that you will join us, and that Gracie will be on your right hand."

"Ay, that she shall."

"We will drink to your healths half-a-dozen times."

"Pooh!" said Goliar, "we will drink to them fifty times."

CHAPTER XXVI.

OF HOW CUNNINGHAM MAKES A JOURNEY TO FOOT'S CRAY, AND OF WHAT HAPPENED AT THE HOUSE OF MASTER WELCH.

THE scene now changes, and we find ourselves, a month after the incidents recorded in the preceding chapter, in the neighbourhood of Wapping.

Here stood one of the largest, and, at the same time, one of the most remarkable hostelries in England.

It was called the "Three Jolly Sailors," and stood close to the river—or, at least, the back did.

In the centre of the house was a huge archway, and this at high tide, if the gates were opened, admitted a boat to pass under.

So it will easily be seen that smugglers could get a cargo of articles into the house.

It was not to be wondered at that the "Three Jolly Sailors" had the reputation of selling the cheapest and best liquors.

The host—a short, burly fellow named Kean—bought up all the smuggled wines and spirits he could get, and heavily bribed officials to keep their mouths shut.

The trade he did was enormous, his house, day and night, being frequented by men of all sorts, but the majority of them were connected with the river traffic.

One night, when very few men were in the house, and when the host was nodding between a couple of his barrels, there entered a man whose age seemed to be about thirty.

His face was bronzed, as if from travel, and so were his hands.

He had a somewhat foreign appearance, and this was added to by his costume, which was partly Spanish.

"What can I do for you?" asked the host, when aroused.

"Oh, a bottle of wine is all I want; and look you, host, have you been long in Wapping?"

"Long! Why, yes—years and years."

"Well, I want a little information about the place, and, if you have a short time to spare, perhaps you will join me in drinking the wine."

"Oh, with pleasure," replied the host.

He called to a serving-man, and having put him in his place, got the wine, and took the guest to a small, and seldom-used chamber.

"I suppose, your honour," said the host, "that you are a stranger hereabouts?"

"It is a long time since I was last here."

"You have travelled much, eh?"

"Ay, been nearly all over the world."

When we tell the reader that the guest was none other than Cunningham Trevanion, he will see what a lie was told.

"Well, your honour, I will tell you what I know about Wapping. I—"

"One moment. I don't want to know about Wapping."

"Eh?" said the host, opening wide his eyes.

"I say that I don't want to know about Wapping."

"You said you did just now."

"Ay, that is true. But I want to know something else. Don't, for a moment, fancy that I am an officer in disguise."

"An officer!"

"I mean, that I am not one of those individuals who want to know how you get this or that, and so on."

The host looked at Cunningham very closely.

It was quite certain that he had become uneasy.

"I can't understand you," he said, after a pause. "Tell me this—have you ever been here before?"

"Oh, scores of times."

"I don't remember you."

"No doubt."

"Well, look here. Just tell me what it is you want."

"I will. I have a little something on hand, and require assistance."

"Assistance! From me?"

"Ay."

"Something on hand? Do you mean that you have a boatload of—"

"Oh, no," interrupted Cunningham, with a grin—"nothing like that. The assistance I require is two or three men."

"Well, I wonder you have taken so much trouble about the matter. If you stay here long enough, you will see plenty of men, and you can choose—"

Cunningham again interrupted him by a wave of his hand.

"I want you to choose *for* me," he said. "You are acquainted with the men—I am not."

The host rose.

"Sir," he said, "are you under the impression that I do anything a stranger may ask me? It is not my custom to select men for *any* purpose."

"Oh, yes, it is."

"*What?*"

"I say that it *is*."

"And I say that you are a *liar*. And so I leave you. Drink the wine yourself."

"All right, my friend—all right. To-morrow I shall inform the authorities where a certain number of bales of silk, smuggled from France and purchased by you, are to be found. Silks are nothing compared with wines and spirits. A man found trafficking in smuggled silks can be sentenced to be hanged. It would be a pity to see the host of the 'Three Jolly Sailors' at the end of a rope."

During this speech, the host had turned very pale.

On its conclusion, he came close up to Cunningham, and looked into his face.

"I can't make it out," he said. "I fail to recognise you. Who the deuce are you? What is your name?"

"I have a dozen, and use them alternately. You have *one*—at least, one *here*—and that is Kean. But you are not always *keen* enough to conceal from curious eyes some of your transactions.

"But why beat about the bush? I want, say, three men who can be relied upon. Provide them, and we will be friends."

"I will do so."

"Good. It will cost you nothing. All I want is your assurance that they are men who can be trusted."

"I suppose you want them to fight?"

"Well, they must not be *afraid* to fight."

"I understand you perfectly. Well, presently, a man, whom I can recommend—"

"What is his name?"

"Dick Haversford."

This was the very same man that Oscar had encountered at the house at Vauxhall.

"Go on."

"He can be trusted to do anything—always provided that he is paid."

"I never allow a man to do *anything* for me without I pay him."

"He is somewhat of a strange man. You see, he makes his own terms."

"I see. He names his own price?"

"Exactly. He comes here to meet two companions, and they also, I am sure, can be relied upon."

"Are you sure he will be here to-night?"

"I am almost certain of it. Do you remain here. As soon as he comes I will tell you."

Not more than a quarter of an hour did he have to wait before the host returned, and he was accompanied by Dick Haversford and his two comrades, who were about his own age.

He simply introduced them, and left them with Cunningham.

"The host told me," said the latter, "that you were men who could be trusted."

"Very kind of him," said Haversford, "but he spoke the truth. But let me introduce my friends. This is Henry Wright, and this Thomas Villiers; and they can also be trusted. And now, your honour, to business, as we generally say. In the first place, what do you want us for?"

"Listen: Maybe you are acquainted with a place called Foot's Cray?"

"It is in Kent."

"Correct."

"I know the place fairly well—or, I should say, that I *did* know it. It is a long time since I went there. And I am not likely to forget it either."

"What happened?"

"Oh, I was simply passing through the place, and stopped at the only hostelry in the village, because my horse was thirsty. While at the hostelry, I was mistaken for a man who, a month before, had committed a robbery.

"In spite of my protestations, I was pounced upon and thrashed within an inch of my life. So sore was I that I could not get into the saddle again, and I had to walk all the way to London."

"Well, well, you got over that. But do you know a house at Foot's Cray called 'Stoneleigh'?"

"I do not."

"The hostelry you just spoke of is called the 'Reaper's Rest'?"

"That is correct."

"Well, the house I speak of is about half-a-mile from here on the right. In this house there lives, and has lived for the past forty years, an old man of the name of Welch."

"A rich man, I suppose?" said Haversford.

"His wealth is said to be enormous."

"Does he live alone?"

"He has one servant—an old woman."

"That is of no importance."

"The house is always kept securely fastened at night. But the four of us can easily effect an entrance."

"Or two, I should say."

"Ay, but the old man constantly carries arms, and from what I can understand, he knows how to use them."

"Oh, that is different. But do you propose to kill the old man?"

"No, I intend to reserve him for another purpose—a purpose you will learn later on."

"Of course," said Haversford, after a pause, "you have made all sorts of inquiries about the old man?"

"I have been at the hostelry for nearly three

weeks. The old ostler there knows him well, and has given me valuable information."

"The principal thing is—does the old man keep his money in the house? I ask you for this reason: If we get into the house, and we find nothing of any consequence there, you will probably be unable to pay us anything."

"You are wrong. Before you start, I will hand each of you the sum of fifty crowns."

"Well, come," said Haversford, "that is handsome, to say the least of it."

"And before we talk further," continued Cunningham, "I will get two or three bottles of wine from the host."

"Don't trouble," said Wright, rising. "I will get it for you."

"No, no, be seated. I want the host to change me a goldsmith's note."

Saying which, Cunningham quitted the chamber.

"Well, now," said Haversford, "who the fiend can *he* be? Looks very much like a foreigner, but there is no trace of a foreign accent in his talk. I have never seen him before. Have you, Wright?"

"Never."

"Have *you*, Villiers?"

Villiers grinned from ear to ear.

"Yes," he replied, in very low tones, "I *have* seen him before, but he has not been disguised as he is now."

"Or do you mistake him for someone else."

"Not I."

"Well, who is he?"

"Cunningham Trevanion."

Haversford started slightly, but it was not noticed.

"Of course," continued Villiers, "you have heard that name before?"

"I fancy I have," said Haversford.

"Fancy! I thought *everyone* had heard it. His father is now in the Tower, awaiting execution."

"Ay, ay, I remember. So this is the son, eh? Ho, ho!"

"He is fairly well disguised," said Villiers; "nevertheless, I recognised him at once."

"He did not recognise you."

"Not he. But he would, if I uttered but half-a-dozen certain words."

"You will not do so?"

"No, because he would have nothing to do with me. And I am in want of a few crowns."

"He pays up?"

"Oh, yes, as a rule. He— But hist! Here he comes."

Cunningham entered with the wine, which he shared among the three.

Then he divided between them one hundred and fifty crowns.

"Now, your honour," said Haversford, "when do we set out?"

"At once."

"But what about horses? It is certain that we can't *walk* to Foot's Cray. If we walked to *Foot's* Cray, we should get sore *feet*."

"Is that a jest?"

"Oh, no, it is a fact."

"Do you know the farrier's close here?"

"I do."

"Four horses await us there. And now as to arms."

"Each of us has a sword and dagger."

"Good. In the holsters you will find pistols, and I am promised plenty of ammunition. Drink now, and let us go."

Four good horses were waiting at the farrier's, as Cunningham had said, and the men were quickly in the saddle.

Just before Cunningham passed out, the farrier handed him a box; and this Cunningham placed under his cloak.

We will not give a description of the ride to the exceedingly pretty little village called Foot's Cray—a place which is quite as retired and quite as pretty now as it was at the time of our story.

The largest house was that in the occupation of Master James Welch, a gentleman possessed of vast wealth.

At one time, many years before we introduce him to the notice of the reader, his house frequently contained many dozens of guests—old friends he had known when in London.

His son—a fine, handsome young fellow—was then alive.

But one night he was killed in mistake for another, and from this blow poor Master Welch never recovered.

He became a completely changed man, dismissed all his servants, with the exception of a woman who had been with him ever since his marriage, and never had but one guest.

That was none other than Gracie's father, Griffin Gaunt.

His visits were, of course, few and far between, but Griffin was always welcome, and he could have stayed there for weeks at a time, if he had so chosen.

Again and again Master Welch had urged Griffin to let his daughter stay at the house.

But how could he do that?

Was it likely that he could allow the only joy of his life out of his sight for any time? No.

To return now to Cunningham and his companions.

They reached Foot's Cray at midnight, when the village was wrapped in slumber.

Dismounting some little distance from the house, they tied their horses to some trees.

Then Cunningham led the way.

Stoneleigh House stood in its own pretty grounds.

The front was comparatively clear of trees, but the back was screened by a huge clump of tall, sombre-looking firs.

It was to the back they went, and tried the doors and windows.

All were firmly secured.

"As I expected," said Cunningham; "but I am prepared. Do you see that second balcony, Haversford?"

"Ay, and should say that it is very unsafe."

"That we must risk. Look here."

He took out the box which had been handed him by the farrier, opened it, and produced a long knotted rope, with a huge hook at one end.

"If," he said, "we can contrive to fasten the

hook to the balcony, we shall soon be in the house."

"True," said Haversford; "but it is possible that we may pull the balcony down. Or it is likely that the throwing of the hook may attract attention."

"That, also, we must risk."

"But if we attracted attention, and any guests were in the house—"

"Don't fear as to that," interrupted Cunningham; "the old man *never* has a guest."

Cunningham now took aim, and threw the hook.

But it failed to catch the balcony, and it was not until he had thrown it at least a dozen times that it caught.

Having hung onto it so as to be certain that it was safe, he directed Villiers to ascend.

He did so, and easily opened the window.

Five minutes after this, he opened the back door, and admitted Cunningham, Haversford, and Wright; and the latter kindled a light, and lit a taper.

"Not a sound is to be heard," said Villiers. "A dead-house could not be more silent."

"They are, of course, fast asleep. Let us examine the rooms."

They did so, noiselessly, but, on ascending, Wright, who was first, stumbled and fell.

He was no sooner on his feet, than the report of a pistol rang out, and he again dropped.

But he did not rise again.

He had been shot through the heart.

It was old Welch who had fired the shot.

He had another pistol in his left hand, but, before he could use it, Villiers rushed up, seized him, and pinned him against the wall.

The old man did not cry out.

Excitement held him speechless.

In but a few seconds, Cunningham had secured his hands behind his back.

While this was being done, the old woman-servant made her appearance.

She was seized upon, hurled into a room, and the door locked upon her, Cunningham warning her that, if she made a noise, she would be strangled.

The old man, who was but scantily attired, was conveyed back to his bedchamber.

"You have shot a man dead," said Cunningham.

"Ay," replied the old man, "and if I had had the chance, I would have shot *everyone* of you dead. You are here to rob me, but I will not tell you where the money is."

"You will directly."

"Never. I will die first."

"You certainly *will* die, if you do not say where it is within a few days."

"A few days!" thought Haversford. "Are *we* to stop here a few days?"

"Tie him in that chair," continued Cunningham.

This being done, he directed Villiers to go below and keep strict watch.

Then he lit all the tapers in a candelabrum standing on a sideboard.

"Now," he said, as he drew a pistol, and placed the muzzle close to the old man's ear, "where is your money?"

"I refuse to say."

"You will answer before I count six, or I will blow your brains out."

"Count away. I will not tell you."

"Will he really fire?" thought Haversford. "No, I don't believe he will. If I thought so, I would soon make him put that pistol down. He is here for something more than the money."

Cunningham counted six, but the old man spoke not.

Nor did he flinch when the cold muzzle of the pistol actually touched his ear.

"Well, on my soul," said Cunningham, as he lowered the weapon, "you are the greatest fool that ever lived. But I don't want to blow your brains out, at present. I will spare your life, on conditions."

No answer.

"Do you *hear?*" thundered Cunningham.

"I do. What are the conditions?"

"That you answer what questions I may put to you. That is the *first* condition."

"Ay, ay."

"And the second is, that you hand over to me the sum of ten thousand crowns."

The old man considered.

Ten thousand crowns was but a very small amount to him.

"I agree to hand you over an order for the amount you mention," he said, "but as to answering what questions you may put to me—"

"We shall see about that. Listen: Is your money in this house?"

"It is not. It is miles away—in London."

"And you can give me an order on a London goldsmith for the immediate payment of the sum named?"

"I can."

"Good. Now, how long have you known Grace Gaunt?"

The old man started at this question.

But he made no reply for some few moments.

Then he said—

"I can answer no question concerning that poor child."

"Poor child!" said Cunningham, contemptuously. "She may not be such a poor child as you think her."

Old Welch looked curiously at Cunningham.

"What do *you* know of her?" he asked.

"*I* am the questioner, not you."

"By heaven!" cried Welch, "I now understand. You are the black-hearted, murderous villain, Cunningham Trevanion."

"I *may* be."

"You *are.*"

"Well, what then?"

"And you actually come here for information!"

"You, no doubt, would like to know how I became possessed of the information that you were long the friend of Griffin Gaunt? Well, I will tell you. In quite an accidental way I came across an old man, who had once been in your service. He is, at the present time, an ostler, near Wapping.

"He chanced to mention the name of Griffin Gaunt, and I at once followed it up. In the end he was richer by some crowns, and I am the possessor of information which is most important to me.

"This house is, from what I can at present see of it, the very place to bring a dainty, particular maiden like Grace Gaunt. And in a very short time she will be here."

"You are a monstrous liar," cried old Welch, his eyes blazing with indignation; "she will *not* be here. She is with friends, who will protect her with their lives."

"Oh, I am well aware where she is, just as I am aware of the fact that they are hunting me down. Ha, ha!"

"And you *will* be hunted down, and probably die a worse death than that which awaits your infamous father."

"Infamous!"

"I say so."

Cunningham dealt the helpless old man a heavy blow on the mouth.

But it brought forth no cry.

Though the tears trembled in his poor old eyes. Haversford placed his hand on his dagger.

"I have half a mind to treat him to six inches of cold steel," he muttered. "A man who strikes a poor old man a blow like that, is *far* worse than a thief. But I'll wait—yes, I'll wait. It strikes me I can see what he intends to do."

"At the present moment," said Cunningham, after a pause, "this superior angel, Grace Gaunt, is not in good health; and if an invitation came from you, there is not the least doubt but that she would come here.

"That invitation you will write."

"Never—never!"

"What! You refuse?"

"I do. Were I to suffer the greatest torture, I would refuse. Do you think, for one moment, that I would cause that girl to fall again into your clutches? No. I would sooner be torn into a thousand pieces."

"I will give you time to consider."

"Give me what time you think proper, you will get the same answer from me."

"We shall see."

Chancing to look to the left, Cunningham noticed a writing table.

It was open, and upon it lay a letter, containing Master Welch's signature.

It was of no importance—simply a letter on a business matter.

Cunningham grinned as he scrutinised the handwriting.

"Ha," he said, "there will be no necessity to trouble you. Your writing is very simple, and it will not take me long to imitate it."

"Abandoned ruffian!" cried Master Welch, who at once saw that Grace might drop into the pitfall, "do you mean to say that you will commit forgery?"

"Forgery! Pooh! that, in my opinion, is a very mild crime."

"It is a crime punishable by death."

"Ay, I know that that is one of the foolish laws of this country, but before the forger suffers death, he has to be caught. Then again, only one forger in a hundred is caught, and I am not so unfortunate as to be the one in a hundred.

"I am quite accustomed to forge a signature, and yours I shall forge with the greatest pleasure."

"Boasting scoundrel, your time will come, mark that; and it will not be long."

Cunningham's reply was a hoarse laugh.

To Haversford he said—

"Remain here the while I select a chamber suitable for him."

He walked towards the door, but suddenly turning on his heel, he said—

"You shall see Grace Gaunt in my clutches, as you call it, Master Welch; and you shall see that I will treat her like the commonest dog that ever crawled through the streets. I will do as I think proper with her. And I will lash her and starve her—do you hear it?—until she stands before you nothing but a mass of skin and bones."

"May the Almighty take her before she can be brought here."

Again Cunningham laughed, and left the chamber.

With the dark stain on his face, and his flashing eyes, he looked a perfect fiend.

Haversford went to the door, listened, and heard him ascending the stairs.

Then, hastily, he returned to the old man, down whose face the tears were now fast falling.

"Cheer up, old man," he said, in a hurried whisper, "cheer up. I will not let him have his own way."

Old Welch looked up and shook his grey head.

"I mean what I say," continued Haversford. "I *know* Oscar—the girl's lover."

"*You* do?"

"I do. But you shall hear how I came to know him anon. I came here to—well, to share what we could get. I admit that, but I'll have no hand in placing a young girl in the hands of that man. That I swear.

"I had a young girl of my own once—a dear little thing—but there! I must not speak of her. Her death drove me to drink, and to doing things I have no business to do.

"But the remembrance of her death will not allow me to see a girl fall into the clutches of a man like this. But be patient. You will, no doubt, be a prisoner here, but you can rest assured that no harm will happen to the girl.

"May heaven take my life this moment if I am not speaking the truth."

Old Welch, as may be supposed, was more than astonished.

He looked hard into Haversford's face, and then said—

"I believe you—yes, I believe you."

"This man, Cunningham Trevanion—for that is undoubtedly his name, though I have not long been certain about it—is a great brute, and will probably give orders that no food is to be supplied to you. But I will supply it. You must, however, be careful lest what I am doing is detected.

"All that transpires you shall know, but to throw him off his guard, whenever he is present, I must speak to you in brutal tones."

"Yes, yes, to be sure. I understand you

entirely. But you shall not be out of pocket. I will well reward you, and—"

"Hist! hist! I can hear him."

They did not cease their conversation too quickly.

Cunningham strode into the room and said—

"I have found the very place. It is an attic, and in that he will remain. His hands will be unfastened, but his legs tied. Now, then, away with him."

Poor old Welch was taken to the top of the house, thrust into a tiny chamber, which, for years, had been used as a lumber-room, and there left, after his legs had been tied in such a way that it was scarcely likely he could release himself.

But that, of course, fully believing what Haversford had said, he determined to make no attempt to do.

The woman servant was next released, and compelled, with Villiers at her side, to bring up to the principal room a dozen bottles of the finest wine, and the whole of the contents of the larder.

More, Cunningham compelled her to wait upon them, and whenever her movements were not quite quick enough for him, he placed his hand on a pistol which he kept beside him on the table.

Not one of them rose until the morning was well advanced, and each was, of course, the worse for the large quantity of wine they had imbibed, though Haversford was the more sober of the three.

They retired to rest, but not before the woman servant had once again been locked in the chamber.

Neither of the three awoke until the day was well advanced, and they then partook of a hearty meal, and more wine.

Cunningham then set himself to "work," and in less than a couple of hours, he had forged a letter to the Armourer.

The forgery was almost perfect; certainly the signature was in every way exact.

Haversford and Villiers examined the writing, compared it with the originals, and confessed that they were much astonished at the close resemblance.

Cunningham grinned as he said—

"This will have the desired effect, I should say. What sounds more genuine than this?"

He then read the letter, which was as follows—

"To MASTER OSCAR RAYMOND. Greeting.

"I have heard that the daughter of my dear old friend, Griffin Gaunt, is, at the present time, at your house. Grieved indeed am I to know that she is in somewhat delicate health.

"I should have written to you before, but I am by no means so young, nor so active, as I used to be.

"By this time, dear Gracie has, no doubt, told you all about me, and perhaps she has expressed some surprise that she has not heard from me.

"But the truth is, that I myself have not been well for some time. I am, however, better now, and should much like to have Gracie here for a few weeks. The air of this place, I feel convinced, would do her a world of good.

"Do you, good Master Raymond, urge her to accept this invitation, and assure her that I shall be much disappointed if she does not accept it.

"Wishing you every success,
"Believe me to be,
"Your friend,
"WELCH."

"Who is going to deliver this?" asked Haversford.

"You," said Cunningham.

"Me!"

"Have you any objection?"

Haversford laughed as he replied—

"Have I any objection? Not at all. I will take it with all the pleasure in the world. But what am I to say?"

"To whom?"

"Why, to the Armourer."

"Nothing—except that you are Master Welch's man-servant. You must, of course, pretend that you know nothing whatever about the contents of the letter."

"I understand that. But I must have the clothes to look like a servant."

"No doubt you will find some that will serve you in the house."

Clothes were searched for, and some, which had evidently been worn by Master Welch himself, were selected.

They did not fit Haversford in any way, nevertheless Cunningham told him to make them do.

When evening came on, Haversford set off, and he reached the Armourer's just as the clock was striking the hour of nine.

He inquired for Oscar, and our hero at once came forward.

"What would you?" he asked.

"Ah," said Haversford, "I thought you would not recognise me."

Oscar looked closely at him.

"I *do* now recognise you," he said. "You are the man I saw at Vauxhall."

"Exactly. But you see these clothes have changed me considerably. The fact of it is, I want a few words with you."

Oscar told him to follow him, and Haversford accompanied him into one of the chambers.

There he told him how he had met Cunningham, and all that had followed.

"You see," he said, "I am by no means a good man—I don't think I ever was a good man —but I draw the line at decoying a girl to a house. So when I said I would bring this letter, I made up my mind to tell you all."

"You have acted well," said Oscar, warmly, "and I will reward you for your trouble. Remain here."

In a few minutes he returned, and placed upon the table a bag.

"That," he said, "contains the sum of two hundred and fifty crowns. Take the money, f or you have earned it."

"I thank you, your honour, and I must say

that it will be of great service to me. I don't think I will return to Foot's Cray."

"But you must. If you do not return, he will become suspicious, and that would spoil all."

"Ay, ay, so it would. Well, I will return. Do you tell me what to say."

"Say that you saw the Armourer, and that he is delighted at the offer. Say that he at once consulted Mistress Grace, and she was eager to go."

"And shall I say when the Armourer proposes to bring Mistress Grace?"

"Yes—to-morrow night, at about this hour."

Haversford departed, mightily pleased with the result of his journey.

He stopped at a hostelry on the way, partook of a bottle of wine, and purchased some provisions for Master Welch.

It was not until the early hours of the morning that he reached Foot's Cray, but Cunningham was eagerly awaiting him.

"Well," he said, "the result?"

"The Armourer was delighted with the offer, and went to give the news to Mistress Grace. When he returned, he said that she was so pleased to have a change, that she would be delighted to see Master Welch, and that she and the Armourer would be here at about nine of the clock to-night."

"Good," said Cunningham, as he gleefully rubbed his hands together, "you have done well."

"Oh, it was the letter. The Armourer never doubted but that it was written by Master Welch. He considered it was most kind of him to think of Mistress Grace."

"In a few hours," said Cunningham, "we will discuss exactly how we are to act when they come here. It may be that, instead of the Armourer, the girl will be escorted by Oscar. Ah, if that were so! if that were so! But we shall see—we shall see. Remain here, and Villiers shall bring you some provisions."

He left the chamber, but had not gone many steps when he heard a faint crash.

The fact of it was that Haversford had taken out his bag of money, and accidentally dropped it on the floor.

At once Cunningham paused.

"If that wasn't money," he muttered, "then I am a Dutchman. What does it mean, eh?"

He crept cautiously to a little window near the door, and looked in.

He saw Haversford in the act of trying to thrust a bag of money into his cloak.

At once his suspicions were aroused.

"Ho, ho!" he thought, "I fancy I can see through you, clever though you think yourself. You have sold me, you hound! That bag is full of money. Oh, yes, he's sold me, sure enough. Now I will wait and see what passes between him and Villiers."

He told Villiers to take Haversford food and wine.

"After that," he added, "we will retire. I am now going to have a conversation with old Welch, but I shall not be more than half-an-hour. The letter I sent to the Armourer was a success."

Villiers took what he was told to Haversford.

"I hear that the letter was a success," he said.

"So *he* thinks," grinned Haversford; "but where is he?"

"Gone up to have a conversation with old Welch."

Villiers was wrong.

Cunningham, with the stealthiness of a cat, had descended, unfastened the back door, seized a ladder, and placed it against the window of the chamber in which Haversford and Villiers were seated.

There was a curtain over it, but as it did not quite cover the window, he could easily see into the room.

More than this, though the two conversed in little above a whisper, he could hear what they said.

And what Haversford said startled him.

"I repeat," said the latter, "that he *thinks* so. I told him that the Armourer and the girl jumped at the offer. But it is not so. As a matter of fact, I saw neither the Armourer nor the girl."

"You did not?"

"No. The one I saw was the girl's lover. But we will be plain with each other, Villiers. No good can come of this business, we are well out of it. I told Oscar—that is the lover—all about it. He thanked me, and handed me the sum of two hundred and fifty crowns, and here it is. Now I will give you half, and we will quit this place."

"Agreed—agreed."

"To-morrow night, Cunningham Trevanion will be caught in a trap. That is very certain. How this young fellow will act I know not. He did not even hint what he would do. But I should say that the house will be surrounded. In that case, there is no chance that I can see of his making an escape."

"Suppose we go now?"

"Ay, ay, I would go now, only you see, if we went at once, it would arouse suspicion. No, we will wait until to-night."

* * * * *

The day was well advanced when Haversford and Villiers descended, and they found Cunningham awaiting them.

His face showed no signs of the actual state of his mind.

The first thing he did was to hand Villiers a letter.

It was addressed to a barber, supposed to live a mile away, but really there was no such person.

It was done with the object of getting Villiers out of the way.

Cunningham chatted freely about having Grace once more in his power, and again and again said that Haversford had played his part well.

Haversford, of course, was thrown completely off his guard.

Cunningham, after a long talk, left Haversford to finish a bottle of wine.

But a few seconds afterwards, he crept into the chamber through an inner door, and stole behind Haversford, who was stretching his limbs in a huge easy chair.

Raising aloft a heavy pistol, he brought the butt down with all his force on his bare head.

Haversford, with a wild cry, leapt up.

But he only stood erect for one moment.

Then he dropped like a log to the floor.

"I am far more clever than *you*, my man," chuckled Cunningham, "and I fancy I have well paid you for your treachery. If you get over that blow—which, by all the fiends, has destroyed a good pistol—you must have a head harder than stone. And now I will help myself to the two hundred and fifty crowns which Oscar thought proper to hand you. They will be of service to me."

The money was still in Haversford's cloak, and Cunningham transferred it to his own pocket.

Next he went to all the rooms, and pocketed what he could of value, including a very valuable diamond brooch, once the property of Master Welch's wife.

"I have enough to go on with, at any rate," thought the abandoned, murderous scoundrel. "And now what next shall I do? I have burned down a few houses in my time. What if I add this one? But, no. I will not take the trouble. I will go as fast as I can."

He was speedily in the saddle, and avoiding the main road, took to the fields.

"I know not where to go," he muttered, "but I have plenty of time to think. I must, however, put a good many miles between myself and London."

* * * * *

It was just after the hour of nine, that a coach rolled up to Master Welch's house.

Some distance away, the giant brothers were in waiting.

Oscar, who was inside the coach, and the giants made certain that they had Cunningham this time.

But Oscar speedily learned that once more Cunningham had slipped through the noose.

Villiers was the one who answered the summons, and he speedily informed Oscar of what had transpired.

"Haversford is not dead, your honour," he said, "but he has not recovered consciousness. The blow must have been a fearful one. I don't think he can recover."

"I would have given anything to have secured the wretch," said Oscar.

"Oh, he has got clean away," said Villiers; "but which way he went I know not."

Master Welch had been released, and though unnerved at what had taken place, he was not injured.

Oscar and the giants, who again and again sighed to think that Cunningham once more had escaped, spent a long time with Master Welch.

A physician was summoned to Haversford, but he at once saw that the case was hopeless.

"I don't think it possible that he can recover from such a wound," he said. "Even if he did, he would be a lunatic for the remainder of his life."

Haversford did *not* recover.

Early the following morning he breathed his last, never having uttered a word the whol time.

CHAPTER XXVII.

WHEREIN IT IS CLEARLY SEEN THAT CUNNINGHAM TREVANION'S SCHEMING BRAIN IS NOT BY ANY MEANS DULLED—OF HOW HE ATTEMPTS TO "LEAD A NEW LIFE."

CUNNINGHAM TREVANION rode on for miles—now fast, now slow—and never stopped until he had put at least twenty miles between himself and Foot's Cray.

Then, and then only, did he consider himself safe.

The place at which he stopped was a small straggling village called Hayes, and here he looked about for a hostelry.

Not seeing one, he made inquiries, and was informed that there was not a hostelry within four miles.

But his informant added that, at the other end of the village, there was a barber of the name of Woodstock, who was in the habit of accommodating a traveller or two.

There Cunningham went.

Master Woodstock he found to be an elderly, short, thin, sharp-visaged man—a man who looked more like an attorney than a barber.

"I am told," said Cunningham, "that you sometimes accommodate a traveller at your house?"

"You have been told correctly," was the reply; "but it all depends upon who the traveller is."

"Oh," said Cunningham, "I am a person of no importance, but I am able to pay fairly well for what I have. I suppose that is what you mean? It is not so much the traveller, as what the traveller can pay."

"Exactly, that is just it."

"Well, I repeat that I am able to pay fairly well."

"I believe you, and will give you the accommodation you desire—that is, if you have no intention of staying long?"

"A matter of hours. I should not have troubled you, but for the fact that there are no hostelries hereabouts."

"There never was—yes, there was, though. One, and one only."

"What became of it?"

"It was burned down, and the host was burned with it. But that was many years ago."

"You have been here a long while, then?"

"Forty years. But enter, and I will take your horse to the stable."

When the barber returned, he showed Cunningham into a small chamber adjoining his shop—a mouldy-looking place, which seemed as if it had not been cleaned for years.

"Have you such a thing as a bottle of wine?" asked Cunningham.

The barber smiled.

"I have scores," he said, "and of various brands. Tell me the brand you prefer. It may be that I have it."

"I care not a straw about the brand, so that it is worth drinking. And perhaps you will join me?"

"With pleasure. Though I have plenty of wine here, I can't afford to drink it."

"Bring up three or four bottles of the best, for I am thirsty. Then tell me the price, and I will pay you before you open them."

The little barber speedily brought up the wine, and also a tray of eatables.

Of the latter, Cunningham eagerly partook.

Then, when the table was cleared, he started on the wine.

"You have, no doubt, travelled a long distance?" said the barber.

"Ay, ay."

"From London?"

"No, all the way from Highgate."

"Well, I don't wonder that your horse is fit to drop. He ought to have a rest of a couple of days, at least."

"I am able to give it him, for I am in no particular hurry. A few hours or days is a matter of little importance to me."

"I see, you travel for pleasure?"

"Ay. But I don't suppose you see many travellers this way?"

"Very few. This is quite an out of the way village. Then again there is no hostelry, and many would not be content with a barber's shop."

"I suppose you haven't seen a traveller of late?"

"Oh, yes. There is one here now, and *only* one—a young gentleman of about your own age. Ah, it is a most romantic story," he added, as if to himself.

"Romantic story!" said Cunningham, pricking up his ears; "what is?"

The barber indicated with his thumb the floor above.

"You mean that the young man has a romantic story attaching to him?"

"Exactly. I have known him ever since he was a boy—a mere child."

"Come, to pass away the time, just tell me what the story is. But drink—drink."

"Your health. Well, you see, this young gentleman, James Mayfield, is the son of Master Mayfield, of Mexley Abbey."

Cunningham shrugged his shoulders.

"I know no more of the place than the dead," he said.

"Mexley is about twenty miles from here. It is a village not much bigger than this, and there it was that I was born. There it was that my father carried on the business of a barber, and it was while there that I used to attend upon Master Mayfield. So in that way I learned all the affairs of the family."

"To be sure you did. And sometimes a little knowledge of that sort is very useful."

"Master Mayfield married a Spanish lady of great beauty. But she did not remain at Mexley Abbey more than about three years, beautiful though the place is."

"It was far and away too dull for her."

"Master Mayfield was not a man who cared for company, but at last he yielded to the entreaties of his wife, and again and again had a brilliant company at the Abbey."

"He is rich, then?"

"Rich! Enormously. But two days after the last of these gatherings, Mistress Mayfield disappeared, leaving her two-year old child behind her.

"Master Mayfield heard nothing of her for some two months, and then came a letter, saying that she did not intend to return to the Abbey—that it was too dull for her, and that she intended to go to Spain.

"She *did* go to Spain, but it was not alone, for inquiries showed that she had gone with a gentleman who had more than once been a guest at the Abbey.

"From the day of her flight, Master Mayfield never spoke of her, though it was a very long time before the villagers ceased to talk of the affair.

"Master Mayfield could not bear to look upon his son. Likeness to the mother there was none, but every time he saw the child, he was reminded of the woman who had proved such a traitress.

"He sent it to London—to a woman who had acted as nurse. He remained with her until he was about seventeen, when he commenced to travel; and abroad he remained until very recently, when his father, who has long been ill, and who, they say, is not in the full possession of all his faculties, caused a letter to be sent to a goldsmith in London—where the son, when in London, is in the habit of calling to receive the money allowed him—telling him to at once go to the Abbey.

"I suppose the old man has relented. James Mayfield came this way yesterday afternoon, and, like you, wanted a hostelry, and he was shown here.

"Of course, I knew him not. But he recognised my name, and asked me whether I was not the Woodstock of Mexley.

"When I told him that I was, he revealed his identity. But he had very little to say—treated me as a sort of dog."

"He don't intend to stay here long?"

"Oh, no—until the morning only. I don't suppose he would have stayed so long, only his horse went lame, and there was not another to be had hereabouts."

"Well, we can do with a little more wine. Get a couple more bottles, and here is the money."

When the barber had quitted the room, Cunningham muttered—

"Well, here is a chance which ought not to go. Here is a man who has never seen his son since he was a child! By all the saints, I think I am in luck's way. If I could only get the barber to assist! A plan struck me while he was telling the story."

The barber was not long in bringing up the wine.

"You," said Cunningham, "have not much business here?"

"Business! I don't earn a living."

"Then it is a certainty that you have not saved much money."

"I have saved nothing. I never had a chance to do so. And I am an old man now. When I can't work, I don't know what will become of me."

There was a brief pause, during which Cunningham shot more than one keen glance at the barber, as he sat with his long bony hands clasping his goblet.

"I believe it will be all right," he thought. "At any rate, I will try.

"Suppose," he said, "that this young man had met with any accident and been killed—who would the property go to?"

"There are no relations, I believe, so, no doubt, the property would go to Margaret Page."

"Who is she?"

"A young girl old Mayfield adopted some few years back. She is the daughter of an old and valued friend, who died in Ireland."

"Has she been living at the Abbey?"

"Oh, yes."

"Have you seen her?"

"Several times—on horseback."

"What is she like?"

"Well, I suppose an old man like me would not be considered much of a judge of beauty; but I should think that any young man would rave about her. The villagers call her Fair Margaret."

Again there was a pause.

Then Cunningham said—

"Listen to me, Master Woodstock: I tell you candidly that I am a person in search of fortune."

"Well, all I can say is, that I hope you will be more successful than *I* have been."

"And since I have been here, I see a way to become possessed of an *excellent* fortune."

The barber looked up in astonishment.

"Since you have been *here?*" he asked.

"Ay, *here.*"

"I don't understand."

"Think."

"I am not a good hand at solving riddles."

"Oh, this is no riddle. I have no doubt that you, as well as I, could do very well with a few thousand crowns."

The barber smiled.

"Such a sum," he said, "is as far off as the moon."

"Not at all."

"Well, do you explain."

Cunningham leaned over the table, and, in low tones, said—

"What is there to prevent my personating James Mayfield?"

The barber fairly jumped at this, and his wrinkled face turned pale.

So startled was he that he could not reply for a few moments.

At last he said—

"I understand exactly what you mean. It would be a bold game to play, but I don't see what there is to prevent you. The old man, as I have said, has not seen his son since he was a child, and therefore, recognition would be impossible. On my soul, I should never have thought of such a thing."

"I have played many a bold game in my life, and have always come off victorious. I can personate James Mayfield easily, and in a few hours, you can tell me all it is necessary I should know. That need not be of an elaborate character, since, as you say, the old man is not in full possession of all his faculties."

"But what of the son?"

"Drug him, bind him hand and foot, and keep him in one of your cellars. Now say, shall we make the attempt? Remember, success will mean a fortune to each."

"I must have time to consider. I must think over—"

"There is no time for consideration. But what do you want to consider? The thing is as simple as can be. Have you such a thing as a drug?"

"I have a powerful sleeping draught."

"That will do. If he should call for wine, put that in the bottle. Then leave the rest to me."

"Good. I agree, on condition that what is obtained is shared equally."

"To be sure. You shall have a fair half, and here's my hand on it. But you well understand that I shall have to remain at the Abbey?"

"Of course. And it may be that you will be able to make some impression upon this young lady, Margaret. She, I have been told, will inherit a fortune under her father's will."

"Good. I certainly will try to make an impression—if by good luck I can obtain an entry into the Abbey."

It was while they were thus conversing in whispers, that a voice was heard calling the barber.

It was Master James Mayfield.

Hastily Woodstock quitted Cunningham and ascended.

"I am about to retire, Master Woodstock," said Mayfield, "but I should like a small bottle of good wine. I feel rather sleepless, and a bottle of wine may have the effect of sending me to sleep."

"I will get it with pleasure," replied Woodstock.

"To-morrow I depart. It may be, however, that you will see me again before long."

"I trust so, your honour."

The wine he took up to Mayfield contained a powerful sleeping draught, but it was tasteless.

Young Mayfield consumed the whole of the wine, and then retired.

In one hour from that time he lay in the bed like one dead.

The discharge of cannon would not have awakened him.

Both Cunningham and Woodstock took good care to assure themselves of this fact, and the first thing they did was to open the leathern bag he had with him, and rifle his pockets.

The bag contained letters, written by old Mayfield, and from them, of course, Cunningham obtained information which would be of great value to him.

But the letters were not all.

There was a somewhat thick book—what, in a different form, would, at the present day, be called a "diary."

This was nearly filled with writing.

It was, in brief, a sort of history of the various places young Mayfield had visited, and his impressions of them.

This would also be most valuable.

The next thing they did was to clothe young Mayfield as well as they could, and carry him down to one of the cellars—a filthy hole, not fit for a dog to be in.

Here they tied his legs and feet, and left him.

The following morning Cunningham devoted to the study of the letters and the book.

So many times did he read them, that he nearly got the contents by heart.

When evening came round, Cunningham set to work, and with the book before him as a guide, imitated James Mayfield's writing to such perfection, that a cry of astonishment burst from the lips of the barber, who had been closely watching him.

"Ah," smiled Cunningham, "I see you are ignorant of these matters. Fear it not, my friend, the old man's property will be *ours*. As easily as I can imitate this writing, so can I impose upon the old man."

He then read the letter, which was as follows—

"BELOVED FATHER,

"Your message reached me a few days ago, and already I am close to you. By this time I should have been with you, but for an accident. Just as I entered this place—the village of Hayes—my horse threw me. But I am glad to say that I only received a slight shock, from which I shall recover in the course of a few hours.

"Fortunately, I was taken into the house of a man with whom you were formerly acquainted, namely, Master Woodstock, the barber. To-morrow night, at about the hour of nine, you may expect me.

"I assure you I am longing to see Mistress Margaret, of whom you speak so lovingly in your letters.

"Accept, my dear father, the assurance of my deep affection for you.

"JAMES MAYFIELD."

This letter was despatched to Mexley by a well-paid messenger.

The reply he brought was that James would be eagerly looked for on the following evening.

The remainder of that day, and a great deal of the next, Cunningham continued to study the letters and the book, and to arrange the plans for the future with the barber, who, now fully believing in Cunningham, was eagerly looking forward to the time when he should be the possessor of a small fortune, and able to leave the dull, dead village of Hayes for a more lively spot.

In the meanwhile, young Mayfield remained a prisoner in the cellar, and was fed by an old woman whom Woodstock, for a long time, had occasionally employed to clean his house.

She had strict orders not to answer a single question, and she did not, although Mayfield implored her to tell him who was the author of the outrage.

He even offered her a large sum of money to tell him.

But the old woman never uttered a word.

Just before the hour of nine on the night following the delivery of the letter, Cunningham arrived at Mexley Abbey.

Woodstock, of course, was well acquainted with the place, and he had again and again described it, but Cunningham had no idea that it was such a magnificent mansion.

It stood in its own grounds, of many acres, with a well-wooded park stretching far away in the distance, though, in consequence of the darkness, Cunningham was unable to see this superb piece of country.

He rang the great bell at the gate, and soon he saw a couple of lights moving rapidly towards him along the avenue.

They were carried by a couple of men-servants, who greeted him with profound respect, and opened the gate.

"By the soul of the Virgin," thought Cunningham, "if luck should be with me, and I become the possessor of this property! By all that's good, I'll lead a new life. I will, and no mistake. Here, under the name of James Mayfield, I can settle down, and live the life of a country gentleman.

"And it maybe that I can win this gentle Margaret for a wife. Who knows? Certain it is that, with this property, plenty of money, and a beautiful wife, I could easily forget Grace Gaunt."

He was received at the door by the butler, who welcomed him with great warmth.

It was while talking to him that a vision of loveliness appeared upon the stairs—a beautiful girl clothed all in white.

"This, I feel sure," said Cunningham, "must be Margaret?"

"Yes, your honour," replied the butler.

Cunningham at once introduced himself, declaring that his "father's" letters had set him on fire to see Mistress Margaret, and he sincerely trusted that they would be good friends.

It was quite evident that Margaret was disappointed.

Disappointment was written upon her lovely face as clearly as it *could* be written.

Her greeting—intended to be warm—was cold in the extreme.

She expected to see a young handsome fellow —a young man like the portraits of his father when *he* was young—but instead, she saw before her a very ordinary-looking person, whose face bore unmistakable signs of continued dissipation.

But this Cunningham did not notice.

"In what state of health is my father?" he asked the butler.

"But poorly," was the reply. "Your return, however, may prove beneficial to him. Follow me, your honour."

He took him upstairs to the bedchamber, where, in an easy-chair, sat Master Mayfield.

That he had long been suffering from ill-health could be seen at a glance, but his mental faculties were in no way dulled.

But his eyes were.

For years he had suffered from extreme weakness of sight, and he was able to see but little of Cunningham's features.

Warmly indeed did he greet his supposed son, and again and again did he express his regret that he had not sent for him long before.

He added that he would have done so but for his continual remembrance of his (James's) mother.

"But," he said, "I have now succeeded in plucking her entirely from my memory; and I intend, during the short time I have to live, to make you happy. You have been a wanderer for years; it is time now that your wanderings should cease."

"I am glad indeed that they are to cease," said the arch-impostor; "but the account of my wanderings will interest you for many a long day to come. And I can assure you that I shall never tire of sitting beside you and telling my stories."

"I am sorry you met with an accident on the way."

"Oh, it was of no importance whatever. This Master Woodstock, once a barber in the village here—"

"I remember him well."

"Gave me shelter and every attention. I only regret that I had no money with me to repay him."

"Open yonder secretaire," said Master May-field. "Take out one hundred crowns and forward it to him."

"But to-morrow—"

"No, no—*now*. The man who attends to my son must be paid well, and at once."

Cunningham opened the secretaire, which he saw at a glance contained a very large amount of money, and counted out a hundred crowns.

"Write him a letter," said Master Mayfield, "and say that I thank him sincerely for his attention."

Instead of this, Cunningham wrote as follows—

"Success. Here is a hundred crowns for you already. Keep your tongue quiet—do not let the money be seen, and carefully guard *the young man*. Anon I will tell you what is to be done with him."

"What have you written, my son?" asked Master Mayfield. "Alas! I am unable to see the largest writing."

Cunningham held up the letter.

But what he read was this—

"My father is extremely obliged to you for your attention to me, and sends you a slight acknowledgment; and, once more, I myself thank you.

"JAMES MAYFIELD."

"Good," said the poor old man, "that will do. One of the servants must take it at once. It is a long ride, but the horses are fresh."

So, in a little over three hours, when he was thinking how Cunningham had got on, Woodstock's heart was rejoiced by this, to him, large sum of money.

He rubbed his hands with evident glee as he counted the money.

"It is what I should earn in two years as a barber," he chuckled.

"Ah, that young man is clever, sure enough. He will become the owner of the Abbey, I am sure. As regards James Mayfield, well, we will remove him. That is bound to be done. But there is plenty of time—plenty of time."

"SEIZING WOODSTOCK BY THE THROAT, HE HURLED HIM TO THE GROUND."

CHAPTER XXVIII.

A WEEK passed away, and during that time Cunningham had made great progress at the Abbey.

But it was with the old man only.

The servants detested him, and so also did Margaret, who avoided him as much as she possibly could.

Cunningham saw this, but he pretended to take no notice.

"She will come round directly," he thought. "She has got to get used to me first. On my soul, she is a dainty damsel—far and away before Grace Gaunt. And then, she has a fortune. That is worth fighting for.

"Oh, I shall manage her, by-and-bye. I wonder, though, whether she is already in love with anyone? Well, I shall, no doubt, be able to ascertain that from the old man. What an utter fool he is! Ha, ha! he is like a child. And I can twist him round my finger."

One evening, when alone with Master Mayfield, Margaret was brought into conversation.

"Margaret," said Master Mayfield, "is the daughter of an old and very valued friend of mine, and I have often dreamed of your coming together. You understand what I mean?"

"Perfectly."

"You have not told me what you think of Margaret?"

"I think her the most charming girl it was ever my lot to encounter."

"I am pleased to hear you say so."

"My happiness would be complete, if I could lead so charming a girl to the altar. But I am afraid she does not care for me. Perhaps she looks upon me as an interloper."

"That is impossible. You are my son, and have the first right to be here."

"Do you think it possible that she is in love with anyone else?"

"No. Margaret is a thoroughly honest, upright girl—a girl who would not keep a secret, however trifling, from me. No—there is no one in your path. But you must be patient."

* * * * *

Meanwhile, quite a different conversation was taking place elsewhere.

When Cunningham ascended to Master Mayfield's bedchamber, Margaret left her apartment, and descended to the butler's quarters.

She found the butler—old Searle, as he was called—busy going over a list of the provisions, and so on, required for the following week.

He looked up in astonishment as Margaret entered, for it was very seldom indeed that she invaded his quarters.

He was more astonished than ever, when Margaret closed the door.

"Searle," she said, "I want a little conversation with you."

"With pleasure," replied the butler, as he hastily dropped his list.

"Perhaps, if you think, you may guess what I want to speak to you about."

"I can guess it at once, mistress. You have come to speak about Master James?"

"Exactly."

The butler shook his head gravely, as he said—

"I never, in all my life, saw a young man drink so much. You have no idea, Mistress Margaret. He has bottles of wines and spirits in his bedroom."

"No doubt. It is my opinion, and has been my opinion from the first, that he is a confirmed drunkard."

"Well, Mistress Margaret, I don't think you are far wrong."

Margaret came close, and laid her little hand on the old man's shoulder.

In low tones, she said—

"Has any suspicion arisen in your mind as to him?"

"Suspicion?"

"Ay, suspicion."

"Well, I believe he is not the steady young man he tries to make his father believe."

"Have you had no other suspicion?"

"No, mistress, not that—"

"Has it ever occurred to you that this young man, who calls himself James Mayfield, is not James Mayfield at all?"

The face of the old butler turned a shade paler, and it was a few seconds before he made any reply.

At last he said—

"I am bound to tell you the truth. That has occurred to me. But then, how can that be possible?"

"Some strange things are done in the world, as you, at your age, are aware. What is more likely than that he should have been simply the associate of James Mayfield—an associate who considered it would be to his advantage to learn all the particulars of James Mayfield's history?"

The butler was now profoundly agitated.

"What you say, mistress," he said, "is quite feasible. Heaven! if it should so turn out! Ah, but how is it possible that such an enquiry could be commenced?"

"Leave that to me. Listen to this: On the night of his arrival, James Mayfield sent a letter to a barber, at Hayes."

"Yes—Master Woodstock, who used to live in this village. He attended Master James for a slight accident."

"Well, that letter, the servant told me, contained a goodly sum of money. Now, James Mayfield has left this house four times since he arrived, with the object, he has said, of a little exercise. But on each occasion he has ridden to the village of Farrowdale, and from there he has sent letters to Master Woodstock."

"You astonish me!"

"I am sure of it. Now, what can be the meaning of these letters?"

"For the life of me, I could not tell you. But what is your opinion?"

"That there is something between these two."

"Are you sure that the letters have been taken to the barber?"

"Yes. I had the messenger watched."

"You are a clever, courageous young lady, Mistress Margaret. There is little doubt about that."

"You are, no doubt, able to advise me what to do next."

"The barber should be suddenly pounced upon, and compelled to reveal all he knows."

"Such was my idea. And it shall be done, ere long. Take this money, Searle. Go to the clothier's in the village, and get a man's costume which will fit me."

"Great heaven! Mistress—"

"Hush! hush! I have made up my mind how to act. Get the costume, and three masks."

"I will do as you say. I am bound to do as you say, but I am fearful for your safety."

"I am well able to take care of myself. I am determined to find out the truth."

"He has pestered you with his attentions during the past day or two, I am told?"

"He has endeavoured to draw me into conversation. But I cannot bear the sight of him. I seem to see, on that man's face, the word 'Impostor,' most clearly written. But what can poor Master Mayfield see of him? Nothing."

"Be careful you utter no word to cause him to be suspicious. If he is an impostor, he should be caught red-handed, and properly punished."

"I will be careful. But do you see about the costume and the masks, at once."

"I will," said the butler.

When Margaret ascended to what for many years had been known as the grand banqueting-room, she found there Cunningham.

That day a magnificent costume had arrived for him, and he had donned it.

He considered that he looked simply splendid in it, and had no doubt but that his changed appearance would now make an impression upon Margaret.

But when she saw him, there was still the same cold distant look upon her face.

"Margaret," said Cunningham, assuming very soft tones, "I am desirous of having a few words with you."

"Say on, sir," replied Margaret. "I will listen."

"My father and I have been talking about you to-night. Can you guess what the conversation was?"

"I cannot. I am, and always was, a very bad hand at guessing."

"Well, the fact of it is, since my father asked me almost directly, I was compelled to admit that I loved you."

Margaret smiled.

"Yes," continued Cunningham, "I love you, Margaret, with all my heart, and grieved indeed am I that you treat me so coldly. I am sure that I have done all in my power to gain your esteem.

"When I assured my father that I loved you, he was delighted, and said, over and over again, that he had dreamed of a union between us.

"But you do not answer."

"Such things as this are not usually answered at once."

"It has occurred to me that someone has been before me."

"Before you?"

"Yes—in other words, that you love someone else."

Margaret shook her head.

"Love is a thing which has commanded but little of my thoughts," she said—"that is to say, the sort of love you mean. Up to now, my affection has been divided between Master Mayfield, the servants who have known me from a child, and this old house."

"You do not think it possible that you can love me?"

"I assure you that I have never once devoted a thought to the matter. But why trouble about such an insignificant person as me? As Master Mayfield's heir, you will soon find yourself surrounded by scores of ladies, who will be quite ready and willing—"

"It is impossible that I could care for anyone but you," interrupted Cunningham. "You are the only one I have ever loved; and heaven knows that, from time to time, in various places, I have been brought in contact with many beautiful women. I ask you to consider the matter. In the course of time, I shall become the owner of a vast property, and I ask you to share it with me."

"I am sure you do me a great honour," said Margaret, freezingly, "but, for your father's sake, I will give the matter my earnest consideration."

"I may tell my father that I have made a little impression on you?"

"Nay," replied Margaret, "you may assure your father that you have made a deep impression upon me."

Little did the rogue dream what she meant.

Margaret, shortly after this, left the chamber, and Cunningham went to old Mayfield, to boast to him that he had made a deep impression on Margaret.

On the following day, Margaret saw Cunningham several times, and conversed with him somewhat freely.

It would never do to cause him to become in any way suspicious.

Cunningham was thrown into the seventh heaven of delight.

What a prospect seemed opening out before him!

A mighty fortune—as it would be, if his own and Margaret's fortunes were joined—to do as he thought proper with, and a most lovely girl for a wife!

And here, in this quiet place, he would be perfectly secure from his enemies.

He could afford to snap his fingers at Oscar; he could laugh at the giants.

No one would ever think of searching for him at this quiet, out of the way village, he thought.

The monstrous crimes of which he had been guilty never troubled him in the least.

He ate well, drank well, and slept well.

Drank well? Oh, yes, enough to startle all the servants in the house.

They never, in all their lives, saw a man drink such a vast quantity.

When evening came on, Margaret told old Mayfield that she had a bad headache, and should lie down awhile.

She certainly did retire to her bedchamber, but it was not to rest.

Her maid was awaiting her, and speedily Margaret doffed her own clothes, and donned those the butler had procured for her.

She did not look at all bad in them, though somewhat *petite*.

When completely attired, the maid left the chamber.

In a few minutes one of the men-servants entered, and he was followed a short time afterwards by another.

These two men had been thoroughly instructed in what they were about to do, and they entered into it heartily.

"Are the horses ready?" asked Margaret.

"Quite ready," replied one, "and, as they are fresh, it will not take very long to get to Hayes—perhaps not more than two hours if you feel able to ride fast."

"Able? Ay, that I do."

"I mean, that it will be somewhat difficult for you, because you must ride like a man."

"To be sure. I am ready to do anything—to risk anything so that I can satisfy myself. I am more than ever convinced that the man here who calls himself James Mayfield is a rogue."

The two men were the first to leave the house, and they took the three horses some distance down the road, the butler having first seen that "James Mayfield" was with his father.

Margaret then, having placed a pair of pistols in her belt, hurriedly left the house.

In a few more minutes she was in the saddle, and she and the two servants were riding at a rapid pace in the direction of Hayes.

Thither we shall precede them.

The barber, Master Woodstock, had received in all four letters from Cunningham, and two out of that number had contained money.

What he had received quite contented him.

He was well aware that a small fortune could not roll into his lap in a short time.

He must wait.

Cunningham had given him no orders in reference to the real James Mayfield.

All he did was to continually urge him to keep his mouth shut, and to go about his ordinary business as usual.

The sufferings of the unfortunate young Mayfield did not enter his thoughts.

He never even visited him once.

The old woman did all that, and saw that he was fed.

The sufferings of James Mayfield were indeed acute, and he was fast breaking down under them.

His legs and arms continued to be tied, and he was left alone in that cellar night and day in the darkness.

The only light he saw was from the lantern carried by the old woman when she brought his food—food scarcely fit for a dog to eat.

Try how he would, he could not get the old woman to utter a word.

She was as immovable as a stone.

It was about two hours after Margaret and the servants quitted the Abbey, and the barber was partaking of a meal with the old woman, when a knock came upon the door.

Both started up, and Woodstock told the old woman to see who it was.

When she returned, she said—

"A messenger."

"Ah," chuckled Woodstock, "from the Abbey, I'll warrant. Show the man in, and then descend to the kitchen awhile."

The "messenger" was one of the servants.

The old woman admitted him, and then went below.

"You, my friend," said Woodstock, "are from Master James Mayfield?"

"Ay, ay," replied the servant.

"I fancy I can remember your face. You have been there some years?"

"Near twenty."

"And you have come here for—"

"For the purpose of unmasking a rogue!" cried the servant.

Seizing Woodstock by the throat, he hurled him to the ground.

Then he rushed to the front door, and admitted Margaret and the other servant.

"What is the meaning of this?" gasped Woodstock.

He looked first at Margaret, who was masked, and then at the two servants.

Though provided with masks, they had not donned them.

"Stand up," said Margaret, "and answer the questions put to you."

As the barber did not get up quickly, the servants dragged him to his feet.

"Answer questions?" stammered Woodstock. "What questions? I can't understand the meaning of this outrage."

"Listen: Where is Master James Mayfield?"

"At the Abbey, I suppose."

"No. James Mayfield is not at the Abbey. It is an impostor who is there."

"Sold!" thought Woodstock, trembling in every limb. "It is evident that something has been discovered. But how much? I must be cautious. I will answer no questions."

"You hear what I say?" continued Margaret. "The man there is an impostor. But you know all about it. You have been in the conspiracy. Answer me."

Woodstock made no reply.

Thereupon Margaret took out a pistol, cocked it, and placed it close to Woodstock's ear.

"If you do not answer," she said, "I will send a ball through your head."

This had the desired effect, for Woodstock turned ghastly pale, and seemed as if about to fall.

"Yes, yes," he groaned. "He is not James Mayfield."

"I thought so," said Margaret, triumphantly. "Who is he?"

"I know not. He came here as a traveller. I chanced to tell him James Mayfield's story, and he laid a plan before me by which he should take Mayfield's place. He promised to handsomely reward me, and as I am a poor man I consented to act as he told me."

"Like the miserable rogue you are! Where, then, is the real James Mayfield?"

"He is here."

"Where?"

"In the cellar."

"James Mayfield a prisoner in your cellar?"

"I could not help it. I was bound to do as I was told."

"It is a lie. You had a right to go to the Abbey, and tell Master Mayfield all that had taken place."

"I wish I had, now."

"No doubt. Do you know what you have rendered yourself liable to?"

Woodstock made no reply to this.

Margaret continued—

"You have rendered yourself liable to be hanged. Secure him!"

Woodstock was bound hand and foot.

By this time, the old woman made her appearance.

As soon as she saw what had happened, she uttered a frightened grunt, and turned to go.

But one of the men seized her by the hair and pulled her back.

"Who are you?" asked Margaret.

"Nobody."

"Who is she?" Margaret asked the barber. "Is she your wife?"

"No; only a woman I have to clean the place up. She has the key of the cellar."

The old woman was made to hand it over, and the two servants descended to the cellar.

It was not long before they returned with James Mayfield.

Ghastly pale and dazed he looked.

Margaret then, to the amazement of the barber, revealed her identity, and she warmly welcomed James Mayfield.

The latter fervently thanked her, and complimented her upon her bravery.

It was then, for the first time, that James was made acquainted with the true facts of the case.

"Well," he said, "it occurred to me that some plot of the sort was in progress, but though confined in that cellar, I did not despair of getting free."

"Spare me, Master Mayfield!" groaned the barber. "I only did what I was told."

James gave him no reply.

The orders he gave were for the old woman to be confined in one of the chambers, and for the barber to take his (James's) place in the cellar; and these orders were speedily carried into effect.

A long conversation then took place, and it was decided that, until the next day, James should remain at the barber's.

It would never do to pounce upon Cunningham too suddenly.

But he remained at the house under different circumstances—for provisions of all sorts were brought in—and with one of the servants for a companion.

With a heart overflowing with gladness at having been the means of confounding a rogue, Margaret returned to the Abbey, and reached her apartments without her absence having been discovered, either by Cunningham or the old man.

On the following morning, Cunningham wrote another note to the barber.

This one was very different to the others, for this is what the cold-blooded wretch wrote—

"I am successful in everything—far more so than ever I hoped for—though I must admit that the old man is not so fond of me as I should have expected.

"Nor can I get the girl to devote much attention to me. But, patience—patience, and all may come right in *that* direction.

"I have decided what is to be done with the young man. He is to die, and you must set about this at once.

"Barbers, as a rule, are able to get from apothecaries what they will not sell to ordinary people, and you can easily obtain a poison of some sort, which you can put in the young man's drink.

"Let there be no hesitation about the matter. Do it at once. I give you twenty-four hours, and I will come and assist you in disposing of the body."

This astounding document, we may mention, fell into the hands of James Mayfield.

Cunningham rode off himself to place it in the hands of the man who acted as his messenger.

He always did. It would never do to trust it with a servant, male or female, for he was well aware of the fact that each and everyone despised him, though it never struck him, for an instant, that he was regarded with the slightest suspicion by anyone.

That morning he met Margaret, and he considered that she was most gracious with him—she even smiled.

Oh, yes, Margaret certainly acted her part to perfection.

"The ice is broken," thought Cunningham; "it will be all right directly. I like the girl immensely, and would not mind the trouble of going through the marriage ceremony with her, though I confess that I like the idea of her money better."

About half-a-mile from the Abbey, Cunningham had to rein in his horse, so as to let pass a beggar—a man clad almost in rags, though he had half a mind to ride over him for having the impudence not to get out of the way.

"*Good* sir," whined the man, "a crust from your saddle-bag, for I swear to you that I hunger."

"Fool," replied Cunningham, "do you think it is the custom for gentlemen to carry crusts in their saddle-bags ? Here is a crown for you—go and get drunk, and be hanged to you."

With that, he threw a crown into the road.

The beggar pounced upon it, muttering his thanks, which, however, Cunningham did not hear, for he rode on.

But when he was out of sight, the beggar, as he looked down the road, muttered—

"Oh, yes, it is right enough. It is no other than Cunningham Trevanion. So then this long journey, after all, has not been in vain. Now, the question is, where does he come from ? It seems to me as if he has stumbled into some good luck, for he is well attired. I will await his return."

And so he did—behind one of the hedges—and there he remained a considerable time.

His patience was rewarded at last, and when Cunningham returned he followed him, using the hedges and trees as covers, to the Abbey.

He got so close to the entrance, that he overheard a servant say—

"Master Mayfield, your father is desirous of speaking to you."

"Oh, oh," thought the beggar, who, we may at once inform the reader, was none other than Villiers, the associate of Haversford—"he is called Mayfield here, eh ? His father ! Ha, ha ! another plot. I wonder what it is now ? "

He hung about the place, at a loss what to do, for he was afraid that, if he ventured to speak to one of the servants, he should get a thrashing, but at last he espied in the garden—Margaret.

He made up his mind to speak to her, but he knew that he would have to approach her cautiously, or she would fly.

But Margaret was not at all of a timid nature, and when Villiers got close to her and spoke, she was not startled.

"Mistress," said Villiers, "may I have a few words with you ? "

"What is it you want, my man ? " asked Margaret. "If it is food—"

"No, no," interrupted Villiers, "I require no food—just a few words."

"Say on."

"Well—er—but, upon my word, I scarcely know how to begin. But just now, mistress, I saw a man enter the Abbey gates on horseback, and heard him addressed as Master Mayfield."

At once Margaret came closer.

"Yes, yes ? " she said, eagerly.

"Well, there is some mistake. He is not Master Mayfield—that is not his name at all."

"How do *you* know ? "

"I am not what I seem, lady. I am not a beggar, but a man who has disguised himself on purpose to trace a certain person, and that person is the man who has just entered the Abbey."

"Do you know his real name ? "

"I should think I do. And it may be that you, even in this out of the way spot, have also heard of it. His name is Cunningham Trevanion."

"Heaven," cried Margaret, "is this possible ? Yes, I *have* heard the name, many a time. His father is under sentence of death in the Tower ? "

"He is. You see, mistress, this man murdered a companion of mine, and I swore that I would

leave no stone unturned to trace him. But I searched and searched in vain until yesterday, when I met a man who came from this neighbourhood.

"I told him what I was engaged upon, and gave him the description of Cunningham Trevanion, with the result that he assured me that he had seen a man answering to it several times in the roads about here.

"And so I set off, and I had the good luck to speedily stumble across him."

Margaret, without reserve, told him exactly how Cunningham had contrived to obtain an entry to the Abbey, and how all had been discovered, adding that he would meet with his deserts at the hands of the real James Mayfield.

But Villiers told her of Oscar, and the prior claim he had, and urged her to wait until he could inform Oscar of Cunningham's whereabouts.

Margaret considered that Oscar most certainly had a prior claim, and she consented to wait until the following evening.

But this was not all.

She handed Villiers sufficient money to get changes of horses, and change of clothes.

In an hour from this Villiers quitted Mexley, fairly well attired, and mounted on a good horse.

When he was gone, Margaret wrote a long letter to James Mayfield, setting forth all that had occurred, and then joined Cunningham and old Mayfield in the latter's bedchamber.

No human soul could have suspected, from her demeanour, what important events were transpiring.

Little did Cunningham think that, in this magnificent Abbey, he was in a trap, and that it was a thousand chances to one he would never get out of it alive.

* * * * *

In the meanwhile, Oscar, the headsman, the giants, the wizard, everyone had been trying to discover the whereabouts of Cunningham.

But he had vanished as completely as he had on other occasions, and it seemed that search would be in vain.

He had seen Villiers several times, and he had told him that, if successful in unearthing Cunningham, he would be well rewarded.

But he never thought for one moment that he would be successful.

Villiers would probably have dropped the search, but Haversford's death rankled in his heart and spurred him on.

It was about nine o'clock in the evening that he arrived at the giant brothers' smithy.

There was no sound of the ponderous hammers, but he heard loud laughter, and knew that it could be caused only by these two enormous fellows.

He dismounted, and thumped upon the door, which was quickly answered by Sampson.

"Well, my friend," said Sampson, "what is it you seek ? Do you want a shoe for your horse, or an iron safe to hold what never belonged to you ? "

"Neither. I am come in search of Master Oscar Raymond."

"The Armourer ? "

" No, the Armourer's son."

" Well, then—but come hither. I have seen your face before. Why, you are the man Villiers ? "

" I am."

" Well, it so happens that you are just lucky. There is Oscar."

He pointed to the forge, beside which, on one of the bright anvils, sat Oscar.

Goliar sat before a large barrel of ale, into which he occasionally dipped a tankard of most respectable dimensions.

It was marvellous how rapidly measure after measure of the ale went down his capacious throat.

He was always in good health, yet continually ale-ing.

The only thing he—and Sampson—were regretting was the absence of a good tray of eatables to keep the ale company.

" Master Oscar," said Villiers, " at last, I have been successful,"

" What ? " cried Oscar, standing up. " Is it possible that you have discovered the whereabouts of that scoundrel ? "

" I have, at last."

Sampson seized Villiers's hand, and wrung it until he danced.

" Well," he cried, " you are not what can be called an honest man, but if you have found that villain, I am compelled to shake hands with you."

" And I," said Goliar, " as he rose and held out his enormous hand, " I will shake thy hand for thee."

But Villiers declined.

One was quite enough. He had to pull his fingers apart to get them right.

At once he told them all, including what had passed between himself and Margaret.

" It is enough ! " said Oscar. " We have him. He cannot escape this time ! "

" No," said Sampson, as he rubbed his horny hands together with glee. " I don't fancy he will get away this time—that is, if we proceed cautiously to work."

" Oscar," said Goliar, " if fortune so far favours you that you meet him face to face, make the hound fight."

" Ay, ay," said Sampson, " no arrest. I shall never be happy until the wretch is dead."

" Yes," said Oscar, " you may depend upon it that I will make him fight. You, Villiers, have earned the reward I promised you, and to-morrow it shall be placed in your hands. But we will lose no time. Our plans must be prepared at once, and prepared carefully. But not a word to the Armourer—not a word to Grace."

* * * * *

Once more night came on, and again Cunningham sought the chamber occupied by Master Mayfield.

But he did not remain there long.

He was now firmly convinced that he had made a great impression upon Margaret, and resolved to have an understanding with her.

For that purpose, he took himself to one of the withdrawing rooms in which Margaret was seated.

She seemed to be busy knitting, but in reality she was awaiting a signal from the butler—the sound of a whistle, which was to tell her that the hour of vengeance had arrived.

He put on what he intended to be gentle manners, and for some considerable time spoke to Margaret, telling her the biggest lies he possibly could.

Margaret replied quietly, and sometimes smilingly—but how her heart was beating !

Cunningham was telling her how happy they would be if she would but consent to be his, when a shrill whistle was heard.

Margaret started up.

" What the fiend is that ? " cried Cunningham, forgetting himself.

" That," said Margaret, in ringing tones, " is a signal, which tells Cunningham Trevanion that the hour of retribution has come ! "

Before Cunningham could reply, the door was pushed open, and our hero entered, pistol in hand, and Margaret withdrew.

Cunningham, giving utterance to a loud yell, drew his sword.

CHAPTER XXIX.

OF CUNNINGHAM'S TERRIBLE DEATH, AND OF HOW OSCAR STRUCK OFF TREVANION'S HEAD ON TOWER HILL—HAPPINESS AT LAST !

CUNNINGHAM'S surprise and consternation can be better imagined than described.

For some seconds, he could not speak.

He looked hard at our hero, in wonder—yes, and something *more* than wonder.

" Oscar Raymond ! " he said, in tones which were scarcely above a whisper.

" Ay, you are right," replied Oscar, " and you are the rascally ruffian, the wretched *murderer*, Cunningham Trevanion ! Villain ! Once more we meet face to face, and there is no one to interfere with us.

" For what you have done to me and mine, I should do right if I lodged the contents of this pistol in your scheming brain. But I will spare you that. You have a sword, and you shall fight. Prepare ! " thundered Roderick, as, thrusting his pistol in his belt, he drew his sword.

Cunningham made no movement.

But when the two enormous giants entered the chamber, he started back with a loud yell.

Oh, yes, he was trapped, sure enough.

"Advance, wretch!" said Roderick.

"If I refuse?"

"Then I will not parley with you. I will blow out your brains, as I would blow out the brains of a mad dog."

"No doubt you are under the impression that I am afraid of you?"

"You make a mistake. I am under no such impression, I do assure you. I have not allowed myself time to form any impression whatever."

Cunningham drew himself erect.

He must fight.

He was *bound* to fight, or it was more than likely that the giants would tear him limb from limb.

With what he intended to be a firm tread, he advanced towards Roderick.

The weapons crossed.

The house rang with the clash of steel.

Our readers, by this time, are perfectly acquainted with the fact that Oscar was an expert swordsman.

While Cunningham's thrusts and parries were furious in the extreme, our hero maintained his calm demeanour.

He *waited*, and his time came.

Cunningham grew tired and disheartened, and being, for an instant, thrown off his guard, Oscar, with the rapidity of lightning, disarmed him.

But before our hero could make another movement, Cunningham turned, and tearing aside the curtain of an inner door, was gone in an instant.

But Oscar and the giants at once followed him.

The door led to a passage, the right leading upwards, the left downstairs.

In his hurry and confusion, Cunningham took the right, and he was thus compelled to ascend the stairs.

Had a howling pack of wolves been at his back, he could not have moved himself more quickly.

But Oscar was close behind him.

Up the stairs rushed Cunningham, past the chamber occupied by the now terrified Master Mayfield, and presently found himself before a small window.

Without waiting to undo the fastening, he hurled himself through it.

Oscar never paused to see where this window led.

He followed Cunningham instantly.

Both were now on the roof of an outbuilding.

Cunningham could go no farther unless he threw himself over, a thing he was very unlikely to do.

He was baffled, and compelled to turn at bay.

"You miserable coward!" said Oscar; "but I will give you one more chance. You have a dagger at your girdle. Unsheath it."

As he spoke, he drew his own dagger.

"Nay, nay," gasped Cunningham, "I am unable to fight further. I—"

"I will not force you. But if you do not choose to use your dagger, I will certainly send a ball through your brain."

"Mercy!"

"Mercy for you, villain? Not a spark! Prepare!"

"You are merciless!" groaned Cunningham.

"Yes," replied Oscar, "as grim death itself."

Cunningham took the dagger from its sheath, and in another moment Oscar was upon him.

From one side of the roof to the other, they dodged about until the very windows below rattled violently.

But at last they closed.

They swayed together for some few seconds, and then Oscar's dagger was seen to flash for an instant in the moon's rays.

The next it was buried to the haft in Cunningham's body.

With a despairing cry, he fell on the lead of the roof.

"The fate you deserved has overtaken you, Cunningham Trevanion," said Oscar. "And you may die now with the knowledge that I am no longer to be known as *Oscar Raymond.* My true name is Roderick, Lord Wyncherley, only son of Lord Eustance Wyncherley, who was murdered in the Tower by his infamous cousin, Greville Trevanion, your father, now lying under sentence of death."

"Curse you! curse you!" groaned Cunningham.

"Ay, curse away, vile wretch!" replied Oscar; "your curses will have no effect."

"Come," said Sampson, who, with Goliar, had been watching from the window—"come away, and leave the dog to die."

"I will leave him," replied Oscar, "but not here on the roof of a house occupied by an honest man."

He dragged Cunningham to the edge of the roof and threw him over.

When they descended, they found that he was dead.

It is not necessary to say what followed at the Abbey.

Old Mayfield soon had the pleasure of receiving his true son, and a long conversation took place between all.

Oscar and the giants remained at the house all night.

In the early morning they took their departure to London, James Mayfield promising to see that the body of Cunningham was placed beneath the ground.

*   *   *   *   *

We now go back to Trevanion at the Tower.

The day of execution had been fixed for the cruel and cunning schemer—the wretch whose very soul was stained with many a horrible crime.

He was to be decapitated on Tower Hill.

He did not hear the sentence pronounced unmoved, for up to the last he was in hopes of escaping death.

Banished from England for ever he thought he might be, but he considered it probable that the queen would interfere to prevent his being publicly executed.

Ay, Trevanion actually thought this! The man whose brain had conceived the idea of assassinating the queen!

Since he was sentenced to death for treason, it was considered unnecessary that he should be tried for the murder of the unfortunate Lord Wyncherley; and, after all, this was a great relief to our hero, who was now well acquainted with all particulars.

It was also a great relief to the Armourer and the Wizard.

It was not until Trevanion had been placed in the chamber reserved for those who were to suffer death in a few days that he heard of his son's terrible end.

It was the Wizard who told him.

Calmly, deliberately, the burning words fell from the lips of this mysterious man.

Like red-hot irons they entered the soul of the beaten, baffled, and now utterly crushed schemer.

The eve of the execution—seven days after Cunningham's death—came round.

Oscar—or Roderick, as we will now call him—had, in the meantime, been fully restored to all his rights and privileges, and the queen had made him a present of a site for a new house.

With that site our readers are acquainted. It was Blackburn House.

It wanted but a quarter to the hour of ten in the evening, when the Wizard, who was attired exactly as we saw him on the night of the murder of Lord Wyncherley, stepped from a coach, and entered the house of the Armourer, where he was awaited by Roderick, Grace, the giants, the Armourer, his wife, and the Headsman.

They greeted him in respectful silence.

"The last scene is about to be enacted," said the Wizard. "Now let us prepare for it."

As he said this, a loud thud fell upon their ears, then another and another.

"What is that?" cried Grace.

"'Tis the carpenters erecting the scaffold for Trevanion," replied Sampson, in a whisper.

Grace shuddered, and clung closer to Roderick, who whispered in her ear.

It was evident that the Armourer was about to say something, for he moved and shuffled in a most uneasy manner.

At last he said to the Wizard—

"Sir, Master Mervine—"

"Go on, Armourer."

"I pray you tell me—cannot this contemplated act of Roderick's be done away with?"

"Nay, it is impossible. I tell you that heaven has willed it so. If, at the last moment, he withdraws, it will be a curse upon his house for ever."

"Let me strike the blow for him," said Sampson to the Headsman. "On my faith, I will have his head off at the very first blow."

The Headsman shook his head.

"The question was asked because Grace, who is about to become my wife," said Roderick, "is horror-stricken at the idea."

"Would she fly in the face of Providence?" asked the Wizard, sternly.

"Heaven forbid it," said Grace.

"'Tis well," said Roderick; "it must be done."

"You will sleep in the Tower to-night," said the Wizard.

"To-night!" cried Roderick, in astonishment.

"To-night!" echoed all present.

"Ay, to-night. But no one will know you are there. You will be made up like the Headsman here. The vision conjured up by me must come true. Roderick, bid your friends adieu for the present."

They tried to persuade the Wizard to allow him to remain for supper.

But the Wizard replied—

"It cannot be. He has but ten hours ere he takes his place on the scaffold."

"Heaven," cried Mistress Raymond, "this is terrible!"

But the Wizard was not moved.

Waving his hand, he said—

"Roderick, your cloak, and follow me."

A hurried good-bye, and they were gone.

*   *   *   *   *

The fatal morning came. Trevanion had not slept. No, his heated brain was continually conjuring up the vision of that cousin he had murdered.

"Fool that I was to persist in my search for that child!" he muttered, again and again. "Fool, fool! And yet for years I suspected the Armourer. And so many times, when I looked upon the youth who was called *his son*, I traced the likeness to Wyncherley."

At seven o'clock he heard a strange noise, but he soon found out what it was. It was a mighty concourse of people waiting to see him executed.

Presently the door of his cell was thrown open, and the Wizard stood on the threshold, a strong guard of halberdiers around him.

"It wants but one hour to the time when you are to die," said the Wizard, in solemn tones.

"I know it, wretch—I know it," replied Trevanion. "And you, like thousands more, are here to feast your eyes upon the scene."

"I am here in fulfilment of—"

"Wretch, away! Devilish prophet of Satan, away!"

"I have brought with me a clergyman, who—"

"I require not his services. Away! A reprieve may arrive at the last moment."

"Dispel such illusions. No reprieve will arrive."

Trevanion waved his hand, and the Wizard turned and departed.

At eight, the chapel bell began to toll.

Drums rolled, hoarse commands were given on all sides; the rattle of arms was heard above the shouts of the mighty multitude waiting for the appearance of the condemned man.

In a few moments, Trevanion was conducted from his cell by the lieutenant and a strong guard, and taken to the middle tower, where he was formally handed over to the sheriffs and their officers in waiting.

With but a brief pause, a procession was formed, and an advance made to the scaffold.

With trembling limbs Trevanion walked to the fatal spot.

He looked about him on all sides.

Almost as far as the eye could reach was a vast sea of expectant faces, and as Trevanion looked, a mighty howl greeted him.

"Traitor! villain! murderer!" were the cries.

Below the scaffold stood the giant brothers, next to them the Wizard.

The Armourer was not to be seen.

Standing by the side of the block, which was surrounded with straw, was the Headsman.

He was attired in a dull black costume, wore a black cowl upon his head, and a mask concealed the upper part of his face.

His right hand rested upon the handle of the glittering axe, and he seemed to be surveying the vast concourse of people in front of him.

Advancing to the edge of the scaffold, Trevanion essayed to speak to the citizens.

But they laughed at him, mocked him, and cursed him.

"He fears to die!" roared the people. "He is a coward."

With a deep, bitter groan, Trevanion stepped back.

As he did so, the Headsman moved his face round, and snatched off his mask.

"Ah!" gasped Trevanion, starting back, "the vision!—it has come true. But you—you are no headsman! I will insist—I—"

Again the citizens roared.

Fulmore hastened up. He was not in the secret.

"This is no headsman!" cried Trevanion. "It is—"

"Peace!" cried Fulmore. "Are you ready?"

Uttering a terrible cry, Trevanion half fell, and was half forced upon his knees.

Trevanion burst into a flood of tears as he laid his head on the block.

Profound silence reigned now. Nothing could be heard save the deep tolling of the chapel bell.

"*Strike!*" said the lieutenant.

Roderick—for he it was—raised the axe high above his head, and whirled it once over his shoulder.

Then down it came.

The aim was true—Trevanion's head rolled from the block.

Roderick seized it, and holding it aloft, cried out, in clear, ringing tones—

"Behold the head of a vile traitor!"

The crowd answered by a series of deafening shouts and yells, and then the horrible scene was over.

* * * * *

The last scene of the last act in this tragic drama is over, but, ere the curtain finally descends, it is our duty to inform our readers of what was the future welfare of our characters.

On the spot where Blackburn House—the scene of many tragedies—had stood, there arose a magnificent pile, the property of our hero, who named it Raymond House.

It was most sumptuously furnished in every part, including the kitchen, in which, our readers will be pleased to hear, "Carroty Charles" was installed as "kitchen clerk," and his sweetheart that was, but whom he had married, was one of the cooks.

Some few months after the execution of Trevanion, Roderick and Grace were married.

The wedding feast was on a scale of great magnificence, and the board was graced by the presence of a large number of the principal nobles of the land.

The Armourer, his wife, the Wizard, and even the Headsman (who was attired in a gay Court dress for the occasion, and who was not recognised by any of the guests) occupied posts of honour.

On a side table sat several curious personages, one of whom was known as Captain Cartridge.

The giants had positions on each side of Roderick and Grace.

The giants remained many years in Roderick's service as "gentleman stewards," and they drank and ate and joked as much as they thought proper.

The Wizard became a queen's councillor, and though frequently at Roderick's house, he was nearly always in attendance on the queen.

Roderick repeatedly urged the Armourer and his wife to take up their quarters with him, but they declined, until well advanced in years, when the Armourer sold his business, and resided permanently at Raymond House.

The Author, in bidding adieu to the many thousands who have read this work, has now only to assure them that, although Roderick rapidly became a great Court favourite, and, with his lovely wife, moved in the highest circles, he never forgot that, in a certain sense, he still remained "THE ARMOURER'S SON."

NOTE.—*For further particulars of the Tower of London read the great Romance entitled "*TRAITOR'S GATE,*" by the Author of the "Armourer's Son." Of all Booksellers, One Shilling; or post free from 173, Fleet Street, One Shilling and Twopence.*

EDWIN J. BRETT'S LIST OF PUBLICATIONS.

BOYS' COMIC JOURNAL.—1d. Weekly; 6d. Monthly. 1s. 4d. Quarterly. Cloth Volumes, 4s.

BOYS OF ENGLAND.—The oldest and best conducted book for Boys. Weekly, 1d.; Monthly Parts, 6d.; Half-yearly Volumes, 2s. 6d. and 4s.

YOUNG MEN OF GREAT BRITAIN.—An Interesting Journal of Love, War, Romance and Adventure, for Men of all ages. Price 1d. Weekly; 6d. Monthly; Half-yearly Volumes, 2s. 6d. and 4s.

SOMETHING TO READ.—The New Double Weekly Journal, containing Stories of Thrilling Interest, together with a full-sized Complete Novelette with each Number. Price 1d. Weekly; Monthly Parts, 6d.; Quarterly, 1s. 6d.; Cloth Volumes, 4s. 6d.

THE PRINCESS'S NOVELETTES.—Profusely Illustrated. 1d. Weekly; Monthly Parts, 4d.

The Postage of any of the above Volumes, 6d.

Interesting and Complete Stories every week, price 1d.; or in Volumes, 1s.

BOYS OF ENGLAND NOVELETTE. | BOYS' WEEKLY READER NOVELETTE.

Complete Volumes now publishing at 1s. each. Illustrated. Post free, 1s. 2d.

KING OF THE SCHOOL.
JACK-O'-THE CUDGEL.
RIVAL SCHOOLS.
FRED FROLIC, HIS LIFE AND ADVENTURES.
NIGHT GUARD; OR, THE SECRET OF THE FIVE MASKS.
GILES EVERGREEN; OR, FRESH FROM THE COUNTRY.
POOR RAY, THE DRUMMER BOY.
TOM DARING; OR, FAR FROM HOME.
WALTER, THE ARCHER.
WILDFOOT, THE WANDERER OF WICKLOW.

JACK STEDFAST; OR, WRECK AND RESCUE.
DICK AND HIS FRIEND DUKE.
ISABEL'S FORTUNE.
OXFORD AND CAMBRIDGE EIGHTS.
UNLUCKY BOB.
EVERY INCH A SAILOR.
FATHERLESS WILL.
CHEVY CHASE.
STRONGBOW.
TOM FLOREMALL IN SEARCH OF HIS FATHER.
JACK RUSHTON.
BY THE QUEEN'S COMMAND.

PAT O'CONNOR.
RIVAL CRUSOES.
BICYCLE BOB.
THREE BOY CRUSOES.
RUPERT DREADNOUGHT.
CAPTAIN OF THE SCHOOL.
GALLANT JACK.
ON AND OFF THE STAGE.
TRAVELLING SCHOOLBOYS.
CAPTAIN OF THE GUARD.
ARMOURER'S SON.
COMIC HISTORY OF LONDON.
NOBODY'S DOG.
WHITE SQUAW.

Complete in Two Volumes, 1s. each. Postage 2d. each Volume.

TOM FLOREMALL'S SCHOOLDAYS.
TRUE TO EACH OTHER; OR, BOYHOOD'S TRUST.

SCAPEGRACE OF THE SCHOOL.
SCAPEGRACE AT SEA.
SCAPEGRACE IN LONDON.

ENGLISH JACK AMONG THE AFGHANS.
PANTOMIME JOE.
WHO SHALL BE LEADER?

Harkaway Series, price 1s. each Volume. Postage 2d. extra.

Vol. 1.—JACK HARKAWAY'S SCHOOLDAYS. Complete in One Volume.
Vols. 2 and 3.—JACK HARKAWAY AFTER SCHOOLDAYS. Complete in Two Volumes.
Vols. 4 and 5.—JACK HARKAWAY AT OXFORD. Complete in Two Volumes.
Vols. 6 and 7.—JACK HARKAWAY AMONG THE BRIGANDS Complete in Two Volumes.

Vols. 8 and 9.—JACK HARKAWAY'S ADVENTURES ROUND THE WORLD, AMERICA AND CUBA. Two Volumes.
Vol. 10.—JACK HARKAWAY'S ADVENTURES IN CHINA. Complete in One Volume.
Vols. 11 and 12.—HARKAWAY IN GREECE. Two Volumes.
Vol. 13.—HARKAWAY IN AUSTRALIA. One Volume.
Vols. 14 and 15.—HARKAWAY AND HIS BOY TINKER. Two Volumes.

American Series.

HARKAWAY AT SCHOOL IN AMERICA. | HARKAWAY AT THE ISLE OF PALMS.
HARKAWAY AMONG THE PIRATES.

Ned Nimble Series of Stories, Price 1s. each Volume, postage 2d.

Vols. 1 and 2.—NED NIMBLE'S SCHOOLDAYS. Complete in Two Volumes.
Vol. 3.—NED NIMBLE AMONGST THE INDIANS. Complete in One Volume.
Vol. 7.—NED NIMBLE AMONGST THE TARTARS.

Vols. 4 and 5.—NED NIMBLE AMONGST THE MORMONS. Complete in Two Volumes.
Vol. 6.—NED NIMBLE AMONGST THE PIRATES. Complete in One Volume.
Vols. 8 and 9.—NED NIMBLE AMONG THE CHINESE.

Vols. 10 and 11.—NED NIMBLE AMONG THE BUSHRANGERS.

BOYS OF ENGLAND SWIMMING GUIDE, 2d.
BOYS OF ENGLAND CRICKET GUIDE, 2d.
BOYS OF ENGLAND TRAINING GUIDE, 2d.
BOYS OF ENGLAND FENCING, 2d.
BOYS OF ENGLAND ROWING AND GYMNASTICS, 2d.

BOXING AND WRESTLING, 2d.
SOMETHING TO READ DREAM BOOK. Illustrated. 2d.
PRINCESS'S INFALLIBLE FORTUNE-TELLER, 2d.
BOYS OF ENGLAND ANGLING, 2d.
BOYS OF ENGLAND CONJURING BOOK, NEW EDITION, 2d.

OFFICE: 173, FLEET STREET. AND ALL BOOKSELLERS.